ACCLAIM FOR THE NOVELS OF LEILA MEACHAM

SOMERSET

"Bestselling author Meacham is back with a prequel to *Roses* that stands on its own as a sweeping historical saga, spanning the nineteenth century...[Fans] and new readers alike will find themselves absorbed in the family saga that Meacham has proven—once again—talented in telling."

—*Publishers Weekly* (starred review)

"Entertaining...Meacham skillfully weaves colorful history into her lively tale...SOMERSET has its charms."

—*Dallas Morning News*

"Slavery, westward expansion, abolition, the Civil War, love, marriage, friendship, tragedy and triumph—all the ingredients (and much more) that made so many love *Roses* so much—are here in abundance."

—*San Antonio Express-News*

"A story you do not want to miss...[Recommended] to readers of Kathryn Stockett's *The Help* or Margaret Mitchell's *Gone with the Wind*. SOMERSET has everything a compelling historical epic calls for: Love and war, friendship and betrayal, opportunity and loss, and everything in between."

—*BookPage*

"4½ stars! This prequel to *Roses* is as addictive as any soap opera...As sprawling and big as Texas itself, Meacham's epic saga is perfect for readers who long for the 'big books' of the past. There are enough adventure, tears, and laughter alongside colorful history to keep readers engrossed and satisfied."

—*RT Book Reviews*

"With this novel [Meacham] has become a national treasure and one can only imagine the great novels still to come. She will, however, have a difficult time topping the joy of SOMERSET."

—Huffington Post

"Meacham's fans—and she has many—will be glad for this prequel."

—*Kirkus Reviews*

"This much-anticipated prequel to Roses surpasses all expectations with its exquisitely detailed and character-driven narrative…altogether an engrossing and unforgettable tale, ending with a perfectly primed setting for those who have not read *Roses*. This book is highly recommended for those who love historical sagas!"

—HistoricalNovelSociety.org

TUMBLEWEEDS

"[An] expansive generational saga…Fans of *Friday Night Lights* will enjoy a return to the land where high school football boys are kings."

—*Chicago Tribune*

"A talented author."

—*Dallas Morning News*

"Meacham scores a touchdown…You will laugh, cry, and cheer to a plot so thick and a conclusion so surprising, it will leave you wishing for more. Yes, Meacham is really that good. And TUMBLEWEEDS is more than entertaining, it's addictive."

—Examiner.com

"Larger-than-life protagonists and a fast-paced, engaging plot… Meacham has succeeded in creating an indelible heroine."
—*Dallas Morning News*

"[An] enthralling stunner, a good, old-fashioned read."
—*Publishers Weekly*

"A thrilling journey…a treasure…a must-read. Warning: Once you begin reading, you won't be able to put the book down."
—Examiner.com

"[A] sprawling novel of passion and revenge. Highly recommended…It's been almost thirty years since the heyday of giant epics in the grand tradition of Edna Ferber and Barbara Taylor Bradford, but Meacham's debut might bring them back."
—*Library Journal* (starred review)

"A high-end *Thorn Birds*."
—TheDailyBeast.com

"I ate this multigenerational tale of two families warring it up across Texas history with the same alacrity with which I would gobble chocolate."
—Joshilyn Jackson, *New York Times* bestselling author of *gods in Alabama* and *Backseat Saints*

"A Southern epic in the most cinematic sense—plot-heavy and historical, filled with archaic Southern dialect and formality, with love, marriage, war, and death over three generations."
—Caroline Dworin, "The Book Bench," NewYorker.com

"This sweeping epic of love, sacrifice, and struggle reads like *Gone With the Wind* with all the passions and family politics of the South."
—*Midwest Book Review*

"The kind of book you can lose yourself in, from beginning to end."
—Huffington Post

"Fast-paced and full of passions… This panoramic drama proves evocative and lush. The plot is intricate and gives back as much as the reader can take… Stunning and original *Roses* is a must read."

—TheReviewBroads.com

"A very enjoyable page-turner… A fine story, which steps right along at a lively pace, making *Roses*, even at a hefty six-hundred-plus pages, a surprisingly speedy read."   —BookReporter.com

"The story is epic, the cast of characters is manageable, allowing the reader to get to know the players well."

—*Historical Novels Review*

"Fans of historical family sagas will enjoy this entertaining epic."

—*Sunday Republican* (VT)

"May herald the overdue return of those delicious doorstop epics from such writers as Barbara Taylor Bradford and Colleen McCullough… a refreshingly nostalgic bouquet of family angst, undying love, and 'if only's."   —*Publishers Weekly*

"Strong characters and plenty of conflict… moves smoothly from modern times to several generations back."

—*San Antonio Express-News*

"Superbly written… a rating of ten out of ten. I simply loved this book."   —ANovelMenagerie.com

SOMERSET

Leila Meacham

GRAND CENTRAL
PUBLISHING

NEW YORK   BOSTON

Grand Central Publishing
Hachette Book Group
237 Park Avenue
New York, NY 10017
www.HachetteBookGroup.com

Printed in the United States of America

RRD-C

Originally published in hardcover by Hachette Book Group.

First trade edition: July 2014

10 9 8 7 6 5 4 3 2 1

Grand Central Publishing is a division of Hachette Book Group, Inc.
The Grand Central Publishing name and logo are trademarks of Hachette Book Group, Inc.

The Hachette Speakers Bureau provides a wide range of authors for speaking events. To find out more, go to www.hachettespeakersbureau.com or call (866) 376-6591.

The publisher is not responsible for websites (or their content) that are not owned by the publisher.

The Library of Congress has cataloged the hardcover edition as follows:
Meacham, Leila, 1938-
Somerset / Leila Meacham. — First Edition.
     pages cm
ISBN 978-1-4555-4738-8 (hardcover) — ISBN 978-1-4555-7621-0 (large print hardcover)
1. Cities and towns—Texas—Fiction. 2. City and town life—Texas—Fiction.
3. Lumber trade—Texas—Fiction. 4. Cotton trade—Texas—Fiction. I. Title.
PS3563.E163S66 2013
813'.54—dc23
                                   2013017542

ISBN 978-1-4555-4739-5 (pbk.)

For all those who came, stayed, made a difference,
and earned the right to be called Texan.

LINEAGE OF THE TOLIVERS
(1806-1900)

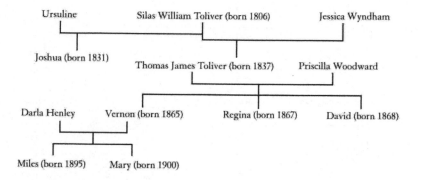

Ursuline — Silas William Toliver (born 1806) — Jessica Wyndham

Joshua (born 1831)

Thomas James Toliver (born 1837) — Priscilla Woodward

Darla Henley — Vernon (born 1865)   Regina (born 1867)   David (born 1868)

Miles (born 1895)   Mary (born 1900)

LINEAGE OF THE WARWICKS
(1806-1900)

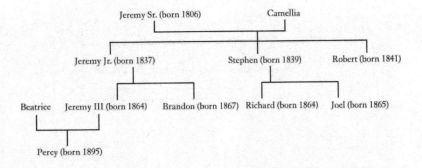

LINEAGE OF THE DUMONTS
(1808-1900)

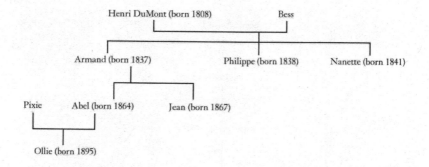

Henri DuMont (born 1808)   Bess

Armand (born 1837)   Philippe (born 1838)   Nanette (born 1841)

Pixie   Abel (born 1864)   Jean (born 1867)

Ollie (born 1895)

JASPER'S LINEAGE
(AS APPLIES TO THE STORY)

Jasper (born 1818)

|

Petunia (born 1839)

|

Amy (born 1856)

|

Sassie (born 1876)

SOMERSET

PART ONE

Chapter One

Elizabeth Toliver observed her younger son, Silas, from under the wide, floppy brim of her gardening bonnet. He stood by the verandah railing, staring down the oak-lined road leading to the family's plantation home, his posture expectant, his gaze intense. It was the beginning of October 1835. Elizabeth watched him from one of the rose gardens flanking the house, clippers in hand to cut a basket of the red Lancasters she'd babied and worried about in January. Amazing what water, mulch, and manure could do for spindly stalks—and for most growing things—left too long without care, she thought. Nature was full of such examples of regrowth and new strength when their requirements were met, if only man would take notice and apply to the human race.

If only her husband had noticed and applied to the needs of his second son.

"Who are you waiting for, Silas?" she called.

Silas turned his head in her direction. It was a very handsome head favored with the striking Toliver features that proved him a descendant of the long line of English aristocrats whose portraits greeted guests in the great hall of Queenscrown. Silas's green eyes narrowed, as fiery as emeralds under brows a fair match to his rambunctious black hair, but it was the dimple set square in the middle of the family chin that left no doubt of his lineage.

"For Jeremy," he answered, his tone curt, and returned to his surveillance.

Elizabeth's shoulders sagged. Silas blamed her for the stipulations in his father's will. "You could have gotten him to change his mind, Mother," he'd accused her, "and now you must suffer the consequences." He would never be convinced of her ignorance of the *possibility* that his father would write his will as he had, even though her son knew—must surely know—she'd never sacrifice his happiness to ensure hers. She now heard the "consequences" of her failure arriving on pounding horses' hooves: Jeremy Warwick astride his white stallion, come to lure her son and four-year-old grandson and future daughter-in-law to a faraway, dangerous territory called Texas.

Jeremy thundered to a stop, and even before he greeted Silas and dismounted, he called to her, "Mornin', Miz 'Lizabeth. How do your roses grow?"

It was his usual form of greeting, no matter the setting, and was meant to inquire after her general well-being. The reference to roses had further meaning in that both the Warwicks and the Tolivers were descended from royal houses in England identified by the elegant, prickly-stemmed flower that served as their emblems. The Warwicks of South Carolina hailed from the House of York, represented by the white rose; the Tolivers, the House of Lancaster, symbolized by the red. Though neighbors and close friends, neither grew in their gardens the other's badge of allegiance to their aristocratic roots.

This morning *How do your roses grow?* was not intended to ask the condition of her beloved plants she'd nurtured back to health after months away tending her husband during his illness in a Charleston hospital, but the nature of her spirits now that he had been in his grave these four weeks. "Hard to tell," she called back. "Their endurance will depend upon the coming weather."

They had exchanged these *entendres* since the boys were children and Elizabeth had discovered Jeremy Warwick's quick, ironic, but never mocking, wit. She adored him. Tall and strapping in contrast to her slim, sinewy son of equal height, Jeremy was the youngest of three brothers whose father owned the adjacent cotton plantation called Meadowlands. United by their family pecking order and the commonalities of age, heritage, and interests, he and Silas made ideal friends, a relationship Elizabeth had been grateful for, since Silas and his brother had warred from the time her younger son could talk.

Jeremy's bright pleasure at seeing her dimmed in his gaze, indicating that he understood her meaning. "I'm afraid the weather can't always be what we wish," he said, with an apologetic inclination of his head that confirmed to Elizabeth why he had come.

"Did the letter arrive that we were expecting?" Silas asked.

"Finally. It's in the pouch, and one from Lucas Tanner. He and his group made it to the black waxy."

Elizabeth was of no mind to go inside. If they wished to speak privately, they could adjourn somewhere out of earshot, but she hoped they did not. Sometimes, the only way she knew what was going on in her family was to eavesdrop shamelessly or enlist one of the servants to do it. She heard Silas call into the house for Lazarus to bring coffee. Good. They meant to collude on the porch in the fineness of the fall morning.

"Will I be happy with the letter's contents?" Silas asked.

"Most of them," his friend replied.

Elizabeth knew what they were about. They were now beginning in earnest to fulfill the dream they had shared and talked about for years. As youngest sons, both had grown up aware they were not likely to be the sole heirs of their families' cotton plantations upon the deaths of their fathers. In Jeremy's case, that reality would have presented no problem. He got along well with his two brothers, and his father doted on him and would have seen he received his fair share of the estate. Jeremy simply wanted to possess his own plantation and run it as he saw fit. Silas's fraternal and paternal situation was entirely different. From his birth, Benjamin Toliver had favored Morris, his firstborn, as heir of Queenscrown. "It's the way of it," he would say to Elizabeth, never having entirely shaken off the principle of the law of primogeniture, a throwback to his English heritage that decreed the eldest son should inherit the family property. In South Carolina, the law had been abolished in 1779.

But other prejudices factored in. Benjamin and Morris saw eye to eye on everything, and it wasn't a matter of son wishing to please father. Morris genuinely shared his father's views on every subject from religion to politics, whereas Silas's took a different, sometimes incendiary, turn. Dislike grew between father and son and brother and brother, and it did not help that Elizabeth, to breach the widening gap between them, treated Silas with special affection. Benjamin had known that Silas and his brother, as equal partners, would have been at each other's throats by sundown of his death. To avoid the situation, he'd bequeathed the plantation, all the money, and family property—land, house and furnishings, stock, equipment, and slaves—to Morris, leaving Silas penniless but for a yearly "salary" along with a percentage of the plantation's profits so long as he served as land manager under his brother.

No wonder Silas, now twenty-nine, feeling betrayed and embittered, wished to abandon the land of his birth and head with Jeremy Warwick for the "black waxy" soil in the eastern part of Texas, superb for growing cotton, so the reports came back. How sad that he should leave with his heart harboring unjust ill will toward his father, for Elizabeth knew something that Silas did not. Benjamin Toliver had set aside his love for his wife out of love for his younger son. Her husband had left her in the care of a lumbering bachelor son who most likely would never marry, and she would grow old without the joy of grandchildren to cherish and spoil. She would probably live to regret it, but she'd let Silas—callous to her love for her adorable grandson and the girl who would soon become his second wife—go to Texas without ever knowing his father had fashioned his will to set him free.

Chapter Two

Silas could feel his mother's despair, layered with her widow's grief, waft to him on the crisp, autumn breeze, but it couldn't be helped. He was going to Texas and taking his son and bride with him. Theirs was an age-old argument. Family was all to his mother. Land, a man's inherent connection to his very being, was everything to him. Without his own land to till and sow, a man was nothing, no matter who his family was. His mother had mounted every reason against her younger son leaving the comfort, security, and safety of his home to set out with his family to the territory of Texas on the verge of revolution. Reports had filtered back that the Texas colonists were organizing to declare their newly settled land independent of Mexico, a move that would undoubtedly lead to war with that country.

"What am I to do, Mother? Stay here under the boot of my brother where my son, like his father, will never be master of his own house?"

"Don't put this off on what you want for Joshua," his mother had argued. "This is what *you* want for yourself—what you've always wanted—but now you have Lettie and your little son to consider." She had covered her face with her hands at the monstrous images she'd warned him about: terrible diseases (there had been a cholera outbreak in Stephen F. Austin's colony in

1834), savage Indians, wild animals and snakes, bloodthirsty Mexicans, dangerous water crossings, exposure to extremes of weather. The list of horrors went on and on, the most horrible being the possibility that she'd never see her son and Joshua and Lettie again.

"And don't *you* put this off on them, Mother. If I were offered acreage anywhere else in the South where it's safe, you'd still want me to remain at Queenscrown, all of us together as a family, never mind that my father practically disowned me and my brother loathes me."

"You exaggerate. Your father did what he thought best for Queenscrown, and your brother does not loathe you. He simply doesn't understand you."

"And *I* will do what I think is best for Somerset."

"Somerset?"

"The name I'm calling my plantation in Texas in honor of the Tolivers' forebear, the Duke of Somerset."

His mother had fallen mute, her arguments futile against so powerful an ambition.

She had her husband's last will and testament to thank for her sorrow, Silas had reminded her, but it didn't pardon his brusque behavior toward her these past weeks, and he felt ashamed. He loved his mother and would miss her sorely, but he could not rid himself of the feeling that she had intentionally failed to foresee and therefore prevent the unfair dispensations of his father's estate. If Benjamin Toliver had divided his property equally, Silas would have forever abandoned his dream. He had promised himself to do everything in his power to live peaceably with his brother. Morris, a bachelor, loved his nephew and was fond of his sister-in-law-to-be and her sweet, gentle ways. Lettie and his mother got along gloriously. Elizabeth regarded Lettie as the daughter she'd never had, and his fiancée considered his mother the surrogate for the one she'd lost as a child. They would have made a tranquil household.

Even Morris now realized what he stood to lose by his gain. "We'll work something out," he'd said, but for Silas, nothing his brother could offer would make up for the deficit of his father's affection so hurtfully demonstrated by the terms of the will. He would not take from his brother what their father had not meant for him to have.

So he was going to Texas.

As Jeremy dismounted, Silas looked gratefully down at the man who would be pulling up stakes with him, the stallion still prancing. Jeremy Warwick rarely refused his horse his head, as he was not in the habit of denying his own. Silas prized that quality in him, for while his friend's head was known for its uncommon common sense, it was not averse to risk, and never would his boyhood companion enter a more risky venture than the one on which they were planning to embark.

Before securing his horse's reins, Jeremy tossed Silas the mail pouch he'd ridden to Charleston to collect. Silas unbuckled the straps eagerly and was reading a letter from Stephen F. Austin, well-known empresario of Texas, before his friend's polished boots struck the floor of the verandah.

"Some disturbing reading in there," Jeremy said, lowering his voice so that Elizabeth wouldn't hear. "Mr. Austin is willing to sell us as many of his bonus acres as we can buy so long as we agree to live in Texas, but he warns that war is coming. There's a newspaper, too, describing the growing dissatisfaction among the settlements with the policies of the government in Mexico City, and there's a letter from Lucas Tanner. He says the area is all he could have hoped for—good virgin soil, plentiful timber and water, fine weather—but he may have to fight to hold it. He's already had a few scrapes with the Indians and Mexican militia."

"Since we're not leaving until next spring, maybe the conflict with the Mexican government will be settled at least, but I have to share this news with the rest who are going with us," Silas said. "Let them know the additional risk."

Jeremy asked quietly, "Does that include Lettie?"

The sharp snipping of the rose clippers ceased, the silence carried to the verandah in the pause that followed. Elizabeth had been listening, her ears perked for his answer. *Yes, do tell, Silas. Does that include Lettie?* Her son was saved from responding by Lazarus elbowing the front door open to deliver the coffee. Silas reached forward to open it wider for him.

"Thank you, Mister Silas," the gray-haired Negro said, and set the tray on the table where generations of Tolivers had been served their mint juleps and afternoon tea. "Shall I pour the coffee, suh?"

"No, Lazarus. I'll do it. Tell Cassandra the pie looks delicious."

Lazarus and his wife, Cassandra, would be going with him to Texas. They belonged to him, an inheritance from Mamie Toliver, Silas's grandmother. She had left nothing to her other grandson. Lately, Silas had noticed a heaviness to Lazarus's walk, and his wife no longer sang over her bread kneading.

"That will include Lettie," Silas answered, handing Jeremy his dessert plate. He poured them each a steaming cup of coffee. "When I'm inclined to tell her," he added.

"Ah," Jeremy said.

"What's that supposed to mean?"

"That the pie is delicious," Jeremy said, taking a big bite. "Will you and Lettie be going to Jessica Wyndham's party?"

"Lettie wouldn't miss it. She tutored Jessica before the girl left for boarding school and really liked her. There are only four years' difference in their ages. I can't say I remember her. Do you?"

"Barely. All I recalled until today was a serious-faced little girl with eyes big and brown as chestnuts, but I recognized her at the docks in Charleston this morning when she arrived from Boston. Her mother and brother were there to pick her up. There was quite a scene when Jessica went to the aid of a Negro porter being mistreated by a passenger."

"A white man?"

"I'm afraid so."

"Her father will have something to say about that."

"I hope his displeasure won't put a damper on the party. I'm told the Wyndhams are sparing no expense to celebrate Jessica's eighteenth birthday and homecoming from that finishing school in Boston. They're entertaining relatives from England as well— Lord and Lady DeWitt."

"The Wyndhams can afford it," Silas said, drawing out a map from the mail pouch.

"The *Courier* lists Carson Wyndham as the wealthiest man in South Carolina," Jeremy said, cutting into his pie.

"The poor man will be busy staving off every fortune hunter in the state."

"Maybe Morris will marry her and save him the trouble."

Silas snorted. "Morris wouldn't know a waltz from a polka or a lady's handkerchief from a cleaning rag, so there's no chance of *him* winning the girl's hand. Why don't *you* marry her, Jeremy, and save her father the trouble. A handsome devil like you should have a clear field."

Jeremy laughed. "No offense to Lettie, but I don't think I could interest a young lady of Jessica Wyndham's background and refinement into marrying a man with plans to settle in Texas. Lettie's besotted over you. She'd let you take her to hell."

Silas spread out the map enclosed with Stephen F. Austin's let-ter and frowned over the route the empresario had marked in dark ink. The distance was formidable; the terrain beyond the Red River into Texas daunting. Circled was an area where the trail diverted from a more logical direction. A note in the margin read: *Stay clear. Comanche Indian hunting grounds.*

"Maybe that is where I'm taking her," Silas said.

Chapter Three

"Now where should we place Lady Barbara for luncheon?" Eunice Wyndham asked as her daughter sailed into the loggia amid a flurry of activity going on around a table set for twelve. "Such a quandary. If her back is to the garden, the sunlight will show her thin hair to its worst advantage. If she faces it, the light will expose every wrinkle. The woman is so *vain* about her looks."

Jessica was not listening. Her mother was mulling aloud and did not expect her to answer. She knew her daughter had no interest in such things, even now after two years away at boarding school to correct her dispassion. The luncheon table had been arranged in the loggia to free the dining room for the huge banquet the next evening. Jessica would have preferred her birthday and homecoming celebrated with a family picnic. The person for whom she searched among the Negro maids was not there. She'd not found her in the dining room, either, where similar activities were taking place.

"Mama, where is Tippy?"

"Perhaps I can set her at the head of the table and Lord Henry at the other end. Everyone will interpret the seating as a sign of respect. Your father and I can sit across from each other in the middle."

"Mama, where is Tippy? I've looked everywhere for her and can't find her. What have you done with her?"

Eunice tucked a flowingly inscribed nameplate into a glass rosebud card holder and stepped back to examine the effect. "Should I set out the fly catchers?" she asked. "I bought a lovely pair in crystal when your father and I were in Washington. They do have the most dreadful flies there—worse than here. Is it too early in the season for them, you think?"

"Mama, where is Tippy?"

Eunice gave her daughter her attention. "Goodness, child. Why are you still in your robe?"

Jessica spun toward the doorway.

"Where are you going?"

"To the kitchen. I'm sure that's where you've exiled her."

"Jessie, stop right there. Do you hear me?" Eunice's voice rose in alarm. She picked up the fan she'd brought into the room and waved it rapidly before her face. Jessica halted and turned around. The three maids, dressed in gray dresses overlaid with white aprons, had gone still, the room silent. "I am so glad your father took Lady Barbara and Lord Henry riding this morning," Eunice said, fanning. "I will be spared the embarrassment of my daughter running to the kitchen to fetch a maid when a tug on the bellpull would do."

"I want to see Tippy, Mama."

"She's busy designing your birthday cake."

"Then I'll go help her."

Eunice cast a horrified look behind her at the stock-still maids, their eyes bulging and the whites stark with shock and curiosity. "That will be all," she snapped. "Go make yourself useful to Willie May."

The maids rushed by Jessica in a blur of gray and white. Eunice moved quickly to pull her daughter into the room, then closed the french doors behind them. Once shuttered in, she said, "Do not take that tone with me, young lady, especially in the presence of the servants. You're in enough trouble after that scene on the dock yesterday."

"I simply gave the man a slap on the shoulder with my fan."

"You were defending a Negro against a white man!"

"The man was abusing an overburdened porter. I would have slapped him if the porter had been white as the driven snow."

Eunice's tight, angry face crumpled like a soggy teacake. "I declare, child, what are we to do with you? We've all been so excited about your coming home. You can't imagine how eager your brother was to see you. He insisted on going with me to pick you up from the ship, but you embarrassed Michael terribly yesterday, perhaps beyond reclaim."

"Michael should have been the one to give the man a wallop."

Eunice fanned faster. "I knew we shouldn't have sent you to school in Boston—into that hotbed of abolitionists."

"No, Mother, a breeding ground for freedom lovers."

"Oh, Jessie!" Depleted as always from these arguments with a daughter for whom she'd rip out her heart, Eunice fell with her fan into one of the loggia chairs and sighed hopelessly. "What did they do to you in that school?"

"They confirmed what I've always believed. All human beings are created equal, and no one has the right to enslave another."

"Sssh!" Eunice whispered fiercely, darting a look through the glassed french doors for listening ears. "Listen to me, my willful daughter. You have no idea what's been going on around here in your absence. If you did, you'd realize what's wrong with such feelings, how dangerous such talk could be for Tippy."

"What's…been going on around here?"

"Not on our plantation, but others. Slave rebellions, all unsuccessful, but too close to home for your father's comfort. Planters are on edge and quick to punish any slave—*unmercifully*, I might add—or"—she drilled Jessica with a look—"*anyone* who gives the faintest impression they do not agree with the Southern cause."

"Cause? Abolition is a *cause*. Slavery is a dogma."

Eunice discontinued fanning. It did little to induce air into lungs that felt about to burst. "See, that's the kind of thing I'm talking about. I'm warning you, Jessie, that while your father indulges your every wish, he will not tolerate such views in this house or your flagrant friendship with a Negro servant." She shook her head in self-recrimination. "I should never have permitted you and Tippy to become close when you were children, but you had no one else to play with. She was the only choice of a companion for you. I should never have listened to my sister's pleas to send you to boarding school to be near her in Boston, and, most assuredly, I should *never* have allowed Tippy to go with you.

"However"—Eunice arched a reproachful eyebrow at Jessica— "I was under the delusion you would have the good sense to break your ties with her once you were home." Wearily, Eunice pressed a hand to her forehead. "I'd hoped you'd understand you must let her go, accept that Tippy has her place, and you have yours."

"Mama..." Jessica knelt at her mother's knees, the fullness of her robe billowing about her, bringing to Eunice's mind the red-haired, brown-eyed doll comprised of only a comely torso and bouffant skirt Jessica had preferred as a child. But there the likeness of her daughter to the doll ended. Eunice did not understand it. Her daughter's features were regular, her teeth straight, her flaming hair and large, expressive eyes a dark, lovely brown, but they did not save her fair, freckled face from being— not homely, but plain. Her husband would have liked her to be beautiful but ordinary in her interests like the daughters of their friends, concerned only with clothes and parties and flirtations, delighted to be the spoiled only daughter of one of the richest men in the South. But from birth, Jessica had eschewed the role to which she'd been born. Was it because she sensed that her father's indulgence was compensation for his disappointment in her? Jessica thought too much, questioned, challenged, rebelled. Carson would have found her spirit attractive in a beautiful daughter, but it was merely annoying in one so plain. Sometimes Eunice thought Jessica should have been born a male.

"I do understand," Jessica said, "but I cannot accept. I would never put Tippy in a jeopardous position, but I can't—I won't—treat her as inferior to me. She's brilliant and creative in ways that I could never be. She's kinder and wiser and possesses every quality I admire and need in a friend. I do not wish to cause you and Papa embarrassment, but I will give my friend the respect she deserves. I will not treat her as a slave."

Eunice pressed her hands to her cheeks. "Oh, my God…If your father were to hear you…"

"He would be very disappointed in me, I'm sure."

"He would feel more than disappointment. There's a side to your father you've never seen. I will not be able to prevent the consequences if you continue to flaunt your affection for Tippy. You must think of her, for goodness' sake."

Gently, Jessica pried away her mother's hands from her cheeks and held them. "Don't worry, Mama. I promise not to stir up family distress by sharing my views on slavery in this house. The South is what it is, and one voice will not change it, but please allow Tippy to be my maid. You know she has the use of only one lung, which suffers from pleurisy, and she can't breathe in the heat of the kitchen."

"I will so long as you abide by your promise, child. If you don't, your father will send her to the fields, and she'll be berthed in the slave quarters. He loves you dearly, but you must believe me that he will." Eunice removed her hands and pushed her daughter's fiery hair back from her face. "We missed you so when you were away," she said gently. "That's why we had you come home before the semester was through, but I declare, my blood has not run easy since you've been back. At luncheon and the party, there will be talk of the abolitionist movement. Promise me you'll hold your tongue if your opinion is asked?"

Jessica stuck out her tongue and held it with two fingers. "Ah pomice to uld ma ung."

"Silly girl," Eunice said, a grin sliding across her face that did not quite relieve the anxiety in her eyes. "Now let me up. I have work to do."

"You'll send Tippy to my room? No one in the world can dress my hair like Tippy, and imagine how I'd look if she didn't manage my wardrobe."

"If you'll remember that your father likes to surprise you unannounced. Make sure your hair and clothes are all you and Tippy are discussing should he appear. If he gets involved, it will be cotton bolls Tippy will be tending rather than ribbons and laces."

"I'll remember." Jessica stood and spun around in her satin dressing gown, skirt twirling from a delicate, narrow waist. "Eighteen tomorrow. When did I get to be so old?"

"It's a birthday that should set you to thinking of marriage," Eunice said.

"Maybe thinking, but not *doing*. What man would wish to marry a firebrand like me?"

Who indeed? thought Eunice with a sigh.

Chapter Four

Tippy drew the brush from Jessica's forehead down to the end of a long, waxed lock. She had repeated the movement over and over until Jessica's naturally frizzy hair shone like springy streamers of russet satin on her shoulders. Shortly, Tippy would fashion it into an evening coiffure inspired by the Romantic Era in England called the Madonna. The style called for parting the hair in the middle with ringlets at the crown of the head and sides of the face. A gown of cream brocade hung from a wire dress form shaped to the measurements of Jessica's figure. The frock featured the latest fashion details designed to show off creamy shoulders, small waists, and slim ankles.

"It's a perfect style for you," Miss Smithfield, the seamstress who had sewn the dress, had pronounced in her shop in Boston, but it had been Tippy who had designed it and selected the fabric. Accessories were laid out: square-toed slippers in matching satin, elbow-length gloves, a small evening bag in green to complement the emerald brooch Jessica's father had presented to her in honor of her birthday.

When sitting straight before the mirror, Tippy directly behind her, Jessica could see only the wispy puff of her maid's hair (another oddity since it was not wiry like other members of her race and its light brown shade was in contrast to her dark skin), the flare of her ears, and the sharp points of her constantly moving elbows. Hardly taller than a fireplace broom and wafer thin, Tippy had been bestowed with remarkably large ears, hands, and feet that made her look grotesque to those who did not know her or appreciate her talents.

"Whatever was the good Lord thinking to stick all that extra yardage on my girl's skinny little face and body and then not have enough to make her a second lung?" Willie May was often heard to lament.

Jessica wondered as well. She thought Tippy the oddest-put-together human being she'd ever seen, but she'd found her diminutive frame and disproportionate features enchanting since they were children. With her agile mind and creative imagination, Tippy reminded Jessica of the mischievous sprite in her favorite storybook. Jessica had fancied her a chocolate elf dropped in from another world whose oversized ears and hands and feet, delicate as a fairy's, could morph into wings and carry her back to the realm from which she came. She had worried about Tippy's fragility since she was old enough to understand her friend had been born without an important working part, and Jessica might wake up one morning and find the angels had come for her playmate. Looking at Tippy's swiftly working hands, picturing them picking cotton under the broiling sun, a heavy ducking sack slung from her thin shoulders, was enough to make Jessica nauseated, but her father wouldn't do that to Tippy. Jessica was sure of it. He knew his daughter would never forgive him, but he could—and would—separate them. She must remember that.

"I don't have anything to wish for anymore," Jessica said. "Isn't that awful, Tippy? To be eighteen and out of wishes."

"I wouldn't know nothin' 'bout wishes no mo' 'cept now I'se home, to hope for sugahcane syrup to go on mah co'nbread," Tippy said.

Jessica turned from the mirror to frown at Tippy and lowered her voice. "Must you speak like an ignorant field hand when you're with me, Tippy?"

"Yessum, I do, les' I forget where I'm at. It's safer for us bof."

Jessica turned back around to her vanity. "I'm sorry now that I didn't leave you in Boston with Miss Smithfield at her dressmaker shop. You would have made a fine living with your needle and thread. There you'd have had many wishes, and they'd have all come true."

Tippy placed her mouth close to Jessica's ear and spoke literately, "Your daddy would have sent men for me, but I wouldn't have stayed anyway. I wouldn't let you come home without me."

Jessica listened for her father's footsteps in the hall. He wouldn't enter without knocking, especially now that she was grown, but he still allowed little time to answer. Yesterday morning when Tippy was allowed to return to Jessica's room from the kitchen, Jessica had told her of her mother's warning, one that Tippy had already heard from Willie May. "They want to separate us because we're so close," Jessica had explained, "and Mama has threatened you'll be sent to the fields if I don't cooperate. We have to pretend that you're my maid and I'm your mistress."

"That won't be hard to do," Tippy had said. "I am a maid, and you are my mistress."

"In name only."

They agreed they had to be very careful. Willie May had laid it out to Tippy. No more calling Jessica "Jessie" without the *Miss* attached followed by a little curtsy. No more shared giggles and secrets. No more lazy sessions reading to each other. No more show of friendship. "And," Willie May had added with a stern eye at Tippy, "no more speaking like a white lady or parading your learning for master and slave to see."

The girls had hooked thumbs—their ritual to seal an agreement. Hearing only silence from the hall, Jessica said with a smile, "I'll make sure you get all the sugarcane syrup you want, even if I have to smuggle it up here."

"No, no, Jessie—*Miss* Jessie. Don't show me any—*no*—favoritism. It's too dangerous."

Jessica sighed. "I'm so disgusted with the way things are. The South shames me. My family shames me—"

"Sssh, you mustn't speak like that. You mustn't even *think* like that."

"I can't help it."

"That new teacher comin' from the No'th…I know what she be up to, Miss Jessie. Please don't let her get you into no trouble. I'se beggin' you—"

"Jessie! It's Papa. I'm coming in!"

The strong voice of the man Jessica both loved and feared boomed through the door. Only a few seconds passed before it flew open and Carson Wyndham strode in, the strike of his knee-high boots hard on the wood floor and their shine dazzling. A short, fit, ginger-haired man of powerful build and brusque manner, he inspired the impression that throngs would part at his appearance and woe to him who did not step from his path.

Tippy, reacting quickly, cocked her head at Jessica's startled reflection in the mirror and said loudly, as if continuing a dialogue Carson Wyndham's entrance had interrupted, "…Yoah hair is so pretty jus' like dis. A cryin' shame to put it up."

"I agree," Carson said, coming to stand by his daughter's dressing table to inspect the subject of discussion. "Why the devil does a woman feel she has to torture her hair into twists and turns and God knows what all when it's so much more attractive hanging unfettered as the good Lord intended?" He fingered the delicate mesh of the head covering that hung from a finial of the mirror. Jessica had worn it at luncheon yesterday, her loose hair filling the gold-filigreed, pouch-like bag. "I liked this…whatever it's called, on you, Jessie. Why aren't you wearing it this evening?"

"Oh, Papa, a lady can't wear a *hair net* with a party gown."

It was the kind of riposte her father liked to hear from his daughter—mindless and feminine and vain. He favored her with a smile. "I suppose not. Do you like your brooch?"

"I love it. Thank you again, Papa."

He had presented it to her at the luncheon attended by her parents' closest friends. The affair was to be part of her birthday celebration, but it had really been held to show off her father's distant relatives from England, Lord Henry and Lady Barbara, the Duke and Duchess of Strathmore. Had it not been for the delightful company of Lettie Sedgewick, her only contemporary there besides her brother, Jessica thought she would have died of boredom if not from sheer disgust. Conversation had deferred to His Lordship and his opinionated wife and was all about the deplorable rise of the British middle class, the audacious attempt of farm laborers in Dorset to form a trade union, and grouse hunting. Their listeners and servile admirers, except for Lettie, had hung on every imperious word, interrupted only when Michael proposed a toast to honor his sister's homecoming.

There was much Jessica liked about Lettie Sedgewick. Jessica had looked forward to resuming her association with her former tutor when she returned from Boston, sharing what she had learned in school and exchanging ideas, but Lettie was now engaged to Silas Toliver, a widower Jessica remembered as strikingly handsome who had plans to start his own plantation in Texas. Jessica recalled that Silas's first wife had died in delivering the little boy who would soon become Lettie's stepson. Lettie was the highly intelligent daughter of a Presbyterian minister, well versed in language arts. The Wyndhams, members of her father's church, had engaged her to teach Jessica penmanship and classical literature to supplement her public school instruction before leaving for boarding school. Lettie had gone on to earn a teacher's certificate at a college in Nashville and now taught in the public school in the small town of her father's church, Willow Grove. The community was described as a stone's throw either way between Charleston and the parallel rows of plantations known as Plantation Alley, where the most prominent sugar and cotton estates were located. Silas, like Jeremy Warwick, had not been included in the luncheon party because they did not know Jessica well. They would be attending the ball.

"You would think South Carolina still a colony of the British Empire, considering how slavishly devoted some of us are to all things English," Lettie had said to Jessica with a twinkle in her eye when they finally had a chance to chat privately.

"Except for slavery," Jessica said. "The British have had the humanitarian decency to abolish the slave trade."

Jessica could have bitten her tongue. She'd leaped without looking, but Lettie Sedgewick's tolerant nature and Jessica's experience with the minister's daughter invited controversial confidences. When tutoring Jessica, Lettie had not minded, and had even encouraged, Tippy to sit in on their sessions, albeit secretly. It was against the law to teach slaves to read and write, and the tutor could have endangered her father's position as minister of the First Presbyterian Church in Willow Grove if she were found out.

Humor flitted across her friend's countenance. "Quite so," Lettie said. "I see you haven't changed much, my dear pupil, but may I caution you to think first where you are before speaking."

"I must learn to do so."

"I heard from Silas about the little incident on the disembarkation dock in Charleston yesterday. Jeremy Warwick was in the area to pick up something for Meadowlands. He told Silas that he did not show himself for fear of causing further embarrassment to you and your mother and brother."

"No doubt Mr. Warwick thought the worst of me."

"Not at all. He told Silas he thought you awfully brave."

Or awfully stupid, Jessica thought, looking at her father's sober face in the mirror. Had Michael told him of the incident in Charleston yesterday, and he was here now to chastise her?

"Jessie," Carson said, "I want you to look especially nice tonight."

"We'll certainly try, won't we, Tippy?" Jessica said, relieved. "Is there any particular reason other than it's my birthday?"

"No…no reason. I just want to feel especially proud of my little girl who's home at last after two years, so please appear your best." He bent and kissed her cheek. "See you at the party. And Tippy?"

Tippy stood at attention. "Yessuh?"

"See that it happens."

"Yessuh, Mister Carson."

He strode from the room, and the women exchanged long, interrogating looks. "What was that all about?" Jessica asked.

"Jeremy Warwick," Tippy answered promptly.

"Jeremy Warwick?"

"I heard all about it in the kitchen. Your papa wants you to make an impression on him with the hope you two will get together. You're to be seated next to him at the supper table."

"Jeremy is Silas's age—too old for me—and I understand they're going to Texas together. Why would my father want me to marry him?"

"I don't know. The Warwicks are rich. Maybe to ward off the bucks who aren't?" Tippy batted her lashless eyes meaningfully. "Jeremy Warwick is a good man, so they said in the kitchen. A good master. I can't understand why he's still unmarried. Maybe your daddy wants you to set your cap for him before someone else snatches him up."

"No, Tippy, that's not the reason," Jessica said in sudden understanding. Hurt plunged through her. Her father had learned about the brouhaha on the dock. Michael would have informed him, and her mother, too fearful to keep secrets from her husband, must have told him about her views on slavery. "My father wants to be rid of me before I cause trouble."

But only if taken out of South Carolina by a good and rich man. Her father loved her that much, she thought. Jessica felt anger slowly overtake her hurt. Well, she had news for him. She would never marry a slave owner.

Chapter Five

She was to be presented in a receiving line in the ballroom rather than strike a grand entrance from the top of the staircase. Staircases were for great beauties. The arrangement suited Jessica just fine. Her right glove was smudged by the time she had finished shaking the hands of the fifty guests attending her birthday party, and she could not feel the stem of her champagne glass for moments after she was free to seek out Lettie standing with Silas Toliver and Jeremy Warwick before her five-tiered, flower-bedecked birthday cake.

"It's lovely," Lettie exclaimed in wonder at the cake when Jessica joined them. "Do I recognize Tippy's hand in the design?"

"Of course. She made the flowers from beaten egg whites dipped into sugar and hardened."

"Well, it's exquisite, as are you, birthday girl. What a lovely gown! From Paris?"

"From Boston." Jessica felt her face grow warm under the gazes of the men. She looked the best she possibly could, but by no means would they agree she was exquisite. Lettie saw beauty in everything and everybody and could well afford to do so. *Exquisite* described her, as was plain to see in Silas's eyes. They made a dazzling couple—he, tall, dark, and handsome, a Lord Byron with his unruly raven-black hair and green eyes and attractive chin dimple, and she, petite and blond, porcelain-skinned and dainty, perfectly fitting the subject of the poet's poem "She Walks in Beauty."

"And your blush is becoming, too," Jeremy Warwick said with a little bow and the trace of a devilish grin. Was he making fun of her? Jessica ignored the compliment and said to Lettie, "I can't tell you how delighted I am to be chosen your bridesmaid."

"I can't tell you how delighted I am that you accepted. Shall we go shopping for your dress fabric next week in Charleston?"

"I'd love to, but I'm hopeless when it comes to such things. Tippy has the best eye for material and color. She has marvelous taste. She's responsible for the design and fabric of my gown. I always take her along to help me select my wardrobe. May she come, too?"

"Tippy?" Silas interposed. "That's twice I've heard her name. I don't believe I've met her."

"Uh…Tippy is Jessica's maid," Lettie explained, her look slightly uncomfortable.

"A Negro maid has better taste than her mistress?" Silas said, addressing Jessica incredulously.

Jessica's chin went up. "Mine does."

She felt her elbow taken in a firm, masculine grip. Was its pressure a warning? "I believe that's the supper bell," Jeremy said, placing Jessica's arm through his. "I'm to have the pleasure of your company on my left at table, Miss Jessica. How did I get to be so lucky to sit next to the birthday girl?"

"It was by my father's design, Mr. Warwick," Jessica said, suddenly feeling suffocated. She cast decorum to the wind, or rather to the oppressive waft of perfumes permeating the room. "If at all possible, I'm to entrance and beguile you with the hope you will not find me unweddable."

Her audience stared at her with mouths agape. Jeremy's chuckle broke the stunned silence. "By Jove," he said, "I believe I'm already entranced."

Jessica was combing out her curls from their party do when her father's short, staccato knock came at the door. Jessica saved herself the bother of responding, for it opened immediately, and he entered wearing a smoking jacket and smelling like cigar.

"Well, my girl, did you enjoy your party?"

"Yes, Papa, very much." It had been a stultifying evening, the conversation boring and predictable except for hearing Silas and Jeremy discuss their plans under way to lead a wagon train to Texas in the spring. It was to be half a mile long, and they hoped to make at least two miles an hour, enabling the emigrants to make ten miles a day, depending on the weather and sundry other obstacles. The journey sounded dangerous, fraught with the unknown, and she wondered how Lettie would fare from the rigors they would surely face. The only other interesting subject discussed had been the safe arrival that afternoon of Sarah Conklin from Massachusetts, who would be taking Lettie's teaching position at the local school. The Sedgewicks had picked her up at the dock in Charleston and taken her to her new home in Willow Grove.

"Is she pretty?" Michael had wanted to know.

"Very," the Reverend Sedgewick had pronounced, coloring slightly.

Jessica had offered no information of her acquaintance with the new schoolmarm, though she suspected that Lettie had been surprised her friend had used her influence to secure the job for an outsider and a northerner to boot.

Her father sat on the settee, the height of the seat too low to stretch out his legs comfortably, but its position providing a vantage point by which he could observe his daughter's face in the mirror. "I hope you're not simply telling me what I want to hear and that you did enjoy yourself," he said. "It was hard to tell. What did you think of Jeremy Warwick?"

Jessica teased a strand of waxed hair from its curl with the hairbrush. "I found him pleasant."

"*Pleasant!* Is that all you can say? Why, there's not an unmarried woman in all the South who wouldn't find him stimulating, lively, amusing. Many married women, too, truth be told." He worked his eyebrows knowingly at her reflection, his attempt at drollery so ludicrously foreign to his humorless nature it was hard for her not to laugh.

"Then why isn't he married?" she asked.

"Too particular, I guess, but rumor has it he lost the girl he loved to typhoid fever when he was younger. I must say, Spook, you didn't much try to impress him."

Jessica met his eyes in the mirror. *Spook.* He had not called her that since she was a little girl. The name had come from a game they'd played when she would pop out from a hiding place to surprise him. *Boo!* she'd cry, and he'd laugh and swing her around and call her his spook. Her throat tightened with an almost forgotten ache her father could waken in her.

"I was supposed to try to impress him, Papa?"

A pink flush cropped up around Carson's ears. "Well, yes, Spook. I admit to trying to play matchmaker. Jeremy is the most eligible bachelor in South Carolina other than Silas Toliver, and he's asked for. Besides, Silas has no money. Jeremy does. He would look after you properly."

"Silas has no money?" Jessica glanced in surprise at her father in the mirror. "How can that be? Queenscrown is a prosperous plantation."

"Benjamin Toliver left Queenscrown to his older son, Morris. Silas is no more than the hired help. That's why he's going to Texas."

Alarmed for Lettie, Jessica asked, "How can he afford to do so?"

"He has some money of his own that he's sunk into the venture, and the rest he's borrowing from me."

Jessica shuddered for Lettie. Not only would she be facing untold hardships in making the journey and starting a new life in Texas, but all would be done on borrowed money. It would probably take years to pay back her father before the plantation was up and running and Silas saw a penny of his own. Perhaps love would be enough to sustain them and see Silas through to the dream he and Jeremy had apparently long harbored.

Jessica turned on her dressing-table stool to look at him. "Why are you in a hurry to marry me off, Papa?"

"Well, you...you're not getting any younger, you know. Your mother was married at your age, and frankly, I can't think of another man more worthy of you than Jeremy." Carson pinched at the air with two plump, strong fingers. "You've got to pluck him out of the pot before someone else does."

"That depends on whether Jeremy is willing to be plucked."

"He looked willing enough to me, but you rebuffed him."

"He's nearly thirty, eleven years older than I am."

"What difference does that make? I am eight years older than your mother, as is Silas older than Lettie, and look how happy she is with him."

Jessica allowed that, yes, Lettie's happiness was evident to everyone at the party. She wondered if there was a man alive who could put the stars in her eyes that Silas had placed in Lettie's. She did like Jeremy. She *had* found him stimulating and lively and amusing, but he could never be interested in someone like her. Her father had witnessed merely a gentleman's courtliness toward the daughter of his host, and her indifference had been caused by resentment at being exhibited like a filly at a horse auction.

"He's going to Texas, you know," she said.

Carson's glance fell to his house slippers. "Yes, I know."

Jessica rotated back to the mirror. In this house, more was related—and understood—in the silences of her family's conversations with one another than in spoken words. The moment's lull clearly admitted her father's sad but true willingness to see her married to someone suitable as soon as feasible and carried away as far as possible. Jessica remained silent, the rhythmic sound of the brush strokes censorious in the quiet.

Carson raised his head and asked suddenly, looking around. "Where is Tippy? Why isn't she here to attend you?"

"I sent her to her room. There was no point in her waiting up to see me to bed."

Carson rose, frowning. "She's supposed to be here until you retire—*then* she can go to her room. You spoil that girl too much, Jessie. I won't have it."

"Yes, Papa," Jessica said, continuing to brush. Tippy had pleaded to stay up to hear about the party, but an attack of pleurisy that afternoon had almost brought her to her knees. Jessica would not dare remind her father of Tippy's lung condition, aggravated by the day's sudden cold snap. With few exceptions, he had little tolerance for useless property. "I'll see that she earns her keep," Jessica said.

"You better." Carson paused, locking eyes with his daughter in the mirror. She saw distress in his; felt tears rise in hers. Again, silence fell, speaking louder than tongues. "Spook, my dear, why can't you be more like…a Wyndham?" he asked. "How was it you were born so different from the rest of us?"

"I don't know, Papa," she said, attacked by a sudden apprehension that left her cold, "but I fear my dissimilarity of birth will cost me dearly."

Chapter Six

Willie May sat amidst the piles of unwashed dishes from the party the night before, indulging in a second cup of coffee and relishing the rare opportunity to be alone with her thoughts in the Big House. It was Sunday morning. Everyone in the house— the master and mistress, Miss Jessica, and the servants, including her daughter—and all the field-workers from the Yard were at church services held today by the creek. There was to be a baptism afterwards, celebrated in the shade of the big pecan and cypress trees by the bank, everybody eating the leftovers from Miss Jessica's eighteenth birthday party. The DeWitts had gotten off to Charleston and their departure to England on Saturday afternoon, thank God. At least Willie May hadn't had *them* to worry about in the hustle of getting fifty guests wined and dined and cleaned up after.

"Now, you all go on to bed," Miss Eunice had ordered the house servants last night after they'd cleared the tables and put away the food. "The dishes can wait until after church services tomorrow. Willie May, you go to bed, too. You look like you're dead on your feet."

She was good that way, Miss Eunice was, always considerate of her housekeeper's limits, though the mistress had her boundaries. Boundary lines were fine by Willie May. Life was so much easier and simpler when everybody knew their place and *accepted* it and never bothered about nobody else's. That was the subject disturbing her this morning in the peace and quiet of the Big House. Boundaries. Tippy didn't know hers, and that was the fault of Jessica Wyndham. The master's daughter was going to get her girl in trouble—*big* trouble. She could smell it coming.

A part of Willie May had knotted up tight as a ball of twine from the day her baby girl—ten years old—had wandered, with Miss Jessica, of course, into the drawing room, where the mistress was in a dispute with her decorator over color and drapery material for the Venetian windows. Willie May had been serving tea when she saw her daughter pick up two swatches of different fabric in matching colors and, calmly, without saying a word, hand them to Miss Eunice.

"Well, I declare," her mistress had exclaimed. "I do believe this is the perfect color of green and fabric combination. We'll use the velvet for the valances and the silk for the panels."

They had all stared at her baby girl, and right then, Willie May had felt that tightening of her innards that had hardly loosened a day since, especially when Miss Jessica piped, "I *told* you she was smart, Mama!" and beamed at Tippy.

Willie May and Miss Eunice had watched helplessly as the girls' friendship grew by the day. In the beginning, when the children were blossoming out from infants together, neither mother had paid much attention to their enjoyment of the other's company. On plantations, it was natural for white and black children to play together, especially if the offspring of house servants lived with their parents in quarters in the Big House. Willie May had been mightily relieved to have her daughter, born missing a lung, brought up under her eye rather than in the Yard, where the other slaves' children were put to work, and Miss Eunice had been happy that her little girl, with no sisters for companions, had a playmate. Their growing bond had skipped Carson Wyndham's notice altogether, even when his daughter had insisted that every treat be shared with Tippy and that she be given the same toys and dolls as she. It was Miss Jessica who had given Tippy, christened Isabel, her name. *"Tippy!"* she had squealed as the girls were learning to walk and her tiny daughter had preferred to tiptoe rather than toddle.

Willie May and Eunice had been slow to do anything about their daughters' closeness since, in some ways, it mirrored their own. Carson Wyndham had purchased Willie May, not quite twenty, as a maid for Eunice Wyndham when he brought his bride from Richmond, Virginia, to his huge estate, Willowshire. Alone for weeks while her husband was away minding the business of his many plantations, Eunice would have gone mad from loneliness had it not been for Willie May. Snatched from her parents and her village in Africa at seventeen years of age, Willie May understood about separation from home. She had been taught English and domestic service by Anglican missionaries—a lucky find for the slave traders—and she and the mistress had become each other's confidante, together making their way through new worlds with husbands they barely knew, sharing the joys and travails of pregnancies and childbirths and the management of the most prominent manor house in South Carolina. Eunice was quick to say she didn't know what she'd do without Willie May, but only because she trusted her housekeeper never to trespass on the bounds of their friendship.

Neither woman could say the same for Tippy, thanks to Jessica Wyndham, and the master had begun to notice.

Just this morning, as the household was leaving for the creek, he had asked in the tone they all dreaded to hear, "Where did you get that dress, Tippy?" Everybody had stiffened, including Miss

Jessica, who was finally getting it through her stubborn head that her color blindness was putting Tippy in danger.

"I made it, suh."

The master had rubbed the material between his fingers. The dress was beautifully and fashionably constructed. "Raw silk. Where did you get it?"

"In Boston, suh. It was a remnant give me by Miss Jessie's dressmaker."

The master had shot a glance to his daughter. "Do you have one made of the same fabric?"

Miss Jessica had had the good sense to duck her head. "Yes, Papa."

To Tippy he said, "Go to your room immediately and take it off. No colored maid of this household will wear a dress of the same material as my daughter."

Tippy had run from the hall, holding in a cough like the kind that had erupted from her one lung all night.

A few years ago the master wouldn't have given the dress, or its exceptional tailoring, a second thought. Tippy's sewing and weaving talents, bolstered by her color sense and eye for design, were well known and even praised in the household, but things had begun to change around Willowshire in 1831. That was the year Nat Turner, a Negro preacher, had led a two-day rebellion of slaves against their white masters in Southampton County, Virginia, where Mister Carson owned a tobacco plantation. He had gone to Virginia to witness the trial and hanging of the men involved and come home a different sort of master.

Then in 1833, to slap tar on resin, a man named William Lloyd Garrison had founded the American Anti-Slavery Society in Boston, the city where Miss Jessica was going to school, attended by the colored maid she treated like a sister. It had not occurred to the master that his daughter would be exposed to the radical teachings of the man and his followers, much less influenced by them, but he was wrong, as Willie May and Miss Eunice now realized.

Willie May got up and tied on her apron. Here at Willowshire, she and her kind had it good. Mister Carson believed in taking care of his property, and he made sure his slaves were well fed, clothed, and housed. They got weekends and Thanksgiving and Christmas off, and the field hands were allowed ten-minute rest periods in the shade and all the water they could drink. They were allowed to establish their own customs and lifestyles with no interference from the Big House so long as they stayed within appropriate bounds. The whipping post still stood in the center of the Yard, but it hadn't been used in recent memory and only then because a slave had beaten his wife half to death. The master, unlike other planters, didn't believe in breaking up colored families by selling their children. Carson Wyndham was hard but fair, and he expected his overseers and drivers to be the same. Except for the masters of Meadowlands and Queenscrown, Mr. Carson's attitude was markedly different from other planters and headmen, who could make a slave's life miserable. At Willowshire, the living was stable and fairly pleasant.

But times were changing. You could sense it at every turn. Last July, a mob had attacked the Charleston post office and burned anti-slavery literature sent by northern abolitionists to be distributed throughout the South. President Jackson had backed the protest and tried but failed to make it illegal to distribute "incendiary" material through the U.S. Post Office. Patrols had increased, bad men armed with whips and guns who rode the lanes by the light of the moon looking for runaways and uppity Negroes on whom to mete out punishment. At Willowshire, unlike before, slaves were not free to visit other slaves at other plantations without special permission from the master, and word was that Mister Carson's drivers—slaves put in charge of other slaves in the field—were less friendly to the workers. Several colored overseers had been replaced with white, and "Spit" Johnson, a grumbler whose discontent had heretofore been tolerated, had disappeared one night. Rumors flew that he had been taken away to the auction block in Charleston and sold.

Willie May feared for her daughter under this cloud of changes. Reading and writing and spouting poetry, speaking like a white woman and advising the mistresses what fabric to buy and how to wear their hair were nothing for a young colored girl with one lung to parade before her masters. After today, she wouldn't be surprised if Tippy weren't assigned chores less pleasant than keeping Miss Jessica company. She might even be removed from the room next to her mistress and assigned to a cabin in the Yard that she'd have to share with another family. Willie May prayed for her only daughter to have the good sense to mind herself, lest some night horsemen came and dragged her from her bed to make an example of what happened to Negroes who did not know their place.

Chapter Seven

"Silas, dear, what's the matter?" Lettie said to her betrothed's back. He stood at a window of the church manse that offered a view of a small garden ablaze with golden chrysanthemums. He was to take home a large arrangement of them for his mother's Thanksgiving table tomorrow. "Are you bored with all this wedding nonsense?"

Silas turned from the window, the vision of Lettie at a table overflowing with wedding frippery—lace and ribbons and a swath of something filmy—lovelier than any garden.

"No, my love, though I admit they're more to a woman's enthusiasm than a man's."

"As long as you're not having second thoughts about marrying me."

"Never." Silas came to sit beside her at the table, and she set aside a writing tablet on which she had been checking off an endless list having to do with their wedding date, the first Saturday in February. He could not comprehend why women felt compelled to begin nuptial preparations months in advance (his mother was in a flurry of activity), but he'd been assured that, with the demands of the holidays in between, early organization was critical. He had argued to set an earlier date to settle into marriage before their departure the first of March, but his fiancée's brother was a student at West Point, and he could not get leave to attend the festivities until the first week of February.

"What's troubling you, then?" Lettie ran her fingers lightly over his furrowed forehead. "When your brow gets bunched up, I can tell you're disturbed."

Silas took her hand and pressed her fingers to his lips. The smallest touch of her skin to his could arouse him. God forgive him, he could not remember his first wife's flesh that had borne his son. Were it not for Joshua, he would not have remembered her face. Ursuline, she'd been called, and the rather prudish name had fit her moralistic views, especially those related to sex. That memory of her remained. His wife had been the daughter of a planter and a member of the landed gentry, but in truth, his father-in-law had been a hell-raising brigand. Silas had expected some of the old man's fire to burn in his daughter's veins, but he had been sadly disappointed. Lettie, daughter of a preacher, hadn't a priggish bone in her body and was as eager as he to share a marriage bed. Silas called the difference in their attitudes, so incongruous to their upbringing, quirks of nature.

He was of a mind to tell Lettie the truth, but she was, after all, of Presbyterian stock, Scottish to the bone, and abhorred debt. She was aware that he would have to borrow the money for their expenses to Texas from Carson Wyndham, but, like Silas, she was convinced that with hard work, they could clear the books with him within a few years.

"We won't be sitting on our verandahs like the members of the planter class here," she'd said. "We'll work right alongside the field hands to get the job done. Time to play lord and lady of the manor when our debt is paid."

"My father would turn in his grave to know we were working alongside blacks," Silas had said, laughing, loving her for her courage and willingness to set sail into the unknown—or, rather, into the known dangers and personal deprivations—with no armor of protection but her love for and faith in him.

"Let him. We're going to Texas. Anything goes there."

His fiancée's disposition made him love her more every day, and Silas could not understand why he felt it necessary to protect her from disquieting news such as the latest unrest in Texas and this new development that threatened his dream. Lettie rose to every unexpected roadblock. Where he saw obstacles, she saw challenges. What he considered maddening detours—irritating rearrangements of his plans and desires—Lettie serenely accepted as "mercies in disguise" arranged by some grand design to save people from taking a wrong path. She lived by and taught her students the motto she'd coined to tackle onerous but necessary tasks: "Dread and do, or don't and regret."

Despite her porcelain appearance, she seemed the perfect wife to take with him to a frightening and uncertain country, but as problems continued to pile up, Silas could not brush aside his fear that even Lettie would find them insurmountable when time came to leave her home and father, lifelong friends and her beloved Charleston, so close to the town where she'd grown up. What if she refused to go? Silas couldn't bear to go off and leave her until he forged out a life for them in the new territory, and he couldn't endure remaining at Queenscrown.

Jeremy had stronger faith in her fortitude than he. "Lettie is not going to change her mind, Silas," he had told him more than once, "but it's only fair to give her the reasons to do so, or you'll regret it later on."

Silas had decided to risk the regrets and kept some daunting news to himself—like today's, for example. A new cloud hung over their heads, and he could see no sun peeking through. Eight of the ten families who'd signed agreements to lease his Conestogas had backed out. He'd thought his speculation in the wagons was a sterling investment. He'd bought them to rent to families who could not afford their own transportation to Texas, certainly not the space and comfort the Conestoga offered that regular farm wagons did not. Silas had believed the lure of striking and graceful vehicles to lease would increase the number in the wagon train (the more, the safer), and the rent money would offset part of his investment cost and pay his expenses on the trip. He would still own the wagons, which he would sell upon arrival in Texas, and a clause in the contract agreement stated the renter was to pay him a percentage of his crops for the first two years. He had not counted on the deterrents of war in Texas or the faintheartedness of men seeking a better life but lacking the will to pursue it. He'd have been better off keeping his money in his pocket.

Jeremy suffered no such financial anxieties, but Silas would not borrow from his best friend. The Warwicks and Tolivers were to begin their enterprises in Texas with no indebtedness to each other but dependency upon their mutual friendship. Snow would fly in hell before Silas gave his brother, Morris, the satisfaction of lending him money—and at exorbitant interest, no doubt. Unless he could find replacements for the number who had reneged on renting his Conestogas, he would be forced to borrow more money from Carson Wyndham, and Lettie would strongly disapprove of that. She would loathe being in further debt to a man she intensely disliked.

Soon enough to tell her, Silas decided, when he had time to hear from the advertisements he'd placed in the state newspapers and the *Nashville Republican* publicizing his Conestogas to lease, though he had little hope they'd be answered. There was great turmoil in Texas, the reason the eight families had pulled out.

"Share with me," Lettie urged, smoothing his brow.

Silas chose to relate the lesser of the two disheartening events troubling him. "The scout is back that Jeremy dispatched in late

September to reconnoiter the area where we're headed," he said. "It seems that skirmish in October between the Texians and the Mexican Army kindled a fire that can't be put out."

"It happened on Jessica's birthday—October Second," Lettie said with a trace of wonder that people could be shooting each other while others were enjoying a party.

Silas smiled indulgently and tapped her nose. "Goodness, girl, the occasions by which you remember dates," he said. "But yes, on Jessica's eighteenth birthday, the scout rode right into the fire and took up arms himself."

The papers had carried the story of the October 2 fracas between the Anglo settlers and one hundred dragoons of the Mexican Army in a town in Texas called Gonzales. The skirmish had been incited when the area's military commander of the Mexican forces demanded that a cannon be returned that the citizens of Gonzales had borrowed to protect them from Indian attacks. The colonists had refused and mounted an armed resistance under a hastily sewn flag made out of a wedding dress on which had been written: COME AND TAKE IT!

The Mexicans had tried but were defeated, and the cannon remained in the possession of the colonists.

Lettie's reaction to the story had been typical. She'd laughed. "I believe I like these Texians," she'd said. "They show fortitude and bravery against odds."

Silas draped the swath of gauze Lettie called tulle around her neck and drew her face close to his. He'd found that amorous moments worked best for softening bad news. "Remember how we thought the incident would blow over?" he said, gazing into luminous blue eyes that, come their wedding night, he would watch close in sleep and awaken the next morning beside him. "Well, it hasn't. The newspapers are calling the battle at Gonzales the 'Lexington of Texas.'"

Lettie's eyes fell seductively to his lips, quickening his desire. "And that means?"

"The Texas revolution has begun."

Dismay flooded her enamored gaze, and she pulled against the filmy restriction. "Oh dear. Will that mean we have to delay our departure until things are more settled there?"

"We can't delay. We must head out by March to make our destination before winter. We need to arrive in time to get shelters built and the land cleared for the next spring's planting."

His lips were making a slow descent from her forehead to her lips, and he heard her little sigh of pleasure. "Don't worry, my love," she said dreamily. "The United States was founded on revolution. Can we expect anything less of Texas?"

"You are the most wonderful girl," he said, but before he could kiss her, the manse's maid appeared in the doorway. "The new teacher is here to see you, Miss Lettie. Should I show her in?"

"Yes, by all means."

Lettie rose to greet her visitor with a regretful look at Silas and playfully swiped the length of tulle over his head. Silas felt briefly irritated at the interruption but was glad to be relieved of further discussion of the troubles in Texas. "I can't tell you how happy I am to be leaving my students in the hands of Sarah," Lettie said. "I was doubtful at first, what with Sarah coming to us from the North, but God answered my prayers indeed to send us someone so competent and dedicated to teaching."

"According to Jeremy, it was Jessica's doing more than God's," Silas corrected her without Lettie's enthusiasm. He had to wonder along with Jeremy why a single woman of Sarah Conklin's age and beauty had accepted a teaching post so far from her home in Cambridge, Massachusetts.

"Behind her charming appreciation of us, I sense a woman at

odds with her surroundings," Jeremy had commented. "I can't put my finger on it, but there's something slightly off-key about the lovely Sarah Conklin."

Silas paid attention to his friend's observations. Without passing judgment, Jeremy could assess people better than anyone he'd ever known, but he knew with whom to be on guard.

"Maybe it's the Massachusetts accent that sounds out of tune among us southerners," Silas had suggested.

"Maybe."

"Lettie says Sarah's escaping a broken heart."

"This far south? And why weren't local applicants considered to take Lettie's place? I know several who are qualified."

Silas had guffawed. "I'll bet you do, and they all wear skirts. Lettie says none of those who applied had the excellent references and teaching experience Sarah does."

"Those qualifications had little to do with her getting the job," Jeremy had said. "Sarah Conklin got the position because of Jessica Wyndham. They knew each other from school in Boston. Sarah's the sister of one of her classmates. Papa Wyndham pulled strings to get her hired at Jessica's request."

"Well, as the school's main benefactor, I suppose Carson feels he can take that right, but, in any event, the children of Willow Grove are getting a first-rate teacher."

Originally, Silas had considered that Jeremy's reservation toward a woman who was very much his type—independent and self-contained—was the result of his romantic relationship with one of the "local applicants" who had coveted the position and he was piqued that she didn't get it. There was also the surprise that the comely new schoolmistress had not shown a flicker of interest in Silas's handsome and eligible bachelor friend on the social occasions she had been in his company. Yet, for Jeremy to give her rebuff any more than a second's amused thought was unlike him as well. There was something about Sarah Conklin that persistently did not ring true to him.

Lettie greeted her replacement with outstretched hands when she was shown into the room. "Good morning, Sarah. Father has Jimsonweed all harnessed up for you. You'll find our horse very manageable." She turned to explain to Silas. "Sarah has come to borrow Jimsonweed and our wagon for a ride into Charleston this morning. She's to pick up a shipment of books for the children at the post office. Sarah, are you sure you don't want me to come with you?"

"Oh, no, no!" Sarah held up both hands to emphasize her objection. "I couldn't possibly drag you away from all you have to do here." She gestured toward the overflowing table and then acknowledged Silas as if noticing his presence for the first time. "Good morning, Mr. Toliver."

Silas returned a brief nod. "Good morning, Miss Conklin." There was no mistaking the glacial cast that fell over her features at sight of him before the frost was thawed by an immediate smile he thought forced. Did she dislike men in general after her broken love affair, or was it something about him and Jeremy and Michael, brother of Jessica and son of her powerful benefactor, that doused the warmth in her?

The question was no concern of his, Silas decided. Lettie liked her, and that was all that mattered. He left the women to discuss Sarah's request before his fiancée suggested he drive her into Charleston to collect her books. Silas could think of no one he'd rather less spend time with than the frosty Sarah Conklin, and he had an appointment to meet Carson Wyndham, hat in hand, at noon.

Chapter Eight

Sarah flicked the reins over the gelding's back and waved to Lettie, who had come to see her off from the stable yard. The manse vehicle was a strange-looking contraption commissioned by the First Presbyterian Church and constructed by the village blacksmith into a combination wagon and enclosed carriage. The name FIRST PRESBYTERIAN CHURCH OF WILLOW GROVE, SOUTH CAROLINA on the doors protected it from the likelihood of being searched, the reason Sarah had selected it as the perfect conveyance for spiriting a runaway slave to the port in Charleston under the very eyes of the slave-catchers. Even the most brazen would not stop a white woman on the road who was about the church's business, and Sarah was becoming recognizable in the area as the replacement for the much-loved and popular Lettie Sedgewick, a cover that offered further protection for her activities.

"Can I take the kerchief off now, miss?"

"Yes, but you'll have to stay hidden until we get to our destination. The bounty hunters are about."

Sarah spoke to a Negro man scrunched under the carriage seat. The "kerchief" he removed was a square of black fabric to hide his teeth and the whites of his eyes should anyone have cause to peer into the dark cab. She did not know his name, or he hers.

She did not know the name of the plantation from which he had escaped. He had spent the night hidden in the barn with instructions to climb into the carriage after the Reverend Sedgewick, Lettie's father, had harnessed the horse to the vehicle and left. It was Wednesday morning, not the best day of the week to effect a slave's escape, but in the relaxed atmosphere of the day before Thanksgiving, vigilance over plantation owners' property was lax. Most escapes were arranged for Saturday night. Many masters did not make their slaves work on Sundays, and the runaway would not be missed until Monday morning when he would have had a day and a half's head start to his destination. Notices of the slave's escape and his description would not be published in the newspapers until the next week, by which time the fugitive might be in a safe house closer to his freedom in the North.

Not until the carriage was well on its way did Sarah breathe easier and her heartbeat slow. So far, so good. Many things—tiny, cruel, unanticipated caprices of fate—could wreck the best-arranged plans and lead to her discovery. It was a fear like a chronic ache in her stomach. Today, if things went wrong at the dock and her "cargo" was captured, it would be only a matter of time before he broke under the lash and told the authorities what they wanted to know. The trail would lead back to her. She would be deported to the North, if not subjected to worse, but at least she could betray no one in the escape system. She did not know the name of the agent who, under cover of darkness, had arranged to have the runaway deposited in the Sedgewicks' barn last night. She could not tell the authorities the location of the place where he had hidden before then or the route he'd taken. The success of the Underground Railroad depended on concealment of the identities of those involved. If discovered, she could give her interrogators no information that would jeopardize the network organized to help slaves escape to free states and countries where slavery was illegal, like Canada and Mexico. With luck and God's beneficence, the man under the carriage seat would be stowed away on a boat headed to Montreal by nightfall.

If captured, she'd be asked how she happened to have chosen Willow Grove as a site for her abolitionist activities, and her answer would be simple enough. Jessica Wyndham, her sister's classmate, had mentioned a teaching post coming vacant when the present schoolmistress married and emigrated with her husband to Texas. Willow Grove was located in the soul of the Deep South. What better place to serve as a conductor for the Underground Railroad than in South Carolina? What better cover than as a teacher in a little town in the heart of slave country? She would keep Jessica's involvement to herself. Never would they learn from her lips that the daughter of the state's most prominent planter had not only suggested but had arranged for her to be given the teaching job.

Did Miss Wyndham know you were a conductor for the Underground Railroad?

Of course not! When I learned of the vacant post, I intentionally ingratiated myself to her by pleading a broken love affair and the need for a teaching position far away from Massachusetts.

But Jessica *had* known. When Jessica learned of Sarah's affiliation with a group that trained supporters of abolition to infiltrate the South as cogs in an organized system to undermine slavery, she had proposed the teaching position as the perfect job to conceal Sarah's clandestine activities.

"There's even a small house you can rent ideal for your purpose," Jessica had told her. "It's the property of the First Presbyterian Church in Willow Grove. It's set on the church grounds behind the cemetery, the reason it stays vacant, but it's very private and secluded."

At first Sarah was disinclined to trust her. The school made no secret of its anti-slavery sentiments, and Jessica's wealthy and powerful father could have enrolled her to gather information about the system that assisted slaves to escape from the South. It did not take long for Sarah to realize that her suspicions of Jessica were unfounded. Jessica's parents were ignorant of the school's leanings, or they never would have sent her there, and their daughter genuinely and wholeheartedly abhorred slavery as a cruel and immoral institution. She considered her colored maid Tippy her best friend, and it was for Tippy's sake that once Sarah was ensconced in her position in Willow Grove, Jessica had regretfully explained she could do nothing to help her in her mission.

"My father will send Tippy to the fields if he discovers my involvement," she'd said, and Sarah, having met Carson Wyndham and perceived exactly what kind of man he was, had no doubt Jessica's fears were justified.

"You've done enough," Sarah had assured her. "Keep Tippy safe."

At boarding school she had explained to Jessica that the Underground Railroad was no railroad at all but a highly secret network of escape routes and safe houses strung from the South to the North and farther into Canada or southward into Mexico. Railroad terminology designated the duties of the brave souls willing to help slaves escape. "Agents" were people who infiltrated the South to distribute abolitionist literature, contact anti-slavery sympathizers, and set up routes and safe houses run by "station masters." The houses were known as "stations" or "depots" where fugitives could rest and eat. Conductors led the runaway—or "cargo"—from one station to the next, the job Sarah had been trained for.

When Sarah reported Jessica's offer to the "engineer"—the head of her group—he enthusiastically encouraged her to take the position. An agent was already in place in the area of Willow Grove, he told her. She was not to know his name in case she was caught, but he would know hers and make contact by code. Sarah had mailed her résumé to the school's administrative body, and a return letter granted her, sight unseen, the position and stated a date to begin her teaching duties the middle of October. Shortly afterwards, she had set sail for her destination to get settled before she assumed her post and was greeted by Lettie and Reverend Sedgewick as she stepped onto the dock in Charleston.

The Sedgewicks were another reason why her real purpose in Willow Grove must remain undetected. If suspicion fell on her, it might also fall on them, and they were innocent of what she was about in the secluded house behind the cemetery. There, having learned the secret, silent "language" by which she and the agent communicated, Sarah had received knocks late at night, found notes written in code slipped under her door or odd markings on her front stoop. Within days of taking up residence, she'd hidden a runaway for pickup at midnight, flashed signals by way of candle and lamplight into the woods across the creek, and left several cryptic messages to be collected from the back porch. The number of runaways and successful escapes had increased in the area, but so far no one had tied it to her arrival. The "freight" had slowed now that winter had blocked routes to points farther north. Sarah felt she'd lived a lifetime since her boat had docked in Charleston less than two months before.

"Fellow," she said, barely moving her lips, her lowered voice urgent, "there's trouble up ahead. Put the kerchief back on and lie absolutely still."

"Oh, Lord have mercy," her cargo moaned.

A knot of horsemen had emerged from the thickets on one side of the road. Coiled whips hung from their saddle horns and all carried weapons. Sarah, at the raised hand of one of the riders, pulled at the reins and drew Jimsonweed to a stop. She recognized the heavy, well-tailored shoulders of the most affluent among them: Michael Wyndham, Jessica's brother.

He kneed his fine Arabian stallion toward the wagon, surprise, curiosity, and admiration mingling in his gaze beneath the wide brim of his low-crowned planter's hat. Sarah felt the back of her neck crawl. The man was a perfect replica of his father. Carelessly, Michael brought his fingers to his hat brim. "Mornin', Miss Conklin. What brings you along the road this day before Thanksgiving?"

"I'm on my way to the post office in Charleston," she said. "And you?"

He laughed and threw a glance at his cohorts. "Isn't it obvious? We're looking for a runaway from Willowshire. You haven't by any chance seen a black man running for his life along the road, have you? He goes by the name of Timothy."

A soft grunt came from under the seat. *Timothy.* The runaway was from Willowshire. *Good God, Jessica, what have you done?* Sarah's breath held from alarm that Michael Wyndham had heard the muffled sound, but his attention remained fastened on her.

"I'm afraid not," she said, forcing a light but dismissive tone and regripping the reins to suggest she must be on her way.

The press of Michael Wyndham's muscular thighs urged his horse closer. Sarah knew he was attracted to her as only a man can be who enjoys the thrill of the hunt and satisfaction of the kill. Her patent indifference to him had backfired. If she'd been flirtatious and coy, he would have lost interest, but she presented a challenge he was determined to win. If only he knew how much she loathed him and his kind.

"Perhaps you'll allow me to ride with you to Charleston, Miss Conklin," he suggested. "My cohorts can take charge of my horse and pursue the boy without me, and you and I can dine at the Thermidor after you've finished your business at the post office."

Quickly, her heartbeat pounding, Sarah considered how best to respond to his offer. What argument could she give to dissuade the arrogant toad? Please, Timothy, do not make a sound. "I appreciate your kindness, Mr. Wyndham, but I have already accepted an invitation to luncheon with a longtime friend of mine, a gentleman who is visiting Charleston, and the morning is so fine, I confess to preferring my own company on the ride into town."

Rather than being put off, rebuffed, as she intended, he threw back his head for a hearty laugh. "You seem always to know how to put me in my place, Miss Conklin, but I am not an easy man to stay put." He touched his hat again, an imposing figure in his polished knee boots with his thickening girth minimized by the outward flare of a long jacket pinched at the waistline, a colorful scarf around his neck. "Enjoy your ride and your luncheon with your gentleman friend, and I shall look forward to another time when I have the pleasure of your exclusive company for both."

He signaled with his hand, and the horsemen parted. Head held high and back straight, Sarah directed Jimsonweed through the pack without returning a nod of greeting and shortly heard the sound of hooves cantering off in the opposite direction.

There was a stir beneath the carriage board. "We clear, miss?"

Sarah put a hand over her heart to steady its hammering. "We're clear, Timothy."

Chapter Nine

The Christmas season had arrived in Plantation Alley. The vast fields of the plantation estates sprawling along both sides of the farm-to-market road lay at rest. The cotton had been picked, the sugarcane cut, and the period on the calendar that Eunice Wyndham most dreaded was over. She welcomed the first prolonged spell of cold weather, but it meant that hog-killing time was upon them, when the pigs rounded up from the woods in early fall, penned, and fattened on generous feedings of corn and mash, would be killed and butchered. For the last several weeks, Plantation Alley had been a virtual slaughterhouse. Eunice had closed windows and doors, sacrificing the first bracing air of autumn to spare herself, Jessica, and the women servants the grisly sounds and smells associated with the killings. If the wind was right, the frantic squeals of "stuck" pigs and thick, strong odor of fresh blood, as well as smoke from pit fires burning in the curing houses, could carry all the way to Willow Grove.

Don't come for Christmas until the last ham is in the curing house, Eunice wrote to her sister in Boston. *You won't be able to breathe the air without retching.*

Those with more appreciation for the end result had learned to ignore the bloody business of sticking and killing and gutting, for it meant an abundance of meat for dining tables, larders, and smokehouses, not only for planters and their families, but, if their masters were generous, for the slaves as well. Carson Wyndham was the most munificent among them.

He kept for the Big House the kidneys, valued for their lard; bladders to be used as preserving sacks; pigs' feet for pickling; and the heads from which to make headcheese, but the meat not set aside to be cured for his own use he had distributed to his workers. During the butchering, the slave community of Willowshire enjoyed quantities of fresh sausages, pork butts and shoulders, backbones, ribs, tenderloins, slabs of bacon, and a share of the makings for cracklings—bits of fat taken from beneath pig skin to be fried and baked in buttermilk cornbread—and chitlings, pieces of small intestines cut up and fried as a treat.

Once hog-killing season was over, work eased, and master and slave alike could relax a bit and enjoy the fruits of their labor. At Willowshire, there were many. It had been a season of plenty. Profits from his numerous plantations and business enterprises allowed Carson Wyndham to budget a present of twenty dollars to be given Christmas morning to the head of each Negro household in addition to sacks of candy, popcorn balls, and whittled toys for the children. Pantries and root cellars were full. A mild fall had produced a bumper crop of vegetables, berries, and fruits. Cotton sacks brimmed with pecans thrashed from the most productive trees in years, and no family—planter's or worker's—wanted for sorghum syrup to pour over their cornbread.

Which was why when the alarm went up that somebody had stolen into the master's smokehouse and robbed it of two hams, Carson Wyndham called in his head overseer.

"I want you to find out who did this," Carson ordered, his face the color of his reddish hair. Of all the sins the master of Willowshire could not forgive, stealing was at the top of the list. "It may be a runaway or an itinerant passing by, a vagrant, but if the thief is one of ours..."

"What am I to do then, sir?"

"You know the penalty for stealing, Wilson. Enforce it."

Willie May had been listening while pouring the master his morning tea and she missed the rim of the cup, sloshing tea into the saucer. The door to the outbuilding where he received his overseers and dispensed his orders was propped open, and the fresh, holiday smell of the evergreen wreath tacked upon it was strong. Tippy had bound the cedar cutting with a limber wisteria vine and decorated it with painted wooden fruits and a big red bow. Passing it to enter the building, Willie May had felt a lift of her Christmas spirits. Now they drooped.

"What's the matter with you this morning, Willie May?" Carson asked, but not unkindly. Lately, he'd taken an undue tone with her because of Tippy. Displeased with the daughter, he could not be too friendly with the mother, but his posturing relaxed when he forgot himself and had his mind on other matters. Carson had come to rely on the good sense and wisdom of his housekeeper. She prevented his wife from going off half-cocked and kept the other servants in line without disrupting the order of his household. Other servants could bring him his tea in the morning, but he preferred Willie May, whose presence never jarred. "You're not coming down with the ague, are you?" he asked.

Willie May blotted the spilled tea with a corner of her apron. "No, suh, Mister Carson. I just hit my funny bone."

"Well, you keep yourself in good fettle, you hear? We can't have you sick at Christmas when everybody else is having a good time." He nodded to his overseer. "That'll be all, Wilson. You know what to do." When he had gone, Carson swiveled his chair around to address the main cog that kept his house running smoothly. The redness in his face had eased. "What do you think, Willie May? Who's stealing from us?"

"I couldn't say, suh. I didn't know anybody was. I haven't heard a thing."

There were hot rolls, too, and Willie May kept her attention on spreading butter and molasses on them, just like Carson Wyndham liked. She handed him a napkin, which he tucked into the collar of his crisp cotton shirt to catch the drips.

"Must be a vagrant," he said absently, his gaze diverted to some reading material on his desk. "None of my people have reason to steal from me."

"That is so, Mister Carson."

"Wilson will find out who it is and may God have mercy on the culprit when he does."

"Amen, Mister Carson."

Willie May hoped the good Lord heard the invocation for mercy. She was the culprit. She had spotted the runaway, a boy not older than fifteen, stealing into the barn last week when she'd gone at midnight to check on Tippy, still quartered in the room next to Miss Jessica's. Her daughter had been coughing all day, and Willie May had prepared a hot mustard plaster to place on her chest. It was a clear, moonlit night, and she'd noticed a shadow move out from the cotton fields, hesitate, move forward again, then pause. It emerged once more, and she had a brief glimpse of a skinny boy of her race wearing ragtag clothes, too skimpy for the cold night, before the body melted into the shadows of the barn.

No building at Willowshire except the master's cabin—his outdoor study—was ever locked. The master's arrogance wouldn't have it. Nobody would dare steal from him. Barns, storage and equipment sheds, silos, root cellars, the two smokehouses, one for curing the most recent meat and the other for storing last year's—all were open for anyone to enter without the bother of keys, but none would be so brazen without proper reason to do so. Carson Wyndham's total control over his fiefdom guaranteed that.

So even her brief glimpse of the intruder convinced Willie May the boy was not one of Willowshire's one hundred slaves. A cold feeling stole over her. A runaway, then.

She hurried down the stairs and let herself out the back door, grabbing a shawl from a kitchen hook, and quietly but quickly made her way across the compound to the barn. Slowly, she opened the door. It creaked a warning but not soon enough for the boy to overcome his frightened curiosity and duck his head down. He had found himself a bed of straw in the loft, and when he saw that he'd been caught, he stared back at Willie May like a hare caught in the sight of a hunter's gun until she motioned for him to come down. The boy obeyed, his head hung, his shoulders drawn as if already feeling the lash of the whip.

"Don't be afraid," she said, wondering why she felt no fear. The boy was thin but taller than she and obviously desperate. Her only concern was that someone in the Big House was up and had seen them. "I'm not here to hurt you. Who are you?"

"I . . . can't say, missus," he said.

"I'm guessing I know why. You've run away, haven't you?"

The boy remained silent, and Willie May, seeing in him her own son who had died of tuberculosis at fifteen, felt moved by a maternal impulse to put her arms around him. His shoulders felt knife thin, and his tense, stiff body was shivering in his inadequate clothes, either from fear or because he had not had time to warm himself, probably both. She pulled away and stared into his gaunt, frightened face. Without thinking of her own welfare, she took off her shawl, wrapped him in it, and said resolutely, "I'm going to help you. You must trust me."

Either he would or he wouldn't. Willie May could tell he was trying to make up his mind, but he looked hungry, and hunger took risks. "You can watch me go to the smokehouse, so you know I'm not going to get the master," she said. "I'll bring you some food. You'll have to take it to your hiding place while it's dark to eat it. It's too dangerous for you to stay here. I'll leave you more food and something warm to wear behind the smokehouse tomorrow at dusk, and you can come and fetch the stuff when all is quiet. I'll hide everything under the firewood."

She had snitched a ham and brought it to the boy, who had watched her from a crack in the barn. She exchanged her shawl for a horse blanket she found on a tack shelf and instructed him to leave it in the place where she'd hide the food. Before leaving him, she thought of a code by which they could communicate. Thank goodness it was Christmastime and the holiday napkins were out.

"When you see the corner of a white napkin tucked into the woodpile, you'll know the coast is clear to come to the woodpile. If you see a red one, you'll know to stay away," Willie May told him. "The napkins will be easy to see from a distance. If you see a green one, that means they're looking for you and you're to try to make it to the gazebo where you can hide. Do you know what a gazebo is?"

The boy slowly shook his head, his forehead knotted in an effort to understand.

"It's that white, round-looking structure to the side of the master's house. You can see it from the woods. Most of the sides are open, but there's a shed right next to it for storing extra chairs with plenty of room for you to hide. The gazebo is never used, and no one will think to look for you in a place so close to the house. I'll come to you soon as I can."

The boy had listened in silence, but his round, anxious eyes told her he'd taken in everything she'd said. Willie May wondered if his mama was still alive and worried out of her mind about him. After sunset the next day, she had left the items as promised, finding them gone when she returned with more food the following afternoon. For two days after that, though, she'd had to leave a red napkin in the chinks of the wood bin, and in that time after darkness fell, the boy must have stolen the second ham.

She had heard no news of a runaway or that anyone was looking for him. Willie May guessed the boy had no particular destination in mind when he took off. He'd run blindly on hope and luck, and his strength and courage had petered out somewhere behind the Big House of Willowshire. But now the overseers would be looking, and if they found the boy...

Why, oh why, had she sent Lulu—with a heart the size of a penny and an eye that could spot an overlooked spec of dust on a ten-foot windowsill—to fetch a package of jowls from the smokehouse when she should have gone herself? Willie May had been smart enough not to steal items from the pantry. If the discovery was made, Miss Eunice would suspect a house servant, and that would never do. Willie May had not believed two hams, out of the dozens remaining in the smokehouse from last year, would be missed. She had not counted on Lulu's eagle eye detecting the theft or her nasty delight in tattling on the trespasses of others.

Willie May gazed at the head of her master bent over his paperwork. "What will you do to...the culprit if he's found?" she asked hesitantly.

"If he's a vagrant, he'll be given a good thrashing. He can come to the back door and beg, but he can't steal from honest folks' smokehouses. If he's a runaway, he'll be taken back to his master, where he'll get whatever punishment is meted out for the offense.

Most likely he'll be whipped. That's the penalty for one of ours caught stealing."

"Suppose…the culprit was simply hungry, and his stomach won out over his conscience?" Willie May suggested.

Carson lifted his head from his reading and blinked at her as if the rapid shutting and opening of his eyes would help him understand a question he'd never been asked before. Willie May braced for a chastising, but he said, "Rules are rules, Willie May, and reluctant though I may be to punish a hungry man, if I relaxed the rules for one, I'd have to do it for the others, and people take advantage of Christian charity."

"Yessuh," Willie May said, wondering how he would know, but she'd see the runaway did not strain his "Christian charity." She knew the person who might help her rescue him before his back felt the lash. She would first run to get a green napkin to stick in the woodpile, then she would go to Miss Jessica.

Chapter Ten

Sarah waited in the cold shade of a cypress tree for Jessica to appear from the woods on her roan filly, Jingle Bell. Jessica had sent word to her by way of Lettie to meet her "at our usual spot."

"Good gracious," Lettie had said, appearing a little hurt at being excluded. "You two sound like conspirators. What are you up to?"

Sarah had rolled her eyes mischievously. "Wouldn't you like to know?"

Understanding, Lettie's cheeks had turned pink. "Oh, now, you all don't go planning anything for me, you hear? There will be enough gifts and prenuptial parties as it is. Truly, you honor me enough by being in my wedding."

"We'll try to keep that in mind," Sarah said, giving her friend a patronizing pat on the shoulder.

Lettie assumed their "usual spot" was a tearoom tucked between a bookstore and ice cream parlor where the three women often met after school had dismissed. Sarah had few social distractions from her mission and enjoyed their gatherings. She looked forward to the lively conversation and hot tea and crusty scones before going home to a cold supper and the dangerous tasks that might await her, her homesickness as weighing as the gloom in the corners of her bleak little house. The Sedgewicks offered the diversion of a Wednesday night meal at their house followed by a game of cards, and Jessica was always after her to join her family for supper—"I'll send the carriage to pick you up"—but those invitations Sarah declined. Michael would be sure to offer his services for the drive, and she could not have abided the proximity of him to her in the close quarters of the carriage. She saw the Wyndhams only if the Sedgewicks were invited and she could go and return with them.

It was in the tearoom that Jessica had slipped her a note during one of the group's first get-togethers. *Meet me tomorrow afternoon at the water mill by Lawson Creek,* it read. That occasion had been in October, shortly after Sarah had come to Willow Grove. The spot referred to in the note was secluded but easily accessible by foot and on the route where Jessica took her afternoon rides aboard her filly. At that meeting, the girl had dismounted with a pleased, self-satisfied smile, relieving Sarah's fears that the purpose of their rendezvous was grave. Her hackles had risen. If the girl thought her involvement with the Underground something to play at, Sarah would disenchant her of the notion before she could wipe that grin off her face.

"I hope you'll forgive the mysteriousness of my note," Jessica apologized immediately, apparently realizing the reason for Sarah's scowl, "but I thought it best to establish a secret place to meet in case a situation calls for it. I see you found the spot easily enough."

There was wisdom in her reasoning, and twice they'd met at the water mill by Lawson Creek. Jessica was not a member of the Underground—she'd vowed she had no hand in Timothy's disappearance—but she passed on information vital to the safety of slaves trying to make it to freedom and the security of Sarah's part of the network. Carson Wyndham had put Tippy to work in the afternoons weaving horse blankets at the looming cabin in

the Yard—"no more lollygagging with my daughter all day"—
and the maid learned things she told Jessica, who shared them
with Sarah. Also, pro-slave factions met in the great paneled
library of the Wyndham manor house—politicians, other plantation owners, slave-traders, federal marshals, bounty hunters, and
the ubiquitous Night Riders, of which Michael was the leader.

When they gathered, Jessica's ear was at the door. Who knew
how many runaways had her to thank for avoiding a snare set
by the Night Riders? The group had learned that lanterns or
candles burning in windows of rural homesteads were a signal
that the home was friendly to escaping slaves on their way to station houses, usually a distance of twenty miles apart. Attics, lofts,
barns, even underground tunnels were used to hide the fugitives
until it was safe for them to leave. Michael and his henchmen enlisted the aid of a farmer to place such signals in his windows
to lure unsuspecting runaways into a trap. Jessica got word to
Sarah, who rode out to the homestead on Jimsonweed and left
large, mischievous markings on the fence post to alert the fugitives, believing the farmer would think them the prank of a child.
Runaway slaves knew to look beyond the trusted signals for anything awry that could be a message warning of a trap.

Another time, Jessica had alerted Sarah of a bank teller planted
to get evidence against another employee suspected of being an
active opponent to slavery.

No information was ever passed in writing among those involved with the Railroad. For the safety of the network, it was absolutely essential to communicate by word of mouth, prearranged
signals, codes, or symbols whose meaning could be deciphered
only by the intended receivers. Jessica had been kept ignorant of
them, the reason they must meet face-to-face in secret.

Sarah rubbed at her arms in her woolen cloak for warmth. Here
in the coastal area of the Atlantic winters were mild, with tem-

peratures rarely dipping below sixty degrees during the day, but a lasting cold front had brought the first true feel of winter and, for Sarah, a longing for her parents' fireside, soon to be satisfied. School had adjourned for the Christmas holidays, and in three days' time, Jessica would come by to pick her up in the carriage to take her to Charleston to catch a boat to Cambridge, where she would reunite with her family until classes resumed in January. She had especially missed her seven-year-old nephew, Paul, son of her older brother. Her sister-in-law had written that Paul had asked over and over, "When is Auntie Sarah coming home?"

Lettie had been alarmed at the thought that Sarah would be so glad to be back in Cambridge she might not return. "You *must* come back to us, Sarah! What would the students do without you? How can I get married without you? Don't you let that little nephew of yours convince you to stay."

There would be no chance of that, Sarah thought, much as she loved and missed the little mutt. Sometimes Sarah felt that her effort to put an end to slavery was like trying to empty the ocean with a teaspoon, but she must do her part. She believed that with faith and perseverance, people seeking to right a wrong would eventually prevail, no matter the odds against them.

She heard the sound of a horse's hooves on the forest path, but not the usual gentle jingle of bells and casual clip-clopping that announced Jessica's appearance. Jingle Bell burst out of the woods at a gallop, flowing mane threaded with ribbons in seasonal colors, and Jessica was out of the saddle before she'd reined the filly to a full stop.

Sarah ran to her. "Good Lord, Jessica, what's the matter?"

Jessica almost fell into her friend's arms. Her fair skin was blazing red from the ride and cold air, and she could not catch her breath. "You've got to help us, Sarah," she gasped. "Willie May's found a runaway at Willowshire."

Casting a look over her shoulder, Sarah led her to a tree trunk to shield them from eyes and ears that might be prying from the woods. "Sssh," she said softly. "You must lower your voice, Jessica. Calmly, now, tell me what happened."

Jessica inhaled a deep breath of cold air and expelled it in the flow of her narrative. About ten days ago, at midnight, she told Sarah, their housekeeper had found a runaway in the barn—"not yet grown to a man," she repeated Willie May's description. He wouldn't tell Willie May his name or where he was from or where he hid in the day. Two hams had been discovered missing from the smokehouse, and her father was now aware a thief was about. He'd dispatched their head overseer to investigate and find him. They didn't think the thief belonged to Willowshire but was somebody hiding along the lake or in the woods. Jessica agreed with Willie May that it would be only a matter of time before the overseer and his men flushed the boy out, and then—Jessica closed her eyes as if experiencing sudden pain—"my father will send him back to his master to be flogged. Willie May says it wouldn't take but a few lashes to whip the flesh right off his bones, the boy is so skinny...and young."

"Why did Willie May go to you?" Sarah asked.

Jessica met her direct look with a defiant one of her own. "She knows my heart, Sarah. How can I keep it a secret?"

Sarah shook her head. "I fear for you, Jessica. What do you want me to do?"

"I'm going to get the boy out of there as soon as possible. Scooter, our blacksmith, is willing to help. He'll hide the boy in the wagon when he comes into town to pick up a new wheel. He'll let him out in the church cemetery, and the boy can stay with you until I come by to take you in the carriage to the dock in Charleston. By then, you'll have made arrangements for his escape with those seamen you know—"

Jessica stopped at the look on Sarah's face and pressed her hands to her wind-reddened cheeks. "Oh, my goodness, Sarah, have I presumed? Are you worried that Scooter will connect you to the reason he's to drop the boy off near your house? I assure you, he won't. Cemeteries are preferred hiding places for slaves."

"No, of course you haven't presumed…." Sarah said. She sank back against the tree, gripped by a premonition that this time luck would be against them. There was a second's flash of her nephew's impish face in her mental vision. Perhaps her sense of doom was due to her reluctance to take on a mission so close to her departure for home.

"All right," she said. "I can hide the boy until then. The Sedgewicks have gone to be houseguests of the Tolivers for a few days, a boon for us. When can I expect the delivery? I'll need time to make contact with my source."

"Sometime this afternoon. The boy is hiding in a shed in the gazebo, and we have to make sure it's safe to spirit the boy into the wagon. Will that give you enough time to do…whatever it is that you do?"

"I believe so," Sarah said. She would leave a light in her back window to alert her contact across the creek of a cargo to be delivered. He or she in turn would signal back that her message had been received. She would then be notified, again by code, that arrangements had been made at the dock in Charleston for pickup by personnel of steam ships willing to grant assistance. She never had to wait long for her message to be received and answered. Her instructions would be simple. She was to drop her passenger off at a prearranged spot at the dock and leave. The day she'd deposited Timothy, she had barely turned Jimsonweed toward home and cast a look behind her to see that he'd disappeared. It worried her that "the person across the creek," as Sarah came to call the agent, knew her identity. She could only hope whoever it was would never be discovered, and they could both remain safe to meet the needs other tomorrows would bring.

"I'll make arrangements and be on the lookout for him," Sarah said.

Jessica threw her arms around her. "Oh, thank you, Sarah. Christmas will have more meaning to me this year, knowing we saved the boy."

"We haven't saved him yet, Jessica. In this business, there's always a chance of the train being derailed, and you can't rest easy until conductor and passenger have made it safely to their destination."

Chapter Eleven

In the library at Queenscrown, Silas Toliver threw down his pencil on the pages of columned items and figures spread on his late father's massive desk, now belonging to his brother, Morris, and held his head in his hands. The numbers refused to lie, as did his own inner voice. He had been a fool to speculate in the Conestogas, as Carson Wyndham had unequivocally pointed out when he'd refused him a loan.

"I'm sorry, Silas, but I'm not about to throw good money after bad. What were you thinking to invest your money in an enterprise with so many potential pitfalls? Your mistake was basing your business venture on the trustworthiness of other people to get those vehicles to Texas, take care of them, and abide by the agreement they signed, which, as you've sadly learned, is about as binding as a lady's hair ribbon. You *never* place your expectations for financial success in the hands of other people. They'll disappoint you every damn time. You need to stick to farming, which you're very good at. Leave investing to businessmen like me who know what we're doing."

Silas could have torn out his hair. What in God's name *had* he been thinking? No one had replied to the for-sale ads he'd placed far and wide, and now eight proud, seven-hundred-dollar Conestoga wagons went begging in a field by one of Queenscrown's barns, a humiliating reminder of his failure to turn a profit outside the realm of cotton farming. An armada of them, their high, white canvas tops like unfurled sails, was weathering next to his own wagon and the two awaiting the families who'd agreed to rent them, but what was the guarantee they'd still want them come their delivery date the first of February?

Silas had been counting on that loan from Carson Wyndham to pay for provisions, supplies, and expenses incurred along the way. He was already leaving South Carolina in debt to the man, not an easy creditor to owe. Even if the Conestogas sold at less than what he paid, he and Lettie and Joshua would have to live on practically nothing for the five to six years he would be in hock to the richest man in South Carolina, and Silas hated that for his family. While other settlers, the prosperous among them, would be building their manor houses, increasing their holdings, adding slaves to their workforce, he, in comparison, would still be living in a log cabin minding the few acres of his original land grant with the help of his meager number of blacks. Lettie would have to make her own clothes of the most economical materials while the wife of Jeremy, should he marry, and the wives of his debtless neighbors could afford seamstresses and silk.

But now, without the money he'd hoped from Carson, even that scant existence was beyond his financial reach.

He had no choice but to go to Morris.

In the other room, he could hear Joshua's excited voice as he pointed to the pictures in a storybook Lettie had borrowed from Sarah's classroom. Silas had left his son sitting in Lettie's lap, his favorite place to be, under the fond eyes of Reverend Sedgewick, who sat smoking his pipe next to Elizabeth knitting before the fire. Their peaceful, happy scene jarred with the black mood overtaking him as he pushed away from the desk. He stared up at an oil painting Benjamin Toliver had commissioned of himself when he was young and felt consumed by a bitterness so intense his finger trembled when he shook it at him. "You could have spared me this, Father, if you'd only loved me enough to remember me fairly. I was your son, too—"

"You wronged our father, Silas."

Silas swung around. Morris had quietly entered the room. He was a large man of the bearish build and cloddish movements that made hostesses fear for their fragile whatnots, but on occasion, his brother's eyes were the gentlest Silas had ever seen. They were such now, and Silas thought he saw tear shine in them. He bit back the retort on his tongue and gathered up the sheets of paper. Morris had deeply loved their father. It was another offense Silas laid at the feet of the man who had sired them. He had made it impossible to comfort his brother in his grief.

"I'm glad you're here, Morris. I have something to discuss with you."

Silas moved to another chair, vacating the one behind the desk for its owner, but Morris ponderously lowered himself into the wingback across from him. "I'm glad you're here, too," his brother said, "for where you are, Joshua and Lettie are also."

Morris read his Bible faithfully, and he often expressed himself in the syntax of the King James Version. Lettie thought his tendency poignantly appealing and that it allowed a surprised glimpse into the Morris few rarely saw. Silas understood that his brother was already feeling the absence to come. Without Joshua and Lettie, his house would be barren. It did not occur to Silas that his son and future wife would be the reason Morris would turn him down.

"No, brother. I will not help you," Morris said when Silas had presented his request. "Your place is here at Queenscrown with Mother and me. I would give you the money if it meant that you alone would go to Texas, but I will not pave the way for you to take Joshua and Lettie."

"I will not leave them here, Morris."

"Then you can't go, not on my dollar."

"And you would dispute that our father wronged me?"

"I would dispute that he knew what was best for you. In my opinion, he didn't."

"If that is so, give me the half of Queenscrown that should rightfully have gone to me, and I will—if not gladly—at least, willingly, stay."

"And go against our father's final wishes for what he thought best for you? I'm afraid I can't do that, Silas."

"You speak in riddles, Morris."

"I speak plainly what you are too blind to see, my brother."

Morris could not be persuaded. Silas promised him that if he would give him the money, the Conestogas were his. He could sell them to the federal army, who would probably pay top dollar.

"Why don't *you* sell them to the army?" Morris suggested.

Because negotiations with the army would probably take months, Silas explained, and he hadn't months, not if he left this spring. He needed money now for outfitting his rig to be ready the first of March.

But it was no use. Morris remained adamant in his refusal. Texas was no place for a woman and child right now. Silas could stay another year, save his money, sell his Conestogas, and hook up with another wagon train next spring. Jeremy and his group would have paved the way. Meanwhile, their mother would be spared the agony of another loss, at least temporarily, and Joshua would have more time to be with his grandmother and uncle. Perhaps the memories would stick, and the boy would someday wish to return for a visit. The discussion ended with Silas marching from the study and slamming the door. Startled, the happy group gathered around the fire looked up to see son, father, fiancé, and future son-in-law stomp up the stairs to his room, his handsome face dark with rage.

"Don't run after him, Lettie," Morris advised from the door of the library. "He's inconsolable."

"What happened?" she asked, having been on the verge of setting Joshua from her lap to do exactly what he cautioned against.

"His dream for the moment has been shattered," Morris said.

"What do you mean?"

"Silas will not be singing the Lord's song in a strange land," he parodied from the Psalms in the Old Testament. "In other words, he won't be going to Texas, at least not this spring. It looks as if Mother and I will have the delight of your company a year longer."

Morris strode forward and, to his nephew's exhilarated laughter, lifted him high above his head. "Let's go see the new puppies, shall we, my fine boy?"

In his room, Silas braced his arm against the cold fireplace and bowed his head. What was he to do now? Where could he turn for money? Other lenders might be willing to bankroll him, but once word got out that Carson Wyndham thought him a poor loan risk, he stood no chance of convincing them otherwise. He must tell Lettie of the pickle he'd gotten them into. She would understand, forgive him, try to get him to make the best of it for another year. Easy for her. She loved his mother and liked his brother—"a loving man, Silas, if only you could appreciate that side of him"—and certainly Queenscrown, with its gardens and acres of lawn, servants and horses and dogs, far different from the cramped manse she'd known all her life. But what she didn't understand—wouldn't love—was the man she married if they had to live another year at Queenscrown. That man would not be able to endure his brother's orders—so often wrong for the plantation. Didn't Morris know that land must lie fallow for several growing seasons to replenish itself? He could not bear to be paid a paltry salary while the profits of his labor poured into Morris's coffers. How could he stand to be regarded as no better than an overseer while his brother sat astride his black stallion as the master of the house where he, too, had been born and bred?

He must find a way out, no matter what it cost, what he had to agree to. He would sell his soul to pull out with Jeremy Warwick March first, 1836, as a leader of the wagon train headed for the black waxy region of Texas. He simply had to find someone willing to buy it.

Chapter Twelve

Eunice said, "Willie May, we need to do something with the gazebo. It looks naked as a plucked bird out there without even a bow to commemorate the season. I'll gather the decorations, and I want you to round up some help and Tippy. We'll need her imagination in this, and we'll go out there and see what we can put together."

Willie May was quite sure she turned as white as her apron. "Right now, Miss Eunice?"

"What could be a better time? I want every nook and cranny decorated as festively as possible before my sister arrives from Boston day after tomorrow. They're so *Puritan* in their celebration of Christmas up there. I want her to enjoy a little color in her surroundings while she's here, and she so loves to read in the gazebo." Eunice paused. "What's the matter? You're looking at me with a stare as long as a country mile."

"Oh, why, I—It's nothing, Miss Eunice. I got a funny tickling down my backbone, is all."

"Somebody just walked over your grave, Willie May. Where is your daughter?"

"Upstairs with Miss Jessica. Miss Jessica just returned from her ride, and Tippy is helping her change for luncheon."

"Jessie can change without her. Would you please go tell your daughter I want to see her?"

"Yes, Miss Eunice."

Willie May hurried out of the room and up the stairs. *Oh, holy baby Jesus!* The runaway was still in the gazebo. What in the world were they going to do? The cooking staff was preparing luncheon, and servants would shortly be passing to and from the kitchen to the Big House with items for the table in direct sight of the gazebo and storage shed. It would be impossible to spirit the boy to another hiding place without someone seeing him.

Her heart beating so fast Willie May thought it would fly out of her chest, she paused before the door of Jessica's room to catch her breath and gain control of her frantic thoughts. For Tippy's protection, she and Miss Jessica had deliberately kept her ignorant of the runaway and their plan to help him escape. Willie May didn't like to think what would happen if their scheme was discovered and Tippy was found to be involved. Thank the good Lord the mistress had given her reason to send her from the room, and she could speak with Miss Jessica alone.

"Well, hello, Willie May," Jessica said, turning from her mirror. "What brings you up here?" She was dressed in a knee-length linen chemise undergarment, and Tippy was lacing her into a corset to suit the small, tapered waist of the day dress waiting to be donned. A white pelerine—a lace covering to be draped over its puffy shoulders—lay on a chaise longue. The lace was threaded with red and green ribbons to satisfy her father's desire to see the women of his household dressed in the colors of the season. No other manor house in Plantation Alley decorated for the holidays like Willowshire.

"Your mother has asked to see Tippy," Willie May said.

Tippy ceased her task and said, "Mama, what's wrong?"

"Nothing is wrong, girl of mine. You better go see what Miss Eunice wants."

Tippy dropped the ties and went to her. "Something is wrong, I just know it."

Willie May looked into her daughter's thin face, the bone structure, as with the rest of her body, looking no stronger than a sparrow's, and as usual felt her heart twist like a wrung rag. She took Tippy's delicate, pointed chin gently between her fingers. "Go along now," she said softly. "Nothing is wrong. I need to speak with Miss Jessie."

Her corset half laced, the ties trailing, Jessica said when her maid had gone, "Tippy is right. Something *is* wrong, isn't it, Willie May?"

"I could never fool that child of mine," Willie May said. "It's your mama. She wants to decorate the gazebo for Christmas beginning *right now*, she said. That's why she sent for Tippy. What we goin' do?"

"Oh, Lord," Jessica moaned. "Right now?"

"*Right now*. She wants me to round up some help while she gets the decorations together."

Jessica rubbed her forehead and paced in thought for a minute, then yanked off the corset and grabbed the day dress. "I'll tell you what we're going to do," she said, struggling into its voluminous folds. "Follow my lead, Willie May, and agree with everything I say. All right?"

"All right," Willie May said, having no idea what she was agreeing to as she helped Jessica to button the dress. "Uh, Miss Jessica, you do know you ain't got on the proper underwear, don't you?"

"Who's going to see?" Jessica said and sailed from the room like a ship heading out to sea under full steam with Willie May following in her wake. Halfway in her rush down the stairs, the wind of her flight plastering the skirt to her legs, Jessica called loudly several times, *"Mama!"*

Eunice came running. She and Tippy had been buried in a cupboard under the kitchen stairs where seasonal decorations were stored.

"Good heavens, child," Eunice said, meeting Jessica at the end of the balustrade, Tippy curious-eyed behind her. "Must you scream like a banshee?"

"Mama, you don't know what a banshee is."

"I do, too. It's a female spirit in Irish folklore that sits under a window and howls that somebody in the house is about to die." Eunice sniffed. "Though I didn't sit in on lessons, I learned a few things from Lettie Sedgewick just by keeping my ears open, young miss. Now, what is it?"

"Mama, Willie May tells me you want to decorate the gazebo, but if you do, you'll ruin my surprise."

Eunice looked mystified. "What surprise?"

Jessica ignored Willie May's befuddled look. "Well, now, if I tell you, it won't be a surprise, will it?"

Eunice glanced at her housekeeper. "Do you know what she's talking about?"

"Yes, she does, don't you, Willie May?" Jessica answered for the housekeeper. "But we were going to keep it a secret. All right, all right, here it is," Jessica said as if her arm were being twisted. "Willie May and I decided to decorate the gazebo ourselves, without Tippy's help, to prove to you that I *do* have some decorative sense. I've decided to take more of an interest in… domestic things, and I thought decorating the gazebo for Christmas would be the perfect place to start."

Eunice's mouth hung open. It was a few seconds before she seemed able to speak. Her eye fell to Jessica's limp skirts. "Where are your petticoats?"

Jessica glanced down. "Well, I was in such a hurry to head you off I didn't have time to put them on. Now will you please agree to let me and Willie May decorate the gazebo, and you'll stay completely out of the way? Truly, I'd like to have *something* to show off to Aunt Elfie this Christmas season."

Her tone full of doubt, Eunice said, "Well…all right, Jessie. Your father will be pleased, I'm sure, but…" She shot a painful glance at her housekeeper. "Will you see that she doesn't make too big a mess out there?"

"I promise, Miss Eunice," Willie May said.

"And *no* peeking," Jessica ordered. "We're going to hang up a sheet to make sure you don't. Right, Willie May?"

"Right," Willie May said.

Scooter told his helpers that he needed to get off to town to pick up the wheel a little earlier than planned. It might rain that afternoon, and he didn't want the wagon to get bogged down in the mud. They could have his share of the noonday meal. He wouldn't take time to eat it. Would they explain to the master if he came by?

The day, however, showed no sign of rain and all afternoon, behind a sheet draped round the gazebo, Jessica and Willie May toiled on turning the structure into a seasonal wonder to match the holiday splendor of the Big House conceived in the creative mind of Tippy and carried out under her hand. In the late afternoon, Carson went with his wife to inspect the results of their daughter's and housekeeper's labor and raved to Jessica, "Spook, you and Willie May have exceeded every…expectation."

That night as Carson snuggled next to his wife to sleep the repose of the just, he murmured in her ear, "Do you think you could have Tippy take a look at the gazebo tomorrow and…do a little rearranging?"

"You have read my mind, dear," Eunice said.

Chapter Thirteen

Other than an occasional bump on the wall, there was so little sound coming from the storage room assigned her guest that Sarah was forced to knock on his door from time to time and whisper, "Are you there?"

The answer would come back, so soft and cautious that Sarah could feel her neck hairs tickle, "I'se here."

She had put up a cot in the small supply closet attached to the kitchen. One window in the fugitive's quarters let in air and light, but it was kept shuttered and latched day and night. Sarah was thankful the cold front had brought day temperatures of a steady sixty degrees. At least her guest would not roast or be plagued by mosquitoes, and at night, when the temperature dropped, he had the use of plenty of blankets. Sarah slipped him food through a quick opening of his prison door, but at no time was he to show himself in the house. Someone by chance might glimpse him through the slits of the shuttered window over the kitchen sink or through the tiny parlor's windows, covered during the day by a drawn curtain. The most distasteful chore of looking after her boarder was emptying his chamber pot, a task she met with no less embarrassment than he.

"I'se sorry, miss," the boy would mutter, handing her the receptacle.

"It's all right," Sarah would respond, holding her breath.

She wondered how the boy could endure the cramped, sunless space, with little human contact and activity when she thought she would go mad if she had to spend one more day later than planned cooped up in her house. She felt like a prisoner herself, unable even to take a walk for fear the fugitive, seeing her gone, might venture out into the house or do something to rouse suspicion.

For the same reason, they had not dared talk to each other. Their voices, his with his Negroid dialect, might be heard and they'd be discovered. Carson Wyndham had put out the word that a possible runaway was in the area. There were many who would turn him in—and Sarah Conklin—to have the gratitude of Carson Wyndham. In the brief seconds the boy took the tray of food from her and shut the door, Sarah had only glimpsed his face and skeletal body in the ill-fitting clothes she'd found in the church's rummage bin. She'd have had him come out to stretch his legs, but, again, neither wished to take the risk of his being seen. Well-meaning people—a neighbor, church member, or parent of one of her students, knowing she was alone until her departure—might stop by with food or offer of company. She was grateful the Sedgewicks would be at the Tolivers' until late tomorrow afternoon. Jessica was to pick up her and her cargo after luncheon, and they would be long gone by the time Jimson-weed turned into the gate.

But it was almost over. This was the last night of her and the boy's captivity. She'd packed her steamer trunk and prepared a basket of food for the fugitive to take with him on his escape. It was ten o'clock, pitch black outside with low-cast clouds obscuring the moon. Time to hook her kerosene lantern to the back porch post and await the signal across the creek indicating that all was in readiness at the Charleston Harbor. The agent's code sign would be three long shoots of flame and one short. She would answer with three brief turns of her lantern's knob. Anyone observing her that time of night would think fear of fire had driven her outside to test the wick. If anything was amiss with either side, there would be no signal. Sarah prayed to see three tall spires and one quick burst of lantern light across the creek.

Wrapped in her cloak, she hung her lamp on the post, the wick burning low. She had not long to wait until the signal came, and she turned the knob to adjust the flame once, twice, three times. A huge relief filled her as she cupped her hand around the glass chimney to blow out the wick. She'd let her storage-room guest know that so far everything was going according to plan. Perhaps he'd sleep better, as she certainly would. Then, as she took down her lantern and turned to go inside, she saw another flash of light wink from the darkness and abruptly die. Her heart held. What had happened? Was that last spurt of flame intentional or accidental? Had her contact dropped his lantern and quickly snuffed the wick? She listened, her eyes straining into the dark woods, but heard nothing but the soft lapping of water around rocks. She'd gone exploring across the creek once, led by curiosity, and found the covert from where the agent flashed his coded messages. Crushed foliage had given away the burrow of his hiding place, accessed by a path through the woods.

A little disturbed, Sarah went inside and decided not to tap on the storage-room door to impart the good news. She might jinx their getaway. Her traveling suit hung outside her wardrobe in her bedroom. She'd placed it there last night as a lift to her spirits and a reminder that in eighteen hours, she would be on her way to Charleston to catch a boat bound for home. She undressed and climbed into bed in her night shift but could not sleep. Her thoughts were on Jessica.

Sarah was afraid for her. Strong will and impetuosity did not mix, and her friend had an abundance of both. Pair those traits with an utter belief in her invincible position in her family, and Jessica was like a blind person with a cocked and loaded gun. The girl did not believe her father's warnings. She mistakenly assumed his love for her would protect her from his threats and that he would not risk her affection turning to hate if he used Tippy as a tool to punish her. Jessica did not understand that if she were caught aiding and abetting the destruction of a system—betraying it—on which her family's wealth, social position, and way of life had depended for generations, her sin would not be forgiven. But Tippy understood, and it was for her mistress's safety, not her own, that Jessica's maid was most concerned.

"She may know Carson Wyndham as a father," Tippy once said to Sarah, "but she does not know him as a white man and master of Willowshire."

Sarah agreed, relieved that she had Tippy's understanding of the danger Jessica disregarded. Working together, there was hope they could temper the impulses of their friend's passionate convictions.

Tippy continued to amaze her—and sadden her, too. Jessica should take sharp heed. Her maid's life could be snuffed out by one stomp of Carson Wyndham's handmade boots or by the heel of that son of his, and all that marvelous creative genius in that quirky little head be lost forever—"a *colored* girl's head!"—so Sarah had overheard Carson Wyndham snort his objection to Tippy on one of the few occasions she'd been a guest at Willowshire. In his tone, Sarah had heard the unmistakable notes of jealousy and resentment of the affection his daughter lavished on her Negro maid that she did not heap on him or her brother. From that dangerous quarter, too, Tippy must be on guard.

The moon was waning when Sarah finally fell asleep. She thought she was dreaming when she heard the clip-clop of horses' hooves coming up the lane past the manse, the cemetery, and drawing to a stop before her cottage. Startled awake, she leaped out of bed and grabbed her robe, hearing a frightened exclamation from the occupant inside the storage room as she ran from her bedroom through the kitchen to meet the nightmare she'd long dreaded and was sure awaited the other side of her door.

Tying her robe securely, she threw the latch to find a gaggle of men staring down at her from horseback, mouths clamped hard and eyes steely. The leader of them dismounted and tipped his hat. "Good evening, Miss Conklin, or perhaps I should say good morning, as I believe it is now," Michael Wyndham said.

Chapter Fourteen

I have no idea where your son has gotten himself off to," Eunice said to Carson at breakfast. "He's been gone all night. Elfie will be so disappointed if her nephew is not here to greet her when she arrives."

"He's out with the Night Riders," her husband remarked, intent on reading his newspaper. "He's determined to catch the culprit stealing from us."

"It was only two hams," Jessica said, uneasy at the thought of her brother and his lackeys out and about the countryside when she drove Sarah and their cargo to Charleston.

Carson glanced at her. "How do you know it was two hams?"

Jessica thought quickly. Willie May had told her, but just as well her father did not know the source of her information. He would no longer take Willie May into his confidence. "It's no secret about the theft, Papa. Everybody in the Yard knows it."

"Tippy, carrying tales again." Her father harrumphed.

"You have to admit, Carson, that the girl has outdone herself with the decorations this year. I can't wait for Elfie to see them."

Carson harrumphed again, but there was no denying that Tippy had created amazing holiday wonders from ribbons, pinecones, evergreen branches, mistletoe, candles, colored paper, wooden ornaments, popcorn balls, fruits, nuts, gingerbread, and glass balls from Germany. Eunice had been so pleased that she had rescinded her husband's order committing Tippy to work in the weavers' cabin, where the smoke from the fireplace was not good for her lung.

"It's a waste of her talents, Carson," Eunice had stated in a tone declaring she would not budge on the matter. "The girl belongs in the sewing room. Jessica and I are both in need of new frocks for Silas and Lettie's nuptials."

Her husband never shrank from a battle unless in those rare instances prudence trumped valor. With the exception of Willowshire, his wife was the love of his life, and he would do nothing to jeopardize his demonstration of it at night in their bedroom. He gave in gracefully, conceding, "You're right. We must put her where we get the most value."

Jessica said, her heart beginning to hammer, "Papa, have you ordered the carriage around? Sarah's ship departs at three o'clock, about the time Aunt Elfie's arrives, and I want to get us there in plenty of time."

Carson looked up from his newspaper. "Yes, but I wish you'd wait a little longer for your brother to drive you. I don't trust the weather this time of year, and the almanac says to expect snow sometime this week. Your aunt's trunks might be a problem for the two of you to manage."

"I'll get a porter to help us," Jessica said, folding her napkin and beckoning a servant to draw out her chair.

"But how will you get Sarah Conklin's luggage into the carriage?" her father persisted.

"We'll manage," Jessica said, hoping with all her heart that Michael did not appear. "Now, if you'll excuse me…"

"They want to be alone for girl talk, dear," she heard her mother explain as she hurried from the room.

"In that case, I'd think Jessica would be taking Tippy along since the girls think she's one of them," Carson said with a snap of his paper.

Jessica snatched up her bonnet and cloak and was out the door and onto the carriage seat before her father got the idea to send the coachman with her. Daniel could be trusted, but she would not involve him in her perilous mission.

"Thank you, Daniel," she said, "but no need to fuss with that. I'm in a bit of a hurry," she said when he attempted to spread a blanket over her knees. She must get away before Michael rode up and insisted on going with her. He would not miss an opportunity to have the captive company of Sarah Conklin.

Jessica realized that her arms and shoulders were aching from tension by the time she'd made the five-mile trip into Willow Grove and turned down the lane of the church property to Sarah's front door. She let out a long frosty breath as she drew the carriage to a stop and forced herself to relax. The most stressful part of the journey was behind her. No one was about to see their cargo loaded, and in two shakes of a lamb's tail she and Sarah would be on their way to their destination unobstructed on this bright winter afternoon six days before Christmas. There would be time in Charleston to enjoy a last cup of tea together before Sarah embarked. Jessica would miss her brave friend, but oh, how much Sarah was looking forward to a reunion with her little nephew and rest of her family. Jessica shared Lettie's concern. Would Sarah want to come back to them after being home for the holidays?

She had raised her hand to knock on the door when from around each side of the house quietly emerged a cordon of men on horseback. Some she did not know, but others she recognized as a local gin operator, tanner, tavern owner, and a few farmers. All stared at her in disbelieving silence, their taut expressions dismayed. For a moment she couldn't think. What were the Night

Riders doing here? She heard a familiar whinny and turned to see Michael's black Arabian tossing its beautifully arched neck in greeting and switching its high-carried tail. The saddle was empty, the reins held by one of the men. Fear froze her brain. Her whole body stiffened. Michael opened the door. He stared at her, his jaw slowly dropping.

"No, no, I can't believe it," he said. "Not you, Jessie. It can't be you.... Tell me it isn't you. You're only here to pick up Sarah...."

She could have lied, but all she could think of was Sarah. Blood rushed to her head. "What have you done with Sarah? Where is she?"

"Oh, God. You're the pickup, aren't you?" her brother said in a voice thick with anguish. His face had gone as pale as a bleached headstone. Even his deep, metal-gray eyes had lost their glint. Shock and incredulity had lightened them to the color of brackish ice. "We couldn't get her to tell us who was coming for the boy. We had to wait and see...."

Jessica pushed by the robust figure. "Sarah!" she cried, rushing through the parlor, into the kitchen, glancing into the open door of the storage room.

Michael seized her arm, stopping her. "She's in the bedroom," he said roughly, his face mottling with anger. "Go tend her. I've sent for liniment and bandages. Pack her things and get her dressed and into the carriage. Miss Conklin will not be returning to Willow Grove. I will escort you to the harbor in Charleston. We will bring our aunt home, and then I will deliver you to our father."

Jessica yanked her arm free and ran into the bedroom. "Oh, my God! Sarah!" she cried when she saw the figure on the bed.

Her friend lay facing the wall, her night shift in strips and soaked in blood from the cut of whip lashes across her back. From the other room came a terse exchange of male voices, and

Michael entered carrying a wrapped package. Jessica whirled to him. "How could you do this, Michael?" she screamed.

"You ask that question of me, little sister, when it's the one I should ask of you? Believe me, our father will." Michael threw the package at her. "There. Clean her wounds. My men are loading her trunk into the carriage now. You have thirty minutes to get your little abolitionist friend ready to leave our shores. After that, she's food for the buzzards." He strode from the room and Jessica tore open the package of gauze and lotion.

"I didn't tell them, Jessie," Sarah moaned as Jessica hurried to pour water into a basin from a pitcher on the lavatory stand. "They caught the agent and forced him to betray me. He tried to warn me.... I hoped—prayed—that you would not arrive, that something would prevent you from coming and that if you did, you'd think of something to tell your brother...."

"Sssh, don't talk, Sarah," Jessie said as she knelt to remove the remnants of her friend's night shift to dress her wounds. "Just lie quietly. Think of your little nephew and that you'll be homeward bound in a few hours. You'll never have to see the likes of my brother or his kind again."

"They took the fugitive to Willowshire," Sarah said, as if Jessica's words had not registered. "He'll be returned to his owner. They took him away with a rope around his neck. They made him witness my flogging."

Jessica thought she was going to be sick. There was a tall magnolia tree behind the cottage. Michael and his ruffians had probably strung her up by one of its sturdy branches, and there was no one around to see or hear the sound of the lashing or Sarah's wails, if she gave them the pleasure, but her friend had not betrayed her involvement. Working quickly over the lacerated back, Jessica pressed her lips tightly together to keep from weeping.

Sarah motioned her to come closer and lowered her voice to a whisper in case someone in the other room might overhear. Careful of her wounds, Jessica leaned forward. "I'm afraid for Willie May...."

"Oh God. What does Michael know?" Jessica asked.

"The boy told him he'd heard of my safe house, and he came here. He didn't mention Willie May, but if your brother is skeptical and questions him further...tortures him...he could talk."

Jessica felt the blood plunge from her head.

"I'm afraid for you, too, my brave Southern friend, and for Tippy," Sarah continued.

Dizzily, feeling as if she were kneeling on the deck of a weaving ship, Jessica swabbed at the cuts. "Don't worry about us," she said. "I'll think of something to save us all. My father's bark is worse than his bite when it comes to me. He'll be furious with me, but he'll forgive me. I'm his daughter. He has no choice."

"Oh, Jessica, dear..." Sarah moaned.

Chapter Fifteen

At breakfast in the Toliver household, as well as at other tables in the manor homes of Plantation Alley, the topic of discussion was the unexpected and disappointing cancellation of Willowshire's annual holiday events. They were the Christmas ball, the tea in honor of the annual visit of Eunice's sister from Boston for the holidays, and the New Year's Eve party to which many dignitaries and luminaries were invited. These social occasions were looked forward to all year by those fortunate enough to be on the invitation list and precipitated much advance planning of frocks and accessories and hairstyles by the ladies.

"Whatever do you suppose is the matter over there?" Elizabeth queried those gathered around her table for ham and grits the morning the festivities were to begin. She thought regretfully of the gown hanging in her wardrobe that she'd now not have the opportunity to show off. This morning, in addition to Lettie and her father, who were frequent overnight guests, her family of two sons and grandson had the pleasure of Jeremy Warwick's company. Afterwards he and Silas were to huddle over the growingly bleak solutions to the problem of Silas and Lettie having to remain behind when the wagon train bound for Texas pulled out in the spring.

"I haven't heard anything," Jeremy said.

"It's as if a dark veil has fallen over Willowshire," Lettie commented. "I haven't been able to get in touch with Jessica. When I went to call on her, I was turned away at the door."

"Same for Michael," Morris said. "He and I were to go hunting yesterday, but he sent word around that something had come up."

"Indeed there must be something extraordinary that's happened," Reverend Sedgewick added. "None of the family attended the Christmas cantata Wednesday evening. Most unusual. Mr. Wyndham always leaves a large donation in the offering plate."

"Did Miss Conklin get off to Massachusetts all right?" Jeremy asked Lettie. "I understand that Jessica was to take her to the ship in the carriage."

"We don't know for sure, and we're a bit worried," Lettie answered. "That's why I called on Jessica. When I went to air out the cemetery house in her absence, I found blood on the bedsheets, and some bloody swabs in the waste bin as well."

"Most puzzling," offered Reverend Sedgewick.

"Do you suppose she cut herself?" Silas asked.

"I wish I could speak with Jessica to find out," Lettie said.

"Perhaps it was due to nature," Elizabeth suggested, giving Lettie a look that made her color, and changed the subject. "I was so looking forward to seeing Willowshire dressed for the holidays," she lamented. "That colored girl of the Wyndhams'... what's her name?"

"Tippy," Silas volunteered.

"Is a marvel with seasonal decorations. It's hard to imagine such ingenuity coming from such an ill-favored strip of a colored girl."

Morris took a bite of his buttered biscuit and asked with his mouth full, "Are you talking about that monkey-looking maid with the big feet who looks like she could swing from the chandeliers?"

"Yes, dear," Elizabeth said. "Apparently Jessica dotes on her."

There was a sudden interruption as Lazarus drew back the double doors to the dining room. He went to Morris's chair and bent close to his ear. "Excuse me, Master, but there is a visitor in the drawing room."

"This early in the morning, Lazarus? Who in heaven's name is it?"

"Mr. Carson Wyndham, suh."

To the startled silence of everyone at the table, Morris yanked his napkin from his collar. "I'll go immediately."

"But he didn't come to see you, suh," Lazarus explained. "He came to see Mister Silas."

"My brother?" Morris stared down the table at Silas as if the idea were unthinkable.

"Good heavens," Elizabeth said with a loss of breath.

Silas folded his napkin and rose. He grinned at Jeremy, winked at Lettie. "Maybe the old boy has changed his mind," he said.

Morris raised an eyebrow. "And he came here to tell you in person in the midst of the Christmas season? Don't count on it."

"Find out all you can about what's going on at Willowshire," Elizabeth whispered loudly behind her hand.

Carson Wyndham stood staring out the Palladian windows of the drawing room with his hands clutched behind his back. Lazarus had taken his hat and the riding crop that he was never without. Silas recognized the stance of a man in deep reflection. He was forced to agree with Morris. Why would the most powerful and richest man in South Carolina deign to call at the breakfast hour to grant his request for a loan this time of year when business had come to a halt?

"Mr. Wyndham, sir?"

Carson turned, and only the force of good manners prevented Silas from uttering his surprise. He recognized a face drawn with severe worry and anxiety. His own was beginning to show signs of such agitation in his mirror each morning. Carson Wyndham's dour expression, the snap gone from his eyes, seemed at odds with the freshly starched, perky ruffles of his fine cravat. "Thank you for seeing me with no notice, Silas," he said.

"My pleasure, sir," Silas said with a slight bow.

"I'm not sure you'll think so when you hear why I've come."

"Then perhaps we should sit down and I'll ring for coffee."

Carson waved a hand dismissively, the large ruby of a signet ring catching the light from the fireplace. "Don't bother, but maybe you'd best take a chair. I prefer to stand."

Perplexed, as he sat down in one of his mother's prized Hepplewhites, Silas searched his mind for a possible reason Carson Wyndham stood in his drawing room—Morris's drawing room—on the morning when the social event of the year was to have taken place at Willowshire that evening. He could think of none, but of one matter he was certain: The man had not come to grant him a loan.

His firm conviction was immediately shattered when Carson, standing before him, imperious legs spread, hands clasped behind his back, glowered down at him and said, "What would you say if I told you I'd absolve your loan, pay all your expenses to Texas, give you enough money to start your plantation and build a manor home, and throw in fifty slaves in the bargain?"

Silas gazed at Carson as if the man had suddenly popped the buttons of his finely tailored waistcoat. When he recovered from his shock, he said, "I'd say I was dreaming or that you were in the throes of a nightmare."

"You're not dreaming, and I'm as awake as an owl at midnight."

"Forgive me, sir," Silas said, "but I'm at a loss here."

"What would you do to get what I just offered?"

Bewildered, but beginning to see a small ray of hope in his confusion, Silas said, "Almost anything short of committing murder or robbing a bank."

"That's what I thought." Carson pursed his mouth and mulled over something in silence a moment as if deciding whether to continue. Finally, he seemed to make up his mind and drew a noisy breath through his nostrils. "Well, here it is, Silas. All that I offered is yours if you'll do one thing for me."

Silas's heartbeat held. The enticements the man tendered danced like sugar plums in his head. To start off to Texas with enough money to make every one of his and Lettie's dreams come true…he would almost make a deal with the devil, but nothing came without conditions—not with Carson Wyndham. "What is it that you want me to do?" he asked.

"Marry my daughter," his visitor answered.

Chapter Sixteen

Silas gaped at Carson, dumbfounded. "You're asking me to do *what*?"

"That's right. You heard me," Carson said. "I want you to marry Jessica and take her with you to Texas."

"But I'm engaged!"

"I know. You must figure out how to circumvent that commitment."

"Circumvent it?"

"Silas…" Wyndham drew up his barrel chest, the starched cravat lifting with it. "I'm offering you the chance of a lifetime—an opportunity that will never come to you again. Take it, and you're free to live the life you've always dreamed. Reject it, and you're doomed to live a life you hate, become the man you hate. You'd be doing Miss Sedgewick a favor by setting her free to marry someone whose obsession does not come before his love for her."

Appalled, Silas declared, "You presume, sir, and you are forgetting Miss Sedgewick's love for me."

"A heartache that the years will dull because of the hate she will feel when you choose my offer over her. How important is love over a decision that will determine the rest of your life and the life of your heirs? Think about it."

"I couldn't possibly do what you're asking, and I am sure your daughter shares my aversion to your proposal."

"Jessica has absolutely no say in the matter. She forfeited that right when she betrayed me and her family."

A glimmer of light was beginning to shine on the mystery of the cancellation of festivities at Willowshire. Jessica—that little firebrand—must be at its root. Silas regarded his visitor with distaste. "What did she do, if I may ask?"

Carson related the details of Jessica's crime.

"Good God!" Silas said.

"Exactly," Carson said, closing his eyes wearily for a brief second. "My daughter is not winsome, Silas, I grant you that, and you'd have a tiger by the tail if you marry her, but some men would find her particular temperament…alluring."

"Jeremy apparently does," Silas said, his tone wry. "Why don't you propose *he* marry her?"

"That had crossed my mind, but…"

Silas's mouth twisted. "He cannot be bought, is that it?"

"He is not a man in your circumstances."

Silas did not know which inference was the greater insult—or the truth. "What will happen to Jessica if you don't…marry her off?" he asked curiously.

Carson glanced away, his mouth hard. "I will get her out of South Carolina, one way or the other, before her abolitionist fidelities become well known. I will not have a traitor in my house. Believe me, the *other way* will be less to her liking than the one I've proposed to you." He looked at Silas, his eyes that of a father whose child is pronounced dead. "Please, Silas. Marry my daughter. You will do right by her, I know it. You might even grow to love her, and she you."

"I doubt it," Silas said. "I love Lettie. She has my heart."

"And you will have my money. Think about it, and get back

with me in a fortnight. Otherwise, the deal is off. I will have put into effect another way to deal with my wayward daughter."

Jeremy had come out into the hall when Carson, followed by a grim-faced Silas, stepped from the drawing room. Lazarus hurried to hand their visitor his riding crop and hat. Positioning the brim tightly, Carson said, "Good morning, Jeremy," but not before Silas had read in his expression the wistful wish that it could have been Jeremy to whom he'd made the proposal. Jeremy was indeed a fine specimen of a man, more easygoing and jocular than the man he'd come to purchase. Silas recognized that his own sense of humor had been pinched by recent events and…his obsession, so Carson had called his weakness.

"Happy Christmas to you and your families, gentlemen," Carson said, with a last glance at Silas before Lazarus saw him to the door.

Jeremy had not missed its meaningful glint. "What was that all about?" he asked after Carson had gone.

Silas raked a hand through his hair. From the dining room came Lettie's clear soprano voice, the sound that was like music to his ears. "Jeremy," he said, "there are times I wish I'd never been born."

Jessica had been confined to her room for four days. Apparently, even her mother had been forbidden to see her. She had seen no one but Lulu, the maid who brought her meals and carried tales. Jessica had given her no tales to carry. She did not inquire about her aunt, whom she'd seen only during the tense, silent carriage ride back to Willowshire from the pier in Charleston. She did not ask about Tippy or Willie May or question Lulu for a temperature reading of her father's and mother's moods. The maid would put her own sly interpretation on her words and state of mind in relaying them to her parents, and in her lonely exile with only her thoughts for company, Jessica did not think she could endure the torture of knowing what form of retribution her father had taken against Tippy and Willie May. She knew only that the house was eerily quiet these days before Christmas, when ordinarily it would have been boisterous and lively with the arrivals of callers, preparations for parties, the hurrying and scurrying of household help, conversation and laughter and music.

But of course Jessica worried. Had her father sent Tippy to the fields? Had he punished Willie May as well? Would her mother ever speak to her again? What kind of punishment would her father concoct for his daughter, because punishment was bound to come. For what? For showing decency to another human being? The outline of Michael's vicious grip on her lower arm when he'd marched her through the house to her father's study had only now faded, but Jessica could mentally still see her bewildered aunt looking on in concern and her mother with her hand pressed to her mouth and her anguished gaze asking: *What in the world have you done now, child?*

While Jessica had stood with head held high, her chin jutted, Michael had related the tale of how he and the Riders had caught "a no-good, slave-loving abolitionist" red-handed at his subversive business and asked his father to guess who the bastard was signaling.

Her father had listened to the whole harangue without the bat of an eye, but his jaw hardened to stone and his dark brown gaze on Jessica turned nearly black. Finally, he'd asked, "Did Miss Conklin get on her ship?"

"Yes, Papa," Michael said. "I saw to that. I told her worse would happen if we ever saw her face around here again."

"And the runaway? Where is he?"

"In the barn until you tell us what to do with him. He's just a boy, ignorant as they come. He says he doesn't know who owns him or the name of his plantation. I figure that he never got out of the fields of wherever he's from. His name is Jasper. We got that out of him when he saw what we did to Sarah Conklin. He told us he hid in the wagon when Scooter drove into town to pick up a wheel."

"Then no one from Willowshire helped him?"

"He said not. I'm inclined to believe him."

"How did he know to go to Miss Conklin?"

"He said somebody came into the fields—the agent, probably—where he was working and spread the word that the woman who lived in the house by the cemetery in Willow Grove helped runaways. He was making for that destination."

"Is the agent anybody we know?"

"Not really. He's a northerner who hired on as a clerk at the feed store in Willow Grove last year. We turned him over to the sheriff."

"And this…feed-store clerk and Miss Conklin conspired to spirit the boy away?"

"Yes sir."

"And you were their accomplice?" Carson turned his questioning to Jessica and got up from his desk to stand eyeball-to-eyeball with her.

"I was," Jessica said, returning his stare proudly but inwardly terrified. She saw not a spark of love in the cold, dark wells of her father's gaze.

"I am not going to ask you what you have to say for yourself. I don't want to hear it. I want you out of my sight. Go to your room and stay there until I send for you. If you so much as poke your head out, I will deal with you severely, is that understood, Jessica Ann?"

He never called her Jessica Ann. A shocking awareness, cold

as frozen steel, made its way down to the pit of Jessica's stomach. She remembered Sarah's moan when she'd boasted that her father's bark was worse than his bite when it came to his daughter. Sarah had reacted not from the pain of her lashes, but from her friend's ignorance of Carson Wyndham. Jessica's horrified thoughts flew to Tippy. Her father would punish her maid for her transgression. He did not care if his daughter forgave him or if her love turned to hate.

She clasped her hands beseechingly. "Papa, I beg you. Please, please do not punish Tippy for what I did."

"Michael, take your sister to her room."

"Please, Papa…"

"Go!"

An audience of her mother, aunt, Willie May, and some of the other servants had watched, round-eyed and frightened, as Michael had herded her up the staircase like a soldier directing her to the guillotine. Before leaving, her brother's last words to her, perhaps forever, were, "To think I adored you once."

A hard knock on Jessica's bedroom door, the one she'd been dreading and waiting for, jerked her back to the present. She opened it to find Lulu smirking at her. "The master wishes to see you, Miss Jessica," she said.

Chapter Seventeen

Silas could not sleep or eat. He went for hard rides at dawn, long walks at midnight. In the still, frosty hours, while Plantation Alley slept, he pondered, worried, prayed about what he should do. He was four days into the two-week period he'd been granted to make a decision, and he was as far away from reaching it as he was the moment when Carson Wyndham had proposed the solution to both their problems.

His mother fretted over him. "Cassandra made your favorite pie, Silas. Why aren't you eating it?"

His fiancée had grown pale from worry. "I know when something is deeply disturbing you, my love. What is it? Please tell me."

Jeremy, who knew him better than a brother, said, "Something's taking a bite out of your soul, my friend. I'm listening, if you want to talk about it."

And his brother—obtuse, leaden, impercipient—observed, "Silas, whatever is amiss with you started the minute Carson Wyndham walked out of the drawing room. What did he do— offer his daughter's hand in marriage?"

Morris had laughed at his joke, but Silas, unsmiling, had turned away lest his brother read the truth in his eyes.

The Conestogas were still for sale on the field next to the barn, their number now increased by two. His prospective renters had also withdrawn from the wagon train, a development that had caused Jeremy to send a note saying he believed he'd determined the source of the problem gnawing at him and would like to meet with him to discuss it. His friend was waiting in the drawing room at Queenscrown when Silas, finished with his managerial duties, joined him before the fire. It was two days before Christmas, and the house was redolent with the savory aromas of cooking and the smell of evergreens. At this point, hoping for a miracle, Silas had not told Jeremy he might have to pull out from the wagon train himself.

"I believe I understand what's been troubling you, Silas," Jeremy said. "It's money, isn't it? You're out of funds for the trip."

Frustrated, Silas ran a hand through the thicket of his black hair. "I'm afraid so, Jeremy," he admitted. "I haven't told you because I believed I could secure a loan, and with the money from the rent and sale of the Conestogas, I'd have enough to get us to Texas and provide a start, but neither has come through. I can't take Lettie to Texas with empty pockets."

Looking distressed, Jeremy leaned forward. "I don't even want to think of going to Texas without you, Silas. This is a dream we've been hatching for *years*. Our plans are under way. Put your pride aside and let my family loan you the money."

"No, Jeremy." Silas shook his head emphatically. "Thank you for your offer, but I absolutely refuse it. Being in debt to one's best friend is no way to start out an enterprise together. You know that as well as I do. If our situations were reversed, would you allow me to help you?"

Jeremy averted his gaze to the fire. "No, I suppose not. You'd let me give my life for you, as you would for me, but heaven forbid we owe each other money. This…tacit agreement between the Warwicks and Tolivers started way back in England at the end of the War of the Roses, you know, when the Lancasters and

Yorks decided to share the key to the kingdom as long as it didn't open the other's coffers."

"It is our legacy, Jeremy. Neither a lender or borrower be."

Jeremy glanced at him worriedly. "So what are you going to do? Is there any hope at all? I assume Carson Wyndham turned you down, and that's what his visit was all about a few weeks ago—why you looked as if you'd been given a death sentence."

"I may as well have been," Silas said, getting up to stroll to one of the tall windows of the drawing room. He could not sit long these days, neither could he stand, or lie down. His nerves would not permit it. Did he dare tell Jeremy of Carson Wyndham's offer? What would Jeremy think of his best friend for even considering it? They each had the highest respect for the other's character and integrity. Though they sometimes differed in their view of things, no dispute had ever come between them, even when they embarked on joint ventures ripe for disagreement. As boys, together they'd built canoes, rafts, and tree houses; concocted schemes to earn spending money; planned hiking, hunting, and fishing trips. As men, they'd invested an equal share of money, care, and training in a racehorse, shared the affections of the same girls, and made a committee of two in deciding everything from how best to remove a tree from the road to building a bridge serving their neighboring plantations.

Let Silas and Jeremy decide how to handle it, was the directive from both fathers of the men and now Morris, when a project concerning the juxtaposed estates was involved, deferring to "the boys."

But if Silas accepted Carson's proposal, would Jeremy even *want* him to accompany him to Texas? Would he want a leader of the wagon train by his side who had betrayed the one he loved to fulfill the dream they shared? *If* he agreed to Carson's terms, would Jeremy understand that, given the man Silas knew himself to be, he had done what he believed was right for all?

"Then there's no hope at all?" Jeremy repeated, the question soft with sadness and regret. "You've tried every avenue?"

Silas stared out the window. The flames from the fireplace leaped around his reflection in the glass, aptly showing a man in hell. He turned abruptly to the drinks table. "There is one avenue open to me," he said, lifting the top of a whiskey decanter. It was only four o'clock in the afternoon. Jeremy's brow raised slightly.

"And that is?" his friend asked, shaking his head no to Silas's offer of a drink.

Silas poured himself a glass and sat down before the fire. "You were right about Sarah Conklin," he said. "There was more to her than appeared. Michael Wyndham discovered her to be a conductor in the Underground Railroad. She's been sent packing and will not be returning to her teaching post in Willow Grove. I have yet to tell Lettie."

"Good heavens!" Jeremy exclaimed. "How did Michael find out?"

Silas explained what he knew. He had an idea Carson had left out certain unsavory details of the story.

"The poor girl," Jeremy said. "I hope Michael and his men did not get rough with her."

"Carson didn't say."

"Does Jessica know?"

Silas lifted his glass to his lips. "She knows. She was part of the deception."

Jeremy sat straighter. *"What?"*

Silas finished the story of Jessica's involvement. "Her father is very angry with her," he said in conclusion. "So angry, in fact, that he wants to get her out of his sight. That's what he came to see me about the other day. He wants my help."

"You? How can you help?"

"He wants me to marry his daughter and take her to Texas."

Jeremy's paralytic look reminded Silas of the time, long ago, when they'd been fishing on opposite sides of the lake. Across the water, Jeremy had regarded him with the same stupefied stare, and Silas shortly discovered what had caught his attention on his side of the lake. A bear had arrived to fish upstream, so intense on his task that it failed to notice Silas. Jeremy's harrowed gaze reflected his two choices. Should he climb a cypress where he'd be safe but captive or chance life and limb by making a dash for freedom? Silas had taken the risk and escaped into the trees beyond the bear's reach. He felt himself in a similar position now. Should he stay were he was, secure but bound, or seek liberation at the risk of great loss? At the lake that day, Jeremy had not abandoned him. Would he stick by Silas now if he should decide to take Carson's offer?

"I'm shocked," his friend said simply.

"So I see. Care for that whiskey now?"

As Silas poured his drink, Jeremy asked, "What did you tell him?"

Silas noted gratefully that his friend did not say, as anyone else would: *You told him* no, *of course*.

"I told him I'd think about it," Silas said. "I'm telling you now, Jeremy, for whatever you might think of me after today, that I *am* thinking about it. Carson Wyndham offered me that avenue you asked about."

Chapter Eighteen

Jeremy Warwick slowed his white stallion to a canter as he turned into the tree-lined, moss-draped approach to the Parthenon-looking mansion of his family home. Built of white plastered brick, the manor house of Meadowlands was a palatial, squarish structure of two and a half stories surrounded by broad double galleries supported by monumental columns rising to the roofline. Like a brilliant gemstone, even in the falling dusk, it sparkled in a setting of lush gardens and lawns sloping away to picked-over cotton fields whose expanse reached beyond the range of the human eye. Born to Meadowlands' opulent entitlements and therefore naturally taking them for granted, Jeremy had never paid much attention to the magnificence and scope of his ancestral home and family's property until today. Queenscrown was no less grand. He cantered along, viewing the Warwick mansion and endless stretches of land from a new perspective. What would a man do—what would he risk, sacrifice, forfeit—for the ownership of all of this, he wondered.

All of this was what Silas desired, felt born to, believed he needed for survival as a man. Jeremy was of no such mind. If Morris died tomorrow and left Queenscrown to his brother, Silas would be a happy, fulfilled man. If Jeremy's father and siblings

followed suit—God forbid—and he, Jeremy, were to inherit
Meadowlands, he would be miserable. His reasons for going to
Texas were different from Silas's. He yearned to be the master
of his own source of livelihood, but in a fresh, new, vigorous environment. All Jeremy knew was farming, but he welcomed the
possibility and challenge of turning his hand to some other profitable venture in the land of opportunity Texas was purported
to be. He had come to find South Carolina's planter system—its
customs, traditions, mores, prejudices—stifling and restrictive, as
worn out as the land would one day be. Jessica Wyndham must
find it so as well.

But he could understand Silas's obsessive need to possess *all of
this*. He was a man of the soil—predominantly cotton-producing
soil—and he was a Toliver, born to own, command, lead—not
follow. Silas carried his forebears' blood, and he could no more
change or compromise his conviction of his role in life than he
could alter the color of his eyes.

Jeremy felt enormous pity for him. No sailor on the planet
would trade fifty-foot waves for the dilemma Silas faced. He
stood between a lion and a tiger. Either could eat him alive. If he
chose to remain at Queenscrown with the woman he loved, he
would surely emotionally expire. If he went to Texas, all the land
and cotton in the world might not allay his misery at being married to the woman he did not.

Would Silas sacrifice those he loved to preserve his own life?
He would leave Lettie devastated, humiliated, inconsolable.
Joshua would be crushed. The little boy already thought of Lettie
as his mother, and Elizabeth loved her like a daughter. If Silas
jilted her to marry Jessica, he would leave South Carolina a disgraced man. He could never come home again.

And what of Jessica Wyndham? After the beautiful Lettie
Sedgewick, what chance did the girl have of winning Silas's

heart—that is, if she were of a mind to? From what he'd seen of the feisty Jessica—and now knowing her views on slavery—it might be hate at first kiss between her and Silas.

Jeremy shook his head in sympathy for his friend and impelled his stallion to a faster clip. Too bad he was not in the running. Not since he was twenty-one and met the girl he loved and later lost to typhoid fever had a woman so intrigued him as Jessica Wyndham. Had her father asked *him* to take his daughter off his hands, he might not have had to think about it long.

Jessica met her aunt coming up the stairs. "Aunt Elfie!" she cried as they threw themselves into each other's arms.

"Oh, my dear child, this is all my fault," her aunt exclaimed. "If I'd just monitored your activities closer while you were in Boston..."

Jessica pulled away to look at her. "This is not your fault, Aunt Elfie. I left here with my convictions already conceived. They were simply birthed in boarding school. Do you...have any idea what my fate will be?"

"No, dear niece. Your father does not confide in me, but your mother is very worried."

Lulu had stopped at the bottom of the staircase. "The master is waiting, Miss Jessica," she said with a sharp look of rebuke.

"Certainly not for you," Jessica snapped. "Go on about your business."

"But I'm to take you to him."

"I know the way to my father's study. Get on with you." Jessica waited until the maid had disappeared and asked, "Aunt Elfie, have you seen Tippy? What have they done with her?"

"She's all right, child—for the time being. She's quartering with her mother and has been dispensed to the sewing room. I believe she's working on your bridesmaid's dress. Please, please, Jessica, mind your p's and q's with your father when you see him."

"I'll try, Aunt Elfie," Jessica said, kissing her aunt's cheek. Then she hurried down the stairs, skirt and hair flying behind her.

Since she did not know how to arrange her hair, Jessica had worn it loose for the four days of her confinement. Its naturally frizzy curls fell in long, ungovernable ringlets when not brushed into submission by Tippy's hand. Today, the thick russet mass had been secured away from her forehead by a barrette. She'd dressed hastily and found, too late to change, a noticeable stain on the front of her dress, and she'd been unable to fasten herself into a corset. Her waist was as thin as a blade anyway since she'd eaten little during her incarceration, but her father could surprise her by noting such things. Would her appearance anger or endear her to him?

He was standing by the mantel of the great stone fireplace, smoking a long-stemmed pipe and consulting the flames as if they held the answer to what to do with his daughter. Her mother sat in an armchair by the fire, looking lost and abandoned, and Jessica's heart twisted in remorse for the pain she continued to cause her. Her mother started to get up to go to her, but her father laid a gentle hand on her shoulder and she subsided into the silken layers of her gown.

Carson moved to his desk and set the meerschaum bowl in its holder. Jessica took that as not a good sign. Her father was a mellower man when he smoked his pipe. "Jessica," he said, "you have shamed our family, not only us of its intimate circle, but you've disgraced us to others in the community, people who put store in your parents and brother and abide by our example. You obviously do not agree with the example we Wyndhams set, so I will give you two choices where you may indulge your abolitionist convictions and actions to the fullest—depending, of course, on whether they're tolerated."

Eunice spoke up, her voice thin with grief. "Oh, Carson, must you? Can't we give her another chance?"

"Now, Mother, we agreed," Carson remonstrated her gently, his own voice losing some of its force. "Our daughter cannot stay among us. She's a betrayer and a traitor not only to her family but to her heritage—those who have gone before us and to all southerners who share and support our way of life. That is," he said, still speaking to his wife but fastening his gaze on his daughter, "unless she apologizes to her family and admits her mistake to those she's deeply offended. I'm sure they will understand she was temporarily misguided by her affection for Miss Conklin."

"You mean apologize to Michael and the Night Riders?" Jessica asked, her frozen fear immediately dissolving in the heat of her indignation.

"Precisely."

"Never," Jessica said.

Her mother pressed her fingers to her forehead. "Oh, Jessie, darling…"

Jessica returned her father's hardening stare. "What are the choices of my punishment, Papa? To be burned at the stake or flayed alive?"

Carson turned his back on her, his way of saying he had had enough. Jessica read the message from the squaring of his shoulders, the deliberate withdrawal of his chair from its kneehole, the drop of his attention to papers on his desk, dismissing her. It was possible he would never look at her again, not directly. She was damned to him. He did not address her as he said, "You may recall the punishment your mother's older sister earned for disgracing the family in Boston."

Terror, cold as a steel blade, drove into her heart. The story had become legend in her mother's family. The oldest daughter, for conducting an illicit relationship with a boy of whom her father did not approve, had been banished to a Carmelite convent in Great Britain, one of the strictest orders of nuns in the Catholic Church. Jessica had heard her mother and Aunt Elfie lament the harsh conditions under which their sister lived. The "inmates," as they called the nuns, were permitted to speak for only two hours each day and were allowed no contact with the outside world. They lived in stark cells and took vows of poverty and toil, prayed constantly, lived on only vegetables, and fasted from Holy Cross Day in September until Easter of the following year. Once she was removed from their home, the two sisters never saw their sibling again.

"You wouldn't," Jessica said, glancing at her mother for verification of the threat. Eunice blinked away tears and nodded slightly.

"I would," Carson said. "As soon as I can make arrangements." He took up a pen to scribble his name to a document. "There is an order of Carmelites located in Darlington, a market town in the northeast of England. Perhaps you will encounter your aunt there. She should be around...sixty years old now, by my estimate." He turned the document over and affixed his signature to the next item requiring his attention. "Or..." he added casually, "you may marry Silas Toliver and go live with him in Texas. Take your pick."

Jessica swayed from a sudden light-headedness. Was her father crazy? Silas Toliver was engaged to Lettie. They were to be married in less than six weeks. Did he not remember his daughter was to be her maid of honor? Tippy was working on her bridesmaid's dress. She glanced again at her mother, who had closed her eyes and was biting her lip as if in silent and urgent prayer, and then at the indifferent face of her father, poring over his papers.

"Silas Toliver is engaged," Jessica said, "or have you forgotten? How can you offer him as a choice for me—that is, if he would have me?"

"He'll break the engagement for the price I've offered him," Carson said, "and believe me, he will have you. He has ten more days to agree to it. I have no doubt of his answer."

"Good Lord, Papa! What have you done?"

Her mother rose in a rustle of silk. "Silas is a good man, Jessie," she said, her tone pleading. "He'll take care of you. Your father will see that you want for nothing. If you go to that awful place in England, we'll never see you again."

"But Silas is *engaged*!"

"An easily fixed situation," Carson said.

The horror of her father's manipulation—what he had bullied into place—had begun to dawn. "What about Lettie? If Silas doesn't marry her, she'll be *destroyed*!"

"A fatality of your stupidity and Silas's desperation. She'll get over it."

"I won't choose either one," Jessica said. "I'll run away first— go live with Aunt Elfie in Boston."

"No, you won't, my dear daughter, for if you do, I will sell Tippy and her mother—separately. You must believe me, I will. I cannot have you in Boston where you will continue to work against the interests of your family and the South."

Eunice gave a little moan and put her hands over her ears—in shame, Jessica perceived.

"Papa, I thought you loved me," she said quietly.

He looked at her, perhaps for the last time fully. "I do, my

dear, more than you will ever know or could possibly comprehend from my actions, and that's the tragedy of it. Now go to your
room and think about your choices. Your mother will send Tippy
to you to do something about your dreadful appearance. We must
look our best for our last family Christmas together."

Chapter Nineteen

In the days allotted him before making his decision, Silas observed life at Queenscrown through the eyes of an outside observer, all scales removed from his vision. It was not a difficult challenge. His greatest strength lay in his willingness—and courage—to face the truth, seeing it not as he'd like, but as it was. He did not fall into the trap of believing that, given time and the right circumstances, one day things would be different. A man could waste his life waiting for his fortunes to turn around. In arriving at decisions, Silas weighed the circumstances as they were currently, considered their chances of change, and determined his course.

Thus, he set his attention to observe, in unbiased focus, the people and circumstances that would mark his days for the rest of his life if he remained at Queenscrown and worked as his brother's land manager. Lettie he saw as a wife who would accept her portion without complaint. She would probably continue her teaching duties now that Sarah Conklin would not be returning, a fact he knew and she did not. Her small income would add to his salary, allow her a new frock now and then, perhaps weekend trips to Charleston to dine and take in a play at the Grand Theater. She would never be the mistress of Queenscrown. His mother was the undisputed ruler of the domestic domain, and while they were exceptionally fond of each other, there were bound to be differences in running the household, raising Joshua, and officiating at social events. He saw an erosion of their affection as inevitable, and even a slight discord between two women in a household could make the rest of the occupants miserable. And what if Morris married? Then Lettie would take third chair behind his mother and the new mistress of Queenscrown. Morris's children would take precedence over Joshua. Joshua and his future siblings would be seen as the children of a dependent relative. Silas could take over the land manager's quarters, now occupied by the head overseer, but how could he, a Toliver and a descendant of the aristocratic scion of Queenscrown, tolerate living in a yeoman's cottage?

Silas saw himself becoming ever more frustrated over Morris's handling of the estate. His brother saw winter as a time to relax, but there was plenty that needed doing as the old year ended to keep a plantation running smoothly. There were farm implements and tack equipment to repair, fences and buildings to mend, silos and storage bins to clean, gardens to spade, fields to turn and fertilize…An endless list awaited crucial attention that as land manager Silas would have seen to, but Morris, taking his argument from Ecclesiastes, would have enforced his belief that there was a time for everything and winter was the season to rest and celebrate the birth of Christ. "We've gathered in the sheaves, Silas. Let us rejoice and be glad in our endeavors." Silas perceived that his brother's laxity with the slaves and overseers and slowness in determining the improvements needed for the coming year would in time drive him mad.

As usual, Lettie saw the sunny side of his dark situation and managed to mitigate his disgruntlements. "Darling, at least we'll have a roof over our heads for the year, sit at one of the best tables in Plantation Alley, and have few expenses. We can save our money to add to the sale of the Conestogas and set sail for Texas March after next."

After considering all angles, Silas decided to hold to that star in the east and let it be his guiding light. Lettie's arguments, parroting Morris's, made good sense. Wars and unrest in the new territories would not deter the westward movement. The Conestogas *would* sell, he was sure of it, and there were advantages to the delay. For one, he'd have time to approach the federal army about the sale of his wagons, and for another, the revolution in Texas would most likely be over by the time they arrived. Though he could hardly bear the thought of Jeremy leaving for the promised land without him, by going ahead, his friend could send back firsthand knowledge of the obstacles they would face, allowing him to leave South Carolina forewarned and prepared. Meanwhile, having Lettie by his side and in his bed would make the year tolerable.

By the evening of Christmas Day, he'd made up his mind to stay at Queenscrown and wondered how he could ever for a moment have considered Carson Wyndham's offer. How could he have been so selfish even to think of denying Joshua the maternal affections of a woman who already thought of him as her son? Watching the boy with Lettie (it was to her he ran to show off his presents, not his father), he wished he'd never shared the man's insult with Jeremy but kept it to himself. He felt burned to the bones from the shame of it. How dare Carson Wyndham believe Silas Toliver could be bought? He would not deign to give the man an answer.

His mind relatively at ease, for Lettie's sake, Silas concentrated on enjoying the rest of the holiday season. In the interim between Christmas and New Year's Day, a constant round of parties, many held in honor of their coming nuptials, left him with little time or desire to brood over the change in his plans for the new year. The Wyndhams—for reasons known only to a few and speculated on by everyone else—had withdrawn Willowshire from the manor homes open to callers, but there was much visiting among the other mansions of Plantation Alley, and planters took turns hosting fish fries, log-rollings, barn dances, and corn shuckings in which their slaves participated.

Silas looked forward to the day when he would host such occasions at his own plantation of Somerset in Texas.

The first arctic cold front the second night into the new year of 1836 put an end to the fine weather and high spirits. The sudden freeze was not immediately felt through the thin walls of the cabins in the slave village of Queenscrown, nor did the night seem terribly deep and dark. As a matter of fact, the overseer was awakened by a strange glow dancing on the wall of his bedroom. He leaped to the window and threw open the shutter through which the light had filtered. *"Oh, my God!"* he yelled, jolting awake his sleeping wife. Out in the field by one of the barns, columns of flame-infused smoke spiraled upwards into the cold, black night. The white masts of the fleet of Conestoga ships were on fire.

In the library at Willowshire, Carson Wyndham sat before a softly glowing fire. It was two o'clock in the morning. He wore a smoking jacket against the chill and puffed on a cigar as he stared meditatively into the flames. The visitor he was expecting arrived fifteen minutes later than anticipated, his approach to the great doors of the library soft so as not to disturb the household and awaken listening ears.

Carson glanced at the man, who closed the door quietly behind him. "It is done?" he asked.

"It is done, Papa."

"You made sure no one saw you and there was no one around?"

"I did."

"We must assure your sister's welfare and possible happiness despite her belief we wish the contrary."

Michael Wyndham sat down next to the fire and tiredly drew off his boots. "You are sure Jessica will choose to marry Silas Toliver?"

"Given her choices, I am in no doubt. We must get her out of here before what happened to Miss Conklin happens to her. The Wyndham name can keep in check a lake from overflowing its boundaries, but not a river."

"You believe there's a chance Silas Toliver can make her happy?"

"As happy as any man could make your sister, I suspect. Silas is a remarkably handsome fellow. What woman could resist him?"

"I wonder who will wed Lettie Sedgewick with Silas out of the picture?"

"Why not you? She's certainly comely enough. Intelligent, but smart enough not to show it."

Michael shook his head. "She's too tame for me."

"Ah," his father said. "Sarah Conklin was more to your liking, I take it."

"I found her very desirable. Too bad she was on the wrong side." He shifted his position. "Did you know she never once cried out until the end? I ordered her punishment stopped then. "All I wanted was to hear her cry."

"But she never gave you the name of her conspirator?"

"No. A brave and loyal woman."

"No braver or more loyal than your sister. She could have lied about her part and saved herself—and her family—this tragic turn of events."

An embarrassed silence fell between them. Carson removed his cigar, his eyes narrowing upon his son behind the screen of smoke. "Did you enjoy flogging a woman, Michael?"

Michael pursed his lip as if having to think about the question. "I thought I would," he said, "but afterwards, despite her crime, I felt...sorry that I'd had to do what had to be done."

"Good," his father said, returning the cigar to his mouth. "If you said you'd enjoyed the lashing, I would have disowned you, too."

Chapter Twenty

An investigation into the cause of the fire yielded no clue to substantiate Silas's suspicion of arson.

"A spark from one of the slaves' chimneys must have started the fire, Mr. Toliver," the county sheriff said.

"There was no wind that night. How could it?"

"It don't take but a slight breeze for a spark to travel."

"*Directly* to all *ten* of my wagons?"

Silas received a shrug for an answer.

Two days before Carson Wyndham's deadline of January fifth, smoldering with fury, Silas saddled his gelding and rode to Willowshire. When the butler informed the master of the estate that Mr. Silas Toliver of Queenscrown had arrived, Carson said, "Show him into the library, Jonah. I'll receive him there."

"He did not ask to see you, Mister Carson. He came to see Miss Jessica. He's in the hall. Shall I tell her of her visitor?"

Carson was startled. So, before making his decision, Silas would first test the wind for his daughter's consent to be his wife, would he? He had not considered that Silas's acceptance of his offer would depend on Jessica's acquiescence. A smart and honorable move. Carson felt a gouge of panic. What if his radical-minded daughter refused Silas, a slave owner, and elected to go to the convent? God knew she was capable of falling on her sword.

But she wouldn't, not as long as he held Tippy and Willie May over her head.

"Ask Mr. Toliver to wait in the drawing room and send my daughter to him," he ordered.

Jonah bowed. "Yes, Mister Carson."

Silas rose from the horsehair sofa when Jessica swished into the room, the full skirt of her dress swaying over layers of starched petticoats. She had lost weight and dark circles like half-moons shadowed the sprinkle of freckles beneath her eyes. She looked incredibly young, a mere child, and colorless as boiled pudding compared to his beautiful and radiant Lettie. A pain like a hot poker thrust between his ribs almost made him rush from the room, but he bowed slightly. "Miss Wyndham, I believe you know why I've come?"

"I'm afraid I do, Mr. Toliver," she said. "Shall we sit down and deliberate?"

Silas spread the tails of his frock coat and retook his seat. "Yes, let us do that," he said. "It seems you're in trouble with your father, and I find myself hand and feet in the stocks as well. Has he explained my situation to you?"

"My father does not explain. He commands. I'd like to hear from your own lips why you would consider jilting the girl you love—and who loves you—to marry me."

Silas flinched. The girl may have the face of a juvenile, but she spoke with the tongue of a woman fully in charge of herself. Very well, then. He had come to put all his cards on the table. He would keep none back, as he was wont to do with Lettie. He would not protect this girl from the truth of the man with whom she may be spending the rest of her life. Let *her* decide if she wished to marry someone who could be bought for the price her father was offering.

Silas answered her question, omitting nothing about his ambition and his loathing for his present position at Queenscrown. The girl heard him out in silence, her large brown eyes following his movements when he stood to roam the room and rake his hand through his hair, typical of a Toliver when agitated. A question struck him—one that, in the turmoil of his own situation, he'd forgotten to ask. "What will happen to you, Miss Wyndham, if…you do not marry me?" he inquired, when, emotionally exhausted, he had laid out every card and returned to his chair.

Jessica enlightened him. Silas listened in speechless wonder. "Good God!" he said. "Your father would send you to a place like that?"

"He would, sir, believe me," Jessica said. "In the blink of an eye." She swooped out of her chair to stoke the fire, the flames playing over her pensive face. "This *Toliver passion* of which you speak…that you feel unable to set aside for the love of your life, and for yours, it would seem"—she cast him a small, cold smile—"is all to be fulfilled on the backs of slaves, I take it?"

"That is the way of it," Silas answered.

Her dark eyes flashed. "You are aware of my anti-slave sentiments?"

"I am."

"Then you understand I'd rather copulate with a mule than with a slave owner."

Silas reeled from her candor and, suddenly angered and alarmed—did that mean the girl would refuse to marry him?—he said, "That may be so, Miss Wyndham, but while we're being direct, a mule may be your only choice if you enter a convent."

Color swept over her face. "Does Lettie know of this change in your…plan?"

He had been waiting for the question and answered as deliberately as his pain permitted. "No, not yet. I wanted to make sure of your approval first."

Jessica's lip curled slightly. "You are a man who hedges your bets, I see."

"Among other frailties."

"Well, at least you do not hedge the truth."

"Not in this case."

"Then let me say this, Mr. Toliver. I believe I can relate to the driving force you seem to have inherited, ignoble though yours may be. Obsession is obsession. One cannot spoon it out of the blood like grease from gravy. I loathe your...*passion* that would lead you to the lengths you're willing to go to achieve your goals, but I understand your fervor and feel sorry for you. I, too, am a slave to my own zealotry, and I seem powerless to rectify it."

The poker back in place, Jessica spun decisively from the fire. "So you see, Mr. Toliver, we have no choice but to tie the knot. I will probably not make a good wife, and I doubt I shall ever love you, as I do not expect you to be a husband to me or ever to feel a grain of affection for me. Regarding the issue of copulation, I am willing to consummate our marriage strictly for the reason of bearing children. You understand that?"

Silas nodded numbly.

"We will hurt Lettie beyond measure," Jessica continued, "and your little boy will have lost the loving mother he was expecting and one I could never replace, but I'm assuming you've figured those casualties into your equation."

Silas summoned enough breath to stammer, "Yes, yes, I have." He thought of Lettie and her warm body that he would never know. He thought of Joshua denied her tender care. He thought of living the rest of his life with this little wisp of a harridan beside him. What kind of man was he to make such a bargain with the devil? *A Toliver*, his inner voice answered. He swallowed the acid spittle that had collected in his mouth and said, "You mean—you *accept* my proposal?"

"My *father's* proposal, Mr. Toliver. There's a difference. Now let us adjourn to his study and tell him of our decision."

Chapter Twenty-One

They both drove hard bargains. Silas presented a list of demands that incited an explosive refusal from Carson Wyndham. "Reimburse you for the Conestogas? Absolutely not," he thundered. "Why the hell should I?"

Carson's furtive glance at Jessica told Silas she did not know of her father's involvement in the destruction of his wagons. "I believe you know why, Mr. Wyndham," Silas said, his pointed look implying that his daughter would remain ignorant of the matter if he agreed to his terms. "Otherwise, the deal is off and I bid you good day."

"Now hold on!" Livid in the face, Carson threw down the list. "All right! Consider it done!"

Silas further insisted on participating in the wording of the nuptial agreement within the bounds of the financial arrangements. When the document had been composed, both sides had guaranteed in print the security of their part of the investment. If Jessica ran away or Silas divorced her or she died within ten years of the marriage, Silas would either forfeit his plantation to Carson or return his money in full. "Either way, I get my investment back," Carson made coldly clear to his future son-in-law. For the same length of time, as long as the marriage stayed intact, Carson was bound to the terms of the proposal he had presented to Silas in Queenscrown's drawing room.

Jessica said she would not sign the nuptial agreement unless Tippy was allowed to go with her. Carson looked about to object, but a new, calculating light appeared in his eyes.

"All right," he said. "I'll let her go with you, but don't get any ideas about setting her free. Tippy will keep you safe, and she's additional insurance that you will keep your end of the bargain. You know what will happen to her mother if you don't."

"Considering that you're willing to sell me, Papa, why would I not believe you would put Willie May on the auction block?" Jessica retorted. She made one other demand. "The boy Jasper. What did you do with him?"

"No one came forth to claim him, and we couldn't locate his master. Finders, keepers, as they say. Come spring, he'll be put to work in the fields, but so far he's cleaning the stables and has not received the punishment he deserves. Why?"

"I want you to release him to go with us, too."

Looking into her determined dark eyes that could pierce his heart, Carson hesitated for the fraction of a second. All doubt vanished as to the wisdom of the course he'd set for his daughter. If she stayed among them, she would be branded a "slave-lover," the least of other epithets he could think of, and one day, no matter his far-reaching power, it was possible in these incendiary times he might find her flayed body left on his doorstep.

"Fine," Carson said. "You can have him. Now sign the papers."

Eunice was called in to assist in finalizing the remaining details. It was decided the couple would marry privately in a week at Willowshire, the ceremony officiated by the minister of the First Methodist Church. Silas would remain at Queenscrown and Jessica at Willowshire until the wagon train pulled out March first. Everyone but Jessica looked embarrassed when all agreed a wedding night was out of the question. Cohabitation was a decision the newlyweds would make for themselves as it seemed appropriate. They must be prepared for the scandal following Silas's broken engagement with Lettie.

"May I ask when you plan to tell her?" Eunice asked.

"You may," Silas said, inclining his head respectfully, and did not reply to the question. Eunice and Carson exchanged surprised glances. While their future son-in-law may be a beggar, he felt himself under no obligation to share with them what was clearly none of their business.

When negotiations were completed, Eunice summoned Jonah and shocked everyone by ordering champagne. After Carson, Jessica, and Silas had taken a glass, she lifted hers. Tears shone in her eyes, and her voice cracked. "I never thought I'd toast the engagement of my daughter to a man she does not love nor he her," she said, "but I hope and pray that you can find in the other something to keep you together besides a financial contract, Silas, and the threat of spending your days shut away in a convent, Jessica. I'm sure if you try, despite difficulties to the contrary, you will find all sorts of reasons to care for each other, as there have been in my marriage, and I'm sure, Silas, in that of your parents."

Carson grunted and turned a startled stare to his wife. Difficulties? What difficulties? But he, too, lifted his glass. "Here! Here!" he said.

Eunice drank hastily and set down her glass. "Now if you will excuse me…" She lifted her skirts and made a speedy and teary exit from the room. The only sound in the silence of her wake was the snap of flames in the fireplace. Carson, his gaze sad on the door of his wife's departure, cleared his throat but failed to remove the grit from his voice.

"I will pray for your happiness," he said. "Now leave me, please."

Jessica surprised Silas by waving Jonah away when the butler came to see him to the door and escorted him out to the verandah herself. He couldn't imagine what else she had to say to him not already communicated in the drawing room.

"You believe my father had your wagons burned, don't you?" Jessica stated after she'd closed the door firmly behind her. She barely reached his shoulder, and the cold winter light on her upturned face gave her skin, despite its freckles, the sheen of alabaster.

"The timing of their destruction seems too much of a coincidence not to suspect foul play," Silas said, "but the sheriff could find no evidence to support my allegations."

"The *sheriff*!" Jessica's contemptuous tone dismissed the man. "I wouldn't be surprised if the fool hadn't lit the fuse himself—on my father's orders," she said. "I'm sorry for your loss, Mr. Toliver."

"And I am sorry for yours," Silas said.

"Mine is nothing compared to yours." She peered up at him, her brown eyes sorrowful. "When will you tell Lettie?"

"I'm on my way now."

"I am...so devastated for her. I can't begin to imagine how she will feel. Will you tell her I..."

"Love her? Yes, I will, Jessica. She will know you had no part in this. I will tell her the truth, as I have told you. Though it will give her no comfort, I believe she knows me well enough to understand that if I were to stay, eventually what we have together would be lost."

Jessica bit her lip. "I thought...love could conquer anything."

She expressed the absurdity in the wistful, schoolgirl voice of someone who had no experience with the kind of love of which she spoke and probably never would. She looked even younger than her age, and Silas was moved to touch her in some comforting way, as one would a child, but he resisted.

"There are some other, greater loves that love cannot overcome," he said, his throat aflame. "I wish it were not so."

She said, surprising him once again, "I wish it were not so as well, Mr. Toliver, since the love you and Lettie share most probably will not come to either of you again. You've made a poor bargain, sir."

A groom had brought his horse around. "And you an equally poor one, I'm afraid, Miss Wyndham." He noted she had not bothered with a shawl. "You will get cold," he said.

"I'm quite sure I will, Mr. Toliver, but I will get used to it. I fear I must, for I don't expect ever to be warm again. Good day."

Refusing to think or feel, imagine or speculate, Silas began the longest ride of his life, a canter of insensate oblivion to the house where lived the keeper of his heart. He found her in the tiny sitting room of the manse, a personal space separate from the small parlor where her father was conducting a Bible study. An overflow of wedding paraphernalia and gifts filled every available nook, and, surprised by his visit, Lettie hurriedly fetched a sheet to draw over her veil before he could catch a glimpse of it.

"Bad luck for the groom to see any particle of a bride's dress before the wedding," she said, kissing him soundly. When Silas did not respond, she drew away to look at him worriedly. "What's wrong?"

He willed himself to go blind and deaf to her. He must not remember how the firelight played on her hair or the whisper of her dress as she rushed to throw her arms around his neck. He felt the low-ceilinged walls of the cramped room closing in. "Could we go…outside to the swing?" he asked.

"It's cold and threatening rain."

"By the fire, then."

"We'll keep our voices down. The ladies are so engrossed in discussing the Gospel according to Matthew they won't hear a thing we say. This is about the Conestogas, isn't it?"

She was aware that the loss of the Conestogas would mean an indefinite, perhaps permanent, delay of their departure to Texas. She had been grief-stricken for him but maintained her indomitable belief that something unexpectedly good would come out of the disaster.

"Yes, Lettie. It's about the Conestogas."

He explained, forcing his heart to grow cold to the vision of her joy dissolving in shock and disbelief.

"Jessica? You're going to marry *Jessica Wyndham?*"

"Yes, Lettie."

He hung his head to avoid looking at her. He must not store in memory the heartbreak that filled her blue eyes or the sound of it in her startled cry of pain. He must not carry away, never to be forgotten, the silence of her shocked incredulity as he explained once again, and badly, that he could not survive as things were and always would be at Queenscrown. Day after day, month after month, year after year, he would quietly erode, Silas told her. Pieces of him would slough off until he was barely recognizable as the man she'd married. He would feel like a grounded sailing ship, left to dry-rot where he'd been stranded.

"Then you must go," Lettie said, rising and standing erect and remote as a marble statue. "God be with you and Jessica, Silas."

"Lettie, I…"

"No more need be said. Good-bye, Silas."

"But I must say this…" he insisted, forcing his words through an agony so searing he felt he was burning alive. "I wish with all my being that it was possible to rip out the part of me that could allow me to do this to you, Lettie, my one, my only love. As God is my witness, I would if I could, but I cannot."

"I know, Silas." She stood before the lace curtain of a window through which the last gray light of day outlined her stoic posture, and he was not to be spared the love and courage he saw on her face that would release him to marry another woman. He wanted to go to her for a final, tender embrace, but she turned her back on him, erecting an invisible wall, and he knew he would carry with him the sight of her head finally bowed and shoulders drawn for the rest of his days.

The heavens opened on his return to Queenscrown, a pummeling, repudiating rain from which he did not take shelter, and he was soaked through when he arrived at the plantation. Lazarus rushed to take his hat and coat, clucking that he must get to his room for dry clothes, but Silas told him he wouldn't bother. "Just bring me a towel, and please ask my mother and brother to meet me in the drawing room immediately," he ordered his longtime servant.

"Yes, Mister Silas. Master Joshua, too? He's playing a board game with his uncle."

"No, Lazurus. My son is to be sent to his room until I go up to see him."

Elizabeth and Morris heard him out in drop-jawed silence, Elizabeth's bosom heaving in apparent need of oxygen before Silas was through. Silas had instructed them to hold their diatribes until after he'd concluded what he had to tell them, but neither looked capable of uttering a word when he finished.

Finally, Morris pronounced, "He that hastens to be rich has an evil eye and considers not that poverty shall come upon him. You need to read your Proverbs, Silas."

"And you need to reread Father's will, Morris. Do not speak to me of poverty."

"Son—" Elizabeth staggered up from her chair. "You can't do this to Joshua. His little heart will never mend, and you must think of Lettie."

"Joshua will have a better chance of his heart mending than mine will, Mother, and I *am* thinking of Lettie. Is it better to hurt her now than later, when it is too late to rectify her mistake? In any case," he said, turning from her to pour himself a shot of whiskey, "the deal is made. I am promised to Jessica Wyndham, and we'll marry in a week."

Elizabeth leaned against the back of a chair for support. "I tell you this, Silas William Toliver, son of mine. If you go through with this marriage for the reasons you've contracted it, there will be a curse on your land in Texas. Nothing good can come from what has been built on such sacrifice and selfishness and greed."

Silas threw the whiskey down his throat. The figure of his mother blurred. He would leave without her blessing, completing his alienation from his family. But in her stead, he saw a land blazing with cotton overlooked by a resplendent manor house of which he was the master. His son would take his place beside him and someday beget his own heirs to rule over the dominion of Somerset.

"I already am cursed, Mother," he said. "I carry the Toliver blood."

Chapter Twenty-Two

That Sunday, the usually organized and focused Reverend Sedgewick appeared distracted and rambled in his sermon, and there was the notable absence of his lovely daughter in the choir loft. All was explained when in the week following, those invited to the marriage ceremony of Lettie Sedgewick and Silas Toliver received the return of their gifts and a brief note stating the wedding had been called off. The citizens of Willow Grove, members of the First Presbyterian Church, and the residents of Plantation Alley shared a mutual gasp of shock and wondered if the cancellation had anything to do with the burning of the groom's Conestogas the week before. No one associated the mysterious closure of the Wyndham house over the holidays with this latest development until the news was leaked that Silas Toliver was now set to marry Jessica Wyndham.

The leak had come from Meadowlands when Silas had met with Jeremy to tell him of his decision. The plantation had its own version of Willowshire's Lulu, and the servant was outside the open door of the Warwick library at the moment Silas asked Jeremy to stand with him when he married Jessica Wyndham in five days' time.

"Morris refuses, and Mother says she won't attend the ceremony," the servant overheard Silas say, and got an earful of the why and wherefore he had to marry Jessica Wyndham and jilt his betrothed. The maid carried the scandalous news to the servants' quarters and added her own opinion that eventually reflected the consensus of the whole town. Lettie Sedgewick was the daughter of a poor minister while the daughter of the master of Willowshire, though plain as cheesecloth, was rich. Silas Toliver was broke. It didn't take the sharpest intellect to figure out why he was marrying Jessica Wyndham.

Shock waves immediately rocked the underpinnings of the village and plantation community, and Silas found himself an object of scorn and aspersion for which not even his worst anticipation of the scandal had prepared him. Elizabeth and Morris would not speak to him. The townspeople shunned him. Tradesmen were surly when he went to buy supplies and make arrangements for the wagon train. His worst moments came when he told his son he would not be marrying Lettie.

His child's mouth trembled, followed by tears that filled his large hazel eyes. "Lettie won't be my mama? Why, Papa? Doesn't she like me anymore?"

"She not only likes you, Joshua. She loves you. This is not about anything you've done, son. This is about…what I have done."

"Have you been bad?"

"In her eyes, yes."

"Can you undo the bad thing?"

"I'm afraid not."

Joshua had cried himself to sleep every night and would not eat or respond to any diversion, but, the worst cut of all, he turned from Silas's arms to his uncle's.

"Have you any idea the grief you've caused that child?" his mother reproached him.

"Yes, Mother, but I rely on time to heal it. I fear time will not be so kind to me."

"Nor should it."

Only his friendship with Jeremy, who kept a closed mouth on the situation, and their earnest preparations for the journey to Texas kept Silas from going mad over the suffering he'd caused his son and Lettie. Within days after he'd left his former fiancée with bowed head, she had taken a boat down the coast to Savannah to stay with relatives. According to Reverend Sedgewick's denouncement of him that Elizabeth was pleased to report, she would not return until "Silas Toliver was gone and good riddance to him." Doggedly, Silas thought of himself as a man rowing his boat through darkness, no beam of light anywhere, but he knew the shore was somewhere in the distance. He must keep rowing and trust his judgment of the direction he had chosen. Eventually land—and liberation—would appear.

The five days flashed by with the speed of lightning and dragged with the slowness of a ball and chain. Silas had not seen Jessica since striking the deal with her father five days before, nor had he spoken with a member of her family. He had dealt with Carson Wyndham's banker in settling the financial details of his marriage contract. Little money was to come to him outright, Silas learned to his dismay. He was to be paid for the destroyed Conestogas and the money used to finance his trip to Texas and provide start-up capital for his plantation. Beyond that, funds would be allocated at stages of Somerset's development and for specific purposes. Silas was to keep careful records and receipts as proofs of purchase and evidence of his endeavors. Carson Wyndham would regularly—and unannounced—dispatch an emissary to collect them and check on his daughter's welfare. If all were in order, Silas could expect another deposit into his bank account.

Silas had believed the cash he required at the outset would be deposited as a lump sum into his account to be drawn upon as he saw fit, rather than doled out in increments. He was enraged to discover that the original agreement he signed after careful study had loopholes that allowed Carson to maneuver him into a position where he was indeed a beggar divested of his former leverage. Silas had burned his bridges with his fiancée, his family, town, and society, and now, too late to mend fences and without financial resources, he had no recourse but to marry Carson Wyndham's daughter—and abide by the man's dictates. Every time Silas signed his name to a bill for supplies that would be forwarded to his future father-in-law for payment, he hated the man even more.

He and Jeremy arrived at Willowshire ten minutes before the ceremony was to take place. Only the Wyndhams and the minister were gathered in the drawing room. It appeared there were to be no other witnesses to the nuptials. Silas nodded to a dour-faced Eunice, but he did not exchange handshakes or pleasantries with Carson and Michael as he and Jeremy took their place beside the minister to await the entrance of the bride.

Carson was apparently not to escort his daughter into the room. The practice of "giving away the bride" must strike too close to reality. Lettie had made a study of the history of wedding customs and told Silas the tradition had begun in feudal England when fathers literally gave the property of their daughters to a man to be his wife. Today, the gesture was to show approval of the groom and serve "as a symbol of the father's blessing of the marriage." Neither was true in this case. Mentally Silas could hear Lettie explain that the tradition of the groom standing to the right of the bride went back to medieval days—"so his sword arm would be free to defend her from attackers. Isn't that the noblest thing?"

Silas shook his head to free it of her voice, and the reverend of the First Methodist Church gave him a strained smile, which he did not feel the least compunction to return. Rather, he eyed his "benefactor," as gossip described Carson, with undisguised contempt. Carson ignored his glare, while Michael seemed to find something on a far wall to hold his attention. The few visual attempts to suggest the purpose of the occasion—probably achieved by the reputed creative hand of Jessica's maid, Silas figured—depressed and mocked him beyond despair. Intertwined with white satin ribbons, the first narcissus, tulips, hyacinths, and crocus of the season stood upright in large containers about the room, and an elaborate, three-tiered wedding cake, bearing the maid's signature sugar roses, reigned from a tea trolley along with a bowl of punch. Silas felt a minor relief to see the piano bench empty. Apparently there was to be no music to usher in the bride. Lettie had spent weeks deliberating on the music she wished sung and played at her wedding.

Servants opened the heavy paneled doors to the drawing room, signaling the entrance of Jessica. She floated in wearing a white dress that shimmered as she walked but no veil to hide her pale face and freckles that stood out like small, rusted nail heads. Silas temporarily lowered his lids, feeling a loss so great it left him faint. Opening his eyes, he saw that Jessica had not missed his moment of pain. There was a fraction of a second when she almost stumbled, and pink daubs of embarrassment glowed briefly on her cheeks. She raised her head an inch or so higher, focused her gaze hard on the minister, and the flush disappeared. Oh Lord, Silas sighed to himself as he, too, faced the minister when his bride-to-be drew beside him.

Hours later, Silas remembered hardly anything about the wedding ceremony. It was as gray and lackluster as the weather outside. His and Jessica's emotionless responses to the vows were mumbled in monotones hardly above whispers. There were no smiles and certainly no trading of long, amatory looks since the bride and groom did not glance at each other. Wedding rings were shoved on fingers with indifference. Silas had sent the bill for Jessica's plain gold band to Carson and returned the diamond solitaire he'd chosen for Lettie to the huffy jeweler for a refund. Silas could not silence his former fiancée's commentary on wedding tradition in his head that made a travesty of the rings he and Jessica had traded. "The wedding ring has been worn on the third finger of the left hand since Roman times. The Romans believed the vein in that finger runs directly to the heart."

When the Methodist minister declared them man and wife (timidly, looking as if he feared being struck) and gave the groom permission to kiss his bride, Silas barely touched his lips to her impassive cheek. Jeremy gave the moment some semblance of traditional merriness when he put his hands on Jessica's shoulders and said with a smile, "Now it's the best man's turn," and kissed her other cheek.

"Well, that's that," Carson announced with a relieved sigh when it was done and patted his stomach. "Let's have some punch and cake, shall we?"

"I'd like to invite Tippy in to have some," Jessica said, turning from Silas as if his act in the play was over and she was ready for the next performer.

Eunice gave her a look of annoyance. "Oh, Jessie—"

"I'd like to meet this Tippy I've heard so much about," Silas intervened, thankful for a diversion to fill the space before he and Jeremy could civilly leave.

Jessica cut him a sharp look. "As you know, she'll be going with me to Texas," she said, "but as my friend, not my maid, and certainly not as a slave. Is that understood?"

For a moment, Silas did not. Then he realized that this... Tippy of whom Jessica was obviously so fond was his property now. Everything that belonged to Jessica now belonged to him. Marriage made it so. Jessica could speak with the growl of a tiger, but she lacked the teeth to enforce her commands. But he would be gracious. He bowed his head a trifle. "As you wish."

Eunice addressed a servant in attendance at the tea table. "Send Tippy to the drawing room."

Afterwards, cantering away together from the scene of the disaster, Jeremy threw Silas a measured glance. "Want to get drunk?"

"It wouldn't help."

"She's a fine girl, Silas."

"I haven't noticed."

"Time will take care of that," Jeremy said.

Arriving at Queenscrown, Silas instructed Lazarus to round up Joshua. He had allowed the boy the comfort of his grandmother and uncle to assuage his loss of Lettie, but now Silas wanted the company of his son.

"He's with Mister Morris, sir."

"That's as may be, Lazarus, but now I wish my son to be with me. I'll be in my room."

"Very good, Mister Silas."

Waiting for Joshua, sunk in gloom before the fire, Silas reflected on the events of the afternoon. The only bright spot had been the odd little creature of a maid servant called Tippy. There was something about her not of this world. She had the widest smile and brightest eyes he'd ever seen on a human face. The girl radiated a light that even he could see would be a shame to extinguish. It was plain that she and Jessica were closer than the grip on a pistol, and he didn't know what to think of such a friendship between a white girl and a Negro slave, but he would do nothing to interfere with it. He was grateful that Jessica would have companionship on the trip to Texas. Small and delicate-looking creature that the maid was, she looked like she could weather anything, and Jessica would need a sustaining friend to endure the hardships of the trail. Used to the finest comforts, Jessica had no idea what she was in for, and he should make an appointment to educate her.

Silas studied the circle of gold on his finger. Make an appointment. He felt no more married to Jessica Wyndham than if he'd said *I do* to an empty sheet. He *felt* like an empty sheet. Lettie had told him that in many places in the world, the bride and groom did not meet until their wedding day, pawns of an arranged marriage. He had thought the idea bizarre and barbarous. Never in a million years could he have imagined himself marrying not only a stranger but a woman who thought of him as an enemy—an advocate for all she was against. Was she really sincere in supporting the abolition of a system that had provided her a life of privilege, or had she chosen her path to rebel against her father? Jeremy was of the opinion that daughter and father loved each other but—like roses and thorns on the same stem—were born to abide in conflict.

Silas could handle Jessica Wyndham's toothless bidding, but how would the girl take to his son? What would be Joshua's reaction to her?

Slight footsteps approached his door. A small hand pushed it open. "Papa?"

Silas held out his arms, his chest swelling with love and need. "Come here, Joshua, and crawl into your papa's lap. It's been a while since I've held my son."

"You're sad, too, Papa?" Joshua said, climbing up on Silas's knees.

"Yes, Joshua, I am very sad," Silas said, tucking his young son's head beneath his chin. He had already caused his child a great deal of pain. Was he selfish to inflict more by uprooting him from those he loved and the only home he knew to take him to a foreign land in the company of a stepmother neither of them knew?

But if he left his son at Queenscrown until the time was safe to bring him to Texas, Silas might never reclaim him. Joshua was in the most sensitive, impressionable stage of a boy's life. What would be between father and son must be established now or forever be lost. Silas well remembered the period when he was Joshua's age. Between his fourth and eighth years, he had felt himself a mere shadow out of the corner of his father's eye. Their chance to know each other slipped away. He would not make that mistake with Joshua. Besides, he must think of Jessica. How could the boy ever accept her as a mother figure if he were not weaned from Lettie now?

But all questions regarding Joshua narrowed down to the one most important: Was Silas wrong to ensure for his son the birthright and future his own father had denied him, no matter what the cost might be?

Only time held the answer.

Chapter Twenty-Three

Something was bothering Jeremy. Silas could read his friend like a well-thumbed book. Jeremy was the only one of his clan to inherit its patriarch's Greek-god features (Lettie had called him Helios), and his friend's face, for all its golden, sculpted handsomeness, was as open as a clear day rarely disturbed by clouds. Today, something had caused the clouds to gather.

"What's got ahold of you, Jeremy?" Silas asked as his friend followed him up to his room at Queenscrown. It was past the supper and reading hour, and his family and servants had retired for the night.

Silas prayed it had nothing to do with Jeremy deciding to go off and help the Texians fight their revolution. His comrade-in-purpose had hinted at the desire some time back. "Caleb Martin is as capable of helping you organize and lead the wagon train as I am," Jeremy had said, "and I'll meet up with you at the point where you cross the Red River."

Jeremy's grandfather had fought in the American Revolution sixty years before and while he lived, never let his offspring and their children forget the reasons the war with England was fought. The concept of a citizen having certain innate rights in his own country had been inbred in them, more so than in the Tolivers' line, who in their heart of hearts still felt some fealty to their

Royalist pasts. Jeremy seethed at the gall of the Mexican government to levy taxes on the Texas colonists without representation and to pass sudden and arbitrary civil policy and laws it enforced by the use of military power. "I have no one but myself to see after," he'd said to Silas. "I ought to go help the Texians. It's our war, too."

Silas had used all his powers of persuasion to convince Jeremy that the Texians could do without his proficient gun arm for now. Many of those who had signed up to join the wagon train in his group had done so because of Jeremy's known courage, cool head, and keen intelligence. For the same reason, Silas's flock had signed on and stuck with him. The scandal of his marriage may have tarnished his image but not his leadership abilities. The feeling was that if anybody could get them to Texas, Jeremy Warwick and Silas Toliver could. Not so if one-half of the team was turned over to Caleb Martin, a strong, tough man but of untested abilities without knowledge of the pertinent information Silas and Jeremy had collected and studied over a year. And what would happen if Silas were rendered incapable of leading the train along the way?

Jeremy had granted that he'd been thinking only of himself even to consider turning his charges over to Caleb, but today, so close to departure time, Silas wondered if his friend's old yearnings had come back to possess him.

"I apologize for the late hour, but Tomahawk rode in an hour ago and brought the worst news yet," Jeremy said.

Tomahawk Lacy, a Creek whose tribe lived in Georgia, was one of two scouts Jeremy had hired and trusted to bring back reports from Texas. As one returned, the other rode out, so that the leaders of the wagon train were kept abreast as much as possible of the current perils they would meet. "Let's hear it," Silas said, ushering him into his sitting room where he had a new map spread out on his desk, the first topographical map of Texas prepared by a man named Gail Borden, a surveyor for the Stephen F. Austin colony.

"Santa Anna's brigades have fanned out along the Rio Grande," Jeremy said, placing his finger on the drawing of the river that served as a border between Texas and Mexico. "Tomahawk estimates the number of troops at several thousand, probably more, along with hundreds of wagons, carts, mules, horses. It must be a heart-freezing sight. He says they'll cross at various points and times in the next week and gather on the Texas side of the Rio Grande. Santa Anna himself is leading the army and will cross with his battalion from a place called Laredo in the south. His intent is to retake Texas and put down the rebellion like he did in the separatist states in Mexico."

Silas felt a chill creep over his skin. He understood Jeremy's meaning and reference to the "separatist states." Santa Anna meant to show no mercy to the upstart Anglo colonists as he had shown none to the rebels in the Mexican states who had opposed his taking over the government and declaring himself dictator of the country. On the long march toward Texas, he and his armies had blazed a path of terror through the provinces that had separated themselves from his rule, systematically burning villages, killing livestock, raping women, and massacring the rebels and their families and communities without quarter. A handful of survivors had carried news of the atrocities into Texas to warn the Texians of the kind of wholesale slaughter and brutality that awaited them when General Antonio Lopez de Santa Anna and his Mexican Army crossed the Rio Grande.

Silas thought instantly of Joshua and Jessica. "So he'll take no prisoners, women and children included?"

"That's the report. Everyone in arms and their families will be treated as pirates, unworthy of mercy."

"The son of a cur! I'd like to string the bastard up by his go-
nads and stake him over a slow fire," Silas said, realizing how
ineffectual he sounded. In Toliver fashion, he swept his hand
through his hair. "So what do we do—take the tide while it is
upon us or decline? We're on a full sea, Jeremy. The wagons are
packed. If we delay, even for a month, we may lose the current."

Jeremy offered the flicker of a grin. "You and your Shakespeare. As bad as Morris and his Bible." His tone sobered. "No
matter the full sea. You would risk Joshua and...your wife?"

"This news gives me reason to suggest another route I've been
considering," Silas said, and turned the map toward Jeremy.
Once upon a time, they favored a specific table at the Wild Goose
in Willowshire to study maps and discuss their plans over flagons
of ale, but that was before Silas's disgraceful conduct became the
topic of tavern talk. These days they met in the Warwick library
or in Silas's rooms at Queenscrown, not the most cordial venue
since Elizabeth and Morris were aware of the reason they had
gathered.

"What if we drop down to New Orleans and cross the Sabine
River into Texas?" Silas said. "It will be out of our way, but
the advantage is that the Mississippi will be easier to navigate
there, and we'll have cheaper and more convenient access to water transport than we're likely to have at Shreve Town farther
north. Ferries are in place in New Orleans, and flatboat construction is a flourishing and competitive business."

Silas pointed to the river's mouth on the map. "We can cross
the Sabine here at its estuary and make our way up through the
bayou country through the pine forests north, then cut west to
our land grants. If we cross where we'd intended"—he indicated
a place farther up on the map—"we might run directly into Santa
Anna's army. He's bound to be headed toward the eastern part of
the territory where the largest settlements are located."

"And by entering Texas from the south, should that madman have taken the territory, we'd have the biggest chance of retreat," Jeremy said.

"That's right."

"I like it. The Comanche will be less of a threat as well."

"We'll need to call a meeting for tomorrow night to inform everyone of the change of route and to assure them we're still going," Silas said.

Jeremy turned away to pour himself a glass of brandy.

"What's the matter?" Silas asked, rolling up the map as Jeremy took a seat before the fire. "You still seem…daunted by the news."

"Not for myself, Silas, you know that, or even for those who have entrusted their destiny to our care. We've kept them apprised of the risks they're taking, the price they may have to pay for the rewards they seek, but there are those innocent of the dangers…who are totally unprepared to deal with them."

Silas joined him with his own brandy glass. "You're speaking of Jessica, of course."

"I am. Far be it from me to tell a man how to deal with his wife, but it seems to me Jessica ought to be given some training in how to defend herself if need be. She doesn't even know how to load or fire a gun."

"How do you know this?"

"I ran into her while she was out riding last week. By the way, she should leave her filly at home. That silly little horse is too dainty for the trek to Texas, tethered to the back of a wagon."

To his surprise, Silas felt a pang of some unidentifiable emotion at Jeremy's interest in Jessica's welfare. Not jealousy, surely, but he found the feeling unfamiliar and unpleasant. "I'll send word to her father that she should be instructed in shooting a gun and to include a firearm in her belongings. I'll also advise that Jingle

Bell be left behind. Let Carson deal with her tantrum when she's told."

Silas had intentionally and familiarly dropped the name of Jessica's horse in rebuttal to his friend's implication—accurate and unintended, though it was—that he had neglected his wife. "What else did you and she discuss?"

"Only that she wishes she could be privy to more information about what to expect. She says she reads the newspapers and knows what's going on in Texas but not to the extent we do and share with the others. Jessica is aware of our meetings and that wives are invited. She feels...excluded."

"She'd only be the object of gawking if she attends. The girl ought to be grateful to have been spared the embarrassment, and she needn't be concerned for her well-being, nor should you. Believe me, Carson will see to her every comfort, and"—Silas took a sip of the brandy—"I plan to drop Jessica and Joshua off at a hotel in New Orleans—the Winthorp—until it's safe to send for them."

Jeremy raised a sandy brow. "Ah. Another reason to change the route." After another taste of his drink, he asked casually, "What if Jessica refuses to stay in New Orleans? She's proven a girl who doesn't mind being in harm's way."

"It's not harm's way she'll wish to remove herself from, Jeremy, but me," Silas said.

Chapter Twenty-Four

"Jessie, do you think this is a good idea?" Eunice asked, the question carrying a note of reproach as she watched her daughter pack a number of small, brightly colored, hand-carved blocks into a sack. "Your *husband* should be the one arranging this first visit with his son."

"If I depended upon my *husband* to introduce me to the boy, I might have to wait until we're in Texas. Cowardliness is not fast overcome."

"In that opinion I believe you've wronged Silas, Jessie. He's probably thinking of his son, who is still pining for Lettie, and Elizabeth, who had hoped she would become his stepmother. Perhaps he's waiting for the appropriate time to introduce you to Joshua."

"And just when would be the appropriate time, Mama? In one week when we leave for Texas? How awkward would that be for the boy?"

Jessica slipped the last colored block into the sack. The blocks made up a set of twenty-six with letters of the alphabet drawn on one side, numbers on the other, and farm animals, fences, pastures, sheds, and equipment on the others, all exquisitely painted by Tippy. Jessica had gotten the idea of them as an introduction gift to her stepson one night when she was lying awake wondering how she could manage, not to replace Lettie in Joshua's affections, but at least to make friends with him. She knew nothing about child rearing and had never experienced a second's maternal longing to produce a child. She'd gone to Tippy with the idea.

"I want something to be a learning tool as well as a toy," she'd said, and Tippy's imagination had immediately taken off in collaboration with Willowshire's talented carpenter to produce the result Jessica would be transporting to Queenscrown today. Along with it was a stick horse whose head had been carved and painted as a facsimile of her beloved Jingle Bell whom she'd been told she must leave behind.

"Besides," Jessica added, "my *husband* has forgotten about me." She'd seen Silas only once after they'd said "I do." Two weeks later, the first of February, the day he was to have married Lettie, he'd sent word by one of the servants to expect him that afternoon, and she'd stood on the upstairs gallery to watch for his approach up the lane. She'd expected to view him with disdain, but her heart had flown to her throat when he came into sight on his high-prancing gelding, the handsomest man she'd ever seen—her husband—and among the *oldest*, too, Jessica reminded herself, *and* an advocate of slavery to boot, she must remember.

Shocked and angry at herself, bewildered, she'd escaped quickly inside before he saw her and mistakenly believed she was eager to see him. By the time she met him for tea in the small parlor, she'd set her face against him. Uninspired by his reception, Silas was no less impassive to her. There was no sign he was aware of the significance of the date. He had come to give her a list of dos and don'ts to consider in preparations for the trip and outfitting her Conestoga wagon, delivered the day before. Apparently they were not to occupy the same "camel of the prairie," as the vehicle was called. Her father had bought her and

Silas their individual wagons as a wedding present. The scandal that the married couple was not cohabiting—now fodder for every gossipmonger in South Carolina—would travel with them to Texas.

"Well, frankly, I hope your husband *has* forgotten about you," Eunice said. "There is no *telling* what the train will run into in Texas, even if you make it there. Elizabeth agrees. She's frightened out of her mind for Joshua."

Jessica turned away from the mirror where she'd been adjusting her bonnet to prevent her mother from reading her same worry. The *Charleston Courier* weekly carried news of the rebellion in Texas, and yesterday they had read a report that 6,000 Mexican soldiers led by Santa Anna, Mexico's ruthless military commander, had crossed the border of the Rio Grande to crush the Texian forces once and for all. Silas had estimated that the trip to Texas would take five months, barring disastrous delays, which would place the date of their arrival at the site of their land grant no later than the end of July. But what would they find when they got there? Burned lands? Hostile Mexican soldiers waiting to take them prisoner? Would their land grants even be honored?

She shrugged off the flurry of worries for her more immediate concern and asked, "Where is Tippy? She's to go with me to Queenscrown. I want her to see the look on the boy's face when I present him his toys."

"For God's sakes!" Eunice moaned. "Must Tippy share everything? This is to be a private moment between you and your stepson and Elizabeth when you meet her as her daughter-in-law. What will you do if Elizabeth invites you to stay for tea? Will you insist Tippy share that, too? Spare the girl and allow her to remain here."

"Tippy will take herself off to the kitchen on her own accord, Mama," Jessica said, picking up the sack. "To spare me, she respects the place others have assigned her. I don't want her to miss the boy's reaction."

Silas felt a small start when he recognized the Wyndham coat of arms on the two-seater, single-horse trap tied before the verandah of Queenscrown. It was not a conveyance he'd think favored by the Wyndham men. It must be Eunice Wyndham come to offer an olive leaf to her old friend and her daughter's mother-in-law after a strained stand-off between the two plantations. Or—surely not—could it be Jessica come to call?

Silas hastily dismounted and slapped his horse's flank. The gelding took off for the groom to look after when he reached the stables.

The sound of voices came from the drawing room—voices threaded with laughter he had not heard in a long time. Silas peered around the door to see Jessica and her maid sitting on the floor with his son, gazing on as he stacked little blocks of colored wood on top of one another. His mother watched the activities from her chair before the fire, looking amused despite that it was not Lettie on the floor playing with her grandson.

"*A, B, C*—what follows *C*, Joshua?" Jessica was saying.

"*D!*" his son squealed delightedly. "My uncle Morris taught me!"

Tippy, the maid, applauded with her floppy hands. "You is so smart!" she cried.

"I know it," Joshua said matter-of-factly. "Can we make a farm?"

"Of course," Jessica said.

Silas cleared his throat and stepped forward. "May I join the party?"

Joshua, seeing him, jumped to his feet. "Papa! Papa! Come

look what Jessica and Tippy have brought me!" He grabbed his father's hand and pulled him to the scattering of colored blocks on the floor. "There are numbers and pictures, and I can build a farm with animals and everything! See?" Joshua grabbed up a barn and a cow for his father's inspection.

"I see," Silas said.

"And, look, look!" Joshua straddled the stick horse. "I have a pony with a real head. Gee haw, horse! Gee haw!" And with a whoop and a cry he galloped off to ride the terrain of the room on his handsome-headed stallion.

Jessica had gotten to her feet. Tippy, too, had hopped up. The maid folded her hands before her apron and stepped back from the group into the dusky shadows of the room, her head down.

"Good afternoon, Mr. Toliver," Jessica said, adjusting the folds of her dress. "I hope you do not mind the intrusion into your home."

"It is a visit most welcome, Miss Wyndham."

"The toys were an idea I had that Tippy made possible as a means to introduce myself to your son."

"A very gracious gesture, Miss Wyndham."

Joshua reined his pony in beside them. "*Jessica*. Her name is *Jessica*, Papa. She and Tippy are going with us to Texas."

"So I've heard," Silas said, his eyes holding Jessica's.

Elizabeth rose from her chair. "Let us be off to the kitchen to see about tea, Tippy, and perhaps you can show our cook how to cut the sandwiches in those designs that were served at Miss Jessica's birthday party."

"I be happy to," Tippy said.

Joshua was back on the floor engrossed with the blocks, his horse temporarily hitched. "Thank you," Silas said to Jessica, taking her by the elbow and drawing her from his son's play. "I…didn't quite know how to arrange a meeting between you and Joshua. It should have happened sooner. Forgive my irresolution."

Jessica waved away his apology. "Perfectly understandable, Mr. Toliver. Your son is adorable. I believe we'll become very good friends."

"Does he know you're…my wife?"

"I thought it less confusing for him not to know yet. Our… situation will easily conceal the fact until the time is suitable to disclose it to him."

"Very wise…Jessica."

She smiled slightly, a flickering light quickly extinguished, but not too soon for Silas to see its benefit to her face. "Silas…" Jessica said his name musingly. "I'll have to get used to calling you that."

"It will not be as hard as hearing yourself referred to as Mrs. Toliver."

"Not any more so than believing I am," Jessica said, and Silas understood the cause of her blush. She had wandered into marital territory in which they might never venture. The possibility—probability—of their never sharing a bed was fine by him. He had his heir to Somerset.

"I'm glad you came over," he said. "I was meaning to come by tomorrow with information which should make you very happy."

A leap of panic flashed in her dark eyes. "You're not canceling the trip, are you?"

Curious, surprised by her reaction, he asked, "Would that make you happy?"

She looked perplexed, but only momentarily. Silas saw her quick mind make short work of her confusion. "I dare say that would put us in a pickle neither of us would prefer, so by logic that news would not make me happy. I was silly to ask such a question."

"I can't imagine you ever being silly, Jessica. The information

is this: Our route will take us to New Orleans, and I propose that
you stay comfortably there in a hotel with Joshua until I can get
the lay of the land in Texas. Of course your maid will remain
with you. When all is well, I will send for you. You will like the
Winthorp. I've stayed there before. It is in the Garden District
and run by an English couple who understand the niceties of
southern hospitality. I'll give you the address to leave with your
mother and friends in case they wish to mail you letters there."

Silas had expected to see her blow out a breath of relief. Instead, her small, freckled face tightened. "Of course I will stay
behind for Joshua's sake," she said, her voice thick with what
sounded like disappointment. "I'm sure you're worried about the
danger to him." She raised her chin to a lofty angle and turned
away from him. "It really is time we were getting home. If you'll
be kind enough to direct me to the kitchen, I'll go fetch Tippy."

Silas was astonished to see that he had somehow wounded her.
Her hurt feelings were as easy to perceive as the bright blocks
scattered on the floor. Lord have mercy, what had he said to in-
jure her so? At a loss, flustered, he inquired, "Are you all packed
and ready for departure? Remember that three-quarters of your
wagon is to be reserved for supplies."

The one time he'd seen her since their marriage, he had
strongly advised her not to bring anything along she could live
without. Later, when they were established, things could be
shipped to their settlement upriver from the Gulf of Mexico,
he'd told her. As a leader of the wagon train, he had met many
times with his group and preached keeping their conveyances
as light as possible. Guidebooks, newspaper articles, and letters
from those who had already made the five-month journey told of
settlers having to discard nonessential items to lighten loads because of various problems with terrain or in case of emergency.
The trails west were littered with abandoned items—furniture,

clothes, bedding, books, equipment, musical instruments—that travelers coming after them found and picked up for their own use. He had left Jessica a list of suggested substitutes for heavier and less practical items, such as candles in lieu of oil and a few sets of sturdy, warm clothing rather than trunks full of silk and satin finery. Silas was sure that half of Jessica's elegant possessions would be left in the wake of the wagon train.

"I am ready, Mr. Toliver," Jessica said crisply. "You may rest your concerns about that, and I am relieved that news of that dreadful despot bent on humbling the Texians has not dampened your will to go. At this point, I am ready to say to Plantation Alley, Willow Grove, my family, and the whole state of South Carolina what Mr. David Crockett said to his constituents when he was defeated for reelection to Congress: 'You may all go to hell. I am going to Texas.'"

Chapter Twenty-Five

A pall fell over the three leading manor houses of Plantation Alley. In each household, owners and servants moved quieter, talked in soberer voices as the final days approached for the departure of the wagon train. The youngest member of each family, nurtured and thought of as "the baby" from infancy, was about to set forth into unknown territory rife with danger and hardship. God only knew when, or if, they were likely to be seen again. At Meadowlands, Jeremy's favorite foods began to appear on the table, picked at by his father and brothers, energetic, talkative men grown uncharacteristically taciturn and short-tempered.

Jessica released Tippy to be with her mother in her quarters at night. In the bed they shared, Willie May lay on her side next to Tippy's back and stroked her daughter's hair. It puffed around her head as fine as gossamer and thin as cobwebs. An ear stuck out like a conch shell washed up on the shore, and sometimes Willie May pressed hers to it, as if expecting to hear the sound of the sea. Most nights she lay awake until early dawn listening to her daughter's breathing, storing its rhythm in memory, worrying about the defect of her child's missing lung as tears trickled into the neck of her night shift.

At Queenscrown, Elizabeth's cold manner toward her younger son thawed. She knocked on his room door one evening when he and Jeremy were visiting. Before Silas could open it, she bustled in to interrupt the men, who, as she'd expected, were discussing the forthcoming journey. "Oh, good. I've caught you in time, Jeremy," she said as they hastily rose. "May I sit? I have a proposal."

"Oh, Mother, not again," Silas moaned as he and Jeremy retook their seats.

"I've not come riding that old horse, Silas," Elizabeth said. She sat down and folded her hands before her in the manner of a schoolmarm about to deliver a lecture. She had not seen Jeremy to speak to in some time. Elizabeth noticed that he did not ask how her roses grew. He knew very well her garden contained nothing but thorns. It was about that subject that she had come to speak.

"I wish to propose that each of you carry the roses of your ancestors to your new land as your forebears carefully brought them from England to be replanted in South Carolina. They are a symbol of your heritage, and I..." Tears welled; Elizabeth's voice trembled. "I could not bear to think you will have nothing tangible by which to remember your family. You boys will have your memories, but your children...Joshua and the children I will never see...will have nothing." She whipped a handkerchief from the pocket of her dress and dabbed at her eyes while the two men looked on in helpless embarrassment. "Your mother would advise you the same, Jeremy, God rest her sweet soul. She so prized her Yorkist roses as I do my Lancasters."

Elizabeth had expected an objection from Silas—space was scarce in the wagons—but to her surprise, he nodded agreement. "A splendid idea, Mother. I should have thought of the roses myself. I was planning on asking for the portrait of the Duke of Somerset to take with me."

"We'll have to ask Morris, but I'm sure he'll agree," Elizabeth said. "He doesn't place the stock in his forebears as you do."

Jeremy had risen to his feet again. He took Elizabeth's hand and bowed over the network of blue veins. "I agree with Silas," he said. "A wonderful thought. I'll have our gardener see to it. He's a master at tending the roses now that my mother has gone."

"I'll come over and personally oversee the digging up. The roots must be wrapped carefully in burlap and kept moist," Elizabeth said.

"I'd be most grateful," Jeremy said. "Good night, Silas. I'll see my way out."

Alone together for the first time since Silas had declared his intention to marry Jessica, mother and son regarded each other, the merrily crackling fire mocking their awkward silence. After a moment, Elizabeth said, "I'm not going to see you and Joshua off, Silas. I simply can't. You understand?"

"I do, Mother."

"You go without my blessing, you know that, but you will always have my love."

"I know, Mother."

"But you go with your father's blessing. I couldn't let you leave without telling you that."

Silas's gaze flickered skeptically. His mouth arched in derision. "You've had some communication with Papa from the grave?" But at the flare of pain he saw in his mother's expression, he added more gently, "Or is this some new knowledge from your mother's heart?"

"From neither," Elizabeth said. "By leaving you out of his will, your father all but pushed you on your way to pursue the dream you've had since you were a boy. He knew you'd never stay here to obey your brother's commands, and that's why he left you with no choice but to leave. What he didn't know was the lengths to which you'd go to do so."

Elizabeth got up while Silas, his brow drawn, reflected on this new information. "It is hard for you to believe your father loved you, Silas, but he did. I can only hope his machinations will not result in fate taking an unkind view of yours. Ill-begotten gains always have a way of costing more than they're worth."

Elizabeth turned with a sway of dark wool toward the door. "Good night, my son. Oh, and by the way...you may have wondered where Morris has gotten himself off to."

Silas, disconcerted, said, "I've been too busy with last-minute preparations to concern myself with Morris's whereabouts."

Elizabeth's lips twitched. "It seems he, too, cannot bear to say good-bye. He loves Joshua as his own, you know. He's with the only person who can comfort him in his coming loss. They share a mutual pain. Morris has gone to Savannah...to be with Lettie."

"Tippy, do you think it's possible to love a man you don't respect or like?"

"How would I know about such things, Miss Jessie? I'se had no experience lovin' nobody but you and my mama."

"Because you were born a celestial being that ended up in your mama's womb, and you know everything."

They had almost reached the Yard, a half-mile from the Main House, on this the next-to-the-last day before they might never see Willowshire again. The sun was warm, the air balmy for this date in February, perfect for a final stroll over the grounds and through the plantation compound to bid farewell to the only home they'd ever known.

"Well, then, seems to me it's possible, like a wildflower growin' out of rock. Can't make no sense of it. Nothin' there to feed it." Tippy eyed Jessica quizzically. "Youse speaking of Mistah Silas?"

"I'm speaking of Mister Silas," Jessica admitted, blushing. "And there most certainly isn't anything there to feed it. I have

no idea where this...*ridiculous* feeling has sprung from. My...
husband traded the most wonderful and lovely woman in the
world—my beloved friend—for a piece of land, Tippy. How
could I not hate him for that alone?"

"I'se don't know, Miss Jessie, but some wildflowers, they impossible to kill. Youse might think you pull 'em up by de roots,
but they be back next year."

Jessica hated it when her friend spoke in the dialect of the field
Negro, but they were within earshot of the open doors of the slave
cabins, and Tippy was determined to give her mistress's father no
further cause to find disfavor with his daughter. When they left
here, though, Tippy would never have to talk beneath the level
of her literacy again, no matter what Mr. Silas Toliver dictated.
Before Jessica could deliver this assurance, her attention was diverted by a restless gathering in the Yard. Something had drawn
the slaves to a point of interest in its center.

"What do you suppose the commotion is all about?" Jessica
wondered aloud, and then, as the group parted at her approach,
she saw.

"You cannot let her go, Carson. You simply can't. She's our
daughter, our *only* daughter." Eunice's emphasis was clear. Jessica
would have had a sister, but she had died minutes after birth.

She had hit her husband on his weak flank. As the date had
drawn nearer for the wagon train to pull out, coupled with the
harrowing news from Texas, Carson had grown more and more
morose. Eunice, recognizing he was having second thoughts
about their daughter's safety, made her move. "It's not too late to
stop her," she said. "We can have the marriage annulled. Jessica
and Silas have never...well, you know."

"And then what, Eunice?" Carson said, his face red with agitation. "We're back to where we started with her. You would prefer we send our daughter to a convent?"

"I believe Jessica has learned her lesson. You've scared her sufficiently for her to realize what will happen if she engages in speech or action that would put her in peril and embarrass this family again." Eunice's words had the convincing ring of a mother who knows her child.

"If we back down now, Jessie will think she can get away with her outrageous sentiments and behavior next time," Carson disagreed, but he delivered his argument in a tone of halfhearted conviction.

Eunice moved closer to hold her husband's eye. "If there is a next time, Carson," she said softly, "I promise I won't interfere with what you must do. I'll make sure Jessie understands that."

Carson inhaled loudly and stepped away from the lure of his wife's wiles. "I made a deal with Silas. I can't back down now. There's been scandal enough without my being perceived as a blackguard who'd set up the boy to believe he was headed to Texas on my money, destroyed his engagement to the woman he loved, then yanked the rug out from under him two days before his departure." He shook his head firmly. "I can't do that to Silas."

Eunice grasped her husband's chin and compelled him to look at her. "Abide by your agreement with Silas. Let him go, but without Jessica. All he wants is the money. He'll be happy to be rid of her because he'll still have the chance of marrying Lettie. You can afford it, Carson." Her tone turned pleading, her look amorous as she took his face in her hands. "Isn't our daughter worth it, my love?"

Carson folded his hands around her forearms, the nearest to an invitation to hold her since the whole blasted mess began. "She's worth it," he said huskily and drew her closer.

His lips did not quite make it to hers. The door of the library burst open, and Lulu ran in, panting. "Pardon me, Master, but you better come see. It's Miss Jessica. She's done gone and done it again."

"Done what?" Eunice cried.

"She done taken the side of a black man."

"What?" Carson threw off his wife's arms. "Who? Where?"

"A lazy piece of colored trash, that who. He be at the whupping post. The overseer, Mr. Wilson, was 'bout to lash him, and Miss Jessica, she step in, say he has to whup her first." Lulu paused for breath. "It all goin' on right now."

"Run and send somebody to tell Wilson to hold off. I'll be right there." Carson turned to his wife, his jaw rigid, his gaze implacable. "Proceed with our daughter's packing, Mrs. Wyndham. She is going to Texas."

Chapter Twenty-Six

In the hour before dawn, March first, 1836, the vehicles bound for the eastern part of Texas began to assemble in a field behind the town of Willow Grove, South Carolina. Groups of family and friends had gathered to wave the wagon train off, and some stores and shops were open for last-minute purchases or for their owners to bid farewell to longtime customers they were not likely to see again. There was a festive air about the occasion, mixed with melancholia and concern. On February twenty-third, the Mexican general Santa Anna and his troops had laid siege against a garrison of 187 Texians bivouacked in a mission called the Alamo on the San Antonio River. Their commander was one of their own, a South Carolina boy born in Saluda County named William Barrett Travis. Alongside him was his cousin, also of South Carolina, James B. Bonham. The Alamo had been under siege seven days, and the *Charleston Courier* held out little hope that the brave defenders—the South's Davy Crockett and Jim Bowie among them—could hold out until reinforcements arrived.

Among the most solemn groups waiting to say their good-byes were the Wyndham and Warwick families and beloved members of their household staffs. Missing were Elizabeth and Morris Toliver, but standing in their stead were Cassandra and Lazarus, holding a still-sleeping Joshua. In a last-minute decision, Silas had freed the elderly couple to stay behind with his mother and brother, and they watched on with eyes still swollen from tears of relief and gratitude. Willie May and Jonah stood with Carson, Eunice, and Michael, and Jeremy's two brothers and father had brought along the Negro nanny who'd cared for all Warwick sons as infants.

A cub reporter from the *Charleston Courier*, pen and notepad in hand, moved amidst the din and activity and, by the light of the moon and stars and campfires, attempted to put on paper his thoughts and impressions of the scene he described as "a sight to behold and a memory to hold." His first pages recorded the awesome cost of pulling up stakes for the uncertain promise and dubious success of driving the same stakes into soil in hostile territory thousands of miles away.

"Six to eight hundred dollars to assemble a basic outfit of wagon and oxen, goods and equipment—a fortune," he informed the reader. He went on to apprise his reading audience that the Willow Grove wagon train would consist of approximately two hundred people, counting the slaves, and an undetermined number of conveyances because the tally changed weekly. They were of all sorts, sizes, and value, ranging from expensive Conestogas and prairie schooners (a lesser version of the desert camel) to market wagons, buggies, carriages, traps, carts, and pack mules. Many would walk, sleeping under wagons or under the stars, and take their food from the land. It was estimated the train could make ten to fifteen miles a day.

Managing this conglomerate group, the reporter wrote, were the wagon masters he described as sitting their horses like princes commanding minions whose trust in them was as clear as the day breaking over the remarkable sight. "Silas Toliver and Jeremy Warwick wield the whip of leadership like men born to authority with the knowledge and skill, if not the experience, to enforce it," his notes read. "Upon their shoulders rests the responsibility to get the travelers where they are going as safely as possible." He quoted Jeremy as declaring, "We have studied every map and chart of the terrain, perused every article and guidebook, read every letter shared with us from correspondents in Texas, and interviewed dozens of people who have been there. We are as informed as we can be to guide the train successfully to our destination. The rest is up to God."

Silas declined to be interviewed, but the reporter followed on his heels and furiously jotted down the wagon master's orders, calmly but firmly delivered. The leader would give his group two hours to settle down their families and animals, attend to last-minute details, say their good-byes, and take their designated place in line. Those who were late in doing so would be left behind. He would tolerate no dawdlers or laggards. A personal item of interest crept into the reporter's notes when the wagon leader went to collect his son to place in the care of the driver of his Conestoga, one of Queenscrown's most trusted slaves. The reporter quoted Joshua as saying, "Please, Papa. Can't I ride with Jessica and Tippy?"

Silas Toliver obliged the tearful plea and, carrying his son, strode to Jessica Wyndham's—Mrs. Silas Toliver's!—matching Conestoga, where she sat, dressed like a peacock among sparrows, on the wagon seat with her strange-looking pixie of a maid and a young colored boy named Jasper. The wagon master repeated his son's request to his wife, who said happily, "Of course," and, almost too slight for the boy's weight, took him into her arms. "Don't worry, Silas, we'll look after him," she said, and smiled into Joshua Toliver's droopy eyes. "It's nap time for you, young man," she said further, and without another word to her husband, spirited the boy away under the spanking white canvas.

The reporter noted that Silas Toliver's stern features relaxed a little as he walked away, and the writer for the *Courier* admitted to himself he would have given a month's salary to know the thoughts of a man who had yet to consummate his marriage to his wife, so gossip had it, but tittle-tattle had no place in serious journalistic reporting. Instead, the young man fixed his courage on getting Carson Wyndham to answer from a father's perspective the question of how he felt about his daughter going to Texas.

"How do you think I feel?" the formidable cotton baron and business tycoon snapped, and, with a glare, stalked off with his wife and son before the reporter could position his pen to record his reply.

At the fixed moment for departure, a bugle sounded. The wagon masters were already in position at the head of the two motley lines of conveyances, farm animals, slaves, and those who would walk in the dust of churning wheels. As the last notes struck the cold morning air, both Silas Toliver and Jeremy Warwick raised a leather-jacketed arm and signaled forward. The wagon train was off.

The cub reporter, along with those remaining behind, watched the cavalcade pull away to the cacophony of creaking wheels, suspended pots and pans banging from the sides of wagons, babies crying, dogs barking, and livestock mooing, bawling, clucking, and bleating—"the sound of the westward movement," he would ascribe to the spectacle in his article. The young man wished them well. In a week he would report on the fall of the Alamo in Texas and then later the revenge of the Texians at San Jacinto where, under the leadership of Sam Houston, they would defeat Santa Anna and his army and pronounce the territory independent from Mexico. The Willow Grove wagon train was headed toward the newly declared Republic of Texas.

PART TWO

1836—1859

Chapter Twenty-Seven

From the first night the wagon train formed a circle for shelter and a corral for the animals, Jessica learned that nothing was expected of her. The other women were hardly out of their wagons before they set about preparations to get their families fed and bedded down for the night. Jessica watched the organized industry in awed dismay, feeling helpless and totally useless as mothers sent their smaller children off to gather firewood and fetch water, the older ones to dig a fire pit while the men unhitched, hobbled, and fed the animals. Dutch ovens and roasting spits, frying pans and eating utensils appeared, and in no time at all, pots were simmering and coffee brewing. A slave couple named Jeremiah and Maddie whom Silas had brought along in lieu of Lazarus and Cassandra were assigned to take care of camp duties for the Toliver family.

Watching the activities wrapped in her fashionable blue cloak of merino wool, Jessica said to Silas, who had drawn to her side for the first time that day, "I feel rather…pointless."

"No need to. You were such a help with Joshua today. You kept him occupied."

"Keeping him engaged is a pleasure. What are my duties?"

"None, except to stay well."

"Ah, yes, we can't have me dying on you before you build your plantation."

Silas looked ready to explain that she'd once again misinterpreted his meaning but thought better of the effort and said, "Tell Tippy that in the future she's to set up your washstand in the light of the campfire. The shadows are private but dangerous—a good place for a silent abduction with no one the wiser until you've been discovered missing."

"Me? Why—why would anybody want to abduct me?"

"Perhaps your imagination can assist you in taking my word for it, Miss Wyndham."

Jeremy had drawn up to their campfire. "Ransom, Jess," he explained quietly, addressing her by the shortened, friendly version of her name he'd elected to call her, "or a Creek warrior desiring a white squaw."

"Or worse," Silas added, an eyebrow arched meaningfully.

"You—you're trying to frighten me."

"No, Miss Wyndham," Silas said. "We're trying to protect you. Stay in the light of the fire."

Jessica did not dare dispute the order and washed in the Conestoga, keeping ears and eyes open for strange sounds and shadows outside the wagon. With Tippy sleeping on a pallet beside her, she hardly closed her eyes for two weeks because of watching for a skulking figure or the feathered headdress of an Indian warrior outlined against the canvas.

From the outset, Jessica realized the privileged daughter of Carson Wyndham was not to be invited into the close-knit community of the wagon train. Besides her dubious standing as Silas Toliver's wife, she treated her black driver and maid as equals, confirming gossip of her anti-slavery leanings that had leaked to the cavalcade before it pulled out. Members of slave-owning families, especially the men, gave her wary looks and, Jessica was certain, discouraged their wives from mingling with her, "quite as if they expect me to unlock their slaves' shackles and set them free," she told Tippy. The others did not seek to befriend her simply because of the great distance between her status and theirs, and Jessica was at a loss how to bridge the barrier of their social differences.

She would have liked to discuss the matter with Silas, for she was willing to enter into the activities of the community, do her share, but she rarely saw him except in the evenings when they gathered for supper around their campfire, and then not for long. His council and attention were in constant demand. When he could take time to enjoy a meal, Joshua was the main focus of conversation between them. Jessica had reluctantly granted Tippy's request that she and Jasper eat later with Jeremiah and Maddie—"It looks better that way, Miss Jessie"—but often Jeremy and Tomahawk joined their group, and her hope to have Silas's attention was disappointed. Jessica came to resent the intrusion on her only opportunity to speak to her husband.

To occupy her time, she would keep a journal—a type of logbook—of their migration, Jessica decided. One day she might write a book of her experiences for posterity.

"What will you name it?" Tippy asked.

"I don't know yet. I expect inspiration will come."

Writing the journal was the ideal solution to fill the empty hours of bouncing along on the seat of the Conestoga behind Silas's wagon while Tippy was busy under the canvas sewing a buckskin jacket like Silas's to present Joshua on his fifth birthday in May. Tippy had made the request for the skin from Jeremy, who had procured it from only the wind knew where, and the secrecy with which the four of them—Jeremy, Jasper, Jessica, and Tippy—kept the garment concealed from the little boy and his father lent a little air of mystery and excitement to the long days.

Silas did not drive his Conestoga, since he was at the head of the wagon train with Jeremy. He had put a longtime slave of

Queenscrown in charge of it, and when the wagon's back flap was open, Jessica could see the woody branches of roses the driver was to mind carefully. Jeremy had also brought along burlap-wrapped root balls of roses from his garden. Tippy had told him and Silas to have them mounded with used coffee grounds to keep them strong. Since wagon space was so valuable, Jessica had been surprised that the men had allotted some of theirs to roses.

"What is their importance?" she had asked Jeremy.

"They are symbols of our family lines that began in England," he told her, and explained their significance. "Silas brought his Lancasters along in honor of his heritage."

"And you? Why did you bring along your White Rose of York?"

"In memory of my mother."

Against her husband's better judgment, thin, spindly Jasper drove Jessica's spirited four-horse team, a present from her father. Silas would have preferred the gift had been oxen. They were slower, but more manageable and made better farm animals.

"The first bobble, Jasper, and you're out of that seat and on foot, understand? I'll have somebody else take over the reins."

"Yes suh, Mister Silas."

"Did you hear that?" Tippy said to Jessica. "Your husband is concerned for his wife's safety."

"My husband is concerned for the safety of his bankroll."

There was much to record, and Jessica was discovering she had a flair for narrative beyond reporting mundane particulars like road conditions, weather, and features of the terrain, usually the sole details found in travel journals and logs. She included such information only if it affected life on the trail, which it often did, sprinkling her accounts with personal reflections and impressions of people and places and items of interest so that within days she realized her journal was taking on the tone of a diary.

I sometimes recall myself in my other life and can hardly remember who that girl was. I remember she rose from a down-
filled bed no earlier than nine o'clock, washed her face in a room
warmed by a good fire prepared by a servant, combed her hair,
and joined her family for breakfast served from a heaping sideboard. There were always ham and gravy, bacon and eggs, grits,
and biscuits kept hot under their sterling lids and served on fine
china, and jellies and jams and sugar cane syrup and coffee and
cream. Afterwards, that girl took herself off to be bathed and
dressed and coiffed at the hands of her maid and best friend, her
only dilemma that of choosing what to do with her day.

The girl I am now rises from a hard pallet while still dark on
days so cold she can hardly keep her teeth together. She sleeps
in the clothes she wore the day before, and bathing is out of the
question because the water is icy. There are mornings the attempt
to comb her hair is not worth the time or energy since it will be
hidden under a bonnet needed for warmth and not removed until time for bed. Breakfast is hot mush sweetened with sugar cane
syrup, of which our supply will soon be depleted, and eaten out of
borrowed tin bowls that replaced the china we had to leave by the
side of the road.

Still, I do not miss that other girl too much, despite the rigors of
the trail. I never had reason to be vain anyway, so to do without a
fresh change of clothes each day or my hair dressed mean little to
me, though I do long for a hot bath with scented soap—any bath!
A creek would do, but I've been told—*ordered* by my husband—
never to venture beyond the compound at night, the only time
for privacy. It is too cold now even to consider sneaking out of
my wagon for a dip in whatever watering place we camp by, but
spring is coming. There are days you can almost feel the old earth

turn over to warm its back in the sun, and clouds write poetry against the blue sky.

My husband. How strange to think of Silas Toliver that way since, of course, he will probably never be mine to claim as such. His heart belongs to Lettie, perhaps forever. He must miss her sorely. How can she not occupy his thoughts during the empty hours at the head of the wagon train? But even if it were not for Lettie, Tippy describes my countenance when Silas and I do meet "about as welcoming as a hot skillet on a bare bottom" and suggests that I smile at him occasionally.

He wouldn't notice, I say to her.

Try it, she says, and then I know that with her uncanny perception she's aware of my growing feelings for him.

APRIL 1, 1836

For the company of Silas, I would prefer my Conestoga to be at the head of the wagon train, but no, he has decreed it rumble along smack dab in the middle of the line. I could voice my dissent, but then Silas would ask my reason, and I'd be at a loss how to answer him. His basis for my wagon's place in line is simple: It is safer. The lead driver has responsibilities that Jasper has had no experience to handle. The lead driver must navigate problems in the terrain, set an even pace, and be ever alert to the wagon leader's signals to stop, slow down, speed up, or change course. It is not uncommon to come across a snake or animal in the path that can startle the teams, and without a cool head handling the reins, a runaway wagon or possible stampede are sure to result. Also, the lead driver is the first target of an Indian arrow.

Jeremy's Conestoga at the head of the Warwick line is driven by a slave named Billy who is one of the most famous teamsters in South Carolina.

Do I dare write of my feelings in my journal? What if Silas should read it? Then he would know that I resent hardly having a glimpse of him until nightfall unless he reins back to check on Joshua sharing my wagon seat on those days he does not permit him to ride beside Billy.

When Silas does appear, I still can't keep my chagrin from showing. Mercy, if it were not for his son, I do believe my husband would never show his face to ask after his wife. What is *happening* to me? Every time I see Silas so confident and authoritative in the saddle, so calm and judicious in meeting the concerns of others that flare up daily, I feel this dreadful gush of warmth and pride that angers and bewilders me. How can I be victim to such wifely emotions when I share no bond with the man who causes them?

I wish I had a confidante who possessed the knowledge and experience to help me understand these untoward sensations that leave me weak and feeling helpless. Sometimes I am so filled with them I believe I will explode like an over packed pig's bladder.

Tippy told me I am in love and all my woman's juices are flowing. The stars told her so.

Ask them what I'm to do about it, I told her.

Be nice to Mister Silas and see what happens was her reply.

I told her that I had said terrible things to him at Willowshire, and he's bound to remember.

Tippy replied that men take no mind to what women say, not when *their* juices are flowing.

I lamented that my appearance was not liable to make him forget or to start his juices flowing.

You might be surprised, she said, and grinned.

Indeed I would be.

Chapter Twenty-Eight

By the time they reached Georgia, Jessica had exchanged her corset for one petticoat and her fashionable day gowns with their down-filled sleeves and full conical skirts for simpler cotton dresses. She had now joined the sparrows if not their nest. The importance of preserving the "empire silhouette," so flattering to her figure, her only asset, seemed ridiculous when attempting to walk beside a mud-slinging wagon in pouring rain to lighten the load or to maintain a seat while driving on a washboard road or navigating forests, rivers, and swamps. The large brim of a calico bonnet she'd purchased from a general store in a small town before leaving South Carolina sheltered her freckled face, and Silas had surprised her with a sturdy pair of women's work boots he'd seen in a store window. "I hope they are not too big, he'd said. "You have such dainty feet."

Jessica had been overcome by the compliment. The boots were the ugliest looking footgear she'd ever seen, and indeed too big, but thick stockings would fill them up, and they were so much more practical and comfortable than her lightweight kid leather slippers.

"Thank you," she'd said shyly.

He seemed pleased that he had pleased her. "You're welcome."

"Of course I will pay you for them," she said.

His face showed an instant's disappointment, then hardened. "They were meant as a gift from my own pocket, but if you prefer, you may consider them purchased by your father, who has already paid for them." His tone had been clipped, and he'd stalked away before he could see her bite her lip in self-reproach.

Why, Jessica had wondered, did she persist in slamming doors in the man's face he seemed to want to open to her? Was she afraid he might see the truth of her feelings for him, whatever that truth was? The day would come when he would no longer bother, and she could not blame him. Indeed, as she noted in her diary a week later, the exchange marked his last attempt to win her friendship, but by then, his days were too busy and fraught with anxiety to try. Their last encounter had happened on the eve of the dreadful news that reached them the next day.

APRIL 7, 1836

Oh me, oh my, it is rumored that the Creek Nation may go to war against the whites for the fraudulent theft of their land, and we've been told we must be on constant alert for attack as we pass through Georgia and Alabama. What did the greedy whites expect when they swarmed onto Creek hunting fields and farms, forcing them out of their own homes and stealing their land rights? Appeal to our government to stop the thievery has been futile. The United States government has broken every treaty it signed with the Creek Nation that guaranteed them protection from encroachment on their territory, and now the Indians have had enough.

I am concerned over the mumblings (mainly from the slave owners, of course) that have risen against Tomahawk Lacy, Jeremy's faithful Creek scout, who has been charged to reconnoiter the trail for danger and safer routes. Tomahawk's out-rider skills have been invaluable to the success of the train so far, and now the ingrates question if his reports can be trusted when he returns from a scouting mission. They fear he is torn between his loyalty to Jeremy and his allegiance to his own people. I like Tomahawk so much. He closes his eyes when he talks to you, as if concentrating on every word for its perfect accuracy. It should be an annoying feature of his expression, but it is not. Somehow his habit makes you believe everything he says.

The grumblers did not address their concerns directly to Silas and Jeremy. They muttered them within my hearing distance with the intention that I relay them to Silas, which I did, and he in turn would inform Jeremy. I have observed that the men in the train, including the hotheads, give Silas and Jeremy a wide berth. My husband and Jeremy have proved themselves extraordinary wagon masters, and they have made it clear that those not satisfied with their leadership are welcome to pull out and seek their own way to Texas.

So far none has.

The almost certain possibility of an Indian attack necessitated halting the wagon train for a day so that everyone—men, women, and children—could learn and practice defense and protection procedures. The wagon leaders and Tomahawk addressed the large congregation with information on what to expect if attacked and gave instructions and demonstrations on techniques to stay alive and preserve their property and livestock. For practice sessions, the members of the wagon train were to be divided in groups of eight with each member of the family assigned specific duties to assist others in their section.

"United we stand. Divided we fall," Jeremy quoted. "In an Indian attack, it's not every man for himself. It's every man watching out for the back of his neighbor."

Led by the most seasoned among them, the audience was then dispersed to rehearse what it had learned. Tippy, Jasper, Joshua, Jeremiah, and Maddie were sent to be with Tomahawk's party. Jessica, standing beside her wagon, waited to be assigned to hers. She had begun to get impatient when Silas finally broke away from his supervisory duties. Her heart leaped when she saw the tall, slim figure stride toward her, a reaction she concealed by setting her face in stone.

"I was beginning to think I'd been forgotten, Mr. Toliver," she said, her tone crisp. "To what group am I to be dispatched?"

"Mine, Miss Wyndham." Silas held out a long-barreled gun. "Do you know how to shoot this?"

She gazed at it, nonplussed. "I...can shoot a pistol. I was taught before I left South Carolina."

"But how about a flintlock rifle?"

"I've never held one in my hands."

"Then get down on the ground and lie on your stomach, right here by your wagon's wheel."

"For what purpose?"

"I'm going to teach you how to shoot it."

"Oh. I thought my task would be to keep the guns loaded."

"That, too, Miss Wyndham, but every woman needs to know how to aim, load, and fire a weapon in an Indian attack. Keep your pistol beside you, but it is useless unless your adversary is within close range. We won't waste ammunition today, but you can practice aiming and firing, and I'll show you how to load the gun. Now, please. Get down on the ground."

Jessica obeyed and lost her breath when Silas lay beside her and reached across her to adjust the gun to her shoulder. She willed herself to ignore the press of his body and the closeness of his head as he patiently and softly warned her of the gun's report and fed instructions into her ear.

"Steady the gun in a spoke and aim for the belly of the horse. When the horse goes down, the Indian will, too. You may not have time to reload. When the Indian comes within closer range, that's when you use your pistol."

Jessica listened, appalled. Shoot a human being, an innocent horse?

"That's it. Good. Now try again," Silas said, close beside her, when she aimed and fired at a pretend target.

When finally he was satisfied, Silas showed her how to insert a paper cartridge filled with gunpowder and a lead ball into the gun barrel. They sat knee to knee, their close heads bent over the gun. Jessica was acutely aware of his nearness and hoped that, in his man's way, he did not sense her "juices" flowing.

"All right," he said, too soon, and clambered to his feet. "That's enough for today." He reached down to give her a hand up, and she noticed his gaze sweep over her hair, flaring unfettered over her shoulders. She was without her bonnet since the day was warm and overcast.

"I suggest, in case we're attacked, that you cover your hair completely," he said. "Red-haired white women are prized among Indian warriors and chiefs—not that they're treated as such."

Horrified, Jessica clasped her head. "Do you think I…should have it cut?" she asked sorrowfully.

He seemed as regretful. "What a pity that would be. No, let's see how events unfold before taking such a drastic measure. I'm leaving the gun with you. Practice your aim and assembling cartridges, but keep the gun barrel empty. We'll need every bit of ammunition should worse come to worst. Let's hope it doesn't."

"Yes, let us so hope," Jessica said. "Thank you for your instruction, Mr. Toliver. I realize it is to your advantage that I stay safe, but I...appreciate the lesson for my own sake."

"Instruction in keeping safe is to the advantage of all of us, Miss Wyndham," Silas said and strode off, his parting shot the last he had to say to her of any substance in the long, anxious weeks following. She sensed his watchful eye upon her as they passed through Georgia and Alabama into Louisiana without mishap from the Creeks, who had indeed declared war against the whites, but he kept his distance, and Jessica could only guess at his relief when he dumped her in New Orleans in two weeks' time.

Chapter Twenty-Nine

Silas set aside his account book. He'd hardly had a moment to tally the receipts of the trip since it began. He liked to do his figuring in the privacy of his Conestoga when all was quiet for the night, but he'd no sooner settle down to his ledger than someone requiring his services would knock at the canvas curtain of his wagon. He poured a small measure of brandy into a glass and sat back to savor it with a sense of satisfaction. So far the costs of the trip had fallen below his budget and without the sacrifice of needed supplies and materials. They were out of Creek territory, but he did not regret the expense of extra ammunition and hobbles to keep animals restrained and safe from theft in case of an Indian attack. There would be plenty of opportunities to be glad of their purchase later on in Texas. The savings in his account, composed of the money for the burned Conestogas, had been due to careful spending. Carson Wyndham did not need to know of the surplus or of any other monies saved from future deposits. If Silas had to adjust his receipts to correspond with the expenditures his father-in-law's payments were meant to cover, he would. Silas did not regard the adjustment as deceit. His thrift would benefit Carson because his son-in-law intended to pay back every cent the man had agreed to pay him to take his daughter off his hands.

Silas did not know how he would do it, but he would start by selling his Conestoga in New Orleans and share Jeremy's into Texas, and already he had mentally devised ways he could saw a little off his expenses here, a little there, and store away the savings while using Carson's funds to get Somerset started. The manor house could wait until he could pay for its construction from his own pocket, but he would not sacrifice his land and its development for the sake of Jessica, his pride, or any other cause, such as his mother's warning he'd never completely shaken off. *If you go through with this marriage for the reason you've contracted it, there will be a curse on your land in Texas.*

Poppycock. There was no such thing as a curse, but if there were, he could lift it by setting Jessica free. He would set aside part of his cotton profits to add to his growing bundle, even purchase fewer slaves and land than he intended until the day (he hoped in five years) he wrote a banknote to his loathsome "benefactor" to cover all Silas had sold his soul for—including his daughter. Jessica would have her freedom. She would still be young. She could move up North and live with her aunt, indulge her abolitionist leanings to her heart's content, and her father would have nothing to say about it. It was the least Silas could do for her.

Of course all his plans depended on his arriving in Texas safely and getting started.

Once set free, Jessica might even consider marrying Jeremy. It was clear he admired her greatly. "Never a whimper, whine, or a complaint have I heard from her, Silas," he'd said recently.

"You would be more likely to hear it than I, Jeremy," Silas had commented.

"Only because you do not avail yourself of the opportunity to be around her. Jessica has eyes only for you, Silas. If you'd but set yours on her now and then, you'd see for yourself."

"I would, but I fear she'd spit in them," Silas had retorted wryly. Eyes for him? Jeremy was losing his keen acumen for reading others if he thought that cold little abolitionist felt anything but loathing for him.

"She's writing a diary, you know," Jeremy said. "Women confess all to their diaries. Why don't you take a peek in it and enlighten yourself?"

"Because I'm afraid of what I would read."

"Read the journal, Silas."

But for all Jessica's cool indifference, Silas came to admire her. His wife wanted to pull her weight in the wagon train and found ways to do so. At night she entertained the children by reading to them from his son's store of books. At first, only Joshua cuddled up next to her by the fire, then gradually other children joined their circle. Naturally, Jessica *would* give him a heart-stopping moment when she waved the slaves' children to gather around as well. There were, of course, grumblings.

"You need to tell your wife the readings are for the white children only," one woman, a planter's wife, snapped to Silas.

"I have a better idea. Why don't *you* tell her."

None dared to approach the young, self-possessed, imperious figure in the glow of the campfire, and the mixed gatherings continued.

The sight of Jessica writing in her journal, or diary, on her wagon seat led to hat-in-hand requests from the unlearned to compose letters for them to mail back home, and there were days and sometimes nights when Silas would see her, a humble petitioner by her side, bent over her writing tablet to commit the dictated words to paper. To comfort a sick child, she shared the hard candy and popping corn, nuts, and dried fruits her mother had insisted go with her, and once Silas had overheard Jessica say to Tippy, "Don't let's eat the sweets in this bag. Let's save them for the children."

Spring arrived when the train entered Creek territory, and, to relieve the tension around the campfire, Jessica had Tippy show the young girls how to weave amazing coronets of flowers from the purple wisteria and redbud trees and white dogwood that abounded in the woods. Also, selflessly, showing not the least reluctance, his wife offered the soft material of her fine dresses for bandages when injuries befell members of the wagon train. The inevitable day came when Silas told her she would have to leave one of her wardrobe trunks by the side of the road.

"It doesn't matter," she said. "It is mostly empty."

His wife seemed to meet every danger, deprivation, and discomfort with courage and resolve, reminding Silas of Lettie, but it was her way with his son that earned his greatest appreciation. Joshua thought of her as his special playmate, and Silas could not help noticing the possessive pride with which he paraded around the campground, his hand in hers, as if to tell the other children they all counted, but none as much as he. Jessica eased his homesickness and yearnings for Lettie, soothed his fears, and diverted him from danger, but never with the authority of a stepmother. Her approach was that of a friend. When Silas warned her against imposing her anti-slavery views on his son, she'd said, "I can promise no words from me on the subject, Mr. Toliver, but I can't speak for my example."

So while Silas watched the friendship grow between his son and stepmother, the distance widened between him and Jessica, and by the end of two months, he came to realize that the remarkable young woman who was his wife only by virtue of a signature on a marriage certificate wanted no truck with him. Gradually he formed his plan to pay back Carson Wyndham in full and set her free. He had signed a contract with the man and meant to honor it, though not the terms. If he returned to Carson all he owed him, Jessica would not be bound to stay married to him.

She would be free to seek her own life, lived the way she wanted, beyond the reach of her father.

He desired a smoke before turning in for the night. Now that they were out of hostile territory, he slept in his wagon with Joshua close to his side. Careful not to disturb the sleeping boy, he had dropped softly to the ground to light a cheroot from the campfire when his eye caught a ghostly figure floating in the direction of the creek. It was a woman dressed in a flowing gown with something white flung over her shoulder, and Silas recognized the fall of red hair down her back. *Jessica!* By God, she'd been told to stay within the fire-lit circle of the encampment at night. Damn the stubborn little minx! Didn't she know there were animal predators about, snakes, poison ivy? There were men on watch stationed around the perimeter, but Silas pocketed the cheroot, hurriedly retrieved his pistol, and went after her.

She'd had a good head start but walked carefully, her candle lighting her path but hardly necessary in the full glow of the moon. Where was she going and why? She was headed toward the creek and seemed to know the way. Silas had seen her looking over the area when the train had stopped in the afternoon. He watched the wraith disappear into a grove of trees and hastened his steps, reluctant to call out to her for fear of drawing the attention of a lookout who might shoot first and investigate later. He came upon her at the edge of the creek and halted when he realized her intention. Her back was to him and before he could alert her to his presence, her gown—a robe—slipped from her shoulders and dropped to her ankles. Naked, she picked it up and laid it on a rock along with the towel she'd brought and blew out the candle. Then, with hardly a splash, she slipped into the water.

Silas, stunned by her body's beauty in the silvery light of the moon and terrified of the dangers lurking in the creek, swung around at a sound behind him. One of the men standing watch had come to investigate.

"Oh, it's you, Mr. Toliver. Anything wrong? I thought I heard something."

"It was only me, Johnson. I couldn't sleep. Thought I'd get the saddle kinks out. You can go back to your post."

"Beautiful night."

"Yes, it is."

"Well, have a good stroll."

"Good night, Johnson."

The exchange must have carried to Jessica. Silas found only her red hair fanned out on the surface of the water when he reached the creek bank.

"Jessica!" he hissed. He did not dare raise his voice for fear of drawing further attention from the guard. *"Come out of there before you get bitten by a snake!"*

Jessica's wet head popped up. "Go away," she said, sputtering water, her silvery arms working to keep her afloat below the quiet current. "I'm…I'm naked."

"I don't give a rat's piss whether you're naked or not," he whispered hoarsely. *Get out of there!"* Consumed with fury at the foolhardiness of the girl, he grabbed her robe and the towel and held them behind him. "I'm turning around, and I'll give you five seconds to come out of there before I come in and get you. Understand?"

She did not answer, but there was an immediate splash of water and seconds later the items were snatched from his hand. He could hear her disgruntled shortness of breath as she quickly robed herself.

"I just wanted a bath, for goodness' sake," Jessica said. "It's been so long since I had a proper one and today was so warm and sticky. Is it supposed to be this hot in Louisiana in May?"

Silas turned around. Her hair hung long and streaming, and the robe clung to her wet body, outlining her full breasts and tapered waist. He felt an involuntary pang of desire. "Do you have any idea of the poisonous critters in that creek—along the bank, in these woods? Don't you ever, *ever* go against my orders for your safety again, do you hear me?"

Jessica toweled her hair. "Forgive me for not considering your investment, Mr. Toliver, but for my own sake, I can see it was foolish to take such a risk for a bath. The creek looked calm and crystal clear this afternoon and too inviting to resist, but you have my word that I will not be so foolish again."

"Is that what you think—that I was considering my *investment*?" He took a step toward her. Her eyes grew wide, and her mouth formed a small, startled O. She looked like a nubile water nymph caught out of her habitat by a ferocious land monster. She moved back.

"Well, weren't you, Mr. Toliver?"

He wanted to shake her. He wanted to kiss her. He opened his mouth to explain, then snapped it shut. "Whatever it pleases you to think, Miss Wyndham," he said. "Now get back to the camp before we both get shot."

Chapter Thirty

A rat's piss. That's how he described how little he cared that I was naked. Was I already in the water when he appeared? I can't express what I felt when I looked up to see Silas looming by the creek bank, so handsome in the moonlight, his face locked in a vise of fury. I felt that...way again, and for a ridiculous second I hoped he *would* come into the creek after me. How can I be cursed with such carnal urges for a man who could never feel them for me? Not only am I a sparrow compared to the beautifully plumaged woman he's still in love with, but if my aloof, unfriendly attitude were red meat, it would not attract a green fly.

And how could a man ever have the least desire for a woman who declared she'd rather copulate with a mule than with him?

Slave holders still repulse me, but neither Silas or Jeremy are typical of their breed. If the white man must enslave the Negro, then pray God it be done by compassionate men such as they. They see to their slaves' needs and comforts and are the only owners in the wagon train who provide tents at night for their property. I have recognized several black families from my father's horde he sent along as part of his agreement with Silas.

These, because Silas does not know them, he shackles after dark, but the slaves from Queenscrown he does not, and he allows the Negro children with blisters to ride in his wagon during the day. That says much about the man I've married, which is cause enough to excuse somewhat my change of heart toward him.

We made our trek back to camp in silence. He walked behind me, as if determined to see that I did not deviate from the path by so much as a wayward glance. He saw me to my wagon where he said stiffly, "Good night, Miss Wyndham. Try to stay out of trouble until the morning, if that's possible."

I replied, "It is entirely possible, Mr. Toliver, I assure you."

Tippy, with an I-told-you-so sigh at my behavior (She'd tried to talk me out of my plan to bathe in the creek), went back to sleep, but I stayed wide awake, watching Silas adjust Joshua's mosquito netting through a tiny opening in the flap, then leave his wagon to smoke a cheroot by the fire and drink a glass of brandy. I longed to join him, to ask him what he meant by his response, so filled with incredulity, to my sarcastic request that he forgive me for not considering his investment.

"Is that what you think—that I was considering my *investment*?" he almost shouted. He made it sound absurd of me to think "his investment" was all he had in mind when he came after me, but why else would he be concerned for my welfare? I can still feel the small warmth from the tiny flame that flared in my heart, but naturally, my haughty question: "Well, weren't you?" squelched his desire to explain. "Whatever it pleases you to think, Miss Wyndham," he'd replied.

Well, Mr. Toliver, I have an answer for that. It pleases me to think that you do not consider me so plain that you can find nothing about me desirable. It pleases me to think that you can see through my off-setting attitude as merely a shield to conceal my real, and growing feelings, for you. I am quite sure you would reject me kindly should you discover the truth, but to save my dignity, I'm of no mind to give you the opportunity. Would that you had some of Jeremy's ability to read people's true motives and feelings, but you are obviously as dense as a block of wood.

So there! I believe I've aptly expressed what it pleases me to think, Mr. Toliver. In a week's time when you deposit me in New Orleans, no doubt it will please you to think you do not have to think of me for a long time.

Chapter Thirty-One

The wagon train was five miles from New Orleans when a screeching hawk appeared out of nowhere and dived at the head of the lead horse in Jessica's team. The Conestoga lurched sharply out of line, beyond the capability of Jasper to restrain the four animals, and pitched Jessica overboard. Even at the head of the wagon train, Silas heard Joshua's piercing scream. *"Jessica!"* Turning his horse around, Silas raced to her wagon, in which Joshua was riding, to see Jessica lying motionless on the ground. Silas grabbed the reins of the lead horse and got the team calmed, then jumped from his gelding to run to Jessica. Tippy stuck her head out the back of the wagon, and Jasper and Joshua scampered down from the wagon seat, both starting to cry.

"I'se so sorry, I'se so sorry, Mister Silas," Jasper moaned.

"Stay with the horses," Silas ordered, "and keep Joshua with you."

"Papa, Papa, make Jessica better," Joshua sobbed.

"I will, son," Silas said. "Go with Jasper now."

Jessica lay lifeless on her side, eyes closed, bonnet askew, her calico dress gathered up beyond her knees. Silas turned her onto her back and found blood seeping from a deep gash on her forehead caused by having struck a large, sharp rock. A chill fell over him as if he'd passed through a cold patch of shade. She was breathing, but the wound would require stitching or cauterization to prevent infection, possibly gangrene. Tippy ran to join him.

"We'll need towels, Tippy."

"Right away, Mister Silas."

Sick to his heart, Silas untied Jessica's bonnet to press it to the wound and yanked down the skirt of her dress. Dear God. What was this girl doing here in a wagon train wearing faded calico and muddy boots? What had her father been thinking to subject her to this? What had *he* been thinking to agree to it? Jessica opened her eyes.

"Don't move," he said softly.

"What happened?"

"You were thrown off your wagon seat."

Tippy dropped beside him with a handful of towels, her huge eyes drowning in dismay. "Oh, Jessica," she groaned.

"I'm all right, Tippy."

"Let's make sure," Silas said. He could hear Joshua crying as he hung out the back of the wagon. "Tippy, I'll take care of Miss Jessica. Go be with my son."

"Oh, please let me stay with her, Mister Silas."

Jessica reached for her hand and squeezed it. "Do as he says, Tippy. Joshua needs you."

Silas applied pressure with a towel to stop the bleeding while he explored her shoulders and arms for fractured bones. He pressed her knees and ankles. "Do you feel that anything is broken?"

"No. I just feel nauseated, and my head hurts."

"You've had the wind knocked out of you, and you have a deep cut on your forehead. Try moving your arms and legs."

Obediently, Jessica pulled up one leg, then the other. She wiggled her arms. "See? I'm all right," she said drowsily.

But Silas had doubts.

Jeremy had ridden up with bandages and ointment, and the

driver of the wagon behind Jessica's had drawn a bucket of water from the rain barrel hooked to the Conestoga.

Silas could hear Tippy soothing Joshua as he and Jeremy tended Jessica's wound. She lay pale and listless, and they debated what to do. Once the blood was cleaned away, the cut did not seem as serious as feared. No bone was exposed, but the gash needed immediate attention to prevent infection. Should Jessica be taken in the wagon to a doctor in New Orleans or should a doctor be sent for? They agreed a jolting wagon ride would not be good for her, and much time would be lost trying to locate a doctor in the unfamiliar city.

"I say let's have Tomahawk take a look at her," Jeremy said. "His people have been treating wounds like this for hundreds of years."

The Creek was already hovering in the background, his usually impassive face drawn in concern. Jessica's consideration and courtesy had won his devotion. "Aloe leaves," he called. "They grow here."

"See what you can do," Jeremy called back, but the scout had already vanished into the woods.

The wagon train had stopped and word of Jessica's mishap had passed down the line. Her generosity and way with children had warmed some of the hearts frozen against her, and people had gotten out of their wagons to peer worriedly in the direction of the accident but knew from the many casualties experienced along the journey that it was best to stay out of the way and remain with their families and animals.

Tomahawk Lacy appeared with a plant spiked with thick, dark green leaves. Silas and Jeremy moved away to allow him to kneel by Jessica. She had been moving in and out of consciousness but came alert when he removed the bandage.

"I help you, Miss Jessica."

"Thank you, Mr. Lacy."

The scout cut several of the cacti-looking leaves that released a thin, clear sap that he applied to the wound. "The cut up and down," Tomahawk said, pumping his hand vertically to Silas and Jeremy. "Not straight across." He sliced the air horizontally. "That good. Skin can be pulled to grow back together."

Jeremy immediately began tearing a towel into strips. Tomahawk said, "Wound should be cleaned first with water that has been disturbed over fire."

"Boiled?" Silas said.

Tomahawk nodded. "If no…if no…" He struggled for an English word.

"Pus, infection," Jeremy interpreted.

The scout nodded again. "If no infection, she will get well," he said. He drew a finger across his temple. "Scar, maybe."

"I'm most grateful to you," Silas said, hoping Tomahawk's prognosis was right and there would be no need for the usual treatment against infection. The image of a red-hot iron pressed to Jessica's wound or a needle and catgut sewn through her delicate flesh made him nauseated to contemplate. Boiled water was brought, and Tomahawk cleaned the cut, reapplied fresh aloe, and bound Jessica's head tightly in a strip of towel to draw the flesh together. Silas and Jeremy conferred over the next step. It was decided that Silas, carefully supporting Jessica's head on his shoulder, would lift her up to Jeremy in the Conestoga. When it was done, Silas climbed in rapidly after his friend and together they made Jessica comfortable on her pallet.

"I'll stay with her," Silas said. "If she becomes feverish, someone will have to ride for a doctor. Tell Tippy to stay with Joshua in my wagon."

"You might get an argument from Tippy about that. She'll want to be with her mistress."

"And *I* want to be with my wife," Silas said in a tone that settled the matter.

"I'll see to them both and give the order to camp here for the night," Jeremy said. "Also, I'll bring down some laudanum. Your wife is going to have one hell of a headache."

Jessica opened her eyes as Silas was adjusting her mosquito netting. "Am I going to live?" she asked.

Silas thought he heard a facetious note in the question. He squatted down and stroked her hair back from the bandage. "Yes," he said. "That head of yours is too hard for a rock to get the better of it."

A small smile flitted across her lips. "Too bad for you," she said.

Silas gave a mock sigh. "Worse for the rock."

Jeremy returned with the laudanum in the company of a local farmer who'd come out to meet the train with fresh produce to sell. Silas should hear his news, Jeremy told him. Silas said it could wait until he'd gotten Jessica to take a spoonful of the reddish-brown, highly bitter liquid used to alleviate pain.

She moaned when he lifted her head, the spoon poised before her mouth. "What is this?"

"Something that will make you feel better. Open wide."

She made a face as she swallowed and Silas quickly handed her a ladle of water to wash down the taste. "Where is Tippy?" she asked.

"With my son."

"Why aren't you with him?"

"Because I'm here with you."

Her lids lowered sleepily. "Good," she said.

The farmer imparted news that would cause the dissenters against Tomahawk Lacy to blush with shame from that day forward whenever they thought of him. As the emigrants had passed through Georgia and Alabama, to the disgruntlements of many, the scout had taken the train away from the few existing towns and settlements in the north and guided them through dense forests and marshes and swamps along extremely arduous but safer routes near the states' southern borders. Some took every opportunity to criticize the scout's choice of routes. At one point, a settler lost his wagon on a downhill slope and blamed Tomahawk. The man would have taken a steel pike to the scout, but Jeremy stepped in, wrested away the weapon, and reminded the dissenter that his loss was due to his own laziness. He should have locked a wheel to serve as a brake or at least hauled a log behind his wagon to supply drag.

To add to their discontent, the settlers had learned before leaving South Carolina that Santa Anna was no longer a threat. He had been captured when Sam Houston's army had defeated the Mexicans at a place called San Jacinto. Therefore, for what reason must the train divert to New Orleans and cross the Sabine into Texas, many demanded to know.

Jeremy reiterated that anyone wishing to break off from the train to travel the original route was welcome to do so. Several families did. The Creeks wouldn't dare attack, they declared, and they had kinfolks at Roanoke in Georgia they had promised to visit when the train passed by. Silas learned from the farmer that in late spring, the settlement at Roanoke had been attacked and burned to the ground and most of the white families massacred. There had also been an uprising in Chambers County in Alabama, where many in the cavalcade had hoped to replenish supplies and mail letters. But for Tomahawk's wise steerage, the Willow Grove wagon train most certainly would have been a casualty of the Creek Uprising.

The other news the farmer reported was even more stunning and unsettling. Earlier in the month, a band of Comanche Indians had attacked a community in the eastern part of Texas. They had burned alive families in their homes, raped women, brutally tortured and killed the patriarch of the clan, John Parker, and kidnapped his nine-year-old granddaughter, Cynthia Ann.

"Good God," Silas said, mentally picturing a screaming Joshua carried away on a Comanche buck's swift horse with the pelt of Jessica's red hair streaming from his lance. "And the area is just where we're headed."

"All the more reason for you to leave Jess and Joshua in New Orleans," Jeremy said.

Jessica was sleeping when Silas returned to the wagon. He sat beside her, and from time to time took her pulse, placed a hand on her forehead to test for fever, and watched constantly for signs of stressful breathing. After an hour of intense concentration in an uncomfortable sitting position, he stretched out his legs and relaxed against the side of the wagon. He heard the train settle down for the night, and Maddie brought him his supper. Tippy led Joshua over, and Silas allowed them a brief sight of Jessica before sending them off to bed. Darkness fell, and Silas lit a lamp and decided to make use of a fringed cushion as a pillow for his back. It was one of a velvet pair serving as a reminder of the refinements left behind. Silas positioned it behind him and felt something hard. He withdrew the cushion and found the obstruction to be a book that had been inserted into an unsewn end, forming a pocket. Curious, Silas removed it. It was the red leather volume he'd seen Jessica writing in during the long, boring days on the trail. He held it as if he'd come across the holy grail, remembering Jeremy's words: *She's writing a diary, you know. Women confess all to their diaries. Why don't you take a peek in it and enlighten yourself?*

Silas glanced at Jessica sleeping soundly. Her breathing was regular. The flesh above her binding felt cool to his touch. He readjusted the mosquito netting, sat back against the pillow, and folded his arms, the red book glowing like a ruby within his reach. Occasionally he swatted at mosquitoes, fanned himself, and listened to the nocturnal sounds filling the silence of the night. Finally, unable to constrain his curiosity any longer and after another glance at the closed lids of his wife, he reached for the book.

Chapter Thirty-Two

Silas was dumbfounded. He was indeed as dense as a block of wood not to have seen what Jeremy had perceived all along. As usual, his all-knowing friend had read Jessica correctly, but in all fairness to himself, how could he have remotely guessed her feelings behind the façade of her stony indifference? Silas looked at the sleeping figure under the mosquito netting. Good Lord, the girl was in love with him—or thought she was. How the hell had that happened? And what were his feelings toward her? There was no denying he cared about her—at times lately, even…wanted her—but *for* her? He still cared for Lettie and, oddly, his stirrings for Jessica made him feel the loss of his former fiancée even more.

He suspected that what Jessica felt for him wasn't love at all but physical attraction. She was too young and inexperienced with men to know the difference. Silas was aware of the draw of his looks to women, an endowment of his lineage that in his early, carefree years, he'd not minded using to his advantage in pursuing a woman who'd caught his fancy. He was often disappointed. Women had to be interesting before he could be interested, and he'd found few, if any, of that stamp along the way until he met Lettie and—he must admit—Jessica Wyndham.

Silas studied her. How could Jessica ever believe she was too plain to be desirable? He must somehow relieve her of that delusion. Her body was bewitching. For days after the episode at the creek, he'd been unable to get his mind off its perfection, and when her face lit up with joy or pleasure, or her dark eyes grew round with wonder or awe, she radiated a loveliness far more enticing than the accepted ideal of beauty. He wondered how he could appreciate that distinction in Jessica when he'd been engaged to a woman who was the very definition of feminine allure.

He must also dissuade Jessica from the notion that his concern for her safety had only to do with the condition stated in the contract that her death would nullify his agreement with her father. He must convince her that, as was his duty as her *husband* and because of his fondness for her, he sincerely wished, and meant, to keep her from harm.

Thank God the accident had happened close to New Orleans. By tomorrow, if Jessica were well enough to travel, she would be ensconced at the Winthorp, where she could be properly seen after. There she would have her daily bath. The schedule called for the wagon train to camp outside the city for a week to repair equipment, arrange for water vessels, and replenish supplies before pushing on to the Sabine. There would be seven days for Silas to see her restored to health and settled in the hotel before he left her. By the time he returned, more than likely her infatuation with him would have cooled.

He inserted the book into its hidden pocket, returned the pillow to the spot from which he'd taken it, and took its companion for a cushion.

He seemed to have hardly dozed off before he was awakened at the first ray of light to edge around the canvas flap by Jessica wriggling the toe of his boot. She was smiling at him from her cot. "Good morning," she said.

Silas blinked the sleep from his eyes but caught Jessica's startled look when he sat up and removed the cushion from behind him. Her glance darted to the other one like it lying in a corner.

"Good morning," he said. Carelessly, he laid the fringed pillow within her reach. "How do you feel?"

"As if I need a drink of water and the necessary house."

He assisted her to sit up, and she took the cushion and pressed it to her midriff as if needing its warmth.

"I mean your head," he said. "How is it?"

With a faint look of relief, obviously satisfied with the feel of the pillow, Jessica laid it aside and touched her bandage. "Like it's been hit by a rock but my head got the better of it."

Silas grinned and handed her a ladle of water. So she remembered their banter.

"You've been here all night?" she asked.

"Yes, all night." In the growing light, he saw that a blue tinge had appeared from beneath the bandage along her brow bone.

She peered at him closely over the rim of the bowl. "Were you afraid I might die?"

"No. I was afraid you might live and be a thorn in my side forever. However"—he took the ladle and refilled it—"I don't mind thorns. What would roses be without them?"

Her gaze above the dipper as she drank flickered with amused surprise. "A most thought-provoking observation," she murmured, handing him back the ladle. "Thank you for...your vigilance...Silas."

"My pleasure, Jessica." On impulse, because he could not resist the child-like vulnerability in her large, brown-eyed gaze, he chucked her chin. "I'll send Tippy to help you, then we'll have to change the bandage."

Jeremy and Tippy and Joshua were already standing anxiously outside the wagon when Silas jumped down. "How's the patient?" Jeremy asked.

"She seems better," Silas said. "She needs you, Tippy. After you see to her, boil some water. Joshua, run get Tomahawk. I want him to dress the wound."

Jeremy's eyes narrowed at a sight beyond Silas's shoulder. A rider cantering up the road from the direction of New Orleans had diverted his attention. "We've got company," he said.

Silas followed his curious gaze and for a moment thought he was seeing an apparition. A slim, black-suited figure wearing a plumed hat and riding an ebony, high-stepping filly turned off the trail toward their encampment. The rider sat straight-backed but leisurely in the saddle, his bearing giving the impression that all he surveyed was his domain.

"A Frenchman, I'll wager," Silas said. "Wonder what he wants? Will you go out to meet him, Jeremy? I must relieve myself and get a cup of coffee."

When Silas returned, the man introduced himself with a deep bow and dramatic sweep of his swashbuckler's hat as Henri DuMont. A dandy, Silas thought, but the man's handshake was strong and his gaze direct. He'd ridden out to ask if he might join the wagon train. He had a yearning to go to Texas—"a staunch bunch, those Texians, and I feel I can live comfortably among them," he said.

"Pardon me," Jeremy interposed, his inspection of the Frenchman's elegant attire patently questioning his suitability to plow land, "but to do what?"

The man waved a lace-cuffed hand bearing a signet ring on his little finger. "To open an emporium as grand as my father's here in New Orleans, which I hope you will visit while you are here," he said in a tone conveying no doubt of his success in accomplishing his ambition. "How long do you gentlemen intend to camp here before moving on?"

"A week," Jeremy answered. He exchanged a look with Silas,

who responded with a subtle nod. "Will that give you time to get your gear in order?"

"More than enough time, gentlemen," Henri said, obviously delighted, and again bowed and flourished his hat. "*Merci*. You have my gratitude. May I be of assistance to you while you are here? I can recommend the best establishments for your needs."

"Right now we might need a doctor," Silas said. "My wife has suffered a head injury."

"Dr. Fonteneau," Henri suggested immediately. "He's the best in New Orleans. Shall I bring him here to you?"

"I'd be most grateful," Silas said. The signet ring was engraved with a royal crest, he noted. A French aristocrat, then. "I had planned to install my wife and son in the Winthorp Hotel in the Garden District today to remain there until I return for them from Texas," he explained, "but I'd feel better if a doctor examined her before risking further damage to her injury from a jolting wagon ride."

"It shall be done," Henri said. "I will return with Dr. Fonteneau by luncheon time, and perhaps then you gentlemen can advise me on what preparations to make for the journey to Texas."

The man was as good as his word, but by the time Henri and the doctor arrived, Tomahawk had cleansed the wound and applied a fresh film of aloe oil and pronounced the cut beginning to heal. There was no sign of infection, and only a faint throb in the area reminded her of her ordeal, Jessica said.

After Tomahawk's ministrations, Silas had helped her down from the Conestoga to test her ability to stand without feeling dizzy. In the wagon's shadow, ready to assist her if she were wobbly, he said, "If the doctor approves, it looks as if you will be well enough to travel to New Orleans today," and watched her face for a sign of how she took the news that the trials of her journey were nearly over. He was not surprised to see her mouth droop slightly before she brushed dried mud from her skirt with exaggerated care. She was still wearing the calico dress from the day before.

"I'm sure Joshua's safety is your foremost concern right now as well as mine, of course, but your son will miss his father," Jessica said, her tone stiff. "He has expressed his desire to continue with you to Texas. You must be prepared for his tears."

"And yours?" Silas could not resist asking.

Jessica glanced up in apparent surprise that he would ask such a question. "I do not cry over decisions in which I have no say, Mr. Toliver."

"So then I take it my decision to leave you in New Orleans disappoints you as well?"

His mind cautioned to let the matter drop before he opened a door too late to close, but something beyond curiosity would not let the moment and opportunity go.

His question flustered her, he could see, and for a girl with so agile a tongue, she seemed utterly at a loss how to answer. Finally, she raised her chin a notch and returned his gaze. "I have become…accustomed to the rigors of the trail, Mr. Toliver, and I fear a long interruption spent in a New Orleans hotel will undo the progress I've made in adjusting to life without a bath."

"And is that the only reason you regret not pushing on?"

Her face blossomed a traitorous pink. "I can think of no other," she said.

"I see."

She was not about to allow him a peek into her feelings for him, Silas recognized, and felt a strong urge to take her into his arms to melt her resistance to them. He pressed her arm instead. "Please be assured that I'm not leaving you in New Orleans to get rid of you, Jessica, but to ensure your well-being and safety. Your death would be a loss to me far greater than the terms of a contract."

He left her in visible shock as he went to meet Henri DuMont and Dr. Fontenau riding up the trail. He smiled to himself. Let her chew on *that* revelation for a while, he thought.

Chapter Thirty-Three

A concerned audience gathered to be on hand for the doctor's prognosis. Jeremy had shooed Tippy, Tomahawk, Jasper, the driver Billy, Joshua, and his friends and their parents a good distance behind the overturned bucket where Jessica sat to be examined. Dr. Fonteneau had directed the bandage be removed outside Jessica's hot, cramped wagon to have more room to work and to avoid the heat triggering the blood to flow again.

Only Silas, a fan in hand to cool Jessica and wave away flies and mosquitoes, and Jeremy and Henri DuMont, who already seemed to have become one of them, were privy to Dr. Fonteneau's assessment of the injury. The doctor had been told of Tomahawk's treatment and the scout's conviction that a tourniquet bandage would close the wound without more drastic measures having to be taken.

"Your Indian friend was right," Dr. Fonteneau confirmed in admiration, and declared Jessica fit to travel but suggested a delay of two more days to be on the safe side. "By then," he explained to Jessica, "the flesh will have knitted nicely if you've kept the binding tightly drawn. I know your head must feel caught in a vise, Mrs. Toliver, but it is a necessary discomfort for the broken skin to bond."

"I feel its discomfort not nearly as much as the need for a bath and change of clothes," Jessica said, glancing down at the soiled skirt of her calico dress. She felt her grubby state more keenly in the presence of the immaculate, urbane Henri DuMont, but his manners were such that not for the world would he have her aware he noticed her appearance. When they were introduced, he'd bowed over her hand with all the gallantry of a courtier meeting a bedecked lady of the royal court.

The Frenchman immediately won her heart by exclaiming when he met Tippy, "What an adorable creature you are! How do you do, my child, and tell me please who is responsible for the excellent construction of your dress?"

"I am, sir," Tippy said with a curtsy and a smile that devoured her face. "It's kind of you to notice."

"*Kind*? An *oaf* would take notice."

"Tippy is a wizard with needle and thread, not to mention her genius at clothes construction and design," Jessica had informed him, impressed that he recognized the skill in the fine tailoring of Tippy's simple muslin dress.

"*Really?*" Henri had trilled, eyeing Tippy with greater interest.

The gathering burst into applause as Jeremy related the doctor's news, and Joshua broke from the group, Tippy following, and flew to Jessica's side. Henri said to Silas, "When the time comes, you must permit me to lead you the shortest route to the Winthorp, where Madame will be relieved of at least one of her discomforts. I know the hotel well. A bathtub in every room. The proprietors have long been customers of my father's establishment and personal friends to boot. Henry and Giselle Morgan. They will see that your wife has every attention."

Joshua, his arm proprietarily around Jessica's shoulders, piped up. "Oh, Jessica isn't my father's wife. She's just our friend, aren't you, Jessica?"

Silence fell like a bomb. Silas drew in an audible breath,

Jeremy studied his feet, Tippy cast her eyes heavenward, and Henri and Dr. Fonteneau exchanged glances that hiked their eyebrows to their hairlines.

Jessica was still sitting. She relieved the awkward moment by putting an arm around Joshua and drawing him close to her side. "I most certainly am your friend, my little soldier, forever and always," she said, nuzzling his nose. "Now go gather your friends, and I will read to you."

Silas was glad of the two days' delay before he had to leave his wife and son at the Winthorp. He would return to camp afterwards and remain throughout the week, making periodic visits to the hotel to assure himself of their welfare before pulling out with the train in six days' time. A kind of darkness entered his soul. He would feel untold relief in knowing his son and Jessica were safe from the horrors that might await them. The details of John Parker's diabolical torture and the abduction of his granddaughter made the blood of every household head in the wagon train run cold. No pangs of separation would induce him to take his son and Jessica with him, but how he would miss them! His loneliness apart, he was aware of what he risked in leaving them behind. He and his son had developed a bond that months apart from each other could weaken. Joshua was growing up fast. He'd turn five in three days' time, and at that age, a boy needed his father. He was a tender child who forged bonds quickly but deeply and felt a terrible severance when he was torn from them. Joshua still missed Lettie and his uncle and grandmother and often asked, "When can we go to see them again, Papa?" Silas had not told him of his plans to leave him in New Orleans, and he cringed to imagine the child's pain when he left him, even to the care of Jessica, his "friend."

Jessica. How had that wisp of a girl managed to get under his skin? How—why—had she, an abolitionist, come to care for him and he for her—even if it were infatuation on her part and admiration on his? Was he so fickle that he could forget his anguish in forsaking Lettie for his pain in leaving another woman—a girl he barely knew—for months, maybe a year, before he saw her again? Would time and separation cure Jessica's feelings for him? Would she read her journal months down the line and wonder why she'd ever thought she was in love with him?

For a short while, he had briefly, faintly, considered buying land in Louisiana for his plantation, but the purchase would be costlier and of less acreage, and he could not set aside the view of his empire in Texas that lay constantly at the forefront of his mind. That sweeping, majestic vista was the spur that drove him on, and he must consider no sacrifice that would jeopardize its reality.

Still, for all his practical reasoning, his depression did not lift in the two days before he was to escort Jessica and Joshua in her Conestoga to New Orleans. His time was spent in huddles with Jeremy and Henri and family heads over arrangements and preparations for the journey, always with an eye on Jessica, who seemed to be recovering nicely. By night's end of the last day, having been awake for most of it, Silas rolled over and kissed the crown of Joshua's head. For their last night together, he'd permitted his son to sleep with him outside by the fire. Silas spoke to him from the silence of his heart. *It's for your own sake your father must leave you, my boy, and your friend's, too. I will be back for you and Jessica and take you home to Somerset, but first I must make sure to leave your friend a memory to remember me by.*

The day of departure, Jessica submitted to Tippy's attempts to bathe her in the wagon, barely cognizant of her maid's chatter. A pity Jessica's bandage would prevent her from wearing a bonnet since there was not much to be done with her hair until it could be thoroughly washed, Tippy prattled on. She would arrange it in her mesh hairnet and press Jessica's finest day dress for her to wear into New Orleans. First impressions were important. Also, she'd rigged up a pretty headband to cover the bandage, an idea that might start a whole new fashion trend. She'd see what Mr. DuMont—*Monsieur* DuMont—had to say about it. He did seem awfully impressed with her sewing abilities—she'd shown him the buckskin jacket she'd made as a surprise for Joshua for his birthday—and, given Henri DuMont's line of business, it was no wonder he was the sort of man who would appreciate her work.

Finally, Tippy sighed in resignation. "You're not listening to a word I say," she said, knowing on whom and what her mistress had her mind. "Now, Jessie, Mister Silas is right to leave you and Joshua in New Orleans, so you might as well accept the idea and stop moping about it."

"I know," Jessica conceded. "It's selfish of me to want to risk both your and Joshua's lives for my desires. It's just that I am afraid Silas will…forget about me while he's gone. We are making…*progress* with each other."

Yesterday, after Silas had declared her death would be a loss to him, Jessica had wondered if she'd heard him correctly. When he left her, she'd looked around breathlessly for Tippy, bursting to share his every word with her, to examine and analyze each one for tone, expression, nuance, but the sudden rush of blood to her head, pumped by the possibility—the *joyous* possibility—that Silas Toliver had come to care for her, had made her dizzy.

She was still leaning against her Conestoga when Silas brought Dr. Fonteneau around. He'd let out a little startled grunt and taken her by the shoulders to study her face in concern and demanded to know, like any caring husband, if she'd had a setback.

"No, I just…suddenly lost my breath," she'd said, staring dazedly into his alarmed green eyes.

Tippy said, "Well, you know, of course, what you have to do to keep yourself in Mister Silas's thoughts while he's gone for only God and His angels know how long."

"I haven't the faintest idea. Do you have something in mind?"

Tippy cocked her head and a meaningful spark lit her eyes.

"Oh, Tippy, I couldn't," Jessica said, reddening. "I—I wouldn't know how to go about it—what to do. I've had no experience with that sort of thing."

"Just remember how your mama goes about getting your papa to do most anything, and it'll come naturally to you."

"I'd be afraid Silas would reject me."

"I'd be more afraid at not taking the chance he wouldn't," Tippy said. "Many a triumph is lost through cowardice."

Tippy's mention of cowardice, coming from her trusted friend who knew her to swoop in where angels feared to fly, struck at Jessica's heart, but it stiffened her backbone. Tippy was right. Better to know defeat from courage than safety through chicken-heartedness.

But seduce Silas? With no skills in lovemaking, how could she manage it? Where? When? And what would Joshua have to say when he learned that his father and "friend" were really man and wife? *Many a triumph is lost through cowardice.* A fact of truth for sure, but one other fact was true as well: She, Jessica Wyndham Toliver, was no coward.

Chapter Thirty-Four

They set out for New Orleans in the afternoon, Silas driving Jessica's Conestoga. Jessica sat on the wagon seat next to him, Joshua wedged between. Henri rode along next to her side on his prancing filly; Jeremy flanked the driver's side mounted on Silas's gelding, and Tippy rocked along in the wagon. Jasper had been left behind with the other slaves under the watchful eyes of overseers charged to make sure none escaped into the jungle growth of the surrounding woods and bayous and disappeared into a city not unfriendly to blacks. The plan was for Jeremy to return the Conestoga and horse team to the campsite once Jessica's belongings were unloaded at the hotel. Silas would spend the night and rejoin the train the next day. Jessica had seen his overnight stay as an opportunity to make her move.

As she bumped along on the wagon seat, Tippy's ruined efforts to have her appear at the hotel looking fresh and enticing were giving Jessica room for doubt. She had been bathed, powdered, perfumed, and dressed at the appointed time for an early morning and cooler departure to New Orleans, but one problem after another had caused delay. To avoid mussing her appearance, Jessica had been forced to stand around beyond noon under her parasol wilting in her taffeta day dress and three stiff petticoats, feet burning in kid slippers and her hair itching under its mesh covering while everyone else bustled about at chores she'd ordinarily be sharing. The day grew steaming hot and cloyingly still. She could feel every one of her freckles standing out against her flushed skin under a shine of perspiration. The only shade available was either in the stifling wagon or beneath cypress trees bordering the open campground, and to stand under them risked an invasion of chiggers under her pantalets. Jessica had never been so uncomfortable in her life.

By the time she boarded the Conestoga, disappointment had turned to irritation. If they had left when planned, they would have already been shown to their rooms and her luggage stowed. They would have had luncheon in the dining room and, afterwards, Joshua sent off with Tippy to explore the city. Still looking her best, except for the bandage and slight tinge of discoloration around her injury, Jessica and Silas would have had a chance to be alone. She planned to invite him to her bed. Two rooms had been booked, one for her and the other for Silas and Joshua. Tippy was to occupy the maid's quarters. Jessica planned to change that arrangement. She and Silas would occupy one room while Tippy and Joshua shared the other. He would need looking after, and the little boy would think it great fun to spend the night with Tippy, who had the imagination to keep him entertained.

As it was, they would not arrive until supper time, and she and Silas would have no opportunity to be alone. It would be too late for Tippy to take Joshua out and about. Silas would have to feed and water the horses, Jeremy would stay to share a table with them in the dining room, and the men would spend the rest of the evening unloading her wagon. After a long day, Silas most likely would retire, rise early the next morning, and return to camp after breakfast.

They were not the only members of the wagon train heading

to New Orleans for a few days' diversion from the trail. To ensure as little dust as possible from the dirt road enveloping the wagon and affecting Jessica's injury, Silas had arranged for the Conestoga to lead the small cavalcade. Jessica had been more concerned about her dress and face, but by the time she took her seat, road dust would have been of little consequence. The havoc on her appearance continued. In the heat, she felt as if she were suffocating in a taffeta cocoon. The material clung to her damp body and wrinkled on contact with her hands, which were constantly fighting to keep her skirt under control. Flying insects, too small to see and bat away, buzzed annoyingly around her bandaged head. Eventually, feeling an additional tightness from the ribbon that Tippy had tied over the dressing, Jessica removed it and yearned to do the same with the hot hairnet and pelerine over her shoulders. How she wished for a calico dress and one muslin petticoat and her hair wound off her neck in its customary knot, and the devil take her hope to show up at the Winthorp looking too desirable for Silas to resist.

Joshua and Silas and Jeremy were seemingly unaware of her discomfort, but Henri apparently sensed it. He had complimented Jessica's taffeta dress profusely, praising specific details Tippy had designed and sewn, once again setting the maid's face aglow. Ambling his horse closer to Jessica on the wagon seat, Henri described the pleasures that awaited her in New Orleans: delicious food, lovely restaurants, exciting entertainments, wonderful shopping (she would love his father's emporium!), delightful people. He would introduce her to his friends, and they would take her under their wings in her husband's absence. If it pleased her, he could arrange for a tutor for Joshua, too, and he could assure her the boy would not want for playmates. Madame would find the Garden District much like

Savannah and Charleston and should feel right at home at the Winthorp, built on rolling grounds surrounded by gardens. The St. Charles Streetcar, put in operation last year and powered by a steam engine, ran right by the hotel to take her down to the old town known as *Vieux Carré* of the Creoles, or the French Quarter, a most amazing place, but not an area to linger in after dark.

Now and then Silas cut in with questions, aimed, Jessica realized, to reassure himself of Joshua's and her safety while he was gone. For the last two days he had been attentive but reserved toward her, causing her to wonder if he regretted his statement in their moment of intimacy by the wagon. Really, whatever did she see in the man?

"No racial unrest to speak of, is there, Henri?" Silas asked.

"Avoided entirely, my friend, by the simple and practical measure of the whites and native Creole population agreeing this very year to live in different areas of the city," Henri answered. "The Creoles, who colonized New Orleans, will continue to live in the French Quarter while the wealthy American newcomers have chosen to reside in the developed Garden District. The area actually belongs to the city of Lafayette, and there is little interaction with the old town. Jessica and your son will be quite safe from its inhabitants, I assure you."

"And the inhabitants safe from the whites," Jessica piped up. "Actually, I've never been afraid of black people," she continued, "and from what I've read of the culture of the native Creoles, I can well understand why they would wish to live apart from the newcomer Americans in order to preserve their way of life from corruption."

Her little speech was met with pointed silence, and Jessica felt a warning poke in her back from Tippy. Jessica saw Silas's jaw tighten and his quick glance at Joshua to determine if he'd registered her remark. Early on, he had said to her, "You are entitled to your feelings about slavery, Miss Wyndham, but do not influence my son to share them." Well, no matter. These slaveholders must be reminded that while she must live among them, she was not one of them.

As Jessica expected, wagon and horses did not rumble into the courtyard of the Winthorp until the air was savory with the aromas of roasting beef and baking yeast rolls. "Ah, the pleasures of civilization," Jeremy declared as he dismounted. "My mouth is watering already."

Joshua pleaded, "Papa, I'm hungry. Can we eat now?"

"In a little while, son. Let's get registered."

Jessica had withdrawn into a sulk, unnoticed by anyone but Tippy. Now there would be no opportunity to consummate her marriage to Silas. He would return in two days' time for Joshua's surprise birthday party and one visit after that, but by then any trace of affection he'd felt for her would probably have vanished and perhaps even her own ardor cooled. She would be left as she'd arrived, a married virgin, she and her husband strangers.

The proprietors came out to meet them, a kindly man and his jolly wife, round and clucking as a pigeon. Henri swept the way for introductions with his hat. "The fine people you've been waiting for," he announced—to avoid the awkwardness of introducing her and Silas as Mr. and Mrs. Toliver, Jessica surmised.

"I understand you're to require two rooms, Mr. Toliver, each with ablutions closets," Henry Morgan said.

"That is correct," Silas replied. "One for my wife and me, and one for my son with a maid's quarters attached as I asked Henri to request. I'm assuming that will be no problem?"

"None at all, Mr. Toliver. All has been arranged," Henry said.

Jessica, irritably attempting to smooth the wrinkles from her dress, lifted her head in astonishment.

Silas glanced at her, a wry smile tugging at his lips. "Is that all right with you, Jessica?"

Jessica's mouth turned dry. "Why, I—yes," she said, swallowing quickly. "That…arrangement is quite all right with me."

Chapter Thirty-Five

"Come sit here by me, son, I have something to tell you," Silas said. He took a seat in one of the tufted chairs in Joshua's room and pulled another close to him. Joshua plopped tiredly down, ready for bed. He had eaten his surfeit at supper after an hour of play while luggage was carried to their rooms. His expression had wondered why certain of his belongings had been brought along, but he had not inquired further. Joshua assumed they were staying in the hotel for only a week while the train replenished supplies and made repairs. Two shocks were coming to the boy. One could wait until later. Silas had decided to deal first with the one he considered more important.

"Yes, Papa?"

Silas leaned forward to engage Joshua's droopy attention. "I've kept something from you because I believed you would not understand. You may not understand now, but you will later when you're older."

Joshua listened with drowsy interest. Silas continued. "Jessica is more than your friend, son. She is my wife and your stepmother. We were married at Willowshire in January."

Joshua came alert. "You and Jessica are married? But you don't act married, like Grandmother and Grandfather used to."

"I know. That's why I won't be sharing your room tonight. I

will be with…my wife next door. That's what married people do. They…sleep together. Tippy will be in her room, right next to yours if you need anything."

Joshua's brow wrinkled. "If Jessica is my stepmother, does that mean she will be only half a mother? She won't love me as much as a whole one?"

"No, that's not what that means at all, son," Silas said, drawing the boy onto his lap. "Jessica loves you with her whole heart, I can tell. You were not born to her, but by Jessica becoming my wife, you become her son."

"My real mother died long ago when I was born, didn't she?"

"That's right."

"She never had a chance to love me."

"No, she didn't," Silas said, his throat tightening. Tenderly, he attempted to subdue a cowlick on the soft crown of his son's head.

"But Jessica will make up for it."

"I have no doubt."

"And she can still be my friend?"

"Forever and always. That's what she promised, and I figure her for a woman who keeps her promises."

"Will she let me call her Mother, like my friends do theirs?"

"I'm sure she'd like that very much."

"I would really like a mother."

All at once, to Silas's surprise, Joshua scooted out of his lap to stand facing him between his knees. He clasped his father's face with both hands to ensure his attention. "Papa…" he said, staring hard into Silas's eyes.

Amused, Silas said, "Yes, son?"

"Promise me you won't take me away from Jessica like you did from Lettie and Grandmother and Uncle Morris."

Silas felt tears burn his eyes. He lifted his son back into his lap and held him tightly. "I promise, Joshua. We will keep Jessica with us forever if she will stay."

So it was done, Jeremy thought. By tomorrow, Silas and Jessica would be husband and wife. Jeremy had heard his instructions to the innkeeper, and had drawn Silas aside out of earshot of the others.

"Tell me to mind my own business, if you like," he'd said, "but I must ask. Did you mean what I think you meant about sharing a room with Jessica, or was that said for the sake of appearances?"

"I meant it."

"What changed your mind?"

"I took your advice and read her diary."

"Ah. I see."

"I hope you do, Jeremy. You were right. Jessica is attracted to me, and I've come to care for her. Neither of us yet know where our feelings will lead, but I want to do right by her. I want to make her happy if possible."

Jeremy had clasped his friend's shoulder. "I've no doubt you will, my friend. I wish you every happiness. My best to you both."

Jeremy was happy for Silas, he really was. His friend didn't deserve Jessica, having gained her in the way he did, but Silas would grow to love her—never as much as his plantation, but close enough. Silas's remark, *I hope you do, Jeremy,* had let him know that Jessica was his. Jeremy could put aside his private hope that Jessica might fall into his hands. That possibility was now not likely to be. A pity. He would have set his slaves free for Jessica's sake. She was an extraordinary person who had won his admiration more by the day. Now there was nothing for it but for him and the woman he would gladly have married to become the greatest of friends.

* * *

"How did you know I'd be…willing," Jessica asked as Silas unbuttoned the last obstacle to the other barriers in the way of their mutual desire. Jessica stood still while his hands did their work.

"I read your diary," he said.

"What?"

He kissed her astonished mouth. "While you were sleeping," Silas said afterwards while her lids were still closed in pleasure. He kissed them, too. "Thank God I did. I would have continued under the delusion you hated me."

Her eyes flew open. "I tried to. I don't know why I don't."

The corset was next, followed by a camisole. "I don't for the life of me know either," Silas said, unlacing the ribbons that held the garment together. "I shall do my best to give you no reason to as…a husband."

The gentle implication was clear. Jessica accepted it. He might give her cause to despise him as a slave owner, but as her husband, her lover—how could she hate a man who filled her with such physical longing?

The corset fell away, and Silas pulled the camisole over Jessica's head. "Dear God," he said in awe at the second sight of her exposed breasts.

"I'll do the rest," Jessica said, hurriedly stepping out of the petticoats and her pantalets. Watching her, Silas untied the sash to his dressing robe, and it dropped to the floor. He touched her bandage.

"Are you sure you're well enough for this?"

"I'm well enough," she said, giving him her hand, and Silas took it and led her to the bed.

Chapter Thirty-Six

Silas was gone by the time Jessica awoke. She reached over to his side of the bed and found a shocking void. Her first thought was that he had fled from her, too embarrassed by their unrestrained ardor the night before to face her. How could she blame him? She had behaved appallingly for a bride...a virgin. He must wonder if she hadn't had experience for him to have satisfied her need so naturally and easily.

Jessica threw back the sheet to take advantage of the ablutions closet and remove her head binding, which Silas had been careful not to disturb. Still it was a miracle the cut looked none the worse for her exertions except for its unpleasing discoloration. She left the dressing off until Tippy could replace it and returned naked to bed, not yet ready to leave its warmth or memories from her first sexual experience.

Little about it was as she'd expected or been warned of in the long discussions of wedding nights with her classmates at boarding school. She had bled slightly but had felt no pain, only an intense pleasure that made her feel as if she were floating among the stars. When Silas discovered the virginal stains, he'd gone at once to soak a cloth in basin water and bathed her as tenderly and unselfconsciously as if he were tending a baby. He placed a clean towel under her, and they turned their backs to the other to seek sleep, but their need—or lust, Jessica didn't know which—got the better of them, and they turned to each other again.

She should be ashamed of her abandonment to a man she barely knew, even if he was her husband, but she did not. For the first time in her life, she did not feel plain and undesirable. Silas made her feel beautiful and wanted, and, against her instincts and better judgment, that tribute to her vanity alone might force her to be happy with him. Love was a long way off and may never come for either of them, she realized that. She was not so young that she did not know time and familiarity and irreconcilable differences could snuff the strongest attraction, but she would not borrow tomorrow's trouble. She would live for today.

Where had Silas gotten himself off to? She missed him so, ached for him. He had told her he had business in New Orleans today and would not return to the hotel prior to leaving for camp, but that was before last night. She had hoped for them to have breakfast together, a civilized and appropriate formality to the consummation of their marriage.

Jessica sighed ruefully. Here she was, already fuming like any wife disappointed at her husband's dereliction of his connubial duties.

A soft knock on the adjoining door of her bedroom startled her from her musings. Hastily, she drew the sheet over her exposed breasts. Tippy, she thought, chomping at the bit to find out what happened.

"Come in," she called.

The door opened and Silas entered. He was dressed in clothes suitable for a drawing room and looked fresh, rested, and unbearably handsome. "Good morning," he said, a sheepish glimmer in his eye. "How's the head?"

Quickly Jessica covered the spot of her injury with her hand, her heart beginning to pound. "Don't look. It's starting to go an ugly color, but otherwise it survived the night."

"A wonder." Silas came around the edge of the bed and removed her hand to judge for himself. "It doesn't look ugly to me," he said. "It's a sign of the healing power of youth and health, but to be on caution's side, it should be rebandaged. I'll send Tippy in. And...uh, are you all right otherwise as well?"

"I find myself perfectly all right."

A moment's awkward silence hung between them. Jessica pulled the sheet higher and burrowed her head deeper into the pillows. "You must think I'm a wanton," she said, peering at him over the edge of the bed linen.

A grin relaxed his countenance. "I think nothing of the kind. I was intensely flattered by your...response to my enthusiasm."

"I'm sure I'm not the only woman who has aroused yours, but be assured you're the only man who has ever aroused mine."

Silas grinned wider. "What an enormous compliment. I hope you found the experience better than copulating with a mule."

"I can't say since I've had no comparison," Jessica said loftily.

Silas chuckled and withdrew two letters from inside his coat, one secured by a wax seal and the other protected in a handmade envelope. "Here. These are for you. I collected them from the reception desk. The Morgans forgot to give them to you last evening. From the seal, I see that one is from your mother. I hope she sends good news but not enough to make you homesick. Now I must leave you, but I'll be back at noon to have a meal with you and Joshua, then I must get back to camp."

He leaned down again. Jessica thought he meant only to kiss her cheek and be on his way, but a mischievous glint appeared in the emerald irises, and before she could anticipate his move, he pulled at the sheet.

"Lord have mercy, Jessica." He sighed and pressed his lips to the voluptuous curve of her breast.

It required all her willpower not to thread her hands through his black hair and pull him down to her, but she must think of Joshua in the next room. She pushed him away and restored the sheet. "Where's your son?" she asked.

"Downstairs," Silas said, straightening reluctantly. "He's had his breakfast and found a playmate, Jake, one of the boys from the wagon train. His parents are staying at the hotel."

"Joshua doesn't know...about us, does he?"

"I told him last night that we're married. He wants to call you Mother."

"Oh, Silas, really?" In her joy, Jessica almost sat up. She could hardly believe it. She'd anguished over the real possibility that Joshua would reject her as a mother when he learned that she and his father were husband and wife. "He wants to call me Mother?"

"That was his expressed wish."

"I'm honored," Jessica said and tried the name on her tongue. *"Mother..."*

Silas bent down once more, and she saw his teasing intent to pull at the sheet again, but she held it firmly despite a flush that warmed her thighs. "Go away so I can read my letters," she said, pushing him away with her free hand.

Silas laughed and tweaked her cheek, but obeyed. With her eyes, Jessica followed him to the door and they were on him when he opened it and glanced back, his gaze serious and still. "Let us not question what has happened between us, Jessica, or why. Let us simply accept it and be...grateful."

"I will, Silas."

"I will return at the noon hour," he said. "Rest now."

Tippy burst in a minute later, eyes growing huge when she saw

Jessica still in bed and apparently naked under the sheets. "Don't tell me it happened," she said excitedly.

"It happened," Jessica said, "and no, I'm not going to tell you *what* happened, but it was divine."

"Well, thank the stars and moon and all heavenly bodies," Tippy said, and tugged the bellpull twice to request bath water. "Now maybe Mister Silas will reconsider his intention to leave you here. Once a man has tasted honey, you think he's going to leave the bucket behind?"

"I've reconsidered my desire to go with him, Tippy. Joshua knows we're married. Silas says he's happy about it and wants to call me Mother. Isn't that wonderful? So now I not only have to think of you, but also of my responsibility to my little…stepson and"—Jessica gave Tippy a look—"I may have to think of me, just in case."

"What do you mean, just in case?"

"I'm in my fertile period."

"Glory be!" Usual for her in moments of elation, Tippy covered her small face with her large hands, leaving nothing but wisps of hair and ears showing. Behind the enclosure she asked in a muffled voice, "You going to let Mister Silas know?"

"We'll see," Jessica said, removing the letter from the envelope that had been posted from Boston. Jessica did not recognize the return address. Her mother's letter could wait. Jessica was hungry for every word from Willowshire, but the letter's contents might sadden her, and she wanted nothing to disturb her euphoria.

"It's from Sarah Conklin!" she exclaimed, surprised. "She's moved to Boston. She writes that she made it home safely but regrets that her nephew, Paul, had to see her in such a state when she arrived. She says her back took a long time to heal, but she's fine now. Paul wants to attend West Point and be a soldier when he grows up."

Jessica frowned and Tippy asked, "What's wrong?"

"Sarah says we may not live to see it, but she predicts that in time there will be a war between the North and South over the issue of slavery."

Tippy, preparing the bandage to redress Jessica's wound, said quietly, "We will live to see it."

Jessica glanced at her, and a feather-light chill ran over her naked skin. Tippy was from the stars. They told her things, and her prophesies were never wrong.

In her mother's envelope were two letters. "Tippy, here's a letter for you from Willie May!" Jessica cried. "Bless Mama for enclosing it. I'm sure Papa didn't know."

Tippy snatched it from her hand, and the two exchanged news contained in each mother's letter until Jessica came to the last paragraph in hers. As she'd dreaded, her mother had enclosed matter that disturbed and saddened her. "Oh, no!" she gasped.

"What is it?"

"Silas will be heartbroken…devastated. How I loathe to tell him…."

"Tell him what?"

"Tell him about Lettie," Jessica said. "She's married to Morris and is now the mistress of Queenscrown."

Chapter Thirty-Seven

Their luncheon together as a family perfectly complemented the night before. Joshua had approached Jessica shyly when his father brought him to her room before they went downstairs. She sat before her dressing table, and Silas led him to her chair.

"You get to be my mother, Papa said."

Jessica took his hands into hers. Her voice pitched low and gentle, she said, "It doesn't mean we can't still be good friends."

"That's what Papa said, too, but I want you to be my mother first. I don't mind if you tell me what to do. My friends say their mothers tell them what to do because they love them."

"That's very true," Jessica said.

"But you'll read to me like always?"

"Until I teach you to read. Then you can read to me."

Joshua glanced up at his tall father. "Is it all right if I hug her now?"

"I don't think she'll break," Silas said, with a slight wink at Jessica layered with private meaning. She ignored him and gave herself up to the embrace of the little arms around her neck. How had this miracle happened that she was now a wife to the handsome man beside her and a mother to this adorable child she had already grown to love? Wisdom cautioned her to beware of such heady happiness built on the uncertain ground of her marriage, but for the moment she would follow Silas's advice and not question what had happened—was happening—between them. She felt wanted and needed. She would enjoy this new, delicious experience as long as it lasted.

Chatting merrily, they'd trooped down the stairs hand in hand and entered the dining room like any normal set of parents with their offspring between them and selected a table next to the family from the wagon train. They were Lorimer and Stephanie Davis and their son, Jake. Like the Tolivers, they were dressed as people of property, the woman one of the few slave-holder wives who had become somewhat friendly with Jessica. But for a faint show of curiosity at Jessica and Silas's new marital situation (their fellow travelers were aware the couple, heretofore living separately, had shared a room), the Davises greeted them as one of them—parents with sons who had a grand time playing together.

Jessica had determined to wait until Silas was ready to depart for the wagon train to relate the news of Lettie's marriage. She did not want a second of their time together marred before he had to return.

The moment came too fast. They had left Joshua taking a nap, Tippy also. Her one lung was feeling the oppression of the New Orleans humidity. Silas had said good-bye to his son as he'd seen him to bed. Jessica had accompanied him to the courtyard, where his horse was bridled and saddled. Like any husband and wife, they apprised each other of their plans. Silas would return day after tomorrow to attend Joshua's birthday party. He would drive his Conestoga back in the company of another wagon loaded with children for his son's party, and post the wagon to sell. He had already lined up a potential buyer who was willing to give him a fair price. Jessica would be busy with hotel personnel arranging the birthday luncheon, and she had accepted Henri's offer to squire her and Tippy and Joshua around New Orleans. The

Frenchman wanted to show them his father's emporium and the St. Charles Hotel that was near completion and touted to be the largest and grandest hotel in the United States. Joshua was excited about riding the streetcar with his friend Jake.

Then Jessica said, "Silas, I have something I must tell you."

"I hope it's nothing to disturb my illusion that you are happy."

"It has nothing to do with my happiness, but it may yours. Your brother and Lettie are married. My mother wrote of it in her letter."

Jessica held her breath. The next seconds would tell if he still cared for Lettie and mourned her loss as now irrevocable. Jessica had often wondered if Silas would return for Lettie should she still be unmarried after he fulfilled the terms of the contract and divorced her.

"Is that so?" he said, and saved Jessica two days of agony during his absence wondering if Silas was awash with regret. He took her hands and kissed them. "I wish my brother and his wife well," he said, "and hope the disparities between them can be settled as satisfyingly as ours."

He said no more, and his face went expressionless except for the small smile he gave her as he tipped his hat and rode away. Jessica covered the back of her hand with her palm, preserving the touch of his lips on her flesh. Silas was bound to feel pain, she thought, and perhaps a sense of betrayal and sadness that things had turned out as they had. But Lettie was gone from him forever, and she was here, at least for as long as it took Silas to fulfill the terms of his contract with her father.

Silas was glad he was alone and on his horse miles from camp. He would need solitude and time and distance to adjust to his shock and the feelings that followed. So Lettie had settled for Morris.

The picture of his beautiful, passionate, exuberant former fiancée married to his Bible-spouting, laconic dullard of a brother was almost too painful to imagine. His shock gave way to dismay. Talk about copulating with a mule! Good God, what had Lettie been thinking to marry Morris?

But as his horse's hooves ate up the miles, Silas came to a new awareness. It lightened his sadness for Lettie's fate and his guilt for his part in it. His former fiancée had known exactly what she'd been thinking to marry Morris. For the sacrifice of her beauty and body to his blockhead of a brother, she'd gained the Queenscrown she'd always loved. Silas recalled her excitement at the prospect of living a year at the plantation before leaving for Texas. Even then he'd suspected that when it came time to go, for all her adventuresome talk, she would be reluctant to leave its luxury and comfort. Lettie was never more radiant than when she graced the rooms at Queenscrown, never looked as if she felt more suited to a place. Queenscrown was her consolation prize, and Morris, of whom she was fond, not a bad substitute for the man who had jilted her.

His mother had gained the daughter-in-law she thought she'd lost. There would be grandchildren to hold and adore. With the exception of a minor adjustment, the lives and futures of the girl and family he'd left behind would continue as planned.

By the time Silas reached camp his pain had been assuaged, his guilt all but forgotten. His thoughts were on Jessica. He wished he could have ridden back to draw her into his arms and assure her his former love was only a chapter in a book he'd started but returned to the shelf unfinished. He had no interest or desire in taking it down again. His old life was gone and everyone in it. He doubted he would ever return to South Carolina and Queenscrown, even to see his mother, who would turn her full affection and attention to Morris and Lettie and her grandchildren. Her younger son and grandchild would become only a memory that claimed her thoughts now and then.

Jessica was in his future, whatever that held. The inevitable shadow of slavery hung over their happiness together. He must prevent her from corrupting his son—*their* son, now, and all their children to follow—to her way of thinking. Slave labor was essential to his dream of Somerset, and he would not permit his wife to interfere with raising his heirs to understand that their way of life and the perpetuation of their land-owning heritage depended on it. When Silas was putting Joshua down for his nap, the boy had asked if he'd bring Josiah, Levi, and Samuel back for his party, slaves' sons he treated as equal to Jake Davis. When Silas had explained that would not be possible, his son had asked why.

"The party is only for you and your friends," Silas told him. "Josiah and Levi and Samuel are Negroes."

"But how does being Negroes keep them from being my friends?" Joshua had asked.

He was too young to understand, as Silas had been when growing up playing with slaves' children and thinking of them as friends. Eventually, by the natural influence of the institution that had bred him, he had learned and accepted the difference in their stations. He had not had to be taught, but then there had been no Jessica Wyndham Toliver whispering her contrary views into his ear.

For now, though, he would not anticipate the problems ahead for him and Jessica in their marriage. He would be thankful the obstacle he'd expected did not exist. For the time being, the slip of a girl he'd married who had blossomed into a woman before his eyes did not hate him.

Chapter Thirty-Eight

The next morning Tippy took a message for Jessica from a hotel maid who appeared at her door. "A gentleman is downstairs requesting to see Mrs. Toliver," the maid told her.

"Did he say who he was?"

"An agent of her father." She handed Tippy a calling card.

"Just a moment, and I'll inform my mistress," Tippy said.

Jessica read the card, and her mouth turned down. "A Mr. Herman Glover," she recited to Tippy, "a man who works in my father's bank." Jessica remembered him as a thin-faced man with bony hands who looked as if he had never been exposed to a ray of sunlight. He was the employee that Jessica had warned Sarah of being planted to gain evidence against a bank teller suspected of actively opposing slavery.

"Should I tell the maid to have him wait?" Tippy asked.

"No, I'll see him," Jessica said, hurriedly rising from her vanity table. Tippy had given her hair a thorough washing. It was amassed in a towel wrapped around her head, but she'd finished dressing and was sitting before the mirror for Tippy to work her wonders with her damp tresses. "I'll see him as I am and send him on his way. We have too much to do today to waste time on him."

Jessica did not bother to hide her repugnance as she swept into the reception room of the hotel. "You wished to see me?" she demanded of her pale visitor.

"Your father sends greetings, Miss Wyndham," the man said with a deep bow, but not before his expression showed surprise at her turbaned head and the brown-and-blue discoloration of a gash on her forehead.

"*Mrs.* Toliver," Jessica corrected the inaccuracy. "What do you want?"

Flustered, pencil in hand, the man threw open the flap of a small notebook. "Your father wishes me to report back on your condition and...state of mind," he said, and commenced to write.

"What are you writing?"

"Why, that you have sustained a terrible injury to your head, Miss...er, Mrs. Toliver. Could you give me the details, please?"

"Give me that!" Jessica ordered, and snatched the book from his hand. She flounced to a writing table and sat down. *Papa,* she wrote,

the reptile you dispatched will no doubt make the worst of a cut on my forehead, sustained when my lead horse bolted at the assault of a hawk, and I was thrown from my wagon. The cut is healing nicely, thanks to the immediate medical attention I received. I am comfortably ensconced in a fine hotel where I will await the return of my husband from Texas when he departs at week's end. You will be happy to read and impart to Mama the surprise that your daughter has never been happier save for the sadness she expects to feel at the absence of the man you purchased for her.

With hope that you are well,
Jessica

"There! That should be all the report required to assure my father of my condition and state of mind," Jessica said, thrusting the notebook back to the agent. "Anything else?"

"Well, uh, yes, Mrs. Toliver. Now if you please, I must see your slave Tippy in person."

Ah, yes, Jessica thought, her father's additional insurance to make sure she kept her end of the bargain. She marched to the registration desk. "Will you kindly send a maid to summon my friend Tippy to the reception room?"

When Tippy had made an appearance and become another jot in Herman Glover's notebook, he said, "And now, I must speak to Mr. Toliver. Is he here?"

"No, he isn't."

"Uh, does that mean he isn't *here*"—the agent swept his hand to indicate the hotel—"or that he's lying dead somewhere?"

Jessica's mouth twitched. The man was serious. He was too humorless to have been facetious. She lifted an amused eyebrow. "By my hand, presumably?"

"Uh, well, yes, the idea did occur to me."

"He's very much alive and well, thank you, but at the Willow Grove encampment five miles from the city. Shall I give you directions to the site?"

"Will he be returning to the hotel anytime soon?"

"Tomorrow, for his son's birthday party at noon."

"Then I shall wait for him here, since I do not sit a horse well, but I assure you I will not intrude upon the party. I shall visit with him later."

At which time you'll hand over further funds if Silas's receipts are in order, Jessica thought. Her husband's second down payment for Somerset.

"Suit yourself, Mr. Glover," she said, her happy spirits dampened.

The birthday party went as planned except for a few words of disagreement with the proprietors of the hotel. It was one thing for a guest's Negro maid to sleep in an adjoining closet to be near her mistress, but quite another to share a table with her in the dining room. The dispute was settled by Jessica arranging for a private room where Tippy could enter from the back door. Jessica had managed to shop for several gifts for Joshua, but they were no competition for the surprise of Tippy's buckskin jacket. Even Silas, who kept Tippy at arm's distance or gave her a wide berth—Jessica hadn't yet decided—was impressed almost speechless, as was Stephanie Davis, who looked uncomfortable at the inclusion of Tippy in the party. Henri said, "It is a work of wonder, *ma petite*. No wonder my father"—he raised his immaculate hands in the air as if to wave from it the exact word—"was *ecstatic* over your extraordinary design of Madame's dress when you and she visited his emporium."

The chocolate two-tiered birthday cake, topped with a spun-sugar version of a low-crowned, wide-brimmed planter's hat like Silas's, elicited raves as well, especially from Silas. He lifted Joshua to better see the design and said, "Someday, son, you'll wear a hat just like that when you ride the fields of Somerset with me."

Everyone applauded, including Tippy, who did not seem to realize she had worked with the kitchen staff to create the symbol of oppression for her people. Her glee that Joshua and Silas were rhapsodic over her efforts so consumed her that Jessica decided not to mention it.

In late afternoon after they'd seen the wagon off with Joshua's guests to return to camp, Silas left them to meet with Carson Wyndham's agent. After several hours, Jessica went in search of him in the hotel and found him in the saloon alone, staring into a glass of liquor on the bar. The agent must have left. On the bar was a leather envelope, a reminder of the deal he'd struck with her father, the trade he'd made for Somerset. Was sorrow that he'd agreed to it the cause of Silas's gloom? Jessica laid her hand on his arm. "It was a lovely party," she said. "Joshua couldn't have been more pleased. He must be sweltering in that buckskin jacket, but he refuses to take it off."

Silas seemed startled at her appearance and quickly picked up the envelope and inserted it into an inner pocket of his frock coat. "Yes, he's beside himself, and I'm grateful to you and Tippy for making him so happy. It was sensible of her to make the jacket with room for him to grow. She's quite extraordinary, your Tippy."

"She'd like to be your Tippy, too."

"She's colored, Jessica."

"Can you not look beyond the color of her skin to the exceptional person she is and accept her as my friend, one to be loved and cherished?"

"No, Jessica, I can't, but I can appreciate her and respect your relationship with her. I cannot promise more than that."

"Promise me you won't sell her."

"I promise."

"And you will permit our close friendship?"

He grinned. "Do I have a choice?"

"No, but I'd like to hear you say you permit it."

"As long as she lives."

Jessica smiled. "Very good. Now let us go see what Joshua is up to."

They finished out the day with a light supper and, after seeing Joshua to bed and dismissing Tippy for the night, Jessica returned to her room to eagerly await Silas, who had gone to the stable to see to his horse. She was already in her night clothes when she heard a small knock on the adjoining door between the two rooms. She opened it to find Joshua, book in hand, staring up at her in wide-eyed appeal, enhanced by sweeping lashes that Tippy declared "unconstitutional" for a boy. Silas's son possessed no facial feature that could be attributed to him. His eyes were hazel rather than green, his hair an innocent mass of brown curls instead of an aggressive black thicket. His nose was more of a sparrow's than a hawk's, his mouth a tender arch rather than a curved rod.

"I couldn't sleep," he said in his childish voice. "Will you please read to me, Mother?"

Jessica's heart melted. How could she refuse him? "Of course I will, Joshua."

"Thank you," he said, and without another word, as if it were a familiar spot reserved just for him, he clambered into her bed clutching his storybook.

When Silas showed himself a while later in his dressing robe, he stared in astonishment at his son and wife snuggled side by side against the pillows. Jessica glanced up from her reading with a droll look, and Joshua, patting the space beside him, said, "Come be with us, Papa. We're at the good part."

"Well, then, I mustn't miss it," Silas said, and climbed in beside him.

Later, after Joshua was asleep in his own bed and Silas and Jessica had made love, Silas lay awake. The agent was not the only visitor he had met in the late afternoon after the party. Jean DuMont, Henri's father, had come to call. In speaking with him, Silas could understand better than most his new friend's desire to part ways with a man as dictatorial and supercilious as the owner of the DuMont Emporium. Jessica had described the place as magnificent—"surpassing the most elegant retail store Charleston has to offer." Henri had told Silas that his father treated him like a lackey, never allowing him to make the most *petit* decision. Silas had been surprised to find the man waiting for him in the saloon and had thought at first he'd come with the hope that he'd dissuade his son from joining him in his migration to Texas. But Jean DuMont's mission had been entirely different.

"You have in your entourage a strange-looking Negro named Tippy, your wife's maid," the man began. "I wish to buy her."

He had named a price that had caused Silas's heart to leap. The money would give him a huge leg up on his savings plan and shave several years off his schedule to pay back Carson Wyndham.

"I am aghast, sir," Silas had said.

"Then we have a deal, I presume?" Jean DuMont had said, arching an aristocratic eyebrow.

The man was already reaching inside his coat pocket for his bank book when Silas said, "No, sir, we do not have a deal. Tippy is not for sale."

"I will double my price."

Silas had hesitated. By marriage, Tippy was his to sell, regardless of the deal Jessica had struck with her father, but the transaction was out of the question despite its temptation. He did not like Henri's father. Even if it were not for the certainty his wife would despise him for selling her maid, Silas would not trade Tippy's indenture to this man to offer Jessica her freedom. He said unequivocally, "Like I said, sir, my wife's maid is not for sale."

Jessica lay in a sound sleep, her face turned toward him. Silas resisted the urge to stroke her cheek, move his hand to her breast. In slumber, she looked child-like and vulnerable, hardly the woman he believed capable of harnessing the wind. It wasn't only for Jessica's love for Tippy that he had turned down Jean DuMont's offer, but the years he and Jessica would have together before he could pay back her father. Perhaps by then she would have no desire to leave.

Chapter Thirty-Nine

By the end of the week, all was in readiness for the departure of the Willow Grove wagon train to Texas. Supplies had been restocked, repairs completed, medicines and ammunition laid in. Keel boats and rafts had been purchased for crossing the Sabine and arrangements made for those preferring the ferry. The other scout in Jeremy's hire had reported in after many months of reconnoitering the revised route for reaching the black waxy. The way through the bayou country up through the thickly pined area fronting the eastern boundary of the new republic would be tough, but safer. The Comanche were still on the rampage and a constant threat to the settlers, but so far, the warring bands had stayed north of the territory they were seeking.

Silas had sold his Conestoga, adding to his extra pot, and Herman Glover had left him funds more than sufficient to meet expected expenses. The day of leave-taking had arrived. Jeremy had ridden in to say good-bye to Joshua and Jessica with his burlap-wrapped roses slung over his horse's flanks. Jessica had agreed to look after them and Silas's Lancasters while they were gone.

"By leaving them with you, Jess," Jeremy had said when he'd made the request, "we will be sure to make it back to collect them."

"Then I will see they are tended carefully," she said, hardly able to breathe for her pain and anxiety.

Henri had been privy to the conversation and asked, "You gentlemen place great importance on these dead-looking twigs. May I ask why?"

It was Silas who explained. "Amazing," Henri said, visibly impressed when Silas had finished relating the story of how the Warwicks and Tolivers had brought the symbol of their houses across the ocean to the new world. "And now they will be planted in another new world to be conquered."

"God willing," Silas said.

"He'll be willing," Jessica said in a tone that allowed for no dispute to the contrary.

"Or God will answer to Jessica for it, I wager," Jeremy had said, grinning.

Joshua had been told the day before that his father must leave him for a few months to make a home for them in Texas. "Now I want you to take the news like a little man," Silas had said to his son. "You're now five years old."

"Yes, sir," Joshua had said, standing militarily straight before Silas in his oversized buckskin jacket with eyes watering and lip quivering. Later, out of sight of his father, he had buried his head in Jessica's lap and sobbed.

Lorimer Davis stood with his family; Silas with his. Their horses were saddled. Tippy had vanished into the hotel. Jessica had been pleased when Silas had sought her out to extend a personal farewell and admonition to look after his family. Jessica held Joshua's hand tightly. The moment had arrived for last good-byes. Silas placed his arms around his wife and son and drew them to each side of him. "I'll be back for you when it's safe, and I'll write," he said, his voice gruff. "Somehow I'll find a way to get mail to you even if I have to borrow Tomahawk

from Jeremy to do it. Joshua, do you remember what I told
you?"

"Yes, Papa. I'm to take care of Mother."

"And you're to say your prayers and mind your manners. Remember that you're a Toliver."

"Yes, Papa."

"Now will you please go stand with Jake until I can say a few
words to Jessica?"

"Yes, sir."

Jessica had bowed her head as she had a tendency to do when
unwilling for anyone to see her on the verge of tears. Silas allowed
her no such quarter and lifted her chin with his fingertips. In the
months to come, she knew she would remember him standing
tall by the magnolia tree, its dark green leaves and waxy white
blossoms a background for his black hair and eyes that held the
fire of emeralds. She told herself she must not consciously remember every detail of his face and expression, for to do so would
give credence to the unthinkable.

"Jessica," he said, "I have never felt about anyone like I feel
about you, whatever value you place in that."

"I've no understanding of it—none at all." Her refusal to become emotional hardened her words. "I only know that I..."

"What do you know?" he asked, the question soft as the breeze
that stirred his undisciplined hair.

"That I want you to come back."

He brushed his fingers over the healing wound that had
brought them to this moment of hope and despair. "I'm glad.
You must keep writing in your journal, and I will write in mine.
When I return, we'll read them aloud to each other and that way
we won't have missed a day of being together. I won't have been
denied these next months of watching my son—our son—on his
journey of growing up. Do you promise?"

"I promise."

"I leave a happy man. Will you kiss me?"

"I will."

In the shade of the magnolia tree, he bent his head, and Jessica lifted her face, and they kissed. Afterwards, Silas backed away from her with a gaze she believed was meant to lock the image of her in memory. He threw a salute to Joshua, who returned it snapped at attention, and mounted his horse. "Lorimer," he called to his travel companion, his voice brisk, businesslike, "let us be on our way to Texas."

Stephanie and Jake, Jessica and Joshua watched them go. Tippy stole beside them, silent as a shadow, and no one said anything until men and horses and wagons were out of sight. Then Jessica said, "Tippy, we must find some big buckets. We have to get the roots of those roses into fresh soil and do all we can to keep them alive."

For how the roses go, so will Silas and Jeremy, she thought.

It was the first of June, 1836.

Chapter Forty

Excerpt from Silas's journal:

SEPTEMBER 15, 1836

"Man proposes; God disposes." That German writer in the fifteenth century, Thomas Kempis, was right when he penned those words, as Morris would be delighted to hear me admit, though God knows I've experienced the truth of them often enough these past couple of years. I sit here now on the eve of my departure to New Orleans wondering where to begin my narration to Jessica of how handily God disposed of my proposal to settle in the black waxy region of Texas. Unless she received my letter of July that I entrusted a soldier returning to Lafayette to deliver, she will not know that the Willow Grove wagon train did not make it to the black soil of my reserved land grant. Once the train had crossed the Sabine and slogged through the bayou country, our people had endured enough. We had survived accidents to limb, wagon, oxen and horses, treacherous quagmires, snakes, and alligators. Two days after we set up camp, exhausted, on a pine-covered knoll, I said to Jeremy out of the blue, "How about here?"

Jeremy looked relieved. He had already exclaimed over the abundance of white-tailed deer and wild turkeys, clear streams, deep, fertile, sandy loam, and the rich variety of trees, but my admiration of the area was based on an additional attraction. The First Congress of the Republic of Texas was offering immigrants who arrived between March 2, 1836 and October 1, 1837 a grant of 1,280 acres for heads of families and 640 acres for single men, provided they lived in Texas for three years. Why would a man pay 12 and 1/2 cents an acre in the land grants of empresarios such as Stephen F. Austin when the land on which he stood was free?

Even though the pine forests would be much harder to clear than the blackland prairies, I saw other advantages to remaining in the region. Not only would the savings in cost of land add to my secret coffer, but I could return for Jessica and Joshua sooner. This time, I would take the Old San Antonio Road and cross the Sabine at Gaines Ferry into Louisiana and bring my family back the same way for an easier and quicker route into Texas.

Lorimer Davis, who'd been within earshot of Jeremy's and my conversation, asked me to repeat what I'd said.

Jeremy answered for me. "Silas said, 'How about here?'"

Lorimer grinned from one big ear to another and shouted at his neighbor, "HOW ABOUT HERE?"

When the question was passed from wagon to wagon, a chorus of YEA's went up and in a meeting the next day, the settlers cast a unanimous vote to settle here among the pines.

And so, on my thirtieth birthday, I managed to hire a surveyor to stake out my acres and to provide me with the necessary figures of location and boundaries to file my claim at the Texas General Land Office when it opens in Austin in December. I made sure to have witnesses to the surveyor's report testify to my arrival in Texas and should have no trouble obtaining a conditional certificate to possess the land until I take official ownership of it in three years. Even before the surveying was completed, I set about building shelters, fences, barns, and—most important—clearing land for the planting of cotton seeds in early spring. I am glad Jessica was not here to witness how hard I worked our slaves, but we now have a semblance of the beginning of Somerset. I look forward to carrying her over the threshold of our log house. It is rude at best, but it is weatherproof because I made sure the chinks were properly filled. It boasts three rooms and a loft, and a hall from the front gallery to a shed in back where, at no small expense, I have had installed a bathtub for Jessica! I hope she will be pleased. In time, I plan to join another cabin to the original to double our living space, but the addition will have to wait until I address other, more urgent needs.

Sam Houston of Virginia was elected the first president of the Republic of Texas two weeks ago. Perhaps now the new nation will know the beginning of stability. The treasury is depleted and credit for the republic next to impossible to obtain. There are no funds to pay for an army, roads, or postal system. Mexico and the Indians present a constant concern. Houston favors eventual annexation to the United States and peaceful relations with the Indians. His opponents support independence and the removal of the Indians from the entire republic. Who will win out? I see myself someday adding my voice to a political body that decides such matters, but at this point in time, I will concentrate on building the plantation my son and his sons will carry into perpetuity in this new land of promise and opportunity.

I fear Jeremy will not be joining me in a like venture, though he has staked out his 640 acres—"the beginning of The Warwick Lumber Company, my friend," he proudly announced to my startled ears within a week of our arrival here. "I'm tired of planting cotton, Silas," he said. "I see my financial future in mining timber." He went on to say that the logging industry was in its infancy now, but he is certain it will grow as the nation grows, and in that growth was bound to come the need for lumber.

I was shocked that he would be so enticed to jump ship—turn his back on his Warwick heritage—but of course, I wished him well. For me, the only calling of a Toliver is to till land—large parcels of it—and that, I and my heirs will do.

Henri picked his plot on the hilliest, least fertile ground a good distance from the river. He envisions his 640 acres as the site of the town we will build together and has already marked the spot where he intends to erect his mercantile store—a sort of general store at the beginning, he says, but later, when the town is established—"Ah, mon ami such an emporium the public has yet to behold!" To him I wish the best of luck as well and count myself fortunate to have within hailing distance two of the finest men I will ever call friends.

This is my final entry in the journal. Writing it has provided solace for my loneliness at the end of many long, wearying days. Once I'm reunited with Jessica and Joshua, I see no need to commit to paper the daily events I will live with them.

(Note to myself: Before sharing my journal with Jessica, mark the parts to be left unread.)

Chapter Forty-One

SEPTEMBER 18, 1836

Silas has been gone now for three and a half months. There are times I believe I cannot endure another day of waiting for his return. Now that I'm feeling better, I've packed and arranged for several trunks to be stored in the Conestoga in readiness to leave as soon as possible to Texas when he does arrive. Stephanie is as much on tenterhooks as I. She, too, is tired of having time on her hands and of being cooped in her hotel room with a rambunctious six year old.

Still, I am glad Silas was not here to see me so sick the first months of my pregnancy. I lived by the chamber pot, not a pleasant sight for a new husband to behold. Only these last weeks have I been able to venture out and about, mainly to take the street car to the DuMont Emporium where my presence is to remind Monsieur DuMont of my threat.

Silas had not been gone a day before Henri's father approached me with an offer to lend out Tippy—"for a wage, of course," he said, "since your husband tells me the girl is not for sale. He turned down a very handsome offer, too," he said petulantly, as if still needled by the insult.

I stared at him, my mouth so ajar he understood at once that his offer to Silas was new information to me. "Didn't your husband tell you? Ah, well, then—" an ingratiating smile heightened the greedy light in his eyes, "perhaps you and I can strike a deal since the girl is *your* maid to do with as *you* please."

I asked him how much he'd offered for Tippy, and when he told me, I very nearly gasped. I do not know how much money my father agreed to pay Silas to take me off his hands, but I would not be surprised if the sum Monsieur DuMont offered did not equal a good portion of it. If Silas had accepted the money, he would have less need for my father's and fewer years to depend on it. He could then throw the contract into my father's face.

He could have gotten rid of me.

But Silas had kept his promise never to sell Tippy and did not take advantage of Monsieur DuMont's offer.

"Well?" My visitor prompted in a tone spiked with impatience.

A heady feeling took hold of me. I would not have been surprised if my body had sprouted wings and lifted me, extra pounds and all, off my feet. "I repeat my husband's words, Monsieur," I told him. "My maid is not for sale."

"Very well then, what do you say to hiring her out to me for..." he pursed his lips in a calculating manner and named a wage. The work would not be hard, he assured me. He rather thought my maid might enjoy it. He wanted to use her in his design room.

I'd see what Tippy had to say about it, I told him. As I saw him to the door, he did not disguise his chagrin that I did not give him an answer on the spot—why was it necessary to discuss his offer with a slave?—but he agreed to return the next morning for my decision.

He could not leave my presence soon enough. I wanted to be

alone to think on the implications of Silas turning down so much money. I remembered that our conversation the late afternoon of the party had followed Jean DuMont's meeting with him, but Silas had kept the reason for his visit to himself. Silas would certainly have realized the consequences to our tenuous relationship if he'd sold Tippy, but why would that loss matter compared to so much gain—including the opportunity to rid himself of the wife he'd been forced to marry!

I placed my hands on the mound that was the fruit of the two nights we'd been together. Here within me was the seed of our destruction. We needed no other. I must accept Silas as a slave owner, but I could not abide our child sharing his endorsement of the purchase and sale of human beings to do another's bidding without compensation for their labor or the freedom to make the choice.

But that conflict would come soon enough, I told myself. For the moment I was warmed—overjoyed—by the sacrifice I believe my husband had made on behalf of our marriage.

Tippy could not hide her delight at the opportunity to work in the design room of the DuMont Emporium. The wage seemed hardly of interest to her. It was the pleasure of handling silks and satins, brocades, and finely woven cotton and woolen fabrics that set her hands to flapping when she imagined herself creating her marvels in such a place.

"But how will you look after yourself and Joshua with me gone all day?" she cried.

"Joshua and I will look out for each other," I told her. Already my stepson was the attentive big brother, often laying his head on the swell of my abdomen and talking to it.

"If you're a boy, I'll teach you to do the things I like to do," he'd say. "If you're a girl, I'll protect you from bad things."

At such times, I plant a kiss on the sweet crown of my stepson's head and wonder if it is possible to love my own child as much as I love this little boy.

Tippy took the job, but only after I had warned Monsieur DuMont that he would answer to my father if she was mistreated or taken advantage of in any way. I also got him to agree to send a carriage to take her to and from his emporium located in the business district upriver of Canal Street. Because people think of Tippy as an oddity, she draws attention wherever she goes, most of it unwanted. New Orleans is exotic, bawdy, sensual, mysterious, an easy city to get swallowed in, and, without my protection, I imagine her assaulted on the street by ruffians, kidnapped by slavers, or spirited away to serve some evil mistress behind locked doors in moss-draped mansions for the rest of her life.

The arrangement has worked well, and were it not for Joshua and the tales Tippy brings home at night of the DuMont Emporium, I might have succumbed to the daily waste of my time and energy in the Winthorp Hotel. Because of boredom and the sameness of the days, there is often little of interest to record. I hope Silas will understand the reason for the gaps between my entries. When I next return to these pages, perhaps I will have something of importance to relate.

SEPTEMBER 19, 1836

Glory be. Last evening I answered a knock on my door and found Silas William Toliver on the threshold.

Chapter Forty-Two

Somerset, January 1841

His father had touted his belief that a man should gauge his life in segments of five years, Silas recalled. Only then did he have a clear view of the gains and losses, rewards and consequences resulting from his decisions that would then determine his resolutions for the future. Bullocks, Silas thought with his usual anger at the memory of his father. He faced a situation that none of the gains and losses, rewards and consequences from the decisions he'd made in the last five years could shed light on, and God knew the journey to this time and place was littered with plenty of each.

The voices of his two sons at boisterous play in the side yard of the family's log house drew him to the window, music that always soothed the beasts that roamed within him. Today's beast conjured up the memory of his mother's blazing face in the drawing room at Queenscrown when she delivered her prediction that his land in Texas would be cursed: *Nothing good can come from what has been built on such sacrifice and selfishness and greed.*

But was it selfishness and greed to wish to expand his holdings for the benefit of his family? A sacrifice, yes. His conscience forced him to see that if he diverted the money he'd saved to pay back Carson Wyndham to buy more land, he would be sacrificing his capability to offer Jessica her freedom. He was certain she would not leave him and the home they'd made even if it were offered, but the feat of paying back her father every penny he'd paid to be rid of her would prove to Jessica that their odious agreement was not the reason her husband stayed married to her. But did his wife need that assurance? Not since New Orleans had she referred to the contract. Jessica loved him, though perhaps not wholly, and he loved her, if not exclusively. The issue of slavery was always between them, like smoke they fanned away at the dinner table and in the bedroom and in the presence of their children, and part of his heart belonged to the mistress lying beyond his house that demanded his attention from sunup to sundown.

So, really, what was the point of returning Carson's money other than as a matter of his own personal pride and the satisfaction of imagining the man's face when his agent handed him a banknote worth the full sum he'd doled out over the years?

Weary from his thoughts, Silas went outside to be with his sons, Joshua, now ten, and Thomas, three and a half. There had been another son, but he had passed from his mother's womb prematurely in September 1836, four months before he was to be born, one of the losses on the journey to this time and place.

This time and place. Silas looked about him at what had been accomplished in the past five years and allowed himself a rare feeling of pride, a pleasure he believed should be reserved for the fulfillment of his dream for Somerset rather than its inception. Still, he was justified in taking pride in the spread of his pine-cleared fields beyond his expanded house, the slave compound he'd built within a footrace distance, and most certainly the cotton gin whose cost he'd convinced his neighbors to share and build on his property. Having their own gin saved ginning fees and the bother of hauling their cotton to the closest one ten miles away. In a few years the gin would pay for itself, and the owners could charge their own ginning fees.

His snug house was bounded on one side by well-maintained barns and sheds and corrals; on the other, a tidy yard where the boys could play, an orchard, and two gardens, their soil recently turned. They looked a bit abject this cold January day, the ground in one awaiting its seeds; the pruned, bare branches in the other dormant until spring when each plot would yield its individual bounties of vegetables and roses.

It had been Henri's idea for Silas and Jeremy to plant both the York and Lancaster roses in each other's gardens as a symbol of unity between their houses. The three of them had been elected the framers of the new community, which the settlers whimsically and unanimously agreed should be called and spelled Howboutchere, named for the more literate question—"How about here?"—that Silas had posed the second day of the wagon train's encampment in the pine trees. He and his fellow planters had recoiled at the folksiness of the suggestion and wangled a compromise: The name of their town would be spelled *Howbutker*, with the sharp accent on the last syllable.

Henri would grow both his friends' roses as well, he announced to Silas and Jeremy in one of their meetings. It was his feeling that, when disagreements arose among them, as they inevitably would, the roses should serve as tokens to express what men of pride such as they could not bring themselves to articulate in speech. "So if ever I should offend you, I will send a red rose to ask forgiveness," he said, "and if ever I receive one tendered for that purpose, I will return a white rose to say that all is forgiven."

Leave it to a Frenchman's flights of fantasy to prompt such a proposal, Silas had thought, but Jessica, recorder of the minutes, had been enchanted by the notion and commenced to write down every detail and word exchanged in the discussion. "What a lovely idea!" she'd exclaimed. "I'm going to include this meeting in my journal, which someday I hope to turn into a history of the Tolivers, Warwicks, and DuMonts of Texas, proud founders of the town of Howbutker."

"And what will you name your book, my dear?" Henri had asked.

"A simple name," Jessica said. "I shall entitle my book *Roses*."

Silas paused a moment to observe another accomplishment of which he was very proud: his son Thomas, born June 1, 1837. "There's no denying who he takes his looks after!" Jessica had said, and indeed, as the year went by, there was no denying the boy was a true descendant of the Toliver line. His dark blue eyes gave way to light green, his chin dimple deepened, and his hair, with its slight but distinctive V-shape on his forehead, grew blacker.

There had been one other miscarriage after the birth of Thomas, but no other hint of pregnancy since. Jessica's thickening journal contained genealogical charts of the three ruling heads of Howbutker's leading families. Jeremy and Henri had married in 1837, and the names of their two children were posted and others were to be added when the men became fathers for the third time in July. The space alongside Thomas's was blank across the page, and Silas had the uneasy feeling it would remain so.

Joshua, seeing Silas come around the house, called beseechingly, "Papa! Come play horsey with Thomas. I'm tired of him riding me!"

"Let him ride your stick horse," Silas said, swinging Thomas up into his arms. At three and a half years of age, he was almost too big for his mother to pick up.

Joshua stuck out his lip. "I don't want him playing with it. He might break it."

Silas rumpled Joshua's hair but did not chastise him for not sharing the stick horse Jessica had presented him when he was four years old. It wasn't selfishness that kept Joshua from allowing his younger brother to play with his possessions, but the value he placed on particular ones. The wooden alphabet blocks and carved farm figures had long lost their paint, which Tippy had collected to restore for Thomas, but the stick horse was special to Joshua, as was the outgrown buckskin jacket Tippy had sewn for his fifth birthday. As young as he was, Joshua had come to know that the sentiment attached to certain things made them too valuable to entrust to other hands.

"It's too cold for you boys to be outside anyway," Silas said. "Come on into the house, and I'm sure your mother will read to you from one of your Christmas books."

"Oh, Papa, I'm too old to read to," Joshua said.

Jessica had come out onto the wraparound porch, drawing a shawl around her. "Then how about reading to your little brother and me?" she said, obviously having overheard the conversation. "I love to hear you read."

Silas looked at his wife, his throat suddenly stung by a rush of feeling that almost brought tears to his eyes. There were days when he was so caught up with the endless demands of the plantation and nights when he was so tired he could hardly remove his boots that he barely noticed her, as a man is not aware of the air he breathes. But she was there, her presence a constant sustenance, and he could not imagine his life without her. They were happy together in this place despite crop failures, Indian scares, never-ceasing labor, and the womb deaths of their unborn children. He had never lost his desire for her or enjoyment of her company. In fact, both had increased over the years until his absences from her to see his cotton to its destination were almost more than he could bear. Would Jessica ever entirely believe it wasn't her father's money that kept him by her side but his love and need of her? Did a woman's heart ever cease to remember what her mind had chosen to forget?

His savings would purchase his neighbor's small land grant that would give him direct access to the Sabine and allow him to build a landing from which he could float his cotton on flatboats down to Galveston and onto commercial steamers bound for New Orleans and ports beyond. He would be spared the arduous transport of his cotton by wagon to a landing farther upstream and the usage fees the owner charged. In time he could charge his own usage fees.

"Silas?" Jessica came down the porch stairs, and Thomas wriggled out of his arms to run to her. "You're lost in thought again. Whatever are you thinking?"

"How much I love you," he said, his voice hoarse from emotion. "If I were Morris I would quote from Proverbs, but I'd alter the verse. 'I have found a virtuous woman, and her price is beyond rubies.'"

"Well, thank God you're not Morris," Jessica said, never one for gushing sentiments, but her face colored from what Silas knew to be surprised pleasure. They did not often speak of love. "Are you coming in?" she asked.

"No," he said. He had made his decision. "I'm riding over to the Wiltons' place to talk with Carl about buying his acres. He wants a decision by this afternoon."

"We have the money for that?"

"I've put a bit aside, and Carl is willing to let his land go for under market price. I'm not liable to get another half-section so cheaply."

"Very good, then, but you'll be back by supper time?"

"I wouldn't miss it, and afterwards"—Silas directed his smile to Joshua, who had gone to get warm under Jessica's shawl—"I'll play horsey with Thomas."

"Very good, Papa," Joshua said, parroting Jessica's familiar expression.

Silas did not go at once to saddle his horse but watched Jessica herd his sons into their log house, smoke from the chimney rising cozily into the winter sky. Before closing the door, she glanced back at him, and he hoped she could not read his guilt at once again favoring Somerset over her.

Chapter Forty-Three

Withdrawing from the crowd that had gathered to celebrate the seventh anniversary of the establishment of the Willow Grove colony, Jeremy selected a bench in the shade of a southern red oak to take stock of his surroundings and to mull over the years that had delivered them to this location and date in July 1843. He gave himself a little credit for the unanimous decision to settle in the spot. From the moment the wagon train had entered the pine woods, he'd been entranced by the area. Another vocation besides farming had called to him, stirred his blood, and he may not have moved on to the blackland prairies farther west. Silas knew him well. He had sensed his friend's hesitancy to push on toward their intended destination, and it may have been that reluctance that led Silas to say, "How about here?"

In any event, he and Silas and Henri had chosen well the location for the town they had hoped to build. Howbutker was gaining in importance because it was the first community this side of the Sabine that settlers passed through when coming into Texas from Louisiana, many of whom stayed, and the only town that could brag of several major stage coach lines offering transportation into the heart of the growing republic. Ground had been broken for a courthouse, church, and school, and the main street had been laid out in a circle around the town common that would become the setting of the courthouse if the land commissioner chose Howbutker for the county seat.

It had been a productive seven years for himself and his fellow founders. Henri had his dry goods store up and thriving, thanks in large part to Tippy's amazing talents that had contributed to its elegant inventory. With Jessica's permission and with know-how gained from working with Henri's father, Tippy had gone straight from Jean DuMont's emporium to his son's visible hope to best him. Henri's establishment had expanded in size and rich display of goods each season until his customers now came from as far away as San Antonio and Houston and the metropolis of Galveston to stock up on items they could never find at home.

Somerset had become the largest plantation in the settlement, and still Silas had plans for further expansion. Jeremy knew from whom the money came that allowed his friend to buy more land and slaves and draft animals, erect more farm buildings and workers' cottages (the timber bought from the Warwick Lumber Company), but Silas could give his own business acumen and land management just due for the prosperity of his plantation.

The Warwick Lumber Company of Howbutker had not enjoyed such prosperity—not yet. The business had been difficult to get off the ground. Jeremy had built a water-powered sawmill and lumberyard, but though there was a large demand for building timber in the expanding republic, getting it to the source of need was a problem. Overland roads were few and the rivers nonnavigable except in prime flowing times. His trees were cut by ax and saw, tediously and slowly dragged by draft animals to his mill or to the river bank, where his timber was joined into rafts and floated to coastal mills that paid him for his haul. Both operations were difficult and at the mercy of slippery soils and frequently bad weather, but Jeremy was inclined to be patient. He saw better times ahead. It was only a matter of a few years before Texas would be annexed to the union, and the financing of roads for hauling commerce to market would be the first item the United States would be petitioned to address. Eventually steamboats would make their way upriver and provide a mode for transporting his timber to coastal cities, and the railroads were bound to come. New tools were being invented to make logging safer and faster, and meanwhile the cry for building timber would continue to grow. Jeremy prepared for the day the Warwick Lumber Company would be among the biggest timber operations in Texas by buying up tracts of pine forests on the Sabine, around Howbutker, and south to Nacogdoches, the oldest town in Texas. To supplement his inheritance and income, he had bought into several thriving businesses on the coast. Also, he had married.

Her name was Camellia Grant, and Jeremy had been introduced to her when he met her father, a banker, in New Orleans in 1837. Bruce Warwick, Jeremy's beloved father, had died, leaving his youngest son his share of Meadowlands in cash. The United States had suffered a monetary crisis that year and few banks were sound and solvent, of which August Grant's was one. Jeremy had remained in New Orleans for a month to court and marry Camellia, then brought her to his modest but comfortable dwelling in the pine woods of Texas. Becoming pregnant on their wedding night, his wife had returned to the more splendid comforts of her parents' home in New Orleans for the nine months before delivery and did so with every pregnancy afterwards. She had delivered their third child two summers ago and come to remain in Howbutker with a husband who was finally getting to know her.

The anniversary festivities were taking place in the center of the fledgling town. The Warwick Lumber Company had provided the rough-hewn benches on which people sat under trees and inside tents for shade. From his bench, Jeremy had a good view of Jessica Toliver inside one of them. She was serving cake and punch to the line of slave children eagerly awaiting their turn, their excited chatter carrying to him across the common. Hard to believe Jessica was now twenty-five and already a legend in her own time, if not the most misunderstood and underappreciated one. Rumors circulated that she'd rescued a Comanche warrior who'd come to some sort of grief beside a creek outside Howbutker. Silas was away with his cotton down to Galveston at the time. Jessica had enlisted Tippy to help nurse the warrior back to health and send him on his way before the community got wind of his presence and strung him up from the red oak under which Jeremy sat. If the rumor was true—and who would doubt Jessica's aiding an enemy warrior since her view of the white man's theft of Indian lands was well known—logic would shout that he had come to scout the place for attack. Jeremy believed the rumor and credited Jessica's kindness for saving Howbutker and the surrounding homesteads from the savage Comanche raids other settlements had suffered.

Jeremy loved his wife. She was gentle and sweet-tempered and soft as a kitten cuddled next to him at night and, furthermore, worshiped the ground on which he walked. She had bravely borne him three sons—they had had their last child, for he would not have her separate herself from him again—but Camellia would have wilted like her namesake if forced to face the responsibilities and challenges Jessica met daily at Somerset. For that reason Jeremy had built his wife a house in town managed by a covey of servants to ensure her the leisure she was accustomed to. Meanwhile, out at Somerset, Jessica administered to the needs of family and slaves, supervised the orchard and gardens, served as nurse, doctor, teacher, and veterinarian as well as oversaw the endless tasks of cleaning, laundering, sewing, spinning, cooking, and preserving. Now and then, her daily routine was disturbed by a wild animal come to call, a poisonous snake in the house, an outbreak of malaria, an accident, a death.

On many occasions, Jeremy had shaken his head in wonder at the strength of the girl he had first met wearing a brocaded gown and satin slippers and an emerald brooch at her eighteenth birthday party.

Excitement began to mount at the appearance of a daguerreotype photographer and his assistant whom Silas had ridden to his landing to collect. The photographer had come upriver from Galveston to take photographs of the families who could afford them. While the man set up his bulky equipment, women gathered their husbands and children together, if not to pose for the camera, at least to watch the amazing invention of a contraption that could capture the likenesses of people and landscapes on a copper plate. Jessica left her station in Tippy's hands to join Camellia and Henri's wife, Bess, both wearing their finest and attempting to corral their two-year-old toddlers while their husbands strolled off to collect their missing six sons. Joshua, aged twelve, would be with Jake Davis and their friends, and Thomas, turned six in June, would be with Jeremy Jr. and Stephen Warwick, aged six and four, and Henri's sons, Armand, six, and Philippe, five.

The fathers found all six boys admiring a stallion in a paddock behind the blacksmith's shop, a white-and-russet pinto with legs of white from the knees and hocks down. The animal was strong-boned but delicate in the head and neck, which at the moment was arched in wary observance of the boys. The horse had caught Joshua's attention particularly. The boy stood on a rung of the fence trying to coax the pinto to his open hand.

"He's for sale at a good price," the blacksmith said to Silas. "He came to me by way of payment for a debt. Your son seems right smitten with him. Isn't it time the boy had a horse of his own?"

Jeremy sensed Silas bristling and backed away from the sparks that were bound to fly. It had not gone unnoticed that Silas was overly protective of his sons. Jessica had suffered two miscarriages in their seven-year marriage, and Silas had confided to Jeremy he had given up hope for another heir.

"He's too young," Silas responded to the blacksmith, his flinty glare advising him to mind his own business.

"Too young?" the blacksmith guffawed. "Why, my boys had their own horses before they were eight. Get 'em in the saddle young, and they never know to be afraid."

"Papa…" Joshua pleaded. "Jake has his own horse."

Silas lifted Joshua, slight for his age, down from the fence. "Maybe next year for your birthday, son. Now let's go get your picture taken."

The photographer instructed his subjects: "You'll have to hold absolutely still for fifteen minutes. No talking. No fidgeting. No smiling. The slightest movement will ruin the daguerreotype. Anybody need a neck brace, my assistant will fit you with one."

The families of the Tolivers, Warwicks, and DuMonts held perfectly still, even the toddlers who had fallen asleep in their mothers' arms during the process. It was the last and only picture of Joshua Toliver. While his parents were enjoying ice cream with their friends in the evening shade, Joshua mounted the pinto saddled for him by the blacksmith.

"Ride him around the pasture to get the feel of him, then trot him on down to the town common. When your paw sees how well you manage him, I'll bet he'll buy 'em for you."

It was the blacksmith who rode to the town common. "Your boy—" he began in a choked voice, startling the Tolivers sitting on their pine benches in a circle of friends. "He—he was thrown from the horse he was looking at this afternoon. You better come quick."

The whole gathering flew to the grassy paddock to find Joshua lying still in the shadow of a giant sweet gum tree, life already gone. Jessica, kneeling by his body, looked up at Silas through a flood of tears and said words to him that would shrill in his nightmares the rest of his life. "We are cursed, Silas. We are cursed."

Chapter Forty-Four

In the spring of 1846, Carson and Eunice Wyndham called on their daughter and son-in-law at Somerset. They had come specifically for the purposes of finalizing the business between Silas and Carson and to meet their new grandson, who immediately won Eunice's heart. "I just wish Benjamin had lived to see the boy," she said. "He'd be pleased to see that his grandson looks a Toliver through and through. Morris's boys...well, they take after Lettie and have little interest in the plantation."

"In that regard, they take after Morris," Silas said dryly, feeling a moment's disloyalty at the thought of Lettie producing three healthy children—two sons and a daughter Eunice described as regrettably having Morris's "heavy bones."

The five of them sat in chairs on the front porch of the Tolivers' log house, and a glance at his wife's stoically expressionless face at this news made Silas ashamed of his brief envy. He knew what she must be thinking. He would have reached for her hand to offer comfort, but that would only embarrass her and aggravate the pain she was trying to hide.

Ever since Somerset's first acre was cleared, even as he rebuked himself for giving a thought to it, Silas had wondered how—when—the "curse" on his land would manifest itself. Where was the curse in his cotton production, which, after a rough beginning,

had increased year after year? Where did it lurk in the abundant
rainfall at just the right times, in the robust health of his slaves and
animals, the deliverance of his family and workers from crippling
accidents and disease, and from fire that could wipe out a farmer's
crops and buildings in the twinkling of an eye? How were all
those blessings jinxed by his mother's prediction?

But sometimes, after he and Jessica had made love, he would
lie awake long into the night assaulted by the demons that rose
from their lairs to haunt the souls of the guilty, and wonder if his
wife's womb held the curse. Nonsense, he would say in the morning light. Jessica was simply…barren. Nothing—certainly not a
curse—was at fault. Joshua had died by the hand of a thought-
less blacksmith who'd allowed him to ride an unknown horse. If
he should feel guilty about anything—and he did—Silas thought
to himself as he watched Carson ceremoniously light the contract with the glowing tip of his cigar, it was that he had gone
back on his intention to hand over a banknote for the sum the
man had paid him to marry his daughter. How he would like to
see the bully's face—and Jessica's—when Carson realized that all
his son-in-law possessed, including his daughter's love, had been
earned by his own hand. Silas Toliver was free and clear of any
debt he owed Carson Wyndham, and Jessica at last had proof that
love alone kept her husband by her side.

But it was wishful fantasizing. The lure to develop and improve his land had been too great. After building his river landing, he'd begun saving again, but a blacksmith in Illinois named
John Deere invented and manufactured a type of steel plow that
could cut through sticky soil without clogging, and Silas had
given in to the temptation to buy several. The single horse-drawn
plows had saved him time and money because the steel blades,
unlike the wooden plow that farmers had used for centuries,
could turn a furrow in any kind of weather or condition of the

ground. Before, he'd have to wait several days for soggy soil to dry, or, if hard, employ three men and several strong animals to plow a field.

There had been other, irresistible "siren songs" to which he'd listened and yielded in the ten years of his indebtedness to Carson until his extra money was depleted. Jessica had never been aware of his intention to pay back her father. It was a secret—and a regret—that Silas would take to his grave. As he observed the contract become ashes in a crockery saucer, the shame of his failure burned like acid to hear his father-in-law, with a condescending sweep of his cigar about his six-room log house, say, "This is all well and good, Silas, but it's time my daughter lived in a proper house. As I promised, the money for it is in your bank, and I'll send a good architect to you."

Eunice, sitting next to Jessica, patted her daughter's arm. "Wouldn't you like a big new house that becomes you, dear?" But even as she said it, a bleak movement in her eyes betrayed again the dismay her expression had clearly shown when she saw her daughter for the first time in ten years. "My goodness, but you've...weathered the years well," she had said, to cover her embarrassment at her reaction to Jessica's thin frame in her simple, countrywoman's dress, her red hair drawn in a severe bun below her bonnet.

"Thank you, Mama," Jessica had said when meeting her parents at the stagecoach station. She had planned to greet them in the one gown she'd allowed Tippy to sew for her that reflected the new bell-shaped skirt and low, pointed waist, but the seam line of the narrower sleeves restricted her arm movements, so she'd elected to wear the type of simple homespun dress she wore every day.

"One that becomes me?" Jessica repeated her mother's question.

"As a Wyndham, as…" Eunice glanced at Silas, and though she appeared galled to say it, added, "the wife of your prominent husband here in the new state of Texas."

Silas puffed on his cigarillo, uncomfortable with the conversation in the presence of Thomas. It was another source of shame that his son would never learn that Somerset and the manor house were financed by anyone else but his father. Thomas was only nine years old, but inquisitive and already able to discern innuendo, moods, veiled conversations.

"What's a contract?" he'd asked when Carson had referred to it and drawn the document from his coat pocket.

"A signed agreement," Carson had answered. "This one is between your father and me."

"What did you agree to?"

"I'll let your father tell you if he's so inclined," Carson said with a smirk at Silas.

"That is business between your grandfather and me only, Thomas," Silas had said. "Go help Jasper with the new foal."

"Jasper!" Carson exclaimed. "Are you talking about that skinny little colored boy I let you have, Jessica?"

"Yes, Papa," Jessica answered between tight lips. She had listened to the exchange between Silas and her father in visible contempt—for both of them, Silas had no doubt. "I don't know what we'd do without him. Jasper is around twenty-eight now, married, and has several fine children. One, a daughter, is especially dear to me. Her name is Petunia."

Carson's faint quirk of an eyebrow at his wife clearly stated their daughter, at twenty-eight, hadn't changed much. With a motion of his cigar, he dismissed the subject of a slave and his offspring. "Let Thomas stay," he overrode Silas's order. "His grandmother and I will have little enough time with him as it is."

"Yes, Papa, let me stay," Thomas begged.

"To the barn, son. I'll come get you in a little while to be with your grandparents."

Glaring at Carson to let him know he'd be damned before he allowed him to embarrass him before his son, Silas was startled to hear Jessica say unexpectedly, "I'd like the house built in town on the street with the DuMonts and Warwicks."

Silas removed his cigarillo in surprise. "Not here on Somerset?"

"No, in Howbutker, on Houston Avenue, down the street from our friends."

"Well, since I'm buying, I say my daughter can build her house anywhere she damn well pleases," Carson said. He stuck his cigar into his mouth and tilted back his porch chair with thumbs hooked into his vest pockets to see what his son-in-law thought of that.

Ignoring Carson, Silas studied his wife. She had lost some of her fire since Joshua's death. She and Joshua had been unusually close, mutually caring of the downtrodden, animals, and nature, interested in books and learning. Thomas was more attuned to the songs and voices of the land, never happier than when accompanying his father into the fields—*Like riding through clouds, Papa!*—and almost from infancy had shown an interest in harvests and ginning. *Why does the soil have to be warm before you plant? How are the seeds separated from the fiber, Papa?*

Unlike Joshua, there was no mistaking that Thomas realized his place as the son of the master of Somerset. He played with the children of the slaves—Jessica saw to that—but he did not call them his friends as Joshua had. His friends were among the sons of the Warwicks and DuMonts and Davises. Slowly, as Thomas evolved from the toddler stage, Silas saw him become what his sweet-natured brother could never have been: a descendant of his Toliver lineage to the bone.

Not long after Joshua's death, Silas had come upon Jessica storing away the boy's treasured stick horse and buckskin jacket. "Shouldn't we give those to Thomas in memory of his brother?" he had suggested.

"No, Thomas would only use them until they were as worn as his memory of Joshua, then discard them," she said, startling Silas with her bitterness. "I prefer to keep them in memory of…my memory of Joshua."

As he deliberated on his wife, the thought occurred to Silas that she desired to live away from the plantation because she did not wish to see the hold the planter system had begun to have on their son. Perhaps she did not wish to remain in the house of Joshua's home and where her miscarriages had occurred. Or…Silas noted Jessica's gaze on the ashes of the contract. After today, could it be that his wife no longer wished to live surrounded by the reminder of the trade that had brought her to live here?

"What about you, Thomas?" Jessica asked. "Wouldn't you like to live in Howbutker close to Jeremy Jr. and Stephen and Armand and Philippe?"

"I like it here," Thomas said.

"Of course you do," Jessica murmured.

That night before he climbed into bed next to his wife, Silas tucked a red rose into a water glass and left it by the stove. The next morning Jessica twirled it at him as he entered the kitchen. "What is this for?"

"To say I'm sorry."

He expected her to say *For what?* But she did not. She knew.

"We'll build the house in Howbutker," Silas said.

Chapter Forty-Five

The Carson Wyndhams—at Eunice's insistence—had brought Willie May with them for a reunion with her daughter, so it was with great pleasure that Jessica conducted another ceremony at the Toliver homestead after her parents' departure back to South Carolina.

"I hereby set you free, Tippy, my dearest friend," she said, handing Tippy a document verifying her release from bondage. "Since I have fulfilled the conditions of my father's contract, he can no longer hold the threat of the sale of your mother over my head."

Tippy folded the paper and slipped it into the bodice of her dress. Her gown was not made of the costly materials of her clients nor as fashionably designed. Even though Tippy had become a partner—albeit a silent and secret one—in the newly renamed DuMont Emporium, it would never do to appear as well dressed as the white ladies who patronized its showroom. She was paid a salary and shared in the store's profits. She lived in a small house owned by Henri located down the street from his store. He and Bess and their three children cherished her.

"I thank you, Jessica, my dearest friend," Tippy said, her dazzling wide-toothed smile tinged with the knowledge shared by the Toliver family that the document tucked next to her bosom did not mean she was free. It would not protect her from the auction block if she were caught outside the lights of the community that held her in a favored position. The color of her skin, regardless of her remarkable talents, amassed as they were in a Negro, still dictated that she must fade into a room's shadows when in the presence of whites.

"You will, of course, assist my wife in choosing fabrics and colors for our new abode," Silas said in the formal tone he used when addressing her.

Tippy responded with a small curtsy. "I be happy to, Mister Silas," she said.

Construction of the house on Houston Avenue began in the summer. Jessica selected a site that would give a view of the entire street, now filling with impressive houses belonging to prosperous merchants and planters whose wives were tired of the arduous duties of overseeing a home and slave compound built in the middle of farm fields. The Warwicks had constructed an edifice on the order of a medieval castle up the street called Warwick Hall, down from the DuMonts' gray-stone, French-inspired château that featured Henri's love for his native country's precisely laid-out gardens. One plot over, the Lorimer Davises had erected a square, colonnaded townhouse in the stately Federal style, and next to them, a mansion of Italianate design was going up, owned by another planter of the Willowshire wagon train. The Silas Tolivers stuck with the Greek Revivalist style traditional to Plantation Alley.

It took almost a year to complete the white, three-storied manor house of pillared splendor that reigned over the avenue from an elevation slightly higher than its neighbors. The elegant entrance hall with its gilded floor-to-ceiling mirror and portrait of the Duke of Somerset, the spacious rooms and high ceilings, graceful curving staircase, marble fireplaces and crystal chandeliers, elaborate friezes, deep moldings, and sash windows drew awed praise from all who entered. Silas and Jessica responded with stiff smiles to the often-voiced opinion that fortune had certainly smiled on the Silas Tolivers.

In the spring a year after the mansion's completion, Jessica watched Jeremy converse with the black men who had delivered a pallet of dressed timber to be used to build a gazebo and rose arbor she had planned for the east side of her new home. "I want to sit in the gazebo in the early morning sun and watch my roses wake up," she had said to Jeremy.

The Negroes were former slaves Jeremy had set free not long after his arrival in Texas. He had given all his slaves their freedom, but though released from bondage, only a few had left. It was not safe for freedmen to walk abroad, and those who remained worked as employees of the Warwick Lumber Company. They were paid a wage and given housing in a trim, company-built compound known as the Hollows.

Jeremy's liberation of his slaves had not set well with the other slave owners, and they'd threatened to boycott the Warwick Lumber Company, but it soon became apparent that Jeremy had enough business outside the county to fill his company's orders without the need for theirs. Besides, they liked Jeremy and his gracious wife, and the inconvenience of buying and hauling dressed timber from miles away became too burdensome.

Jessica had pointed out the successful transition from slave to employee to Silas, who'd responded in a raised voice, "Are you suggesting that I *pay* a Negro in whom I've invested thousands of dollars for his *work*?"

"Let him earn back the money you've paid for him, then hire him as an employee," she'd suggested.

"I couldn't afford such wages."

"Then allow him a share of the crops he tills. It will come to that, Silas," Jessica had declared, standing her ground. "If there is a war, the South will lose. The North will free the slaves, and the only way you'll be able to farm your cotton is to permit our Negroes a fair portion of the profits."

"There will be no war," Silas stated, refusing to listen to another word from Jessica on the subject of the North's growing dissatisfaction with the South on the issue of slavery. Their slaves were happy, he said. They sang in the fields. None in Texas could claim to be better clothed, fed, sheltered, and doctored. Each family had a garden, fruit and nut trees, their own milk cow, and Saturdays and Sundays off for rest. He did not separate families. He reminded Jessica that at the disapproval of the other planters for setting an unwarranted precedent, he had granted her every request for the comfort and safety of his slaves and now wanted to hear no more about it.

Jeremy sent the men on their way, brushed the lumber dust off his hands, and joined Jessica on the Corinthian-columned porch that faced the wide boulevard of Houston Avenue, recently paved with bricks from the area's red clay. It was April 1848.

"Well, Miss Jess, how do your roses grow?" he asked, removing his hat as he sat down and stretched out his long legs.

"I can tell you better after I've transplanted them from Somerset," she said, letting the ironic meaning of her entendre dance between them.

Jeremy laughed. "Ah. Husband and son."

"I'm not worried about the Lancasters and Yorks."

Jessica loved these opportunities to share a chat with Jeremy, another compensation for living in town and on this street. Besides Tippy, Jeremy was her best friend. Jessica could tell him anything, more so than Bess and Camellia, more so than Silas. Strangely, their spouses did not see in their special relationship a warrant for jealousy, which made their friendship even more comfortable. Now that the Tolivers had come to live on Houston Avenue, Jessica and Jeremy could pull up a chair together more often.

"Don't you think it's time to put a shovel to the plants?" Jeremy said. "Until you do, the place won't feel like home."

"Well, like Silas and Thomas, the roses are happier there."

"They'll be happy here, too, Jess. It's a magnificent house."

"But you said it. The place is a house, not yet a home. I may be happy here, such as I'm capable, but I fear Thomas will not. He loves living closer to his friends, but he misses Somerset, and now that our old log cabin has been turned over to Silas's overseer, Thomas has no place to lay his head but in his bed on Houston Avenue."

"Wasn't that the plan?"

Jessica cracked a small smile. With uncanny perception, Jeremy could always see right through to the core of other people's designs. "I want my son to have a few hours' separation from the plantation and...from his father," she added frankly.

Jeremy raised a brow. "You might as well try to split a hair."

"Well, I'm going to try," she said. "I've kept my promise to Silas that I wouldn't voice my contrary views to our son but that I could not speak for my example. So far my *example* has fallen on blind eyes, but Silas agrees with me that at eleven the boy needs more schooling than either of us can give him. I want Thomas to have *choices* about what he wishes to do with his life. How will he know of them if he doesn't have the opportunity of an education? He might wish to study medicine or law, become a journalist or teacher."

"All well and good, Jess, but how will you accomplish that here in Howbutker?"

"Silas has agreed to hire a tutor."

"Ah," Jeremy said, cocking an eyebrow. "With the hope a tutor may achieve what you've promised not to do?"

Jessica smiled. Again, Jeremy had read between the lines, which is what Jessica had done when she received a letter from Guy Handley in answer to her reply to his notice in the Positions Wanted section of the *Houston Telegraph and Texas Register*. In the advertisement he'd described himself as "a teacher of the humanities with special emphasis on classical literature." Jessica had been caught by the word *humanities*. In his letter, Guy Handley had explained that he was from Virginia and a graduate of William and Mary College. He was the private tutor of the children of a prominent landowner in Houston until his employer was killed in the Mexican-American War. The man's widow was moving back to her people in Louisiana, but he wished to remain in Texas. He would be happy to come to Howbutker for an interview if she would please advise him of a time and date.

"He's coming by coach tomorrow," Jessica said to Jeremy, "and I hope so much Thomas takes to him and to his studies. He was none too pleased to hear he'll be in school half a day."

"And so should all our children be," Jeremy said, rising and replacing his hat. "The public school won't open until next year, and we're not likely to lure the talents of a Sarah Conklin."

Jessica glanced up at him, startled, and a chill wafted across her skin at the little knowing glimmer she caught in Jeremy's eyes. Was his remark about Sarah another of his double entendres meant to imply he'd perceived the real reason she hoped to hire Guy Handley? It was as if Jeremy had read the tutor's letter and seen the tiny circle that served as a dot drawn over the *i* in "Cordially yours" at the letter's closing. Ordinarily, the substitution for the proper mark would have meant nothing to Jessica, but in Sarah Conklin's letters she had noticed a similar circle affixed over the *i*'s in both their names. Only those aware that codes were a form of secret communication in the Underground Railroad would pay attention to the coincidence. Was Guy Handley, the tutor she hoped to employ to teach her son, an abolitionist?

Chapter Forty-Six

It may be nothing, that little circle over the letter *i*. It may be only a personal conceit, and not an identification code, but such a whimsical liberty taken with the written language does not seem like Sarah, a purist when it comes to writing and speaking English, nor like Mr. Handley. I would not dare inquire about the practice in my correspondence to Sarah for fear that a postal clerk, seeing a letter addressed to a northern city, would open it to expose a sympathizer. In regard to Mr. Handley, I keep looking for signs but so far there has been no indication "the tutor of Houston Avenue" supports the Northern cause. We—and the DuMonts and Warwicks—refer to him in that vernacular because he now tutors their children in the afternoons following his lessons with Thomas.

Mr. Handley arrived two months ago. I collected him from the coach station and brought him here for our interview. He was not as I, nor Silas, expected. I could tell that Silas was surprised when they were introduced. We discussed the subject later in private. Both of us had thought we'd meet a pale, myopic, fastidious man with lily-white hands and a limp handshake, definitely someone who spent most of his days indoors, absorbed in a book when not tutoring students. Mr. Handley, while slight of build and of no great height, quickly proved our assumptions wrong. We could read his intelligence and zest for life in his clear-eyed, steady gaze and feel his confidence in his firm handshake. His attire was indeed impeccable without giving the impression he was above removing his spotless frock coat and rolling up his crisp linen sleeves if a situation called for it. Silas and I, Jeremiah and Maddie—unerring weather vanes of people—and especially Thomas, liked him immediately, to my great relief. Our son even showed a little jealousy at having to share his tutor with his friends.

We installed Mr. Handley in the apartment above the carriage house, which he says suits him perfectly, and have settled down to a routine. From nine o'clock in the morning until noon, he tutors Thomas. He brought books with him, the latest editions addressing reading, writing, and arithmetic, but Thomas's favorite part of the session is the study of Homer's *Iliad*. It will be interesting to hear from Thomas the slant Mr. Handley gives the poem. Will he emphasize that war is glorious or that it decimates families and property and constitutes a waste of time and human life?

I have tried to sound Mr. Handley out about the growing tensions between the North and South to determine if we have an abolitionist in our midst, and if so, whether he's an active member or a simple believer, but neither by word or deed has he given me a hint of where his loyalties lie. He treats Jeremiah and Maddie with a respect deeper than the common politeness a superior accords a servant, perhaps because he feels he shares their status. On one occasion, he stepped in for Jeremiah, who was ill, and a guest mistook him for our houseman. Our guest treated him with the contempt a man of his self-importance would, and upon his departure when Mr. Handley handed him his cane and hat, the man snapped, "Is this my hat?"

Without missing a beat, Mr. Handley replied, "I wouldn't know, sir, but it's the one you came with."

The Mexican-American War ended in February, and Mexico ceded approximately seven territories to the U.S. that in time will be annexed to the Union. The acquisition has incited another confrontation between anti- and pro-slavery members of Congress. If the territories are admitted as free states, the balance of power will be upset, and the North can outvote the South on issues regarding slavery—could even abolish it.

I asked Mr. Handley straight out for his view of what will be the outcome of the debate, hoping he would confide to me what *should* be the outcome.

"Compromise," he said, "where neither side gets what it wants."

His neutral answer left my curiosity unsatisfied, but not dampened, and so I decided to smoke him out by revealing where *my* sympathies lie. I wanted him to know that he was not alone.

The Warwicks and DuMonts are frequent guests to our house, and Guy Handley has become a welcome addition to our gatherings. He has great wit and charm, and Jeremy and Camellia, Henri and Bess are delighted with his instruction of their children. He even has the boys reciting passages from Shakespeare's plays, and in August there is to be a theatrical performance of *Macbeth* in which our sons and Nanette DuMont are to be players.

My sympathies are no secret among these, our closest friends. They are like family to Silas and Thomas and me. None of them possess slaves, and if truth be told, out of the group, only Silas believes slavery is essential to the southern economy. I picked my moment well. We were all seated at supper, and I said, quite casually, "I understand there is to be a Women's Rights Convention held in New York next month."

"Really?" Camellia said, her blue eyes round. "Whatever for?"

"To declare that women should have the right to vote, to have access to equal education, control of their body and property, and equal pay for equal work," I recited.

"I read about that," Jeremy said. "Good luck to them, I say."

"Sounds fair to me," Henri said.

Silas looked down the table at me, a smile curving his mouth. "I thought our ladies already had those rights except the one to vote. Gentlemen, can you imagine what would happen if we denied our wives anything they want?"

There was laughter at this, and then I said, "That is only saying that we ladies at this table are not called upon to fight for what should rightfully be ours, but the truth is that in this country women have no more rights than a field Negro, may he live to see the day that he is free."

Mr. Handley stared at me while the others spooned up their dessert, no more bothered by my remark than if a mosquito had landed on their dollops of cream. I had no idea what he was thinking. Was he merely shocked that the wife of a slave owner held such an opinion, or that he'd discovered a fellow ally in the enemy camp? Whatever his thoughts, I had declared myself. Now I must simply wait to see what happens.

Chapter Forty-Seven

The fourth Saturday of every month when cold weather set in was among Silas's most happily anticipated days of the year. The tradition of meeting at Somerset with Jeremy, Tomahawk, Henri, and all their sons as they grew older had begun a number of winters back. Tomahawk had stayed on in Jeremy's employ, serving generally as his indispensable right-hand man. His knowledge of animals and nature and terrain fit right in with his additional learning of the timber business and the cattle operation Jeremy ran on his deforested acres, replanted in rye that he sold for feed, but the job he most enjoyed was hunting game for his employer and his friends.

One Saturday morning when the temperature had dropped to thirty-two degrees, he and Jeremy had arrived at Somerset with a couple of field-dressed, blood-drained deer slung over their horses. Tomahawk's kills were especially prized. He could be counted on never to shoot his prey in the belly, not only because of its inhumanity, but because the carcass would spoil rapidly and prevent aging, a process that made the meat more flavorful and tender. Aging was accomplished by hanging the deer up by its hooves for several days to a week to allow enzymes to break down the tough connective tissue. Hunters inexperienced with this step in field dressing were reluctant to hang a deer longer than a few hours for fear the meat would spoil, but Tomahawk knew the exact hour to cut down his quarry and take it home for the table.

Never an avid hunter, Silas and his family greeted their visitors gratefully, and for the rest of the day they stayed to help butcher the carcasses and assist Jessica in distributing a good portion of the meat among the slaves. Before long, spits were turning in the yard of Somerset and the slave compound, the aromas of roasting meat from their individual fires mingling in the distance between them. As a reward for Jeremy and Tomahawk's labor and generosity, nothing would do but for them to remain for supper and a nip or two of blackberry wine.

Jeremy's largesse and Tomahawk's hunting skills led to including Henri in the Saturday ritual, but by then Jessica was living in town, leaving only the men to butcher, dry the meat for jerky, and encase the sausage. Plenty of food and drink, laughter, conversation, and horseplay suitable only for male company took the edge off the labor. Soon after, the fourth Saturday in the colder months was marked on the calendars in the Toliver, Warwick, and DuMont households as "Men's Day at Somerset."

So it was that Silas and his longtime friends and their sons gathered on a clear but frosty Saturday morning the last of October 1850. On these occasions, Silas wished he'd retained the log house now occupied by his overseer. The single-room log cabin he'd erected as an office and sleeping quarters in its place was too small for feeding and sheltering four grown men and six growing sons, but the ground outside was hard packed and suitable for setting up tables and chairs.

By early afternoon, the butchering had been done, and the spits were turning. A keg of ale from the tavern in town, already tapped, stood nearby, and pots of cocoa Jessica had sent along for the boys were keeping warm over the coals of the campfire.

Silas relished these moments of relaxation with his male com-

panions in the heart of his kingdom. He especially enjoyed sharing them with Thomas, now thirteen. The boy was so like him in
looks, manner, and bearing. As much as he searched and yearned
to find it, Silas had not discovered so much as a freckle of Jessica
in their son, a deficit she noticed, though Thomas loved her
dearly. Just this morning he'd come upon the two of them in the
kitchen, Jessica in her robe, Thomas in his hunting clothes. She'd
gotten up early to supervise the hampers of food they'd be taking
to the plantation. Thomas had come behind her and wrapped his
arms around his mother's waist to lay his chin on her shoulder.
He'd become of such a height he'd had to bend down to reach the
niche that had once accommodated his head so comfortably.

"You're too tall for that pillow now, Thomas," she'd said.

"I'm not ready to be," he said.

Thomas's reply had pleased her, Silas could tell. She turned
in the circle of his arms and wet her fingers with her tongue
to smooth the recalcitrant line of his black eyebrows, so like his
father's. As she looked at him, Silas saw the poignant gaze of
someone who must set a beloved bird free, nursed from a fledgling.

"Yes, you are," she said softly and drew his thickly thatched
head down to kiss his brow. "Enjoy your day with your father,
my son."

At such moments, Silas ached for his other son buried in the
local cemetery. Somerset would never have claimed Joshua's devotion as it had Thomas's. Joshua would have stayed close to
Jessica's side.

In a pensive mood, Silas stretched out his legs and laced his
hands over his still firm midriff to look over the heads of the
group gathered around the campfire. A small smile assured his
engagement in the banter without his really listening to it. With
the exception of the manor house he had imagined overlooking

his vast acres, his dream of Somerset had come to pass. There was still much to be done—land to acquire, slaves and animals and equipment to buy, buildings to enlarge, but the essence of the plantation had been established. Everything he owned was his free and clear, even if not all attained by his own hand. Nonetheless, he had no debts, and production had been so abundant the past years he'd been able to set aside a part of his profits not needed for expenses to pay back Carson Wyndham. This time he would not fail. He would not yield to any temptation to lure him from his goal. He figured it would take two more years to settle his account with a man for whom time had not softened his loathing. Silas hoped only that his father-in-law, now approaching seventy, lived long enough to receive his payment in full.

It was something Silas felt he must do: pay back Jessica's father to satisfy that small part of her heart never his. After all this time, Silas sensed that Jessica held a piece of herself in reserve that not all his loving and caring and giving could gratify. There was still that faint but lingering echo of how she'd come to be his wife in the first place and the question of whether he'd have wanted her if he'd had a choice. Silas was determined to put that doubt forever to rest. Having lost to death the stepson she'd loved like her own and the boy she'd birthed to a system she hated, Jessica would at least have the assurance that her husband wanted and desired no other woman beside him but her.

Silas moved his attention to the sons of his three friends. They were good-looking lads all, an amalgamation of their lovely mothers and handsome fathers. The oldest boys—Thomas and Jeremy Jr. and Armand—were as inseparable at thirteen as they had been in their nappy days. The second oldest—Henri's son Philippe and Stephen Warwick, aged twelve and eleven—had forged as tight and long a bond. Robert, the caboose of the Warwick train, somewhat of a worry because of a chronic bronchial condition, and Henri's exquisite little seven-year-old daughter, Nanette, were close in age and had been playmates, but at nine, Robert had moved beyond the little girl's company into the exalted sphere of his brothers and their friends. This was Robert's first year to join the all-male group at Somerset. Silas would like to have included Guy Handley in their gathering, but he had been hired as the teacher of the public school when it opened, and the boys—his students—would have found his presence restricting.

Conversation grew serious as it turned to the provisions of the Compromise of 1850, ratified by Congress and signed into law by President Fillmore in late September. All concurred that Texas had been favored. By the state giving up part of its territory, the United States had agreed to assume the debts of the former republic, a move that could only be good for Texas's economy. But one provision in the compromise disturbed Silas greatly. It admitted California into the Union as a free state, and now both houses of Congress were controlled by abolitionists.

The discussion was suddenly interrupted by the high pitch of barking dogs and the hard clop of horses' hooves headed in the direction of Somerset. It may have been Silas's imagination, but he thought he heard total silence fall over the slave compound a quarter of a mile away.

The men, women, and children housed there would recognize the sound. It was the din of patrols looking for escaped slaves. Silas and his guests were on their feet when a body of a half dozen men, led by Lorimer Davis, rode up. Silas did not miss the flicker in Lorimer's eye taking in the social gathering to which he and his son had never been invited. Though Thomas liked Jake, Silas had never quite taken to Lorimer or his wife. The planter had a mean streak in him. He liked to ply his whip too much, and Silas found Stephanie nauseatingly pretentious.

"'Afternoon, gentlemen," the planter said, tipping his hat. "Sorry to raise dust on your vittles, but we're looking for one of my blacks who ran away last night, and no ordinary field hand, either. He was my houseman at the plantation. That's loyalty for you. Mind if we search your slave compound? He couldn't have gotten far."

"I'll come with you," Silas said, setting down his tankard of ale. In no way would he have Lorimer and his thugs ransacking his workers' cabins looking for the man, scaring the liver out of them with their whips and guns. He was sorry to hear that the runaway was Ezekiel. The Davises' houseman had been with them a long time and had a kind way about him, especially with children. Thomas and his friends were fond of him. Silas could see the boys' distress in their arrested attention on the men.

"I will, too," Jeremy said, squaring his formidable shoulders in his woodsmen's jacket.

"And I as well," Henri volunteered and planted his strong figure next to Silas. "Boys," he said to their offspring, "you stay here and keep the fire going."

The search unearthed no escaped butler from the Davis plantation. The compound was left as it was found, and Silas's slaves, their gratitude to their humane master and his friends almost palpable in the presence of other men whose cruelty they could smell, went back to their dancing and turning spits. On the minds of all of them at Somerset—black and white—was the dreadful image of the punishment Ezekiel would receive when he was caught.

Chapter Forty-Eight

I was reminded of Thomas Jefferson's words in 1782 in his *Notes on Virginia* when I read that abominable tripe," Jessica said, speaking to Tippy of the Compromise of 1850 when her friend finished reading its articles reprinted in the *Democratic Telegraph and Register of Houston.*

Tippy reached to take a sandwich from the plate Jessica offered. "And they were?"

"Jefferson said, 'Indeed I tremble for my country when I reflect that God is just.'"

"Amen to that," Tippy said. "It's only a matter of a few years before the South feels the whip of that justice for enslaving the black man. All this compromise does is to buy time until war is declared between the North and the South. It's inevitable. The North will never abide by the Fugitive Slave Act, and the South will never tolerate its disobedience to it."

"God help us," Jessica said, attacked by the icy fear that knotted her stomach when she thought of the conflict in relation to her son and only child. Thomas was thirteen. In a few years he would be of conscription age.

"Oh, forgive me for blabbing so, Jessica," Tippy said, her look of distress reflecting the one on Jessica's face. "I forget what war would mean to you and Silas personally."

"Whether spoken or not, the truth is what it is, and I must live with it," Jessica said, pouring them another cup of Assam Gold from the rosewood Regency tea table. The tea, like the table and most of the furniture chosen for the elegant rooms of the Toliver mansion, were imported from England.

"We must have in our home those things that reflect our roots," Silas had said when the subject of furniture was discussed with Henry Howard, the renowned architect Carson had sent from Louisiana to design the Tolivers' manor home. Silas had not asked Tippy to be involved in its selection, but she mightily approved the choices the architect had made, especially for the morning room where she and Jessica often sat for afternoon tea.

"Perhaps by a miracle, my apprehensions will never be realized," Jessica said. "Silas maintains there will be no war. Our industry is too important to the North, he says. Their factories are too dependent on southern cotton to spin into cloth for their profitable foreign markets."

"What does Sarah say in her letters?"

Jessica sipped her tea, warm to her cold lips. "That the Abolitionist Movement cannot be stopped. In her view, war is coming. Her nephew Paul will be in the thick of it. He's graduated West Point and has been commissioned a second lieutenant in the United States Army."

Tippy stirred the sugar in her cup. "Lorimer Davis and his men came to my house looking for his escaped slave," she said. "He was sure the poor man would head to my place."

Jessica set down her teacup in horror. "How dare he! Did he abuse you?"

"Wrecked my house. Henri was out at Somerset with your husband and Mister Jeremy, or he'd have put a stop to it."

"I will certainly report this to Silas—"

"No, Jessica…please." Tippy put up a beseeching hand. "Let it lie. I didn't even tell Henri. I've restored order to my home, and all is well."

Furious, Jessica declared, "Oh, if I were only a man, I'd—"

Footsteps—boot heels on the polished walnut floors of the entrance hall—alerted them to Silas's arrival, and Tippy immediately changed the subject. "Henry Howard did a splendid job designing this house," she said. "When I went with Henri to New Orleans to help him dismantle his father's emporium—God rest the man's soul—I saw your architect's work in Baroness Pontalba's town houses in the French Quarter. Mr. Howard designed cast-iron railings for each verandah with the baroness's initials forged in the centers of them."

Jessica bit her lip. It saddened her to no end that Tippy did not feel at liberty to speak freely in her best friend's house before her husband. Tippy had never won Silas's heart, though he tolerated with great politeness her coming and going from his house—and by the front door. He'd never expressed it, but Silas's reserve toward Tippy suggested he could not accept the place his wife had accorded her in their home.

As usual, Jessica cooperated with Tippy's diplomacy. "How interesting," she said, as Silas entered the morning room.

"What's interesting?" he said.

Jessica turned to greet him and felt the leap of sensual pleasure still surprising after fifteen years of marriage and the differences they'd tolerated but never overcome. At forty-four, Silas was handsomer and more virile than ever. His lord-of-the-manor clothes suited his striking Toliver looks and tall, commanding figure. Along with Jeremy and Henri, he had spent the afternoon with other city council members in a meeting to apprise the owner of a proposed bank about Howbutker's architectural requirements for commercial buildings. There were numerous such meetings now that Howbutker was one of the largest and most prosperous towns in the state. At the urging of Silas, the first city-planning commission had pushed through a proposition in 1839 stating that public and commercial buildings be built in the Greek Revivalist style traditional to the South.

"I'll leave it to Jessica to explain," Tippy said, rising, as she always did in Silas's presence, a prelude to her immediate departure.

"Tippy came by to bring me a new invention called a safety pin," Jessica said, opening a box on a side table to show Silas its contents. "Henri managed to get a shipment, and naturally, Tippy had to share a few with me." She held up a fastening device made of wire, twisted in a circle at one end to form a spring and capped on the other with a metal hood to provide a clasp and protection from the sharp point.

"Very clever," Silas said when Jessica demonstrated its use. "Must you go so soon, Tippy?"

"I fear so, Mr. Toliver," Tippy said, the polite exchange an accustomed hail-and-farewell between them. They rarely exchanged more than a few words.

Jessica saw her to the door, and when she returned to the morning room, Silas had picked up the newspaper, left open at the page she and Tippy had been sharing. "You don't need to explain," he said. "This tells the gist of your conversation."

"May I pour you a cup?" Jessica said, ignoring the pointed observation, and spread the skirt of her watered-silk day dress to sit again at the tea table. The stiffly starched petticoats of former years had been replaced with lighter-weight crinolines that Jessica found easier to manage.

Silas took her hand and drew her back to her feet. "You may take me upstairs," he said, his meaning clear.

"What? In the middle of the afternoon?"

"Thomas won't be home until late evening. He and Jeremy

Jr. and Armand are out at Somerset helping Jasper and his men gather up the pigs for penning. Jasper will see they don't get into trouble. Besides"—Silas drew her closer—"I read the look in your eyes when I came into the room."

"What look?" Jessica said innocently, her breath lost in the racing of her heart. "I've no idea what you're talking about."

"Yes, you do, but I'll be happy to translate it through demonstration," he said, playing the sexual game they'd begun long ago at the Winthorp Hotel.

Before he led her toward the stairway, Jessica's glance fell on COMPROMISE in the blazing headlines of the newspaper. Compromise had preserved their marriage. Mutual tempering of their convictions allowed them to make love in the afternoon, and Silas could still take her to mountaintops beyond the clouds. But he and she were basically a country divided. Would war come between them when war finally came?

Chapter Forty-Nine

"I'm sorry to disturb your reading, Miss Jessica, but Mr. Handley is downstairs," Maddie said, addressing her mistress in the sitting room of the master suite where Jessica read most afternoons. "He says it's important that he speak with you."

"Oh, by all means, I'll go down, Maddie," Jessica said, delighted. She had missed the accessibility of her son's former tutor since he had moved from his apartment above the carriage house to a room in a boarding hotel nearer the school. "Prepare a tea tray, if you will, and perhaps I can entice him to stay awhile."

What absolutely perfect timing, Jessica thought, marking her place in the English translation of Marcus Aurelius's *Meditations*, recently mailed to her by Sarah Conklin. There was no better person with whom to discuss the Roman emperor's philosophical views than Guy Handley. What a humane and wise leader the ruler was—the last great emperor of Rome, remembered for his social reforms and laws that gave women and slaves more rights and protections. Those in the halls of power in the United States—whether it be Washington, D.C., or small burgs like Howbutker—could take a few cues from *him* in their thinking: "Let opinion be taken away, and no man will think himself wronged. If no man think himself wronged, then there is no more any such thing as wrong."

Now wasn't *that* food for minds to chew on in leaders who believed that dissenters should be muzzled, if not strung up from the nearest tree!

Descending the stairs, Jessica suddenly halted. Why would Guy Handley be calling on her on a weekday when school was still in session? Oh, God. It wasn't about Thomas, was it?

She hurried with quicker steps into the drawing room. Guy Handley stood before the fireplace, staring into the fire that had been stoked to full blaze to disperse the chill of the November afternoon. He was still in his overcoat, and his walking stick and hat were on a table within quick reach for departure. He did not mean to stay, then.

"Is it Thomas?" Jessica asked from the doorway.

Guy Handley turned quickly, and Jessica pressed her hand to the base of her throat at the sight of his expression. It was the kind of wooden look that presaged bad news. The former tutor of Houston Avenue stepped forward and put up a mollifying hand. "No—no," he said. "I apologize for my appearance giving a false impression."

"Where is Thomas?"

"Still in school with my other pupils. I left my assistant in charge. I have come on another matter, and time is of the most importance."

Jessica sank with relief into the nearest chair. She had brought the book of meditations with her and placed it on a table. "What matter?" she asked, short of breath.

"Jessica...I need your help."

He had never called her by her first name and wouldn't do so now, Jessica thought, if he were not in some sort of desperate straits.

"You have it if I can give it," she said.

"I—" He looked around at the open entrance into the hall and crossed to draw closed the heavy double doors.

"Good heavens, Guy," Jessica said softly. "What is it?"

"I want you to help me arrange the escape of a slave."

Her lips parted in shock. It was a few seconds before her breath returned. "Lorimer Davis's runaway," she said.

"Yes. Mr. Davis sold the man's wife to a planter in Houston, and he ran away in hopes of finding her. I've hidden him in a storage shed at the school, but he cannot stay cooped up there. I know I'm taking a terrible risk coming to you, and if you do not agree to help me, all I can hope for is that you do not raise the alarm."

"You're an abolitionist."

"I am."

"I *knew* it!" Jessica said, thumping the arm of the chair in triumph. "Are you a member of the Underground Railroad?"

"Yes."

Jessica got to her feet and held out her hand. "Shake. I'm an abolitionist, too. What do you want me to do?"

She saw him almost sway from gratitude as he shook her hand. "Will you hide the man—his name is Ezekiel—in my old apartment above the carriage house until I can make arrangements to get him to safety?" Guy asked.

"You think he'll be safe there?"

"I can't think of any place where the patrols would less likely look."

Jessica's mind raced. She thought back to that day at Willowshire when she and Willie May had hidden Jasper in the gazebo. Her father's men had searched every outbuilding without once considering that a slave would choose a hiding place so close to the Big House. From the vantage point of the carriage house, the runaway could look out a front window up the avenue directly onto the verandah of Lorimer Davis's town house. What a delicious irony.

"You're right," she said, taking back her hand. "I'll do it. You have no conveyance for transporting him. I propose that I pick up the man in my brougham once school is adjourned and bring him here."

Guy shook his head, his dire expression dispelled by an awed smile. "You're an amazing woman, Jessica Toliver. I knew I could trust you. That was my proposal as well, but what about Thomas? He'll be coming here after school."

"Only long enough to change clothes and saddle his horse," Jessica said, "then he and Jeremy Jr. and Armand are riding out to Somerset to help with the hog killing. My son and his father will not be home until early evening."

"What about the servants?"

"They can be trusted to say nothing to Silas and certainly not to Thomas if they should by chance discover Ezekiel. They're aware of a slave on the loose, and I heard Maddie at her prayers this morning asking God for his successful deliverance." There were no Lulus in this household, Jessica thought. She'd made sure of that.

"Splendid," Guy said. He picked up his hat and walking stick. "I must get back. I don't dare leave the man long in case someone should stumble upon him. Jessica...Mrs. Toliver...how can I ever thank you? With hope and luck, Ezekiel will be your guest for only a few days."

"You know, of course, what will happen to you if you're found out? They'll horsewhip you out of town."

"I know, but that pales in comparison to what they'll do to Ezekiel."

"You're a brave man, Guy Handley, and please call me Jessica," Jessica said.

Immediately after he left, Jessica sent Maddie off to Bess DuMont's house with a note asking for herbs not grown in the Tolivers' garden.

"What is anise?" Maddie asked, her frown puzzled. "How am I to use it?"

"It tastes like licorice, and I'm going to mix it in cookie dough."

"*You*, Miss Jessica? You ain't baked in years."

"Well, it's time I put my hand in a bowl again," she said, trying to curb her impatience.

The other servants had been assigned tasks to keep them in rooms at the front of the house and Jeremiah dispatched to do some weeding in the side garden out of sight of his mistress carrying blankets and a chamber pot to the carriage house.

When Thomas came home from school, hungry as usual, Jessica shooed him away from the untouched tea tray Maddie had prepared for Guy Handley, saying she'd wrap up the cake and sandwiches to take with him to Somerset.

"You should get out to the plantation while there's still enough light to be of use to your father," she said, a change in attitude that drew an odd look from her son. Thomas was accustomed to his mother prolonging their time together at every opportunity, but he seemed satisfied that she had calls to make. Earlier, Jessica had put together a hamper of food "to take to shut-ins," she'd explained to Maddie. The slave would be given the hamper to be spirited with him up the stairs and it would have to suffice until Jessica could find a safe time to replenish it. Thanks to Henry Howard, the architect, an extra set of stairs to the apartment had been built inside the carriage house to use in inclement weather, and the slave could easily and secretly slip from the brougham and disappear up into the deep darkness.

Jeremiah had her one-horse closed carriage hooked up and ready for her by the time Thomas and his friends cantered off down the boulevard. Guy had been watching for her and directed the horse to the door of the storage shed in back of the school. Their purpose was accomplished in less than a minute, but for the benefit of any person recognizing Jessica's personal conveyance parked in such an odd location, Guy unloaded a number of gardening tools he'd ostensibly asked to borrow.

Back on Houston Avenue, Jessica released her passenger to hurry up the stairs but did not accompany him. Jeremiah would be coming out to unhook the horse. Jessica hoped he did not smell the slave's strong musky scent mixed with sweat and fear that may have trailed after him.

"You'll find everything you need up there," Jessica had whispered to the runaway shortly before they arrived.

"I'm thankful to you, missus."

"Remember. No sound. Not a single one. No sneeze, cough, or movement, and no light. The barn is next to the carriage house, and my husband and son will be stabling their horses there at nightfall and coming and going during the day."

"Yes, ma'am."

She had met the man only on the few occasions the Davises entertained at their plantation home but knew his wife as Stephanie's personal maid in their house on Houston Avenue. "I'm sorry about your wife," Jessica said. "Perhaps…perhaps she will be well treated."

"The man was mean who bought her. *Oh, Della…!*" the man moaned.

How could Ezekiel have possibly hoped to rescue her, Jessica wondered, sickened to hear echoed in his anguish the enslaved black man's plight everywhere. That night as she lay beside her sleeping husband, her heart still pumping in her throat for the safety of the hapless occupant in the carriage house, Ezekiel's lamentation haunted her until dawn.

Chapter Fifty

Guy had said that within two days he would come for his "cargo" in the darkness of night with none in the house the wiser. He would take away all evidence of the slave's presence. It would be best if Jessica would forgo use of her carriage until he appeared at her door on some pretext to say that Ezekiel was away and clear—perhaps to lend her a book he thought might interest her.

It was late morning of the third day and Guy had not appeared. Jessica felt like a cat on a leash. She could not have said how many times she'd peered surreptitiously out the mansion's back windows giving a view of the gazebo, rose garden, and carriage house, careful not to arouse her husband's and son's curiosity. Guy could not have hidden the runaway at a more inopportune time. School had adjourned for the Thanksgiving holiday, and the cold and rainy weather had kept Thomas inside playing euchre, a card game, with Jeremy Jr., Armand, and Jake Davis. Even Silas left for the plantation later than usual each day. He'd hired a land manager to take over many of his duties at Somerset so that now he had more time to enjoy the life typical of the planter class. One of his pleasures of leisure was to stay late in bed with Jessica, but she was too wrought up to respond to his reason for doing so.

As the day lengthened, a series of anxious what-ifs stalked

Jessica like shadows. What if something had happened to Guy? What if he'd been caught and was unable to take possession of his cargo? What if Ezekiel were still in the carriage house? What if the odor of the full chamber pots could be smelled below the stairs? What if the man had run out of food and water?

"Miss Jessica, I declare, the last few days you actin' like a bird with nowhere to land," Maddie observed. "This weather gettin' into your insides?"

"That's it, Maddie," Jessica said. "I'm perishing to work in my garden."

"Your frettin' not goin' make that garden soil dry no faster. Why don' you go visit your friends? Jeremiah's rheumatism ain't botherin' him so much he can't hook up your buggy for you."

Listening to her, Jessica was struck by an inspiration. The servants were accustomed to her considerations. They would think nothing of her hooking up her horse to spare Jeremiah from having to aggravate the pain of his arthritic joints.

"Let him be," Jessica said. "If I wish to go out, I'll see to the carriage."

Now was the perfect time. Luncheon was over. The house servants were having their noon meal in the kitchen. Silas had left for the plantation, and Thomas had taken the card game up the street to the Davises. Jake reported that his father was still searching for their butler. Jessica drew on her bonnet and shawl and took up her umbrella.

She did not announce her departure to Maddie and slipped out a side-terrace door to walk around to the carriage house. Perhaps none in the house would notice she had gone. If she found Ezekiel still in the apartment, she would drive immediately to the boarding house to speak with Guy Handley. For anyone curious as to why the wife of Silas Toliver was visiting the young and handsome schoolteacher—she was thinking of Guy's nosey landlady—her excuse would be that she wished to invite him to join her family for Thanksgiving dinner.

With an effort Jessica drew back the heavy door to the carriage house. She'd have to leave it open to make good her intention to hook up the brougham should she be discovered, but the rain would shield her once inside. No human smell permeated the damp enclosure. Jessica waited and listened but heard only the rain pounding on the roof. Through the rain-lashed windows of the kitchen, lit by kerosene lamps, she could see the servants at their meal around the table, Jeremiah at its head, his back to her. It was highly unlikely anyone would notice the door to the carriage house open.

Quickly, Jessica climbed the stairs to the narrow landing and knocked on the door. "Anybody there?" she whispered.

No answer. She tried the door handle, freezing when she felt it resist the turn from inside. "Who's there?" she said louder.

She heard footsteps move hurriedly away from the door and opened it to find Ezekiel, wrapped in a blanket, hugging the far wall, eyes bulging with fright. Jessica expelled a pent-up breath.

"What are you still doing here?" she demanded, drawing inside but leaving the door open to alert her to the sound of someone entering below.

"The man, he did not come for me," Ezekiel said. "Did he not tell you?"

"I haven't heard a word from him."

"He say he send you a note."

"I didn't get it. That's why I'm here now—to learn what's happening."

The Negro drew the blanket tighter. "The man say it not safe to travel. My master and his dogs and patrols are about. The man say he come for me late tonight. Master Davis is supposed to be busy."

Playing poker with Silas, Jessica remembered. It was the third Wednesday of the month and Lorimer's turn to host in his town house. The game usually lasted past midnight. She looked about her. The slave had kept his "place" even here. He had not slept on the made-up bed but on a pallet of his belongings he'd made for himself on the floor. He had not eaten at the table but from the hamper, nor chanced firing up the Franklin stove, even though the temperature had dipped below freezing two of the nights he'd been confined. There was no smell of body odor or chamber pots. Under cover of darkness, he'd risked the back stairs to empty the pots and wash himself in the downpours of rain.

"When did you last see…the man?" Jessica had noticed the slave did not call Guy by name, nor would she. It was likely Ezekiel did not know that his conductor was the local schoolmaster. If caught, the slave could recognize Guy but not name him to his capturers.

"Around midnight last night. He brought food and a jacket," Ezekiel answered her. He opened the blanket to show her proof of his statement. "That was when he told me we'd leave tonight."

"The note you mentioned…you said he *sent* it to me."

"To tell you I was still here."

Jessica felt her skin crawl. The note would have been sent by a messenger, but who? And to whom had he given it? If one of the servants, Jessica would have been sure to receive it. Thomas, perhaps? Her son could easily have forgotten to give it to her. Had it been written in code to protect their clandestine activity? Where was that note now? Had it been intercepted or delivered to the wrong house?

"Do you have everything you need until you leave?" she asked.

Before he could answer, there were footsteps on the wooden stairs. Immediately, Ezekiel disappeared behind a curtain hung to conceal the chamber pots, but it was inadequate to cover the toes of his shoes. Jessica had only managed to turn toward the open door when Silas appeared on the threshold, rain dripping from his hat and overcoat.

"What in bloody hell?" he demanded.

Jessica stood motionless, her mouth locked open in dismay and shock. "How—how did you know I was here?" she managed to gasp.

"You mean other than you were nowhere in our home, the door to the carriage house was open, and your skirts left a water trail up the stairs? Where is he?"

"Where is who?"

"Guy Handley."

"Guy Handley?"

Silas swung his gaze toward the curtain enclosure and coldly inspected the gap from where the slave had withdrawn his exposed feet. In two long strides, he crossed to the curtain and yanked it aside.

"What in the name of God! *Ezekiel?*" Silas exclaimed, rearing back on his boot heels.

"Mister Toliver," Ezekiel greeted him weakly with a formal nod of his head as if he were receiving him at the Davis plantation.

"Silas, please," Jessica pleaded. She went to him and took hold of his chin to tear his shocked gaze from the slave attempting to maintain his dignity plastered to the wall among the chamber pots. "You must listen to me. If you turn Ezekiel over to Lorimer, you know what they'll do to him. Please, please, Silas, think if it were your wife. What would you do if I were sold away from you? Wouldn't you run away to find me, too?"

Silas lowered his bewildered gaze to her face. "What are you talking about?" he asked.

"Lorimer sold Ezekiel's wife to a planter in Houston, and he ran away to rescue her," Jessica explained.

"Where is Guy Handley?"

"I don't know."

"He's not here?"

Jessica swept the tip of her tongue over her dry lips. She must pretend ignorance of Guy's involvement until she was sure of what Silas knew.

"Why would he be?" she asked.

A deep flush mounted Silas's high cheekbones. "You're not—you're not…meeting him for a—a liaison?"

Understanding at last, Jessica stepped back indignantly. "Silas Toliver! Whatever would make you think such a thing?"

He withdrew a folded note from his pocket. "This," he said, handing it to her. "Not to mention you've been behaving… distant lately. I intercepted the boy delivering it. He said it was to be given only to you, but when I threatened him with my walking stick, he gave it to me."

Jessica read the note: *I'm afraid we will not be able to meet as planned. I will see you soon. Devotedly, Guy H.*

"Oh, dear." So the note had fallen into Silas's hands, and he'd mistaken its content. She had no choice now. Silas knew Guy Handley was implicated, either as her lover or a participant in the slave's escape. There was no protecting Guy's involvement. Jessica gazed up at her husband, feeling a deep plunge of sympathy for the anguish he must have endured, despite her certainty that if he turned Ezekiel over to Lorimer, their marriage would be over.

"It's not what you think," she said, running her fingertips over the flaming ridge of his cheekbone. "I could never be guilty of infidelity to you. Guy Handley is a conductor for the Underground Railroad. He came to me for help in keeping Ezekiel from Lorimer's henchmen until he could be taken to safety. Guy was to come to the house to let me know his mission had been accomplished, but apparently, he's run into a problem. If I'm going to be hanged, I want it to be for the correct crime."

Silas closed his eyes and breathed in slowly. "God, Jessica, you are the death and life of me. When I read that note, I thought the worst...." He glanced at the slave, pinned to the wall by fear, eyes stark as an animal's caught in a trap. Silas turned to his wife. "Am I never, ever to be spared the rod of your will? What do you want me to do?"

"You'll help?" she asked, not daring to hope.

"I will not interfere with Ezekiel's escape."

"You mean it, Silas? You're not going to turn him over to Lorimer?"

"Lorimer can get mired in his own mud trying to find him," Silas said. "He'll get no help from me."

"Bless you, Mr. Toliver," Ezekiel said and crumpled, sobbing, to the floor.

Chapter Fifty-One

He had never looked into a slave's eyes before, not unless he was looking for proof of innocence or guilt, health or sickness. Silas did not pay attention to symptoms of pain or sorrow, want or hope or hungers of the spirit in his slaves. It was not the purview of masters, or in their best interests, to concern themselves with the feelings of their servants, but Silas could not expunge the look in Ezekiel's eyes after Jessica had admonished him to put himself into the man's shoes. *Think if it were your wife. What would you do if I were sold away from you? Wouldn't you run away to find me, too?*

"I raise you one, Silas. Silas? Didn't you hear me? I raise you one."

"What? Oh, yes, of course. Too rich for me. I fold."

"Where have you gone in your thoughts tonight, *mon ami?* Your travels are costing you dearly," Henri commented quietly beside him.

"I have much on my mind, Henri," Silas replied as quietly.

"And the heart, if I'm not mistaken."

"You are too wise, Henri."

There were six seated at the poker table, four planters, of whom Silas was one, and Jeremy and Henri. The smoke was thick and the talk voluble. Lorimer Davis liked to entertain his friends lavishly, so the humidor of hand-rolled cigars was open, the whiskey decanters constantly replenished, and the buffet laden with the best from his larder. Silas had helped himself to a Cuban cigar but had taken little advantage of the food and drink. Earlier, the conversation had centered mainly on Lorimer's elusive runaway and his whereabouts.

"We think he's taken off to Houston to find that wife of his," Lorimer said, "but he won't be at large for long. All the patrols and marshals and bounty hunters from here to Houston have been alerted, including Damon Milligan, the planter who bought Ezekiel's wife. Damon will be on the lookout for him."

"Does the boy know where to find her?" Silas had asked.

Lorimer rolled his eyes. "Yes, thanks to the misguided intentions of my wife. Stephanie felt sorry for the boy and had Damon write down the name of his plantation and mailing route in front of Ezekiel. She wanted to prove to him she knew where to send his wife a letter on his behalf now and then."

"That was nice of her," Jeremy said.

Lorimer shrugged and made a face. "I shouldn't have indulged her, but I'd just sold away the best maid she ever had. What else could I do? The minute Damon laid eyes on Della, he wanted her, and he made me an offer I couldn't refuse. But if I hadn't been so blamed permissive, the boy wouldn't have known where to head and probably wouldn't have run away."

"You can't blame yourself for your good heart, Lorimer," one of the planters said.

Talk had settled on other matters, little of which had penetrated Silas's inner contemplation. His eye kept straying to the mantel clock and the slow progression of the large hand toward midnight, the hour the party would break up and the men would walk to their various homes along Houston Avenue. Surely by now Ezekiel had been whisked away. The night was in his favor. The rain had cleared, but the sky was still overcast, shrouding the moon and stars. Silas had heard no dogs barking. That was a good sign.

Silas's private exchange with Henri was drowned out by the loud voice of Lorimer expounding on the traitorous nature of the black man.

"You can't trust 'em. Not a single one. Now some of you at this table might disagree with how I treat my slaves, but I tell you, that if you handle 'em too leniently or give 'em too much they'll turn on you. My houseman is a good example of that truth. I treated that boy with respect and gave him everything a slave could ask for. A good roof over his head, plenty of food, a position in my household, and how does he repay me—"

"But you sold his wife, Lorimer," Silas quietly interrupted the man's speech to remind him.

Lorimer gaped at him, his mouth frozen open in midsentence. An uncomfortable silence dropped over the table. The other players kept their eyes on their cards.

Lorimer found his voice. "Well, what difference does that make?"

"The difference is, he loved her," Silas said.

"How the hell do you know?" Lorimer demanded.

"Don't we all love our wives?"

Looking dumbfounded, Lorimer clamped his mouth shut, and a few seconds passed before he seemed to find the proper ammunition to load his verbal gun. He drew back his shoulders and took aim. "We are white men," he pontificated. "White men love their wives. Black men merely copulate. They are not capable of the finer feelings associated with love. Therefore, the relationships between them and their women are of no consequence. Do you not agree, gentlemen?"

All but one of his fellow planters nodded their heads. Silas tapped the table with a finger. "I'll take one card."

Walking out together into the dark night at the conclusion of the card game, Jeremy said to Silas, "What was that all about in there?"

"Damned if I know myself, Jeremy."

"You have made an enemy of Lorimer Davis."

"No loss," Silas said.

The cold air cleared Silas's head as he walked along the red-brick avenue. He was the only one of his five neighbors who lived in his direction, and he was glad to be alone. What had possessed him to challenge Lorimer as he had done? He wouldn't change the man's treatment of blacks if he opened his head and threw in white wash. Silas had easily read the question everyone's expression had posed, including Jeremy's and Henri's. Were Jessica's abolitionist sympathies rubbing off on him? No, his wife's personal persuasions had no effect on him. He had simply grown tired of Lorimer's dogmatic oratory and wanted to prick the man's insufferable pomposity.

He awoke before daybreak the next morning and found Jessica missing when he reached for her in their bed. Silas knew where she'd gone and awaited the report. Ten minutes later, she burst into their bedroom, still in her robe and announced, "He's gone. There's no sign that he was ever there. Thank God. Do you suppose Guy will contact us today?"

The schoolmaster tugged the bellpull as they were at breakfast, and the Tolivers rose from their hot cereal flavored with ginger and honey to welcome their visitor in the library, ordering their son not to leave the table. In the paneled room, the former tutor put out his hand to Silas.

"Mr. Toliver, Ezekiel told me what you did—or, rather, didn't do, and I am most grateful to you, sir. I suppose you now know…what else I do besides teach."

"You'll have to leave the county, Mr. Handley."

"I am aware of that. Thank you for not betraying me."

"I cannot say that I won't if you stay."

"I understand."

"Guy," Jessica said, "is Ezekiel on his way to safety?"

"He has been conducted to a station house awaiting transport into Louisiana and from there he'll be taken to a ship setting sail for the north, but he says he's not going without his wife. I have no way to rescue her, and I'm afraid Ezekiel will try the impossible again."

"What?" Silas exclaimed. "Is the man mad?"

Guy raised a brow. "You have to ask, Mr. Toliver, a husband as devoted as you?"

Silas traded looks with Jessica, the woman he could not live without, and saw all hope for Ezekiel fade in her eyes. Silas had suffered a bad night getting reacquainted with his conscience. He knew what he must do. He turned to Guy. "Can you keep Ezekiel wherever he is for a few days more?"

"Why, I—yes, yes, I suppose I can," Guy stammered.

"And is there space in your getaway plans for his wife?"

"Yes, of course. Why? What are you going to do?"

"I'm going to go to Houston to fetch Ezekiel's wife."

Jessica was seated. She looked at him with the puzzled gaze of the hard-of-hearing struggling to make sense of sound. Silas pulled her to her feet and took her into his arms.

"Jessica, I've tried for years to save money to pay back your father the sum he gave me to start up Somerset and for all of this"—with his head he indicated the house—"but I've given in to the temptation to spend the savings on the needs of the plantation. Now I have an amount set aside that will satisfy most of the amount I owe him, but if I buy Ezekiel's wife to return her to him I will deplete those funds, and there may not be time to recoup them before your father's death. Do you understand what I'm saying to you?"

Comprehension slowly widened the dark brown eyes. "You've...been saving money to pay back my father—for—for me?"

"I wanted to prove to you that after New Orleans, I would have stayed married to you without his money."

"And you are going to use...your savings to buy back Ezekiel's wife?"

"I'm sure Damon Milligan will state a price that requires every cent of it."

"Why?" Jessica asked, her voice strained with disbelief. "Why would you buy back Ezekiel's wife?"

"Because if you had been sold, I would stop at nothing to get you back. That's why I know Ezekiel is going to get himself killed."

"Oh, Silas..." Jessica's arms stole around his waist and, with a deep sigh, she closed her eyes and laid her head on his chest beneath the shelter of his chin. The moment gave Silas the feeling of a ship coming home to harbor at last. "Silas..." she murmured again, and he could feel her tears through the linen of his shirt.

Chapter Fifty-Two

A tenuous sun continued to shine over the town of Howbutker and the fortunes of the Tolivers, Warwicks, and DuMonts for the next decade. Sunny times of peace and bliss were interspersed with far-off rumblings of war threats and the tragedies natural to the hand of man and nature. The community burgeoned. The region, with Howbutker its hub, continued to draw land-hungry settlers, among them planters from the southern states who believed that if war was declared between the North and the South, its ramifications would not reach Texas. New businesses seemed to spring up monthly in the town and within a few years, the county seat of red-bricked streets and Grecian-columned buildings could boast of having among its professional residents two doctors, three lawyers, an architect, two public school teachers, a steam engineer, and one artist. Other sources of community pride were the three churches, four-room public school, county library, post office, and newspaper building spread along the spoke streets leading to the courthouse circle, but reigning supreme at its commercial axis was the DuMont Emporium.

By force of public demand, the gilt-and-glass, mahogany-and-marble showplace expanded to occupy a city block. In early 1856, prior to Texas's fifth governor, Elisha Marshall Pease, moving into the newly built governor's mansion in Austin, his wife,

Lucadia, came to visit Henri with hope he could advise her on furnishings for the two-story, buff-colored brick residence of Greek Revival design that she described as a "drafty hull of a place." The $2,500 allocated by the Texas Legislature for furnishings did not go far, but Henri and Tippy did their best. The amazing results were so admired by those who entered the governor's residence that a society reporter for the *State Gazette* of Austin felt compelled to write that "those embarking on any endeavor of social consequence should first visit the DuMont Emporium in Howbutker, Texas, to consult with its exceptionally astute proprietor and his talented assistant."

Such remarks added to the store's growing reputation as the final stop and say before purchasing anything from women's undergarments to cutlery for the dining room table. By the end of the decade, Henri's once-upon-a-time two-room general store had become Texas's leading arbiter in fashion apparel and home décor.

The Warwick Lumber Company saw its business expand as well, though its full coffers were due partly to Jeremy's quiet investments in commercial enterprises beyond his first love of mining timber. In 1843, while on a visit to New Orleans where he had taken his wife and brood to visit her parents, he met a New York University professor named Samuel B. Morse. The portrait painter was on a stump to raise money to fund the production of a machine he'd invented, called a telegraph, that could successfully send messages across wires utilizing electricity. Jeremy understood its potential, liked what he heard, and invested in the Morse Telegraph Company. Within six years, his investment had quadrupled and the price of his stock in the company had soared.

Beginning in 1858, Jeremy experienced similar financial rewards when he joined a team of New York financiers to invest in a factory that produced a long-lasting canned milk derivative that needed no refrigeration. The process was developed and patented by a one-time resident of Texas named Gail Borden, who had created the state's first topographical map. The sales of Borden's condensed milk took off and led to the opening of other condensed milk factories in New York and Illinois that generated enormous revenues for the company's initial investors. While the results of these financial risks provided the luxuries his wife so enjoyed, Jeremy considered himself first and foremost a lumberman with continuing faith that one day his company would stand in the forefront of one of the greatest industries in Texas.

Cotton production, and subsequently Somerset and the planter culture, flourished in the 1850s, despite the Panic of 1857 when the era of prosperity in the western and northern parts of the country came to an abrupt if temporary end. Demand for cotton in the United States, Mexico, and Great Britain was at an all-time high, ushering in the golden age of the plantation system and sparing the South and East Texas from the recession that affected other unrelated industries. Somerset led the region in feeding the jaws of the ever-increasing number of northern factories and textile mills that chewed up the raw bales of "white gold" and spun them into cloth. The phrase "Cotton is king" was coined in the middle of the decade, an apt description of a cash crop that accounted for one-half of all U.S. exports and strengthened Silas Toliver's belief that war would never come.

"The North needs the South to keep a stabilized economy, and how in the world can it do that if slavery is abolished?" he would ask to wave away the argument of those who debated otherwise.

While some of the town's leaders and the Tolivers' friends took heart from Silas's confidence, the majority did not. Throughout the decade, the South—to which Texas was aligned tight as a hipbone—endured what the region considered a glove constantly slapped in its face. Books and articles attacking slavery appeared in increasing numbers. The most inflammatory of these was the 1852 publication of *Uncle Tom's Cabin*, an anti-slavery novel taken by the free states as a true and accurate depiction of the brutal system on which the South's economy and planter class were built. Harriet Beecher Stowe's work of fiction enraged the pro-slavery states, which the *Democratic Telegraph and Register* denounced as "flagrantly biased and totally untrue" and further diminished Southern desire for a peaceful settlement of their differences with the North.

Ongoing troubles resulting from the refusal of the free states to abide by the Fugitive Slave Act, enacted in 1850, were another major source of conflict and rubbed raw the South's growing frustration with its Northern neighbors. The new law created a force of federal commissioners empowered to pursue runaway slaves in any state in the U.S. and mandated citizens to assist in their capture. To protect the fugitives, some Northern states reacted by passing Personal Liberty Laws that nullified the federal act and infuriated Southerners who regarded their passage as unconstitutional.

In its state legislatures, the South pondered how it could remain part of a union that blatantly made a mockery of the Constitution's preamble, which clearly stated that the role of government was to "insure domestic tranquility" and "promote the general welfare" when Northern political leaders encouraged the harboring of fugitives, slave insurrections, anti-slavery riots, the spread of biased propaganda, and the undermining of Southern laws. In other words, how could the South continue to abide the North's elected representatives doing everything in their granted powers to destroy its domestic tranquility and general welfare? How could the homeland not stand by the doctrine expressed in the Declaration of Independence that "whenever any form of government becomes destructive of the ends for which it was established, it is the right of the people to alter or abolish it, and to institute new government"?

The general opinion was that eventually the slave states would have had enough of the high-handed practices of the North and secede from the Union. On Houston Avenue, dubbed "Founders' Row" by residents of lesser distinction, such discussions raised chills along the backbones of mothers, and some fathers, whose sons, should the bugle sound, would be of age and have more reason than any to fight for their heritage and way of life.

But the threat of secession and war talk remained only that, and while the citizens of Howbutker kept an eye on the horizon for clouds of the gathering conflict, they continued to bask in the benevolent sun of prosperity, progress, and relative peace.

There were deaths. In 1853, New Orleans was struck by an epidemic of yellow fever in which over five thousand residents died. Of their number were Camellia Warwick's parents. Attending the funeral, the Warwicks learned that Henry and Giselle Morgan, proprietors of the Winthorp Hotel who had remained friends with Henri's family, had also died from the mosquito-spread virus. In February of 1854, a letter arrived from Eunice Wyndham to inform Jessica that Willie May had "passed away peacefully in her sleep." Jessica was never to forgive her mother for not telegraphing the news immediately upon Willie May's death so that Tippy could attend the funeral.

On August tenth, 1856, while attending a debutante ball at a Gulf Coast resort on Last Island off southern Louisiana, fifteen-year-old Nanette DuMont was swept out to sea when an Atlantic hurricane engulfed the island. Her body was never recovered. The families were devastated at the loss of the beautiful girl who had been like a daughter to all of them. In honor of her memory, Henri and Bess turned out to pasture her horse Flight O'

Fancy that Nanette had ridden in English side-saddle competitions, never to be ridden again.

Tomahawk Lacy rode off to hunt deer in the late fall of 1858 and did not return. Two weeks later, Jeremy headed a search party to scour the woods of the Creek's favorite hunting grounds and found the bloody remains of his body, identified only by his boots and rifle. It was assumed the faithful scout had come to sorrow in the powerful arms and jaws of a grizzly bear.

The founders of Howbutker grieved their losses but rejoiced in the treasures of children and family and friends remaining to them in an age of cholera and malaria and yellow fever, of the still-prevalent threat of Indian attacks and the constant danger of slave uprisings. They took pleasure in the diversions of arranging art shows and musical festivals and theater productions that their fortunes and status required they bring to the community. They had the means and leisure to enjoy books and magazines, reading and poker clubs, parties, dances, and masquerade balls typical of their class. They had the luxury of traveling by improved steam boat and railroad to social events in New Orleans, Houston, and Galveston in a fraction of the time it took to go by horse and coach.

As the 1850s advanced, startling announcements of new inventions such as the sewing machine, the pasteurization of milk, and the rotary washing machine appeared in Howbutker's newspaper, leaving the residents shaking their heads over the marvels of the age in which they were living. Surely no rational country with so brilliant a future would ruin its progress with the outbreak of war, voices of reason maintained.

But as the decade grew to a close, in December of 1859 a firebrand abolitionist who had led a raid on the United States Federal Arsenal at Harpers Ferry, Virginia, was hanged for his intent to provide arms to slaves to mount an armed resistance against their white masters. John Brown had been found guilty of treason against the Commonwealth of Virginia, the murder of five pro-slavery advocates, and instigating a slave rebellion. In the North he was praised as a martyr for the cause of freedom; in the South he was vilified as a madman and a murderer deserving of the hangman's noose. Many important writers of the day—from the South, William Gilmore, Mary Eastman, and John Pendleton Kennedy; and from the North, Henry David Thoreau, Ralph Waldo Emerson, and Walt Whitman—weighed in with their opinions in defense of or against the hanging, but it was Henry Wadsworth Longfellow's comments that raised goose pimples over Jessica Toliver's skin. The famous poet predicted of the execution: "This is sowing the wind to reap the whirlwind, which will soon come."

PART THREE

1860–1879

Chapter Fifty-Three

In August of 1860, a stranger emerged from around the carriage house of the Toliver mansion and addressed Maddie as she was hanging wash on a clothesline. "Mornin', aunty," he said. "Is the lady of the house at home?"

Maddie had never experienced a white man tipping his hat to her. She had the feeling the man had been hanging around the outbuildings of the grounds for some time watching her and the maids at work on washing day. A thread of suspicion wove through her. There was something not quite proper about him, though she couldn't have put her finger on it. He was a handsome man, presentably dressed in a suit and clean shirt, and had a pleasing manner, perhaps too much so to a black woman. Why had he entered the grounds from the pasture road in back of the house rather than from Houston Avenue?

Maddie responded on impulse, hoping the maids, who had ceased work to give the tall, red-haired stranger their attention, would not dispute her lie. Miss Jessica was alone in the house. "No, suh, she isn't. I be happy to take a message for her."

"When will she be in?"

"Not for some time, suh."

The man cast a furtive look at the gazebo, and, alarmed, Maddie wondered if he was considering waiting there for her mistress to return. "Then I suppose I'll have to call again," he said.

"Your name, suh?"

"It doesn't matter," he said, moving off quickly.

Maddie waited until she heard the gate creak before returning to the washtubs.

She would have reported the incident to Jessica, but not long after the man had left, she felt faint of heart and sat down in a back porch chair to fan herself. She closed her eyes and released a sigh. One of the maids found her a short while later, her hand still clutching the straw fan, caught in its final movement upon the earth.

In the cries that went up and the hubbub following her death, the man who had appeared mysteriously in the backyard that morning was forgotten, but a store clerk making a delivery by way of the pasture and service road behind the row of mansions spotted him leaving the Toliver property. The clerk, who knew everybody in town, had never seen him before, a position dangerous for strangers in Howbutker at that time. Local forces were about that did not take kindly to persons of unknown identity traveling around the countryside.

In July, a blaze had started in a small drugstore in Dallas and quickly spread to burn down most of the town's business district. In the already charged political atmosphere of secession and war talk, exacerbated by a prolonged heat wave that had tempers soaring, suspicions flared that the fire had been set by abolitionists. Similar fires had already destroyed parts of several Texas towns, and a document had been found and interpreted as proof that their cause was the work of roving bands of radical anti-slavery groups bent on using fire, assassination, and destruction of personal property to influence public opinion against Texas remaining a slave state. The groups were suspected of arranging slave escapes, stealing livestock, burning gins, barns, and fields, and poisoning wells. Fear was rampant that a plot had been hatched for a full-scale slave uprising. The match that had lit the powder keg was the conflagration in Dallas. Paranoia spread, whipped up by newspaper headlines screaming of acts of outrageous vandalism, whether accurate or not, and articles written by excitable editors calling for immediate and merciless punishment of the perpetrators. Overnight, secretive bodies and vigilante groups, acting without jurisprudence, formed to investigate and interrogate anyone suspected of being a slave agitator or supporter of the Northern cause. Hapless parties were subjected to terrifying treatment, and if they were not convincing of their innocence, more times than not they were hanged from the most convenient tree.

The clerk slowed his wagon to take a long look as the man mounted his horse, noting how he pulled his hat farther down on the exposed side of his face as they passed. The wagon driver was little more than a boy and riding alone. He was punier in size than the rider. Otherwise, the clerk would have stopped and questioned him. He must be satisfied with the report he'd take to the leader of the vigilance patrol of which he was a proud member. At the meeting tonight, he would tell Mr. Lorimer Davis about seeing a stranger on the road outside the Tolivers' mansion and keep the fuzzy picture of him clearly inside his head for future identification.

A few weeks later, Jessica joined her reading club in Bess DuMont's Louis XIV–influenced drawing room, her first outing since Maddie's death. In meetings during happier years, social-hour conversation preceding the book discussion revolved around lighthearted subjects. A tacit rule of the club was that depressing topics such as death, health and political issues, complaints of children, husbands, and in-laws be left at home. But today talk of the merits of the fashionable hooped petticoat over heavier, hotter, multiple crinolines could not keep at bay an anxious discussion of rumors that a conspiracy was in the works to arm slaves for a statewide revolt. Unspoken but deeply felt and shared among the planters' wives, the majority in the room, was the terror of sexual assault by black men seeking revenge against their husbands. It was a fear they and their daughters had lived with since marrying into the planter society, and it explained why some of them chose to live in town away from their plantations.

"Lorimer has taken to mandating that all our slaves learn the ten commandments," Stephanie Davis announced. "He has them recite each one every Sunday morning with stress on 'Thou shalt not kill.'"

"I'm sure that's very effective," Bess DuMont commented, winking at Jessica over the rim of her tea glass.

"And more powerful than the example he sets, I'm sure," Jessica could not resist remarking, but regretted her outburst immediately. She should not have come today. She was in no frame of mind to be sociable. Many concerns weighed heavily upon her heart, and a series of sleepless nights had left her irritable. She felt the pinch of her corset, which she'd taken to discarding when at home, and the wire cage of her new hoop skirt made it impossible to find a comfortable sitting position. The heat in the room was stifling, unrelieved by the constant motion of her fan and the waft from the rotation of the DuMonts' newfangled ceiling units that were somehow driven by a water system that turned the two blades.

"What do you mean?" Stephanie demanded.

"We're all aware of how handy Lorimer is with whip and rope, Stephanie. That's all I'm saying."

"But implying so much more," Stephanie rejoined, her eyes snapping. "Most people around here consider the whip and rope tools of justice which we're all aware *your* husband seems opposed to using. Lorimer was so disappointed when Silas refused to join his vigilance patrol. Perhaps he has no interest in keeping peace and order."

"Perhaps he has no interest in circumventing the law," Jessica returned.

A shocked silence filled the room. All eyes were upon the two women, who, metaphorically speaking, looked to have removed their dainty gloves for bare-knuckled combat. Not an ice chip tinkled; not a silk skirt rustled.

"I've been meaning to ask, if you'd be so kind to answer, Jessica," Stephanie continued with no apparent intention of letting the matter drop, "who was your male visitor of a couple of weeks ago? He was not one of us. He was quite unknown to our delivery boy when he saw him skulking out your back fence gate. My husband would like to know. He's interested in strangers in town, especially those who call at the Toliver residence in times like these."

Jessica set down her tea glass and laid to rest her accordion fan. "Perhaps you'd be kind enough to tell me what you're talking about, Stephanie. There has been no stranger call at our house."

"Apparently not at the front door. Otherwise, why would he leave from the back gate?"

"I'm sure I couldn't say. Maddie would know, but she has left us."

"How very convenient."

"Ladies!" Bess DuMont popped up. "Shall we begin the discussion of *The Mill on the Floss*? I can relate the most divine information about the author, George Eliot. *He* is really a *she*. The author's name is Mary Anne Evans...."

Jessica wasn't listening. Stephanie may spread gossip, but she didn't create it. Now she recalled that one of the maids had mentioned Maddie having died "right after she talked to a white, red-haired man in the backyard." In the shock of her grief, Jessica had dismissed the man as probably a vagrant looking for a handout and thought no more about it. Lorimer saw potential abolitionists lurking behind every shrub and tree, and, as Stephanie had not so subtly hinted, must have speculated the worst about the Tolivers' backyard visitor. Jessica would question the maid when she returned home, but good heavens! Had Guy Handley, from wherever he was based now, sent an emissary to enlist her aid for the Northern cause?

Chapter Fifty-Four

Mounted on his horse, Silas looked out over the drought-ridden expanse of Somerset from his favorite spot on the plantation. His vantage point did not allow a full view of his three thousand acres, but it allowed a vista that gave a sense of the width and breadth of his domain. In the past, the scene filled him with such joy of possession that sometimes when alone, he would shout his exhilaration to the sky. At other times, he rode to this place for its serenity and quiet when he required balm for his soul. Today, the land stretching in his line of vision left his spirits as bone-dry as the endless rows of burned, nubby stalks under his gaze. Today, he felt no peace here in this, his Gilead, and wouldn't for a long time to come.

It was late October 1860.

On his Appaloosa beside him, Thomas said, "Hard to look at, isn't it, Papa?"

"In more ways than one," Silas said. The devastation was harder for Thomas, Silas recognized. Thomas had not lived through as many of Mother Nature's attacks on men's labors as his father, and this one had been the most vicious either had ever encountered. Out of the blue, Silas thought of Morris. His brother would ascribe some apocalyptic meaning to the destruction before him, probably taken from the Book of Revelation, and he

could be right. The drought of the miserable summer just passed
could be a prediction of the doomsday to come.

The year had started calmly, but cruelly deceptive, as things
had turned out. Never had East Texas planters and farmers seen
their crops so green and lush, so full of promise of an abundant
harvest to come. March had delivered the perfect amount of rainfall and sunshine, and its winds, the dreaded enemy of fine, aer-
ated soil and seeds planted just under the surface of the ground,
had been surprisingly mild. They had all gloated, but as April
and May passed without a drop of rain, hope for even a small
yield faded utterly when June ushered in a blistering heat wave
that had scorched the dry earth until hardly a stalk of cotton,
blade of wheat, barley, or corn was left to wither in the hot, dusty
winds—a harbinger of the ruin that would surely lay waste to
Texas and the southern states should they secede from the Union.

Reading his "heart thoughts," as Jessica called them, Thomas
said, "You think secession is inevitable, Papa?"

"As certain as I am that in time rain will come."

"And then war?"

"And then war." Silas could no longer deny it. If secession
came, war would follow. The senator from Illinois, Abraham
Lincoln, had been nominated as the Republicans' candidate for
president and in all likelihood would win. He'd made his political
position clear in a speech delivered to Congress in June of 1858
when he stated that "a house divided against itself cannot stand.
I believe this government cannot endure permanently half slave
and half free." As president of the United States, Lincoln had
vowed he would not compromise on the issue of slavery nor recognize the legitimacy of secession.

"The handwriting is on the wall, son," Silas said. "The South
will secede whether Mr. Lincoln's administration approves or
not. Southern firebrands will never stand for a central govern-

ment overruling states' rights, and men like your grandfather and Texas planters who settled the republic would rather die than submit to any legislative body that would destroy their forebears' way of life." Silas drew in a deep breath of cool fall air, the first relief from the summer heat, but it only aggravated the needles of anxiety in his chest.

Again his son read his thoughts. "What makes you so sure war will come?"

"The Republican abolitionists are determined to free the slaves in this country, and Lincoln is determined to keep the country intact. The South believes it has the legal authority to hold slaves and the constitutional right to secede. The different attitudes make for a lethal conflict. War is inevitable, and the North will win."

Thomas readjusted himself in his saddle, a sign of inner disturbance to his father. "Why?"

"Because it has everything the South and Texas do not."

Silas swatted at a persistent fly buzzing around his head, an annoyance to his enjoyment of the pleasant breeze drying the sweat from his face. "It has industries, railroads, factories, and a huge and ready source of manpower provided by massive immigrations from Europe. The South has a smattering of cities, no railroads to speak of, little immigration, and few factories—all factors that will work against us in a war with the North."

"What will happen then?"

Silas released his horse's reins to allow him to nibble at the few blades of grass. He blamed himself for Thomas, at twenty-three, not being better informed of the explosive civil situation looming over his future and his very life. Thomas did not show interest in matters that did not pertain to the growing of cotton. He religiously read the *Cultivator*, a periodical published in New York for farmers, and devoured every article in newspapers pertaining to the most recent agricultural techniques and advances in farm machinery, but he was not one to pay much attention to current political events. Silas had seen no reason to muddle his mind with articles of bleak forecasts that might never come to pass. Over Jessica's wise counsel, even at the dinner table, the only opportunity for family discussion, he had avoided talking of the growing conflict.

"What can Thomas do about it?" he'd said to Jessica.

"To be forewarned is to be forearmed," she'd said.

"Forearmed? With what?"

"A plan to save the plantation from the destruction the changes will bring if war comes."

Silas watched a prairie falcon swoop down to snatch a lizard in hasty retreat—an appropriate image of the crisis at hand, he thought. "Lincoln will emancipate the slaves, and the plantation system will be over," he answered his son. "The way of life we enjoy now will be extinguished."

Thomas stared off across the distance with a hardening of his Toliver jaw. He had reached his full height and breadth of shoulders, a man in every way, but Silas could not let go of the memory of him as a callow youth, uncomplicated and trusting, innocent of the world that lay beyond Somerset. Silas blamed himself for that, too.

"You have only yourself to thank that he lives for and would die by the plantation," Jessica told him. "Isn't that devotion what you wanted from your son?"

"Yes, but not to the exclusion of everything else."

"He will have to learn, like his father did, that there is more to love than land and growing cotton," she said.

Silas, too, could read his son's thoughts. Thomas was imagining Somerset—his inheritance, land of his father, the one and only occupation he felt born to—gone to ruin.

"So what will there be to come home to?" Thomas asked.

It was the question Silas had anticipated, and its answer was the reason he'd asked his son to meet him out here today in this spot of solitude and reflection. Because of course if there was a war, Thomas would go. He would not exercise his legal right to hire another to go in his place, as was his option as an only son of a wealthy man. It was that numbing certainty that kept Silas and Jeremy and Henri up at nights working long in their studies to occupy their minds, leaving their wives as sleepless in their beds. Silas lost his breath sometimes visualizing his son in the midst of battle, vulnerable to a rifle shot, a knife blade, imprisonment, torture, death. Food stuck in his throat, sweat broke out, blood rushed to his head, his speech stopped in midthought whenever he envisioned all the ills that could befall his only child on the battlefield.

And his sleep was never without the haunt of his mother's prediction.

"We must give him a reason beyond us and himself to stay alive," Jessica had said.

"Like what?" Silas had demanded, feeling the strain of his sleep-deprived eyes glued upon his wife.

"You must save the love of his life for him."

"Somerset."

"You know what you must do to preserve it, Silas."

"Yes, thanks be to you, Jessica."

And so, following Jessica's proposal of long ago, Silas had formed a plan for the salvation of Somerset when the backbone essential to its survival was no more. The plantation—the certainty that it awaited him—would serve as a vision for Thomas to hold on to that might see him safely home. Such a vision had worked for Silas in coming to Texas. The dream of Somerset was always before his path. That image had given him courage. It also had given him wisdom to meet life-threatening obstacles with patience and good judgment, not to give in to terror and desperation. The mental sight of land to call his own had given him reason to live.

That was what he wished to provide for Thomas. Silas did not mean to inspire cowardice—safety at any price—but to influence his son to exercise prudence, to listen to reason, to take no undue, foolish chances that would prevent his return to the place he loved. It was so little in the face of war when panic and despair—and simple bravery—so often prevailed, but it was all he could give his son. Beyond that, he must leave Thomas's fate in the hands of God.

Silas said, "That's what I've brought you out here today to discuss, Thomas—a way to save Somerset. Let's talk about it over there." They dismounted and moved to the shade of a heat-stressed red oak tree, where they sat on the ground and Silas explained.

Thomas listened and afterwards, he said, "This is the only way?"

Silas nodded. "The only way. East Texas planters will choke on my plan, but I suspect it will be adopted by all of them who wish to salvage a portion of the livelihood they knew."

"Bless Mother and her altruistic heart for the downtrodden," Thomas said.

Silas emitted a brief laugh. "Amen to that. God knows, if it hadn't been for your mother…"

Chapter Fifty-Five

The business with Ezekiel had been a pivotal point in Silas's life. For the first time, he saw Negroes as human beings; his slaves as individuals. He had resisted these new perceptions, but it was as if a strong hand had grasped him by the chin and forced him to look upon the landscape of slavery and see it for what it really was. Simply put, it was a law-approved system that forced one group of people to work for another without remuneration for their labor. In the glaring light of that reality, Silas saw that it was wrong.

Well, so be it, he had thought. Somerset could not exist without slave labor, and Somerset *would* exist. But not long after, he directed Jasper, his head man, to inform the slaves that he did not wish to be addressed as *master*, but by his name. Which one was up to them. They must have agreed by unanimous consent, because from that day forward no slave ever addressed him by any other form but *Mister Silas*, a choice that pleased him as it was more affectionate than the more formal *Mr. Toliver*.

He began to make small adjustments in the way things were done at the plantation. As a reward for their loyalty and conscientiousness, Silas allowed his most diligent workers an acre of land to grow their own cotton. At weighing time they were paid for their output, less the cost owed to Silas for seed and the nominal rent of farm animals and equipment. Silas was scrupulously fair in his dealings with these workers, and in time he realized benefits beyond a sop to ease his conscience. The favored bondsmen took on a new stature among their kind, worked harder for their owner, and gave every impression that if offered their freedom, they would not leave. Where would they go? Where would they find work? Where would they get the food, shelter, medical attention, and clothes they had right here? Mister Silas was kind and good. He could be trusted to do right by them.

These sentiments were passed on by Silas's overseers and land manager, and led to other changes. Disputes among workers were heard out rather than all being punished out of hand. Husbands were allowed to stay with their wives during the last days of their pregnancies, and women did not have to work as many hours in the fields as men. Silas did away with the troughs used to feed small children set up in the communal yard. His slaves' offspring were not pigs, he'd have it be known. In their place he hired the Warwick Lumber Company to build a series of long tables with benches where children were to take their meals using proper utensils. Additional measures were taken to increase personal safety, health, and hygiene. Privies were built. Slaves' cabins were kept in good repair. Wide-brimmed straw hats were issued to replace water-moistened towels for keeping the workers' heads cooler under the broiling sun, and gloves were distributed to protect the hands of slaves who worked with ax and saw and machinery. Ground was set aside for a slave cemetery high above water level. A wrought-iron fence draped in red pyracantha enclosed the area, and graves were marked by dignified crosses bearing the names and death dates of the deceased.

Silas loosened his reins on his slaves, but not his grip. The productivity of Somerset was his first and foremost concern. As the year progressed, it had become clear Governor Sam Houston would lose the fight to the secessionists in the Texas state legislature. The supporters of his view—Silas being one—that the United States could get along without Texas but Texas could not get along without the United States was shouted down by shortsighted, hotheaded men who preferred to settle issues with rash and extreme action.

By October 1860, Silas was ripe to accept Jessica's idea of tenant farming as the only way for Somerset to survive the backlash of slave emancipation. Thus the plan he presented to Thomas. To ensure a stable labor supply, Silas explained to his attentive son, he must give his former slaves reason to remain at Somerset. He would offer to rent a tract of land to each head of a family to put under cotton and continue to house, feed, and shelter them as well as provide the seeds, equipment, and animals necessary to farm their acres. When the crop was harvested and taken to market, Silas would give his one-time slaves half the sale price for their crop after deducting the cost of the items he'd supplied during the year.

The plan had its disadvantages. The obvious, of course, was that Somerset's profits would be split. "Your mother calls it '*sharing* the revenues,'" Silas said to Thomas, his lips hovering halfway between a grimace and a grin. Cotton production—notwithstanding the capriciousness of Mother Nature and other disasters that could wipe out a crop—was only as good as the hand that tilled the soil, and once out from under threat of the whip, there was no guarantee the tenant would work the hours required to make the land pay. The call of the North—the promise of jobs, easier living and working conditions, greater respect to members of the black race—no doubt would lure many away. Bad years might discourage the worker from staying. He could walk off at any time, leaving cotton in the field to rot.

But if Somerset could hang on until the nation and markets

were stable once more and profits reasonably good, the plantation would flourish again. In time, inventions of labor-saving farm implements would relieve the problem of unreliable workers and manpower shortages, and—if lady luck smiled—they might have the money to buy up neighboring plantations Silas foresaw as headed for bankruptcy the minute their slaves were freed.

But they were concerns and hopes for the future. To prepare for the inevitable to come, Silas told Thomas, he had decided to increase the number of slave families to whom he offered plots to grow their own cotton. To his favorites who had already proven themselves, he would assign more acres. By the time the war was over, he hoped to have in place a labor force of freed slaves who would prefer to accept the conditions of land tenancy in a place and under a trusted landlord they knew than to take off for a territory and an employer they did not.

"But they're not to know what you have in mind for them until the proper time, is that it?" Thomas asked.

"That's right. I want them to have a taste of what it's like to be paid for their labor rather than see all the profits go to the landlord. It will be good groundwork for the time they're offered the opportunity to rent the land they worked as slaves."

"So when do you intend to put your plan in place?"

"Right now, today," Silas said. He unfurled a rolled drawing and showed it to Thomas. It was a map of Somerset divided into tracts on which names had been inscribed. "Look this over and tell me if you agree with the division of plots and the families I've selected as the best choice for the plan."

Thomas studied the drawing and nodded approvingly. "They're the ones I would have picked. I see you've allotted Jasper's sons an acre apiece."

"We'll need to keep them with us when the time comes, and I know Jasper will prefer his boys to stay at home. We'll go by his place first and tell him the good news. So what do you say to the plan, son?"

"That it's brilliant and the *only* chance for Somerset's survival if what you predict happens." Thomas rerolled the map and handed it to Silas. "I have just one question, Papa. Would the tenants ever be allowed to *buy* the land they rent?"

"Not in my lifetime," Silas said, "and I hope not in yours. At contract signing, I will make clear in writing that the agreement does not offer that option. When he can afford them, the tenant will have the right to buy his own animals and equipment and any other item he needs to run his place, rather than lease them from me, but not the land he's renting. Not as long as I live will anyone but a Toliver ever own a single acre of Somerset."

"Not as long as I live either, Papa," Thomas declared. "You have my word on that."

Silas's stomach clenched at the phrase coming from his son's lips. "Let's go make our rounds, then."

Jasper was thrilled when Silas asked him if he'd like a few more acres to call his own to put under cotton.

"To call my own?"

"By that I mean, to cultivate *as* your own for more money in your pocket," Silas explained.

Jasper broke into a wide smile. By his own calculation, he was approximately forty-two years old, the father of two boys and one girl. Petunia was the oldest of his children and a continued favorite of Jessica. At seventeen, Petunia had given birth to a daughter named Amy, who was now four years old. Her husband had drowned when his boat had overturned in a nearby lake as he was fishing.

"Why, Mister Silas, what could I say but yes," Jasper said. "Other than that, I be at a loss what else to say 'cept thank you, suh. You be the most generous master there ever wuz."

"And one other thing," Silas said. "Talk it over with your wife, but if you all agree and Petunia is willing, Miss Jessica and I would like for her and her daughter to come live with us. As you know, Maddie recently died, and Miss Jessica believes Petunia would make a fine housekeeper, and we'd all enjoy her little one in the house."

"She goin' be thrilled when I tell her, Mister Silas. I declare, you is so good to us."

Silas and Thomas mounted their horses to ride to the other "top hands" to relay the news of their increased acreages. From the saddle, Silas looked down at Jasper. How many years since Jessica, his stout-hearted little wife, had stood up to her father and rescued Jasper from the fate he would surely have known. He had repaid her bravery with loyalty, devotion, and steadfastness of duty to her family. Jasper would have died for her. He had been a caring friend to Joshua, a guide to Thomas, a wise mediator between Silas and his slaves. He was a good man who deserved his freedom, but under the new plan, Jasper would live out his life with hardly a noticeable change in his station but for one glaring difference Silas hoped the man would never see. Unlike before, slave and master would be shackled together, equal partners in the preservation of Somerset.

Chapter Fifty-Six

From her high seat in the gazebo, Jessica gazed beyond the rear wrought-iron fence across the service road to the pasture where the inhabitants of Houston Avenue grazed their horses. The lone horse in the field this late January afternoon in 1861 was Flight O' Fancy, a sight Jessica never beheld without a swell of bereavement over the death of Nanette DuMont. Like clockwork at this hour of dusk, Robert Warwick appeared to collect the filly-turned-mare, halter in hand, his affectionate greeting carrying to Jessica on her swing in the gazebo. The mare perked her ears at the sound of Robert's voice and sauntered toward him to nuzzle his neck in her usual fashion. Her caretaker slipped the halter over her head, and the mare followed him docilely to the DuMont stable.

Jessica swallowed at a prick of tears. She was so weepy these days. The "mid-life plague" was upon her, and moisture could spring to her eyes over just about anything, but Robert's dogged faithfulness to Flight O' Fancy these five years after Nanette's death was enough to set most anybody's tear ducts flowing. Robert had asked to become the Thoroughbred's keeper upon his childhood playmate's loss, and now, even though he had turned twenty, Robert looked after the horse as his connection to the girl he'd vowed to marry when they were grown.

Jessica wiped her eyes with the edge of her shawl. She should not be ashamed of her emotion. There was much to be emotional about these days, and there was nothing on the horizon to relieve the steady stream of heartbreaking news begun just before Christmas when South Carolina seceded from the Union. Ten days later, its troops seized the United States arsenal at Charleston, and in early January, that incendiary action was followed by Governor Francis Pickens, a frequent visitor to Willowshire, giving the order to fire on an unarmed federal supply ship dispatched to reinforce the Union garrison at Fort Sumter in Charleston Harbor.

"It has begun," Silas had said, his voice hoarse with disappointment as he read aloud to Jessica and Thomas his brother's telegraphed message of the assault. The same day the ship was fired upon, the state of Mississippi seceded. A day later, Florida dropped out of the Union and changed "the United States" to "Confederate States" in its constitution. Alabama promptly followed suit. Louisiana was expected to join the pack in a matter of days, and in Texas the political process was under way to take the issue of separation from the United States to the polls. The wind was blowing overwhelmingly in favor of a vote for secession.

"Who is going to defend Texas if all our able-bodied men leave to fight for the South?" Thomas worried aloud to family and friends. "Who will protect their wives and children and property from the Comanche and Kiowa and the Mexicans who are only waiting for Texas to be unprotected before they invade our borders? You know good and well the Federals will try to blockade our rivers and the coast to prevent us from getting food supplies. They'll try to starve us out. I'm for forming a brigade to stay and fight right here in the homeland."

His parents listened in agreement with his rational concerns but could only shrug their shoulders helplessly. Thomas's push to form a home force to guard the rivers and coast and protect the community from Indian attacks struck many of their slave-owner friends, whose sons were already spoiling to take the fight into the Southland, as cowardly. It was just another example of the differences that set the Tolivers apart from the rest of their kind, they said. First, Silas Toliver marries an abolitionist, then he sets a precedent insulting to their culture by coddling his slaves like no other planter would dare run a plantation and expect a profit. Silas's was the lone planter's voice in the county opposed to secession, and he had even carried it to the state legislature in support of Governor Houston's pleas for Texas to remain in the Union. Was it any wonder, then, that his son would prefer to stay home than to join his Texas brothers to protect the folks and property of the lower South against the Northern invaders?

Jessica sighed. The feeling of being an outcast was nothing new to her, but it added to her sadness, making her inclined to cry at the fall of a leaf. Tippy had left Howbutker. One morning last October, on Jessica's birthday, a man dressed like the prime minister of England had wandered into the DuMont Department Store and presented his calling card to Henri. He had come to see Tippy. He was owner of a ladies' clothing design and manufacturing firm in New York and had seen examples of Henri's assistant's amazing artistry in gowns worn by his customers visiting the city.

"I knew it was coming," Henri told their weekly supper group, composed of the Tolivers, the Warwicks, and the DuMonts. "In good conscience I had to encourage Tippy to go. The opportunity the man offered her, the salary…" He shrugged in his Gallic way, but there was tear shine in his eyes. "How could I not?"

"I will escort her to New York City," Jeremy offered. "I have business to attend there."

And so they had parted, Jessica and her lifelong friend, now addressed by her proper name, Isabel, so her new employer insisted. Tippy had balked strenuously and tearfully at going, but Jessica saw something at the back of her eyes—the imagined chance of a dream come true—that would not permit her to listen to her friend's arguments against the opportunity to come into her own.

"You must go, Tippy."

"How can I leave you, Jessica?"

"By the front door, my dearest friend. That's what this opportunity will mean for you."

"I have ruined your birthday."

"There will be others."

Tippy stuck up her thumb in the old way, and Jessica hooked hers around it. "What are we promising to?" she asked.

"The promise to reunite on our fiftieth birthdays," Tippy answered.

Jessica studied the first yellow crocuses and hyacinths showing their heads in the iron planters arranged around the gazebo. The bulbs never broke ground but that Jessica was not reminded of Tippy and the vases of crocuses and hyacinths intertwined with streamers of white satin ribbons she had arranged in honor of an event many Januaries ago. This morning, as Silas had kissed her good-bye, she'd not called his attention to the memory. His face was gray with worry and the effect of many sleepless nights.

"Don't look for Thomas and me this evening until you see us coming," he'd said. "We're needed to help our manager and overseers settle unrest among the slaves and keep them at their tasks."

Jessica had understood. Rumors of the political situation were beginning to reach slave compounds and cotton fields, and planters were on the alert for the slightest sign of rebellion. She'd seen her husband off without reminding him that today was their twenty-fifth wedding anniversary.

"Miss Jessica," Petunia called, appearing waving a letter Jeremiah had collected from the post office. "Somethin' for you that looks important. I wouldn'a bothered you otherwise."

Jessica pulled her shawl closer and took the folded sheet of heavy cream-colored paper fastened with an authoritative wax seal. The return address listed the sender as a law firm in Boston.

"Thank you, Petunia."

"Will you be in shortly, Miss Jessica?" Petunia asked worriedly. "It gettin' cold out here."

"I'm enjoying the temperature. It's such a welcome break from the heat of last summer," Jessica said absently, studying the face of the letter.

"It supper time," Petunia reminded her. "Don't you want to come in for a bite? Mister Silas and Master Thomas won't be in for only the Lord knows how long. They is used to cold suppers, but don't you want somethin' while it hot?"

"No, just a pot of tea will do," Jessica said. "Bring it out, if you please, while I see what this letter is all about."

"It ought to be champagne and cake, Miss Jessica. You be for-gettin' today is your weddin' anniversary."

Jessica regarded her young housekeeper in surprise. "How in the world do you know that?"

"How could I ever in this world forget? In January 1856, I fell sick with pneumonia and you insisted I be brought to your house in town so a doctor be close to look after me. I remember you leavin' your party downstairs and comin' into my room in your pretty party gown to feel my head for fever. When I asked you why you so dressed up, you say it be your weddin' anniversary. That was January fifteenth. I remember 'cause you say the date."

"That's right, January fifteenth," Jessica said, remembering the party. A milestone, Silas had called their twentieth anniversary. *We must host one every five years to celebrate our married bliss.*

"But let's keep it our secret, Petunia," Jessica said. "Mister Silas will feel bad that he forgot. He's had so much on his mind lately. Tell little Amy when you go in that I'll read to her before her bedtime."

"I sure will, Miss Jessica. She'll love that. I'll get that tea now."

Jessica broke the seal of the letter. Its message shattered her resolve to keep her tears at bay. Aunt Elfie had died. Her tenderhearted widowed aunt she'd not seen since her disgrace on the eve of Christmas in her native state had passed away on the day of South Carolina's secession. The letter from her lawyer expressed condolences, details of her aunt's death, and the startling notification that Elfie Summerfield had left her entire estate to her niece, Jessica Wyndham Toliver. The lawyer implored Jessica to travel to Boston to sign papers and deal with the residence "of substantial standing" bequeathed to her in her aunt's will.

Jessica remembered the stately mansion well. During her years in boarding school, she had spent many happy times visiting her aunt in its Victorian parlor, taking meals with her in her sunny morning room, sleeping weekends in a bedroom wallpapered in flowers and designated "Jessica's room." The house and its opulent furnishings now belonged to her.

What was she to do with them? How could she travel north by herself—enemy territory now—to deal with the terms of the will?

Chapter Fifty-Seven

Silas did not arrive home until Jessica had gone to bed, for once to sleep like the dead, and was gone the next morning when she awoke. Lying on his pillow beside hers was a bedraggled red rose with a note. *Forgive me, my love. I am sorry that I did not remember our anniversary, but somehow I will make it up to you, the one who has become my heart. Ever yours, Silas.*

Jessica touched the blossom to her nose to inhale its fragrance. Silas must have brought it from the plantation where several of the original transplants of Lancasters carted from South Carolina still managed to bloom season after season. Jasper's wife saw to their care, the reason there were still a few remaining in Jessica's old rose garden this time of year.

Jessica felt a touch of chagrin. Now she would not be able to tell Silas of Aunt Elfie's death or show him the letter from her lawyer until late in the evening. They must decide quickly if she, a Southerner, a planter's wife, should risk a trip to Boston, that boiling cauldron of abolitionist activity and war fever.

Jeremy offered a possible solution to her quandary when he stopped by the house to deliver the Warwicks' copy of the *Atlantic Monthly* in accord with the agreement among the three families to share subscribed publications to defray the exorbitant cost of postage. Founded in Boston in 1857, the magazine featured articles written almost exclusively from a Northern abolitionist point of view and gave their neighbors further reason to question the families' loyalty to the Southern cause. Jeremy waved aside their criticisms as ridiculous. His opinion was that to know the enemy, read its publications.

He found Jessica pruning her rose bushes as Amy, the housekeeper's five-year-old daughter, played alongside her, happily making mud pies.

"Mornin', Jess. How do your roses grow?" he called.

"Not so good, Jeremy. There's been a loss in the family. Do you have time for a cup of coffee?"

"Always."

"I'll tell Petunia. Let's sit in the gazebo so I can keep an eye on the little one."

Over coffee, Jessica related the news of her aunt's death. "I remember her well," Jeremy said. "A sweet little bird of a woman, and you could tell she loved you dearly."

"She must have. In her will, Aunt Elfie left me all her worldly goods." Jessica told him of the contents of the lawyer's letter and explained her dilemma. "Her lawyer makes it clear that he prefers I dispose of her house and belongings in person rather than make them the responsibility of his firm, but I'm sure Silas would strongly disapprove of my venturing into enemy territory with war so near, and frankly, I'm not sure I have the courage to brave it. If war were declared while I was there, I might not be able to get home."

"I'm going to New York in a few days on business with hope to get in and out before the cannons are lit. Would you trust me to settle your aunt's affairs for you? It would be no problem to pop over to Boston. I'm sure a letter to her attorney giving me authority to act on your behalf would suffice."

Jessica felt her spirits lift. "Oh, Jeremy, would you? Of course

I trust you to act for me, but I'm afraid the process of selling the house, disposing of its goods, the paperwork, all the sundry things involved, will delay you from getting home. You could be stuck up North and no telling what could befall you—"

Jeremy flashed her the charm of his boyish grin. He had aged little since he'd stood with Silas at their wedding, whereas Silas's raven-black hair was now almost entirely silver gray.

"Don't worry about me," Jeremy said. "I'll make it back. My northern business associates and friends will see to that." He finished his coffee and rose to go. "Talk it over with Silas and let me know. I'm leaving day after tomorrow. And Jess—" He hesitated, the space between his eyebrows creasing doubtfully.

"Yes, Jeremy?"

"Remember that in Texas, inherited property that a woman acquires during her marriage is hers, not her husband's."

Perplexed, Jessica said, "And you're reminding me of that for…what reason?"

"I would advise you to leave the money from your aunt's estate in a Boston bank. I believe we're all in agreement that if war comes, the South will get the shorter end of it. Our banks will be hard hit, our currency worthless. Only those who've had the foresight to take their money out of Texas and place it where it will be safe will be able to ride out the aftermath."

"And you have followed your own advice?" Jessica asked. Though the Warwicks would never dream of alluding to the success of Jeremy's financial ventures, it was no secret they had become the wealthiest family in the county, among the richest in Texas. Jeremy was of that rare breed of investor: a visionary with an astute head for business.

"It's the reason I'm going to New York at this time," he said, replacing his hat for departure. "Just a thought. Forget I said anything if the suggestion goes against your grain."

The suggestion did not go against her grain, Jessica reflected after Jeremy had left. She'd needed reminding of the property rights women had enjoyed in Texas since 1840, when a state statute was enacted giving women sole rights to property they possessed at the time of their marriage as well as any acquired during it. Not that Silas would have, but after 1840 Tippy was no longer his to sell.

Thinking hard, Jessica slipped the letter into her pocket and got up from the swing to go into the garden to collect Amy. It was time for the child's midmorning treat, and, partner in crime that Jessica was in encouraging the mud pies, she picked up the little girl and carried her inside to make her presentable for her mother's prune cake and milk. As she washed Amy's face and hands, Jessica pondered the practicality of Jeremy's advice.

It made good sense to leave her aunt's money—*her* money, now—in Aunt Elfie's bank, but she dreaded an argument from Silas. The plantation was prosperous, but they often lived from crop to crop. Silas could not resist the urge to purchase more land as it became available, more work animals and the latest farm equipment, to build more barns, sheds, and fences. They were sometimes short of cash, never to pay their bills and see after their slaves properly, but enough to cause worry if the cotton didn't make it. Last summer's drought had wiped out their cash reserve, an all-too-common example of how easily their pockets could be emptied. After the war, the labor force uncertain, their money worthless and their land valueless, how would they keep the plantation going without Aunt Elfie's money?

Jessica sent Amy off to her mother in the kitchen and went into her morning room to better analyze the astonishing direction of her thoughts. If the money from her inheritance were deposited locally, it would soon be gone in the way of all their extra resources. After twenty-five years of marriage, she knew her husband's proclivities well—and hers, also. Silas would not be able to avoid the temptation to spend the money on the plantation, and she would not be able to refuse him the use of it. Jessica believed in Silas's plan to save Somerset after the war, but all sorts of problems could thwart it, and they would have no financial means to sustain the land that must be held for Thomas.

Jessica removed the letter from her pocket and slipped it into a secret compartment of her secretary. Then she pulled the bell to summon Jeremiah and, after sending him on his way, drew forth a sheet of stationery and dipped her writing quill into a pot of ink.

Jeremy arrived soon after she'd finished composing her letter. "Jeremiah caught me with your message just in time, Jess," he said strolling into her morning room. "I was on the way to the office. I'm assuming this is about my proposal?"

Jessica handed him the letter she'd written, sealed with a daub of dark green wax embossed with a rose, emblem of the Toliver coat of arms. "I have decided to take you up on your kind offer to act on my behalf, Jeremy. Your authority is there in writing. The letter is to Aunt Elfie's attorney empowering you to act in my name to dispose of her house and belongings."

"And what do you want me to do with the money?"

"The letter also authorizes you to open an account in my name at Aunt Elfie's bank."

Jeremy's golden brow rose questioningly. "Silas has agreed to leaving your money in Boston?"

Jessica ducked her chin and cast an upward look at Jeremy.

"I've seen that look on my boxer after he's eaten a whole cake off the tea table," Jeremy said. "What's going on, Jess?"

Jessica gestured that Jeremy take a seat and returned to her chair at the writing desk in a puff of hoop skirt. "Silas doesn't know of Aunt Elfie's death or of her leaving me her estate. He hasn't seen her lawyer's letter. He was gone this morning before I could show it to him."

"As I told you, I'm not leaving for a few days. You have plenty of time to show it to him and discuss what you want to do with the money," Jeremy said.

Jessica's face grew mutinous. "I don't want to discuss it with him. I don't want him to know about the money. I have my reasons, Jeremy, so don't look at me like that. I realize I'm deceiving Silas, but it's for his own good and that of our son—and for Somerset. Silas will run through the money if it's deposited here, may I be forgiven my disloyalty in saying so, but you and I both know that's the truth. The Tolivers have never been as...well, as prudent in business matters as you Warwicks." Jessica raised her chin and added loftily, "If the burden of my deception is too much for his closest friend to bear, I will certainly understand."

Jeremy remained silent for a moment before answering. He had not yet pocketed the letter. "If I don't do this for you, what will be your recourse?"

"I will go to Boston and handle the matter myself. If I'm detained by the war, I will stay in Aunt Elfie's house under Sarah Conklin's protection."

Jeremy stood up. "I see you've thought this out." He turned away as if needing privacy to think, rubbing his clean-shaven chin. Neither he nor Silas sported beards, the fashion of the day for men. After a moment, he swung back around. "For Somerset, you say?"

"And Silas and Thomas."

"Same thing." Jeremy approached Jessica still sitting before her desk and stared down hard into her eyes. "You know what will happen if Silas finds out I've gone behind his back on this?"

"I am aware of the risk, Jeremy, and despise myself for asking it of you. I know the value you men place on your friendship, but I know no other way to save Silas's dream for Somerset. He'll need money when the war is over, and we won't have any."

"I have been longer acquainted with Silas's dream for Somerset than even you, my dear," Jeremy said softly. "All right, I'll do it with the cherished hope that Silas never discovers the hand I had in the matter."

Jessica rose with a swish of silk and stepped toward him. She placed a hand on the lapel of his finely tailored frock coat. "He will never hear it from me, Jeremy. I give you my word along with my deepest gratitude."

"A forceful combination that will win my obedience to your wishes every time," Jeremy said and sealed the pact with a brief press of her hand. "And I suppose you'll want me to look in on Tippy while I'm in New York?"

"If it would not be too much of an imposition."

"And to make contact with Sarah Conklin while I'm in Boston?"

"I do not dare ask," Jessica said, her eyes widening hopefully.

Jeremy chuckled and inserted the letter into an inner coat pocket. "You would dare anything, Jessica Wyndham Toliver," he said. "I'll collect the addresses before I leave."

Chapter Fifty-Eight

The night of April 12, 1861, just before dawn, Silas cried out in his sleep from a nightmare in which he heard his mother's prediction again. *"No!"* he howled, startling Jessica awake beside him. She glanced at the large-faced clock on the mantel made visible by the moonlight streaming through the open window. It was 4:30.

"Silas, wake up! You're having a bad dream!" she said, shaking his bare shoulder. She jerked her hand away. "My goodness, it's cold in here, and you're perspiring."

Silas opened his eyes, the clutch of his nightmare releasing him in the semidarkness chilled by the last breath of a long winter. "I was having that dream again," he said.

"What dream?"

Silas pushed himself up against the headboard and ran his hand through his damp hair. He reached for a glass of water on his bedside table and took a long swallow to relieve his drought-dry mouth. He had never told Jessica of the curse his mother had predicted would fall on Somerset or of his terror that it meant to manifest itself by taking the life of his last surviving child. On and off the past anxious year, his mother had come to him in a dream with her dire threat, and he'd jerk awake with his heartbeat pounding in his ears and his skin clammy from a fear so deep he would rise from his bed for the rest of the night so as not to return to the dream again.

But never before had his imagined horror come to reality in his nightmares. Tonight in his dream he saw his mother pointing to something hidden by tall stands of cotton in the fields of Somerset. *See!* she cried. *I told you your land was cursed!* and the sprawled figure between the burgeoning rows toward which she aimed her finger was the body of Thomas.

Before reason—and his usual caution—could prevent him, he blurted, "Jessica, do you believe in curses?"

There was no immediate response, and Silas turned his blurred gaze to her, alarmed by his outburst and her thoughtful silence. Was she remembering her words at the time they discovered Joshua's still body? Had he disturbed old coals that had lain quietly burning beneath layers of ashes all these years?

"I believe that…what we call a curse is really a withholding of natural blessings," Jessica said. "Like rain that should fall at the proper season, but it does not."

Like women made to be wonderful mothers who cannot conceive or hold their babies in their wombs, Silas thought. "You do not think a curse is punishment administered by God for past sins?" he asked.

He hoped for a breezy dismissal of the subject as nonsense. He did not know if his wife believed in a divine being. Jessica attended church to go along with his belief in Sunday tradition and to expose Thomas to the teachings of the Christian faith their son was at liberty to accept or reject, but she seemed to have no interest in established religion. Silas had never heard her call upon the name of God, even in times of great despair, or seen her read from the Bible. To his knowledge, the King James Version upon which she'd laid her hand at the exchange of their wedding vows had never been moved from whatever shelf it had been assigned.

"I've never thought about it," Jessica said. She cuddled closer to him and laid her head on his bare chest. "Tell me about this persistent dream of yours, beloved. I'm assuming it has something to do with a curse."

Beloved…an endearment soft with solace and the willingness to listen and understand. Silas was surprised by a sensation of tears. Jessica called their son "sweetheart" occasionally, but Silas could count on the fingers of one hand the number of times she'd addressed him by a similar term of affection. She was not the type of woman, like Camellia and Bess, and, Lord have mercy, Stephanie Davis, to drop intimate expressions of address willynilly, and so they carried more value. Comforted, he kissed the top of her head. Did he dare tell her of his mother's prediction that had haunted him since he'd dropped the first seeds into the soil of Somerset? Should he tell her of the drastic solution he was contemplating to eliminate the greatest fear of his life—of *their* lives?

It was not a course to decide alone.

"My mother prophesied a curse would fall upon Somerset for the sacrifice I made to fulfill my ambition of having a plantation of my own," Silas began. "I paid no attention to it. It was the prediction of an angry and disappointed woman for my not marrying the girl she wanted as a daughter-in-law, I thought. But then our first child miscarried, the child conceived in such passion and joy, and there was another miscarriage after the birth of Thomas, and after that…you…seemed unable to conceive. And then when we lost Joshua…."

Jessica stirred abruptly in his arms, and he held her tighter to prevent her from moving away in hurt and pain. He continued. "And you said to me, "'Silas, we are cursed.' Do you remember?"

A nod of her head on his chest indicated acknowledgment. "I remember."

"The possibility possessed me like a demon that perhaps we *were* cursed. I and my innocent wife were being punished for the deal I made with the devil back in South Carolina, the injury I caused to Lettie, the selfish and willful trades I made for the sake of the land."

Jessica lay still, and Silas realized she may have taken his words wrongly. How could she not? He lifted her chin and looked into her eyes. "Not that I regret a second of the decision I made to marry you, Jessica. Tell me you are sure of that."

She removed herself from his arms and adjusted pillows at her back to sit up beside him. "I am sure of that, Silas. Where is this discussion leading?"

"I don't think the curse is through with us yet," he said flatly. "I believe it intends a final stoke of vengeance." He threw back his covers and got out of bed wearing only drawers. "Do you mind if I smoke?" he asked, wrapping a robe around him.

"Not if it will clear your head of this foolishness," Jessica said.

Silas lit a cheroot and drew in deeply. "Is it foolishness, Jessica?"

"Silas Toliver!" Jessica scowled at him, her tone sharp. "I was insane with grief when Joshua died and would have said anything. At the time I *did* feel we were cursed with our inability to have and keep children, but I later realized that such were the quirks of nature. Joshua's death was an accident that could have befallen any inquisitive, adventuresome twelve-year-old boy. Let's be grateful that we've been blessed with a healthy, intelligent, industrious son—a perfect heir to your Somerset. Our only concern should be his survival."

"Exactly!" Silas jabbed the air with the cheroot. "For our son to live—that's what we both want if we could ask for anything in the world. His life is the most important thing on earth—more important than Somerset."

Jessica turned an ear to him as if she had not heard him clearly. "What are you getting at, Silas?"

He placed the smoking cheroot in an ashtray and came to sit beside her on the bed. Jessica drew back uncertainly, doubt of his sanity clouding her dark eyes.

"What if…because of my obsession with Somerset…the curse takes Thomas?" he said. "What if God, as final punishment for the deal I struck with your father, means to leave no heir to possess the plantation?"

Jessica smacked his arm in rebuke. "Ridiculous!" she said. "Absurd. If—if Thomas perishes, a curse will have nothing to do with it. The stupid men who make war will be responsible!"

"But to make sure, I…Jessica…I…" His voice sounded raspy as a saw cutting wood. "I'm…I'm thinking of giving up Somerset—selling it—taking it out of Toliver hands, anything to get out from under the curse and bring our boy safely home."

Jessica, pale as the bed pillows, clutched him by both arms. "Silas, do you hear yourself? You are talking superstitious nonsense. There is no such thing as a curse. God couldn't give a fig whether you give up Somerset or not. Honestly, do you really believe that forfeiting the plantation will guarantee Thomas's safety?" She shook him. *"Do you?"*

Her voice had risen on a note of incredulity and panic. Silas pulled out of her grasp and got up from the bed, putting a finger to his mouth. Their son's room was next to theirs. "Lower your tone," he said. "The window's open, and I don't want Thomas to hear this."

"I should say not," Jessica snapped. "Now answer my question. Do you really believe such a sacrifice will bring Thomas back?"

"I don't know," he said. "In my dream tonight, I saw Thomas lying dead between the cotton rows of Somerset. I saw his body clear as day."

That silenced her. Jessica pressed her lips together, and he could tell she was envisioning the scene. Silas picked up the cheroot and inhaled until he could feel the smoke burn his lungs.

"It was just a dream," Jessica said finally. "Only that, Silas, nothing more. If you sell Somerset, you will be selling Thomas's heart. Whether he survives or not, either way he cannot live without his heart."

"He'll be alive," Silas said.

"But will he live?" Jessica pushed away the covers, drew on night slippers, and went to slide her arms up around his neck. "Silas, if you hadn't, as you say, 'made the deal with the devil,' look at what you would have saved yourself from. You wouldn't have married me. I'd be growing old in a convent in England, never having known what it was like to love and be loved, to have been a wife and mother. You wouldn't be the father of Thomas. You wouldn't be the master of a land that is yours by right of courage and hard work and perseverance. You would never have fulfilled the calling of your heritage, nor enjoyed the prosperity, respect, and happiness you've earned. You would have been spared all that to live the life prescribed for you at Queenscrown. Tell me truthfully, my darling. As it's all turned out—Lettie apparently happy, your mother surrounded by grandchildren, you and I meant to be—where is the curse in all that? Rather than a vengeful God, can you not believe that Providence was looking after you when you made the deal with the devil?"

Tears seared Silas's eyes. He could feel Jessica's recital of all that never would have been—the logic of it—working to release him from the demons that bound him. Could it be that he was guilty of nothing but pursuing the destiny set for him? God knew, the burden of being a Toliver was sentence enough. He laid aside the cheroot and folded his arms around his wife.

"I have never loved you more than at this moment," he said, his voice cracking on the wonder of his shackles falling free.

"Then you may prove it to me," Jessica said, leading him back to bed.

Chapter Fifty-Nine

Thomas stole quietly away from the open window of his parents' bedroom, awed and shocked. He had heard every word of his mother and father's conversation. Unable to sleep, he had gone out onto the verandah and taken a chair by his room to watch the sun rise on another uncertain day when he'd heard his father cry out. He'd jumped up to go to them, but his mother's voice had stopped him. Apparently, his father had been in the throes of a bad dream.

To make sure he was all right, Thomas had hung close to their window, open to allow in the last cold air before the spring turned warm and invited mosquitoes. His father was fifty-five and showing the distress of the past months. A year ago, the jeweler in town, the same age as his father, had died in bed next to his wife, the strain of a nightmare too much for his heart.

His poor father had reason to suffer nightmares, Thomas thought. The events of the last months had taken their toll. Silas Toliver's pleas to the Texas legislature and his friends of influence to oppose secession continued to go unheard. February first, Texas became the seventh state to join the newly formed nation calling itself the Confederate States of America, shortened to the Confederacy for brevity's sake. His father's old friend, Governor Sam Houston, had been deposed from office after he locked himself in the basement of the capitol building in Austin and refused to come out to sign the papers authorizing separation from the Union. Contrary to the opinions of the Tolivers' aghast friends, his father had tirelessly supported the governor's views of the state's inevitable fate if removed from the teat that nourished it. He'd been sickened to his soul when public opinion turned against Sam Houston and forced the hero of San Jacinto, the man to whom the state owed so much, to withdraw from government service and retire to his farm in Huntsville, Texas.

Still his father had persisted in trying to convince anyone who would listen that the South was outmanned, outgunned, and outmatched. Typical of the reception of his views, in a town meeting called to discuss the wisdom of secession and the consequences of an armed conflict, one farmer dared to demand of the prominent Silas Toliver, "Why should we listen to you? For years you said there would be no war."

"That was before Mr. Lincoln was elected," his father countered. "Listen to reason," he'd begged. "Only a third of the population in Texas owns slaves. Why should a few dictate the course that will involve the rest of the state in economic ruin and the waste of life to support a cause bound to be lost?"

Boos and hisses had answered his pleas. No less polite had been the reaction from other planters when his father had encouraged them to follow his plan to save Somerset from destruction should the slaves be emancipated. To a man, they believed the South would succeed as a nation. No Northern president would have a say in the rights of the Confederacy's citizens to hold slaves. Great Britain and France would come in on the side of the Southern states in case of war, and the United States would back off. Those two great European countries were dependent on the region's cotton, and to produce cotton, slaves were a necessity. In no way would they tolerate the disruption of their vital import by Mr. Lincoln's Congress.

Thomas had seen his father pale at these optimistic assumptions. "Don't the fools know that cotton agents in London have warned that England has a stockpile of cotton in their warehouses, whereas much of Europe's wheat harvests have suffered?" he would moan. "Great Britain is far more dependent on the North's grain than they are on the South's cotton!"

His father's anti-separatist stand, coupled with his mother's long-known views on slavery, had made the Toliver family all but social pariahs. To his father's great disappointment, he was not re-elected to the city council. Parents withdrew their children from his mother's Young People's Reading Group. Only their status as first settlers and city founders and the steadfast friendships of the DuMonts and Warwicks prevented them from being cast totally out of Howbutker society. Henri DuMont and Jeremy Warwick wielded such economic power and influence in the county— indeed, in the whole state—that none dared to exclude the Tolivers from their guest lists—not that their invitations would have been accepted anyway.

The cruelest charge—and the one that disturbed Thomas the most—had been the allegation from Lorimer Davis that Silas Toliver had gone crazy from anxiety that in case of war, his son and only heir would be killed. No one need listen to him, the planter declared. Parental alarm and fear that Somerset would pass into oblivion were his sole reasons for opposing secession.

Tonight, drawing away from his parents' window, Thomas was forced to believe he'd heard evidence that Lorimer Davis's theory was correct. He felt almost nauseated from the chilling revelation that his father had considered selling Somerset to ensure his safe return in case of war. Good God, what an appalling, unthinkable idea! He knew his father loved him—too much, he'd thought at times—but sell Somerset? To appease an imagined curse? Thank God his mother had made him see the ridiculousness of it.

Thomas sat down in his room, stunned from the proof he'd heard tonight that certain rumors drifting to him over the years had a basis of truth. Threads of gossip, innuendos, whispers, vaguely familiar names, together with his own impressions and knowledge of family history, began to weave into a sort of decipherable tapestry. He had never questioned the love between his mother and father, but there had been intimations that their marriage had been arranged. His powerful grandfather, Carson Wyndham, had been involved, and money had traded hands between him and Silas Toliver back in South Carolina. The transaction had required that his father abandon the woman he was to wed in exchange for the money to buy his plantation in Texas.

Only wisps of such hearsay had ever reached Thomas's ears, and he'd never been curious enough to wonder or ask about their foundation. But evidently there *had* been another woman in his father's life: this Lettie he'd mentioned tonight. Wasn't she the wife of his brother, Morris? Was she the sacrifice his father had spoken of? Apparently the deal he'd made with the devil had been with the wealthy man who became his father-in-law. Was it true that Carson Wyndham had paid Silas Toliver to marry his daughter? Why? To prevent her from entering a convent? And had his father in fact used the money to bankroll Somerset?

Thomas remembered his "Willowshire" grandparents well— especially his imposing grandfather—even from their one short visit long ago. The only reunion with his mother's parents had been strained. Thomas recalled a contract-burning ceremony that had set his father's teeth on edge, and his parents had not been sad to see them go. He knew very little of the "Queenscrown" side of the family. There was a grandmother named Elizabeth who wrote occasionally, but she had never come to see them or they her. He knew there was an uncle called Morris, and once he'd heard the name *Lettie* mentioned whom Thomas assumed to be his wife, but his parents did not discuss them in his presence.

Thomas now had a fair understanding of why his grandmother had prophesied that a curse would fall on her son's land, but how could his father give a rational, intelligent thought to it? Did he really think Joshua's death or his mother's failure to carry children were punishments from God for whatever deal he had struck over twenty-five years ago? Or that his son's death would be God's final stroke of vengeance? Sheer nonsense! If there was a war, Thomas would go. In what capacity he would serve was another matter. In February, the lieutenant governor of Texas had authorized a committee for public safety to recruit volunteers, but he and Jeremy Jr. and Armand, Stephen, and Philippe (Robert suffered from bronchitis severe enough to preclude war service) had already decided to wait and join the regiment formed that would best defend Texas.

And, yes, he could be killed, and there would be no heir to take over Somerset, but he'd already decided on a solution to defray that possibility. He'd planned to talk to his parents tomorrow about proposing to Priscilla Woodward. He and Priscilla had known each other since her father had hung up his shingle as one of the town's two physicians ten years ago, and he'd courted her for one.

Thomas had been waiting to feel for her what she clearly and unabashedly felt for him, but while he liked her and enjoyed her company, something that he could not put his finger on was missing. She was the prettiest girl in town, with bouncy golden curls and sparkling blue eyes, and she exuded a buoyancy good for his more serious nature. She was a little too impressed with his house on Houston Avenue and his link to English royalty, but he could understand it. Priscilla had grown up in a modest house still home to her two older brothers, who worked as lumberjacks for the Warwick Lumber Company. Meals in the Woodward house consisted of meat and potatoes, eaten at the kitchen table with her brothers still in their work clothes, shirt sleeves rolled up. Mrs. Woodward's finest possession was an English bone china tea set. Priscilla wasn't ashamed of her upbringing—Thomas couldn't have gone with that—but she appreciated the refinements of his home and lifestyle and that was all right with him.

The idea of marrying her had gradually formed when the same realization hit him that had deeply troubled his father. If he should die, what would become of Somerset when his father passed on? The idea of the plantation passing out of Toliver hands was abominable to him. It must not happen, and Priscilla Woodward was the resolution. He would marry her, and they would begin a family right away. He was almost twenty-four. It was time he tied the knot, became a father. He felt much better now about the fact that he did not feel as deeply for his future wife as he would have liked. He had deduced from his parents' conversation tonight that his father had not loved his mother either when they first married, and yet, here the old boy was at his age proving to her he did.

Somewhat at ease, Thomas crawled back into bed for another hour's sleep before the sun fully rose. When he awoke, the news had been telegraphed to the community that Confederate forces had—at the exact hour Silas had cried out in his sleep—fired upon the federal troops stationed at Fort Sumter in Charleston Harbor. The War Between the States had begun.

Chapter Sixty

"He doesn't love her, you know."

Jeremy's sandy brows lifted. "What makes you say that, Jess?"

"It's something a mother knows about her son. The bud is there, but not the bloom."

"Perhaps it will blossom to full glory as happened with you and Silas."

"Perhaps. He's marrying her to produce an heir for Somerset."

"You're sure of that?"

"I'm sure of that."

"Is Priscilla aware of that?"

Jessica shrugged. "I cannot tell."

"Does she love him?"

"I believe she thinks she does. The girl is such a romantic. In her eyes, Thomas is quite a catch—handsome, of a prominent family, connected to royal blood, a subject that enamors her. She sees Thomas as her knight on a white charger, come to deliver her from the yeoman she most likely would marry if he didn't rescue her, but she says she's eager for children, too, and of course that pleases Thomas. Mutual respect and liking and the bond of children can go a long way in making a happy marriage."

Jeremy lit a flame to his cheroot. "Indeed," he murmured.

"And in some ways, her blond beauty aside," Jessica continued,

"Priscilla reminds me of Lettie. The other day she said to Thomas, 'Failure is only experience for success.' Doesn't that sound like Lettie?"

"The way she once was," Jeremy said. "Do you think Silas has noticed the comparison?"

"Silas notices only cotton, as does his son."

It was three weeks after war had been declared. Jeremy, wishing to see his brothers before the Union blockade of southern ports made a visit to the family plantation in South Carolina impossible, had returned with news from Plantation Alley. Today, he had brought a report of Jessica's family to her. In dismay, she'd heard that her father was ill from heart disease and her mother in declining health. Michael had taken the exemption offered to males of draft age whose services were essential to the war effort. Their wily father had anticipated the blockade as a move to disrupt the exportation of cotton, and much of Willowshire was now under crops to sell to the Confederate troops.

"They all sent their love, Jess," Jeremy said.

Jessica's throat throbbed from painful recall of happier days with her parents. She'd had no desire to return to the home of her birth. Her parents' last and only visit and her mother's willful neglect to inform Tippy of Willie May's death had sealed her interest in seeing them. Now she never would. Michael, perhaps, if he survived the war.

"What of the Toliver family?" she asked.

"Not the best news to report there, either," Jeremy said. "Elizabeth is in frail health as you'd expect at eighty-one. Morris has aged, too, and become somewhat of a lay preacher. He spends much of his time 'about the Lord's work,' he says. Silas would be distressed to see the condition of the plantation."

"Are not the sons a help in that quarter?"

"I gather they share their father's lack of management skills and have put their faith in their overseers, a lazy bunch according to my brothers. At the first shot the Toliver boys were off to join General Lee's army in Richmond."

"The daughter?"

"Sweet like her mother but unfortunately looks like Morris with no beau in sight. She's destined for old maidenhood."

"And...Lettie?"

"Lettie has...lost her sparkle. I was shocked at how worn she looked, tell you the truth. Her duties and worries are many. Elizabeth requires constant care, and the servants are little assistance in the household because Morris refuses to discipline them. The management of the plantation has fallen to her. The house is in disrepair, and there's no money to reclaim its former glory. Morris has gotten them into a hole of debt with no way to climb out, and of course, Lettie is worried sick about her sons."

Jeremy paused, seeing Jessica wince as if from a sudden pinch. "Shall I go on?"

"You mean there is more?"

"I'm afraid so. Her West Point brother that she idolized has elected to stay in the Union army. He has become the enemy."

Jessica shook her head sadly. "I am heartsick for her. What of her father? Is he still living?"

"He died last year from a long struggle with tuberculosis."

"Oh dear." Jessica sipped her iced tea. As deeply as she regretted Lettie's grim circumstances, Silas must never hear of them. He would feel responsible—as indeed he was—and his guilt would stir his belief in that absurd curse again and a vengeful God bent on punishing him. She spread her accordion fan, her mind working. No breeze wafted through the open louvered shutters. The summer's heat was upon them. They were sitting in her morning room, where she had persuaded Jeremy to be her ally in deceiving her husband. He had fulfilled his secret mission nobly. Jeremy had seen to the selling of her aunt's house and belongings and deposited a small fortune in a Boston bank under her name. He had brought back news of Tippy's happy entrenchment in New York and Sarah Conklin's continued abolitionist activities in Boston.

"You were in Boston?" Silas had commented to Jeremy in surprise when he returned. "What for? I thought you went to New York."

"I had a friend's business to attend there," he had told him.

Jessica carefully set down her tea glass. "Jeremy, my friend, apart from the report of Elizabeth's health, must you tell Silas all you've told me?"

Jeremy eyed her skeptically. "What are you asking me to do, Jess?"

"You are a man of remarkable insight and understanding. Do I have to explain what news of Lettie's plight will do to Silas?"

"Are you suggesting I not tell him of the situation at Queenscrown? He's bound to ask, and I must relay the truth."

"*All* of it?"

"What part do you suggest I leave out? Even if I don't mention Lettie, he'll deduce the toll Morris's mismanagement and foolishness has taken on her."

"Must you tell him you visited Queenscrown?"

"Are you asking that I *lie*?"

"No. I'm asking that you don't volunteer all the truth."

"Why, Jess? It's been over twenty-five years since Silas and Lettie were...close. She made her bed with Morris. For better or worse, she must lie in it."

A light tap on the door interrupted them. Jessica called to come in, and Petunia stuck her head in. "Pardon me, Miss Jessica, but which china do you want to use tonight?"

"The Chelsea," Jessica answered.

"And where do you wish to seat Dr. and Mrs. Woodward?"

"Dr. Woodward will be to my right and Mrs. Woodward to Mister Silas's left."

"And Mister Thomas and Miss Priscilla?"

"Across from each other. It won't matter which side of the table as long as they have the other in sight."

Petunia chuckled. "Yes, ma'am," she said and withdrew.

Jessica explained. "We're having Priscilla's parents for supper tonight to formalize our children's engagement. Silas is beside himself over the fact that Thomas is getting married. He hopes to be a grandfather this time next year."

"Ah. And have in place that heir to Somerset."

Jessica sighed. "In case Thomas doesn't make it back from the war, you see. I only hope such a design does not carry future regrets."

As usual these days when reflecting on Thomas's motive for marrying, Jessica was reminded of her mother's little toast to her and Silas back in the library at Willowshire when she expressed her hope that they could find something to love in the other that would keep them together besides the commitments of a contract. They had found it. Something told Jessica that Thomas and Priscilla would not.

She rose, too fidgety and warm in her wide-skirted morning dress to sit. Whoever had designed the double-layer pagoda sleeves women were wearing these days should be shot, she thought irritably, wondering if she should divulge Silas's secret fear of a Toliver curse to Jeremy.

"Don't take this wrong, Jess, but people have married for less noble reason than to beget children to inherit the results of their parents' hard work," he said.

Jessica fanned rapidly. "Oh, I have no quarrel with either of their reasons for marrying each other. I'm just less optimistic for their happiness. I'm thinking especially of the girl. She may never know the thrill of setting her husband's heart on fire." She glanced at Jeremy with a small smile. "It's one of the most wonderful experiences a woman could ever know."

Avoiding Jessica's gaze, Jeremy swiped at a curl of ash that had fallen from his cigarillo onto his knee. If asked, his flower-like wife would say that her world was perfect. She was married to a rich, handsome husband and was the mother of three equally handsome, intelligent, responsible sons. Her men treated her like a queen. She lived in a magnificent home with servants to attend her every wish and wanted for nothing. But had she ever had the thrill of setting her husband's heart on fire? Jeremy thought not. Only the small, neat woman standing in the light of the louvered morning sunshine would have had the power to do that—still to this day. Jeremy shook his head. It had never been beauty that had attracted him to her—Jessica was a plain-faced woman—though time in its capriciously merciful way had added a certain loveliness to her unconventional allure. The freckles had faded and her skin had acquired the luminescence of fine china, a porcelain setting for dark eyes as lively at forty-six as they had been at eighteen. She'd maintained a figure that did not require a corset to achieve a slim waist, and the first silver had toned her bright, frizzy hair, worn in a voluptuous bun on her neck, to the tawny hue of red oak leaves in the fall. Her temple still bore a faint scar from her fall off the wagon train over a quarter of a century ago.

"You're shaking your head, Jeremy," Jessica said. "What are you thinking?"

"I'm thinking that once again you're going to talk me into deceiving Silas."

Voluminous skirts swaying, she swirled to his chair. "Not deceive him, Jeremy—*protect* him."

"Then go sit yourself down and explain to me the difference."

Jessica took her seat again. It was absolutely ridiculous, she thought, but Silas's revelation following his predawn nightmare had planted a seed in her mind, usually unreceptive to idiocy. It must not be allowed to germinate. She'd tried to talk it out in her diary with little success, but discussing it with Jeremy might grind the preposterous little kernel to dust. She looked across the room at him, so assured of himself in the world and his place in it. "Jeremy, do you believe in curses?" she asked.

Chapter Sixty-One

They had agreed from the first telegraphed report of the firing on Fort Sumter that they would sign up together—Thomas, Jeremy Jr., Stephen, and Armand—and that they would join the military unit designated to defend the borders of their home state from invasion and the coast from siege. The northern and eastern rims of Texas were especially vulnerable to enemy incursions from the free territories of Oklahoma and New Mexico, as well as from Louisiana, should that state fall into Union hands. There were reliable reports that the Federals had plans to force Texas to supply beef to the Union army and that they possessed detailed routes of ingress. There was also the fear that homesteads would be open to devastating destruction and savagery by the Comanche once the U.S. Cavalry and Texas Rangers, guardians of the frontier, pulled out of the state to join the armies of their respective persuasions. The United States Navy was making its way down the Atlantic blockading southern ports to prevent the exportation of cotton and passage of trade goods, supplies, and arms to the Confederacy. It was only a matter of time before the Union fleet arrived in the Gulf of Mexico and sailed down to the ports of Texas with a like mission in mind. Maintaining a clear waterway to transport Texas's cash crop to Europe and Mexico in exchange for desperately needed munitions was absolutely essential. To meet these concerns, Edward Clark, the state's acting governor, sent a battle-seasoned captain in the Texas Rangers to East Texas to form a home guard unit and named Howbutker as its mustering site.

Captain Jethro Burleson had joined the legendary Texas Rangers at twenty years of age and had spent the last twenty-two protecting the Texas frontier against outlaws, Mexican bandits, and marauding Indians. General Zachary Taylor, under whom he served in the Mexican-American War, called him Wind Rider because he could ride the fleetest mount with the expert horsemanship of a Comanche warrior.

Jessica hated him on sight because he had distinguished himself in the Cherokee War in East Texas in 1839 in which Chief Bowles, the tribe's wise and venerable eighty-three-year-old leader, had been killed. Jessica had championed Chief Bowles's decades-long fight to secure land rights for his people in Texas.

But if anybody could bring her son safely home from the conflict, she thought, gazing at the grizzled veteran holding forth as a guest at her dinner table, it was Captain Jethro Burleson.

Thomas caught her eye and winked. She returned a small smile that did not lighten the visible worry on her face. At the head of the table, his father sat as somberly, flanked by the no less dour men of the DuMont and Warwick households and Jake Davis, who would not allow his family's falling-out with the Tolivers to interfere with his friendship with his childhood friend.

The only women present were Jessica and Priscilla, neither of whom added to the glow cast by the candle chandelier. Thomas was well aware of the grim nature of his mother's thoughts as Captain Burleson spoke of his expectation that the war would be "much longer than those fools in the legislature realize," and of his wife's meditations as well. Priscilla was probably hoping the evening would never end, for that would mean she and Thomas would adjourn upstairs to the room prepared for the newly married couple before he reported to duty, and there she would be expected to perform her marital responsibility.

Their wedding night had been a disaster. Thomas had anticipated Priscilla looking forward to the marriage act, wanting a child as quickly as he, but she had been nervous, afraid, tense in his arms, squeezing her eyes shut and gritting her teeth as if she expected a fist in her face. She had screamed out at the first hint of penetration. "I'm not ready," she cried, pushing him off her. "Please stop!"

He had felt like a monster. "What's wrong? What did I do?"

"You're…it's so…big, so…" Her lips had twisted in distaste, and she'd turned away from him and drawn her body into a rigid ball.

Priscilla had, of course, never seen a man's appendage before, but Thomas would have thought her mother would have informed her of what to expect on her wedding night. Or maybe she had, he'd thought. Ima Woodward was a Puritanical woman. She had probably put the fear of God into her daughter.

"Well, sweetheart," he'd said, "it's normal for a man's…genital organ to…enlarge when he desires a woman."

She'd peeped at him over her shoulder. "You desire me? It's not just to impregnate me?"

"Of course not," he'd lied.

The second night had not been much better. Priscilla had been willing, but he might as well have tried to coax a flame from wet kindling. The third night they had achieved copulation, but it had not been the loving, joyous consummation Thomas had envisioned. Lying afterwards on her side of the bed, he in a fume of disappointment on his, he'd asked, "What is wrong, Priscilla? Can you explain the reason for your reluctance? Don't you love me?"

"Of course I do," she'd said, her voice plaintive, sounding like the cry of a kitten lost from its mother. "It's just that it's all so...frightening."

Frightening? He had known numerous women, and none of them had complained that he frightened them. They'd all loved the way he made love.

He had turned to her, moved by the fragile outline of her body beneath the sheet, the lustrous tangle of her blond hair on the pillow, and caressed her face. It was oval-shaped and sweet as a rose. "It will be all right, Priscilla," he'd said. "It will just take time and patience."

But in the two weeks they'd been married, he was out of both. In a few days, at the beginning of June, his company would deploy to join another group in Galveston to defend the coast, and so far, Thomas had no reason to hope he'd leave his wife pregnant.

From her side of the table, Priscilla suddenly brightened and launched into a subject that had come to fascinate her. "Captain Burleson, be aware that you are carrying off the sons of aristocrats whose forebears acquitted themselves with famous bravery on English battlefields," she informed him.

It was the wine, an anesthetic to dull her dread of the coming night, Thomas thought, only then realizing his wife was tipsy. Priscilla was a fastidiously decorous woman—girl, for she had no claim to the realm of his mother. It was not like her to burst forth with a line of conversation that held no interest to the captain and would have embarrassed his parents and guests if pursued, but Priscilla had an inordinate interest in his family's and their best friends' ties to a royal past.

"How is that, Mrs. Toliver?" Captain Burleson asked, raising shaggy eyebrows in a polite show of interest.

"It doesn't bear telling," Jessica said promptly and rang the small silver bell at her plate to summon Petunia. "Gentlemen, port and cigars await you in the drawing room."

Priscilla looked rebuffed, and Thomas felt sorry for her. He went around to draw back her chair and whispered in her ear, "Another time, sweet, when we're all in a mood for your enthusiasm."

"I was only trying to change the subject, and I'm so proud of your family history," Priscilla said, pouting.

"I know, Priscilla, but nobody cares about it but us. Take the wine up with you. It might help you to relax."

"That would be good," she said, lifting the decanter a little desperately to pour more wine into her glass.

Thomas sighed and left her to join the men.

All through the port and cigars, the war talk, Thomas's thoughts were on the girl he had married. He could not understand it. When a woman loved a man, wasn't it the most natural, normal desire in the world to want to be close to him, to feel him in her body, to possess and hold him? Priscilla said she loved him. Was it that she sensed he did not return her feelings that she could not give herself totally to the marriage act? Or was it because she was simply repulsed by everything associated with sexual intercourse—the sweat and fluids and animalistic coupling, the feeling of personal violation and…pain.

Heat surged to his face as he thought with shame of her pain during penetration long before he could conclude his objective, let alone his enjoyment. What was he to do? He would not force himself on his wife. He had tried to be gentle and considerate, but his patience was running out with the time he had left at home. Had he made a terrible mistake? Had he been wrong about Priscilla's feelings for him? Had it been mere infatuation with his looks, his family's prominence, and the Tolivers' connection to royalty that she'd mistaken as love for him? Had she lied to him when she said she wanted children as much as he?

Thomas looked across the room at his father, still stalwart and handsome at his age, still so attractive to his mother who had adored him long before he came to feel the same for her, if Thomas had correctly interpreted the secrets he'd heard at their bedroom window in the early dawn hours of last year. Henri and Bess, Jeremy and Camellia had enjoyed long and happy marriages as far as he could tell. How he wanted the same for him and Priscilla!

But—he had to remember—those couples had married for love.

He excused himself while the wine was still at play in his wife's bloodstream. Perhaps the alcohol would free her inhibitions, and tonight they would achieve—he admitted it!—the only purpose for which he had married the girl upstairs who waited for him with the sheet drawn to her chin.

Chapter Sixty-Two

I see that my last entries were written in July of 1861. Has it been over two years since I have recorded my thoughts and feelings and the events of these heart-sickening, blood curdling times that have fallen on America. As a mother of a son, I cannot think of the land of my birth as two nations. The tragedies of war combine us as one.

The glaring blank space between years is no reflection of the lack of occurrences around here, simply the lack of heart and scarcity of paper and ink on which to record them for posterity. I laugh, though only in derision, when I remember Lorimer Davis's boast that the Confederates would have the Yankees on the run by May Day of 1862, a little over a year after war was declared. Well, May first came, but there was no cause for ribbons and flowers and ring-around-the-flagpole. No one was in the mood for a festival.

My God, I should say not. By April of that year, the Confederates had suffered untold casualties at Shiloh in Tennessee, and New Orleans had fallen to the North. In July, the Union fleet occupied Galveston, and in September, General Lee's army lost a major battle to overwhelming federal forces at Antietam in Maryland. The wounded are trickling home, some minus limbs, hearing, sight. The butcher's son had his nose shot off. Oh, the stories these young men tell returning from the battlefields, they who had departed to a send-off of bands playing and flags waving, their stomachs full of barbeque and fried chicken from picnics and parties, their makeshift uniforms unbloodied—those who will speak of the killing grounds, that is. Most do not talk at all. Their silence is like a tomb that enshrouds them.

Newspaper accounts strike like a fist to the heart. Most of the soldiers on both sides are barely out of their adolescence with no experience of warfare, weaponry, or knowledge of why they're fighting. Engagements with the enemy are fought Napoleonic style. The young men are lined up to march in ranks toward entrenched opponents. Those in the line still standing then engage those in the trenches in hand-to-hand combat. The bloody aftermath must be the most appalling, ungodly sight on earth, next only to the filthy army camps and the shocking conditions that breed disease of every contagious variety. One reporter wrote that if a bullet did not kill you, disease would. Walter Bates, the barber, lost his son in an epidemic of typhoid fever, and Billy Costner died from bowels destroyed by dysentery. Untreated measles, chickenpox, mumps, and whooping cough are just a few of the outbreaks that can threaten the lives of soldiers confined to camps littered with refuse, food wastes, heaps of manure and offal. Consumption of contaminated food and water are other hazards against the chance of survival.

I listen to the stories and read the newspaper articles without taking a breath, for of course I'm thinking of Thomas and the boys and the conditions under which they're living, the dangers they face. He is in a specialized unit that makes daring strikes into Louisiana to cripple the enemy's ability to cross the Sabine into Texas. By necessity, their camps are without shelter and most often near stagnant swamps teeming with snakes, crocodiles, and malaria-carrying mosquitoes. Our son has given us few details about the deadly nature of his missions on the few occasions he's been home, but his father and I can guess from his hollow eyes and cheeks, his thinner frame, the state of his clothes. On his last visit, Thomas asked for my remaining ink and notepad, for he'd been assigned the task of writing the parents and spouses of the men in his unit who had died in a brush fire ignited during heavy fighting in a dry field.

"You need all my paper?" I asked him.

He replied with a grim mouth, "I need it all."

I find it bitterly amusing that Henri, bless his Frenchman's heart, insisted the boys be outfitted in custom-tailored uniforms, such as their specifications were in the Confederate army at the time. Those uniforms have long seen the dust of the road.

Henri supplied me with more ink and paper, and today I write with the blood of every one of us in the region running cold. Occupation of East Texas will come within weeks unless our troops—among them Thomas, Jeremy Jr., Armand, Jake, and Priscilla's two brothers—can hold off the Union forces at Sabine Pass, a waterway off the Gulf Coast leading into the Sabine River. It is there the Federals hope to push into the interior of the state with the primary intent of plundering everything they can get their hands on to fuel their war machines and confiscate cotton for northern textile mills. Terrifying news has arrived that gunboats and transport ships loaded with thousands of Union soldiers have entered the pass, defended only by an undermanned fort to which the boys have been sent as reinforcements.

If my son should perish, this will be my last entry in my diary. Someone else—a DuMont or Warwick, even Priscilla if she's still in the mood—will have to take up the chronicling of the founding families of Howbutker. There will be no following generation of Tolivers to read it.

At least it looks that way now. Each morning I rise under the weight of a mother's worry for the happiness of her only child and for Priscilla's, too. It was obvious from their first night together that things had not gone well in the bedroom, and after mornings of the children coming down to breakfast with drawn, disappointed faces, Silas and I suspect that Priscilla is afraid of marital intimacy. Never would Silas blame Thomas. "Look at him!" his father will storm. "Can you imagine any young woman not wanting our son. My God, every female he meets practically drops her drawers for him!"

Silas blames Priscilla's mother—"that dried prune of a woman with as much sexuality about her as a wooden spoon!"—as responsible for putting ridiculous fears about men into her daughter's head. But I, too, must shoulder some responsibility for Thomas's befuddlement with Priscilla and therefore his ineptitude in understanding her. He grew up with no sisters and a mother who requires no coddling or celebrating, who does not need love expressed in words or pampering. It would never occur to him that such manifestations of devotion are what Priscilla craves.

But if Thomas loved the girl, understanding of her needs would come naturally. He would have the desire to please her. I do not point out to Silas that by now Priscilla may have realized Thomas only married her to beget an heir and that her disinclination for sex may have something to do with the girl's wish not to be used. As much as she loves Thomas, she has her pride after all. At the very least, if the girl does suffer from an arousal disorder, knowledge of his lack of feelings for her would certainly not help.

I see them moving beyond the other's reach, and I am sad. Distance allowed to grow too long between people can make it impossible to meet again. This I fear for Thomas and Priscilla.

Chapter Sixty-Three

After their sons left for war, Silas, Henri, and Jeremy expanded their "Men's Day at Somerset" to include the fourth Saturday of every month rather than limit their meetings to those only in winter. Tomahawk's death had put an end to the point of the gathering, but by then, fresh meat from the scout's kills had long ceased to be the motivation for the men to collect around the campfire in front of Silas's one-room plantation office. After their sons' departure, the three longtime friends had discussed a change of venue, but nothing had ever come of it. They still hauled food baskets and a keg of beer to be set up under the pecan tree that shaded the hard-packed ground in front of Silas's cabin.

For the last four years, talk around the campfire had been grim for the fathers, whose sons had been involved in nearly every battle and border skirmish to repulse invaders since the capture of Galveston in 1861. Captain Burleson's home guard unit had been engaged in defending internal trade routes, railroads, bridges, telegraph lines, and making sorties into hostile territory with the objective of destroying the same. Thomas and Philippe had almost been captured in Shreveport when they rendezvoused with a resistance group bent on blowing up Union gunboats moored in the Sabine.

Today's meeting was the grimmest yet. It was May 1864. A

vicious battle newspapers were calling the Red River Campaign had ensued between rebel and federal troops on the banks of the river that formed the border between Texas and Oklahoma. It was another attempt by Union forces to invade Texas, and the boys' unit was in the black heart of it. One of the Union's aims was to capture Marshall, a town twenty miles from Howbutker, and destroy its factories that supplied crucial munitions and goods to the Confederacy. Occupation of Marshall would open the door to East Texas and the rest of the state and give the invaders access to its cotton, horses, livestock, and food. They would leave a path of pillage and wreckage in their wake, the destruction setting back the state's infrastructure and economic development twenty years. The Confederates meant to hold the border at all costs, and once again local residents were hunkering in their houses, weapons ready for defense if the Yankees broke through.

The three old friends had been reluctant to leave their womenfolk, but their wives had insisted. Invasion would not come for days if it came, and they knew how much their husbands enjoyed and needed the all-male get-togethers to let off steam, talk business, and damn every politician that ever made war and every general that ever sent men into battle.

The day was too warm for a fire. Petunia had sent the last jar of pickled pigs' feet, a cold corn custard, a salad of cucumbers and onions, deviled eggs, and wedges of her "Petunia bread," made from flour ground from oats and pecans. Henri had contributed a canned plum pudding imported from England smuggled past the Union blockade.

"A feast!" Henri declared, unpacking the basket. "How I wish the boys could share some of this bounty."

"Maybe soon," Silas said. "I don't see how the war can go on much longer."

"By next spring is my guess," Jeremy said.

The men could hear the wistfulness in their voices. Hanging over them like the smoke from their cigars was the unspoken terror that the miracle of their sons still being alive after four years of combat could not last.

Henri and Jeremy heaped their plates. Silas declined, preferring another glass of beer.

"Aren't you going to eat something, Silas?" Henri asked.

"I'm not hungry. I'll try something later."

Silas noticed a look exchanged between his old friends. "All right, what is it?" he demanded. "I sense collusion."

Henri said, "You do not look well, *mon ami*. You've lost weight and your ruddy glow is gone."

"We've all lost our ruddy glow," Silas said. "What father with a son in the war hasn't?"

"We think you need to see a doctor," Jeremy said.

"Woodward is a quack, and I'd cause a family rift if I visited his competitor. I feel fine. It's just that I have...other worries."

"I thought the plantation was managing splendidly under the circumstances," Henri said.

"It's not that."

Jeremy asked quietly, "What is it then, Silas?"

Silas drew in a deep breath and held it. Men were not confiders like women. They managed their affairs without the need for advice or guidance from even the closest of friends, dealt with their problems, kept their secrets. If a man needed a listening post, he usually turned to his wife. But sometimes he could not share his concerns with his wife. He needed another man's ear—a trusted friend's—and Silas had the benefit of the most trusted in Jeremy and Henri. But he could not unburden the grief eating at his heart like hungry fire ants. What comfort could his friends give him? What advice to correct the problem? Silas did not think he could describe even to Jessica the misery of the guilt he felt in encouraging Thomas to marry Priscilla, and all for the sake of an heir for Somerset. Would the Tolivers ever learn?

Silas let out his breath. "I—it's my son and daughter-in-law," he said. He could divulge that. "They're not happy."

"A pity," Henri murmured.

"I'm sorry," Jeremy said. "What seems to be the trouble?"

"They're...not compatible." Silas took a long swallow of beer to chase the sour taste prevalent in his mouth these days. His stomach felt empty. He had no appetite lately, and he could feel the alcohol soar straight to his head. "I once believed Thomas and Priscilla were a well-matched couple," he said.

"Perhaps they've not had the opportunity to be a couple, what with the boys darting home for only weeks at a time on and off these past years," Jeremy offered.

Silas attempted a grin. "Armand and Jeremy Jr. have been married for less than a year and already their wives are pregnant."

"So it's a grandchild you're wanting?" Henri said.

"Yes, but more than that—" Silas stood and jammed his hands into his pockets. Oh, damnation! He must pour out his feelings to someone or burst. He began. "I knew Thomas did not love Priscilla when he married her, but I thought she loved him, and her affection would bridge the gap. Thomas would grow to reciprocate her feelings as...I grew to love his mother. I wanted him to experience the thrill of discovering small, delightful things about the girl he did not know, her mind, her heart, her body, the kinds of things that made me crazy about Jessica when I married her, that I took pride and joy in, that made her become indispensable to my life, but..."

"But Priscilla is not Jessica," Jeremy said.

"No, she most certainly is not." Silas sat down again, the

strength gone from his legs. "There are no sweet surprises or secret desires or hidden passions tucked behind the closed door of Thomas's wife. In my opinion, Priscilla Woodward is an empty room."

"Merciful saints!" Henri said.

Silas was appalled at himself, feeling a traitor to his son's wife, his daughter-in-law, a member of the family. He blushed. "Forgive me for talking so frankly of my feelings. I'm ashamed of myself," he said.

Henri threw up his hands. "*Mon ami*, there is nothing to forgive and no reason to feel ashamed. Feelings are neither right nor wrong. They just are."

Jeremy cleared his throat. "And you feel responsible for Thomas's marriage?"

"I encouraged it."

"But it was Thomas's decision to marry her, Silas, not yours," Jeremy said.

"But it was a decision I prompted because of my…obsessive love of the plantation. Thomas, to please me, wanted to leave an heir for Somerset in case…" Silas could not bear to say it. He scraped a hand over his face, feeling it bony, and went on desperately. "I can't sleep at night for worry that because of me, Thomas is condemned to a loveless, perhaps childless marriage. Now that the war is almost over and there's a good chance he'll make it home in one piece…" Silas left unsaid the obvious implication that if his son had only waited, he might have met and married a woman he loved. "I am haunted by the wasted sacrifice he made on behalf of Somerset," he added dully.

"Again, Thomas's decision, not yours," Jeremy said.

"I concur," Henri said, turning up his palms in the French manner. "The sins of the fathers…the children do not have to bear them. They can make their own sins."

Silas threw them a small smile. "You're trying to absolve me of my guilt."

"No absolution is necessary when no guilt is involved," Jeremy said.

"I just want Thomas to be happy. I want that above all else, heir or no."

"We know," Jeremy said, "and if God is listening, He knows it, too. That's why no curse is involved here. You're thinking of Thomas, not Somerset."

"And we must not give up hope that once the war is over and Thomas and Priscilla are together, time and peace and privacy will solve their problems," Henri said. He held up his glass, and Silas and Jeremy raised theirs. "My friends, a toast to our boys' safe return and their future happiness."

"Here! Here!" the men chorused, and as Silas drank, he thought he must ask Jeremy to explain his comment. What made him refer to a *curse*? But his intent was lost in a flush of gratitude for the loyalty and understanding of his friends and the awareness of a recurring fullness beneath his ribs and a pain in his groin.

Jeremy, as usual, read his mind. "Silas, my boy," he said, "you need to see a doctor."

"I believe I will," Silas said.

Chapter Sixty-Four

The war reached Howbutker in September of 1864 and took one of its most beloved native sons. Jessica, Priscilla, and Petunia were in the kitchen preparing cloth packets of corncob ashes as a substitute for soda to distribute to neighbors when Amy, eight years old and a "mother's helper," was sent to answer the pull of the front doorbell. Wartime shortages and the Union blockade of supply ships had generated ingenious ideas for replacements of coffee, flour, pepper, sugar, and salt. Residents of Houston Avenue had formed a cooperative exchange. Individuals were assigned specific tasks of preparing large quantities of substitute items to be shared by all. As examples, Bess DuMont had become quite proficient at roasting and grinding acorns and okra seeds to make a fairly decent cup of coffee, and Camellia Warwick had refined the art of making passable flour from potatoes. The women of Houston Avenue made a morning social occasion of the exchange, taking turns entertaining the group in their homes. Jessica was to host the following day.

"That's probably Mrs. Davis bringing me an arrangement of her chrysanthemums for the table," Jessica said.

"She sure been nicer to you since Mister Silas been proved right on all accounts, and her husband been proved wrong," Petunia said. "You got to hand it to her. She eat crow without tryin' to sugar it."

"A hollow vindication for Silas, though," Jessica said. Silas's predictions had come to pass. The Confederacy had not been able to sustain itself against the military might of the North, and rumors flew that a major invasion was under way to lay waste to the Southland. France and Great Britain did not come to the aid of the Confederacy in exchange for its cotton as expected, and slaves were running away from plantations by the hundreds owing to the drain of their overseers to the war and having no incentive to stay. So far, Somerset's labor force, but for a few desertions, had remained intact.

But it was a neighborhood boy from down the street who burst into the kitchen, Amy hurrying after him, alarm written across her young face. The boy whipped off his hat, breathless, his face flushed. "Miss Jessica," he panted, "the bluecoats have come."

Jessica jumped up. "*What?* Where are they?"

"In the pasture in back of your house. They're stealing the horses."

"Priscilla, you know where the pistols are. Arm the servants," Jessica ordered. "Petunia, you stay here with Amy. Leon, do you know how to use a gun?"

"I sure do. My daddy taught me, just in case."

"Priscilla, give him a pistol, too."

"What are we going to do?" her daughter-in-law asked, eyes large with fright.

"I don't know."

Jessica grabbed the flintlock standing at the ready by the door in the larder and headed for the back door. All the men on the street were at their places of work, the children in school. The question flashed through Jessica's mind why Leon, son of their banker, was home. She heard a cough from what sounded like a deep chest cold and understood why. Only the women were home, most napping this time of day, their servants oblivious to the scene that met her eyes when she stepped onto the high floor of the gazebo and peered toward the pasture.

A dozen or so men on horseback and wearing Federal army uniforms were twirling ropes in pursuit of Houston Avenue's carriage horses, let out from their stalls for the day. The horses were resisting capture, successfully dodging the rope nooses tossed at their heads. To her horror, Jessica saw Flight O' Fancy among them. The Thoroughbred had caught the attention of the officer in charge. She could clearly hear his orders to *"Get that horse!"*

She stood helplessly. The soldiers mustn't get their hands on Nanette's horse, but what could she do, a lone woman with one flintlock between her and a dozen armed men? She must not risk injury to Leon or expose Priscilla to them. One look at her and no telling what those soldiers might do. She wished for Jeremiah, wise and strong, but he had died two springs ago. Her mind in a lock of indecision, she gasped as she saw Robert Warwick run out to the pasture, pistol in hand. She had forgotten he'd be home, working as he always did in his carpentry shop. He was building a desk for Thomas as a welcome-home gift. *Oh, good Lord, no!*

Priscilla, Leon, and the servants had come outside, the collection from Silas's gun cabinet in their hands.

"Priscilla, run to the next-door houses and tell the neighbors what's happening and to arm themselves," she said. "Tell them to send a runner to alert the house next to theirs and they in turn are to send somebody to alert the neighbor next to them and so on. Hurry now. No time to waste."

"Yes, ma'am," Priscilla said, looking relieved at her task.

The officer in command, a first lieutenant by the parallel bars on his yellow shoulder straps, swung his horse around at Robert's approach and withdrew his pistol from its holster. Without thinking but with enough presence of mind to leave the flintlock behind, Jessica flew down the steps of the gazebo and through the wrought-iron gate across the service road hollering *"No! No!"*

Every man turned to look at her. Flight O' Fancy, seeing Robert, had stopped running and ambled toward him.

"Miss Jessica!" Robert said, his voice echoing his surprise when she reached the conclave. "What are you doing here?"

"Hoping to talk some sense into every mother's son here. Good afternoon, Lieutenant."

The lieutenant recovered the use of his dropped jaw and said, "Madam," and brought his gloved hand to the brim of his cavalry hat.

"Robert dear," Jessica said, "please put your gun on the ground. It will be useless against so many here."

Robert at twenty-three had never outgrown the whistle and rattle in his lungs. His bronchial condition had left him looking as if a strong wind could blow him away. He had no more wherewithal to challenge the mounted cavalry unit than a stick against a battering ram.

"I'd do what she says," the lieutenant said, his tone and the steel in his eye receptive to no argument. Flight O' Fancy had reached them, her flanks quivering nervously.

"You can't have this horse," Robert said, lowering his pistol but keeping it by his side.

"I am going to take her and all these horses here, so drop your weapon and both of you go back where you came from and no harm will come to you."

"You are not taking her," Robert said, his jaw set obstinately. "She'll be no war horse for the Union army."

"She will be when I'm through with her."

"No, never. I'd rather see her dead first," Robert declared and positioned the gun to a spot behind Flight O' Fancy's ear and fired.

Jessica couldn't believe her eyes. From their stunned stares, neither could the mounted men. It took a moment while the horse thundered sickeningly to the ground and the smoke cleared from Robert's pistol for them all to realize what had happened.

"Well, now, you shouldn't have done that," the lieutenant said and aimed his firearm at Robert's head.

"No, please!" Jessica screamed, but it was too late. The bullet struck Robert in the middle of his forehead and he crumpled to a gangly heap beside the body of the fallen horse. Jessica dropped to her knees beside him and cradled his bleeding head in her lap. He had died instantly, defiance locked in his frozen stare. Jessica looked up at the officer through a glaze of shocked tears. "How could you do such a thing? He was just a boy."

"Weren't we all once?" the lieutenant said. "A man who would shoot a beautiful horse like that for the reason he gave doesn't deserve to live."

"The horse belonged to the girl he loved. She died at fifteen. Robert looked after her mare in memory of her," Jessica said, eyes overflowing.

Remorse washed over the lieutenant's face. He looked away across the green space of the pasture for a moment, then back at Jessica. "War is nothing if not a series of tragic misjudgments, madam. My sincere regret for mine."

Jessica heard a commotion behind her and glanced over her shoulder to see the mistresses of Houston Avenue and their servants taking position in a line of billowy hoop skirts and maids' uniforms stretching almost the length of the service road. They held guns and had been trained how to use them in defense of their homes. Among them were mothers whose sons had been lost or wounded in battles in Texas and all across the Southland.

They seemed to be waiting for a signal from her about what they should do.

Camellia Warwick, small, delicate, broke through the file with a shriek and ran toward them, her hooped skirt almost lifting her from the ground. Jessica turned back to the lieutenant. "Leave now, young man, and go home to the mother who will never know the grief you've caused this boy's. Stay, and there will be further bloodshed, possibly yours."

"I make no war against women and servants," the lieutenant said, "but I aim to take the horses. Signal to your people to stand down, and we will be on our way."

Silas had been in Dr. Woodward's office when the tragedy occurred. Afterwards he rode out to Somerset to his favorite vantage point overlooking his plantation and the result of his life's work. The peace that usually calmed his troubled mind and eased into his soul did not come. He did not hear of the grievous events in the pasture or of his wife's heroism until he returned home at dusk. There was sadness enough, he thought. He decided to wait until the brunt of Robert's death had passed to give Jessica the news of Dr. Woodward's diagnosis.

Chapter Sixty-Five

April twelfth, 1865, would always be remembered in the family annals of the Tolivers, DuMonts, and Warwicks as the day "the boys" came home. The War Between the States was practically over. On April ninth, General Robert E. Lee, commander of Confederate Forces, recognizing its inevitable outcome, had surrendered his 28,000 troops to the Union commander, General Ulysses S. Grant, at Appomattox in Virginia to avoid further casualties and destruction of property in the Southland. Both were staggering. Sam Houston's words of warning that in case of war, the state would lose "the flower of Texas manhood" applied in devastating numbers to the Texas Confederates who had defended the South. Jake Davis was among them. Late in the war he had split off from Captain Burleson's unit to join the Texas Brigade that fought in the Eastern Theater under General Lee. It was Jake who sent back word to the Tolivers that Willowshire had been burned to the ground by one of the regiments under the command of U.S. Army general William T. Sherman during his flaming march through South Carolina. Jessica could easily picture the scene of its destruction from the description her brother Michael gave to Jake.

February in Plantation Alley was always a bleak time of year, the color of dusk, and one afternoon, Michael had been startled when one of the servants burst into the library and shouted that the bluecoats were coming. Her brother had stared out his window at a Union colonel on horseback leading a column of blue-coated soldiers at an unhurried gait down the leafless lane of Willowshire to the front of the mansion. Jessica was thankful their parents were not alive to see what happened next. According to Michael's report to Jake, her brother had gone out to meet the intruders and stood on the verandah while the officer in command dismounted and his men remained in the saddle and fanned out around him.

"Good afternoon," the officer said to Michael, removing his gloves as he climbed the steps. "Allow me to introduce myself. I am Colonel Paul Conklin. Perhaps you remember my aunt."

Michael admitted he must have blanched white as a cotton boll, for of course he remembered Sarah Conklin.

The colonel allowed him to remove his family, servants, and hunting dogs from the house before the fires were lit, but he ordered everything else to be left behind. Jessica believed that it was for the sake of her friendship with his beloved aunt the soldiers were not permitted to loot the home of her childhood, and for that, she was grateful.

The boys came home on the eve Silas took to his bed, never able to rise from it again. Before then, he had managed to ride out to the plantation every day, see to his business affairs, and attend meetings of the city council, to which he'd been re-elected. Suspecting Silas's disease from his symptoms, Dr. Woodward had sent him to Houston to a doctor with special knowledge of cancer of the blood. The specialist concurred with Dr. Woodward's diagnosis: Silas was suffering from a condition known as leukemia. There was no treatment or cure.

Thomas was devastated. No grief he'd experienced in the war could compare to the sorrow of the coming demise of his father. He had returned home for Robert's funeral in September, and he had noticed how greatly his father had aged. Something had been amiss, but he attributed it to his father's years of worry that his only child would be counted among the war's casualties, and the death of Robert had left its mark. His parents, more dear to him than ever, his wife a stranger, suffered deeply for the Warwicks. On that visit to his home, he said to Priscilla, "I want a child, Priscilla, and now. Do you understand?"

She'd nodded, fearful, as usual, but Thomas did not care. For God's sake, what had the girl expected when she became a wife! That she would simply be set on a shelf and looked at? What use was she if she was no lover, companion, or helpmate and could not bear him children?

She submitted, and Thomas left her wondering where her tender, considerate, understanding husband had gone, but when he returned for good in April, he found her eight months pregnant. He prayed nightly for the safe delivery of his child and that his father might live to see a Toliver of the third generation who would someday become heir to the plantation of Somerset.

"I do not know how I can live without Silas," Jessica said to Jeremy. They still met around ten o'clock some mornings for a cup of Bess DuMont's bitter acorn coffee in the gazebo when the laudanum had eased Silas's pain and allowed him to sleep.

"It isn't a matter of living," Jeremy said, his voice throaty with grief. "It's a matter of staying alive for those left behind."

He and Henri came every day to cajole with Silas, gossip, bring the latest war news, to assist in his baths, to sit with him when Jessica needed a break. Jeremy read to him as his sight weakened. Henri brought special treats from his store. Their pain behind their jocularity broke Jessica's heart.

Silas lived three weeks after Priscilla delivered a healthy, nine-pound boy. She asked that her son be named Vernon after an obscure member in the genealogy she'd resurrected to the status of hero on the basis of his participation in the War of the Roses.

"Vernon," Silas repeated, his voice hoarse from pain and medication as he propped up in bed to hold the baby for the first time. "I like the name. How clever of you, Priscilla. I see the little trooper has your fine ears. Do you mind that the rest of him has your husband's side of the family to blame?"

"I am thrilled about it," Priscilla gushed, glancing at Thomas, who stood close to his father on the other side of the bed. Jessica caught the look. It was full of hopeless yearning: *I have performed. Now love me.* But her husband's attention was on Silas, obviously impressing on memory his father's joy as he looked into the face of his grandson.

During his lucid periods, Silas called Thomas to his bedside, and they spent every minute in a huddle over accounting books and business papers and plans for the survival of Somerset. Silas warned that Texas and the South were in for a long period of turmoil. "Our state will be slow to bend its knee to Northern dominance and Texas may not be reinstated into the Union for a long time," he predicted between moments of losing and regaining his voice. "Lawlessness will be rampant, and the old order of our social structure will be in ruins. Our money will be worthless and land values will drop drastically, but you must not despair, son. Hold on to the land. Better times will come, and Somerset will thrive."

Unable to bear being beyond the sound of Silas's voice for as long as it was heard, Jessica sat in the sitting room next to the wall by their bed during these sessions and could hear the exchange of every word. She was torn between telling Silas of her bank account in Boston to ease his worry over money and the risk of his disfavor toward Jeremy when he learned of their pact to keep the money a secret from him.

"Don't take the risk, Jess," Jeremy advised during one of their morning interludes in the gazebo. "For my sake, don't tell him."

"You believe it would matter at this point that we were in cahoots together?"

"I'm sure it would."

Jessica heard a strange note in his voice. "Why?"

Jeremy had discovered a loose nail in the swing. He diverted his attention to pushing it back into position with his thumb. "Just trust me, Jess. In some ways I know your husband better than you. He would mind that you took me into your confidence over him and that I acted upon it without his knowledge."

"As you wish, Jeremy," Jessica said. "I would do nothing to damage your lifelong friendship, not here at its end."

Before his death, Silas had been cognizant of President Abraham Lincoln's assassination in April, the capture of Confederate president Jefferson Davis in Georgia in May, news that the possibility of natural gas might replace candles for lighting and wood for cooking, and Jessica's proud announcement that Maria Mitchell, an advocate in the women's rights movement, had become the first woman professor of astronomy in the United States when she was appointed to a teaching position at Vassar College in New York. Silas had grinned and said, "What in the world is the world coming to?" and earned an affectionate swipe at his arm from his wife.

The last day of his life, Jessica heard Silas gasp to Thomas, "Son, I'm aware…that your marriage is…not all you'd like it to be, but will you take…a word of advice from your father?"

"I always have, Papa."

"You may…never grow to…love Priscilla, but you must… respect her love for you. It is not a…trifling thing. It is to be honored. Give her the grace of your...acceptance of it, if...nothing else...."

Jessica rose to her feet, her hand pressed to her lips. It had been a struggle for Silas to get the words out of his mouth, among the last she believed she would ever hear from her husband. Her fear proved justified. Just as day broke the next morning, she woke from an exhausted sleep to feel Silas press her hand. "Jessica..." he gasped.

She was instantly awake and by his side. "Yes, my love?"

"It...was..." His lips formed a word beginning with *w*, but it was never uttered.

"Wonderful," Jessica said. Gently she drew his lids closed and kissed his lips. "Yes, it was, my dearest love."

Silas died at dawn on June 19, 1865, the day the Union commander of U.S. troops in the state issued the order that the Emancipation Proclamation abolishing slavery was in effect in Texas.

Chapter Sixty-Six

There began a period whose events would not make it into Jessica's latest diary for over a year. The elegant, red-leather volume of her first recordings had been followed by black-faced utilitarian journals that gave way to commonplace notebooks when they were available. A stack of her musings, impressions, experiences was arranged chronologically on a shelf in her secretary, begun the first months of her marriage to Silas. Her last recording ended in June of 1865. No other entries followed. The final page read:

We have buried Silas. Thomas wished to inter his body at Somerset, at a place only he and Silas knew about. "It overlooks the plantation, Mother, where Papa often went for meditation," he said to me. "I'd like to visit him there."

I thought of Joshua, alone in the family plot set aside in the county cemetery where a tombstone in memory of Nanette DuMont is erected and Robert Warwick is buried, but I could not refuse my son his heart's wish. I did not know of such a place, but then there is so much of Somerset I do not know.

It is truly a beautiful place where my husband lies. A red oak tree shades his grave and a creek flows close by. The wind is gentle there and carries the hum of the spirituals and songs the workers sing in the fields. I suspect Thomas often stops there to confer with his papa. It is a private place just for them, and I feel excluded, but I am glad I did not oppose the choice Silas would have approved. I was his heart, but Somerset was his soul.

Years later Jessica would read "The Bustle in a House," a poem by Emily Dickinson, that described her activities after Silas's death and accounted for the long period between her writings. When she finally took pen in hand again, she went back to the blank pages of June of that year and inscribed in her diary the poet's immortal words:

> *The bustle in a house*
> *The morning after death*
> *Is solemnest of industries*
> *Enacted upon earth*
>
> *The sweeping up the heart*
> *And putting love away*
> *We shall not want to use again*
> *Until eternity*

Silas lay in the parlor for the last hour of viewing when a copy of the Emancipation Proclamation was put into Thomas's hands from the telegraph office. The order was backed by the arrival of Union general Gordon Granger and 2,000 federal troops in Galveston to see that the order was enforced. Thomas read it and, without a word, passed it to the other planters in the room, then he went to his father and pressed a hand to his cold forehead. "It has come, Papa," he said.

Jessica hoped the memory of the day her son read the proclamation to the slaves never dimmed. From all over the plantation, they gathered for the burial, a sea of black faces, many streaming with tears. The last dirt had been shoveled over Silas's grave and flowers laid before the headstone. It was a mercifully cool day because of a hilltop breeze and an overcast sun.

"Let there be silence," Thomas said, raising his hand and lifting his voice to the assembly. "I have something of importance to read to you."

All tongues ceased and every face turned to fix upon him. He began to recite the contents of General Order No. 3:

> *The people of Texas are informed that, in accordance with a proclamation from the Executive of the United States, all slaves are free. This involves an absolute equality of personal rights and rights of property between former masters and slaves, and the connection heretofore existing between them becomes that between employer and hired laborer. The freedmen are advised to remain quietly at their present homes and work for wages. They are informed that they will not be allowed to collect at military posts and that they will not be supported in idleness either there or elsewhere.*

The slaves looked at one another. A ripple of anxiety curled through the gathering. Jasper and his sons had expected the announcement and been alerted to its contents.

"What does this mean?" somebody asked.

"It means youse is free," Jasper said.

"Mister Thomas ain't my master no more?"

"He's your *employer* if youse stay."

Most stayed. Thomas availed himself of the contracts the agent at the Freedmen's Bureau had prepared for former master and slave, and by the end of the month, Somerset had been parceled into fifty-acre units rented to families under a system that came to be known as tenant farming. Once again, a Toliver had led the way in anticipating the inevitable, and the transition for Thomas from master to proprietor and his slaves from bondsmen to paid workers was relatively painless.

But the Toliver family was not without criticism. Most of the planters had not wanted to inform their slaves of their emancipation until the harvest was in, but Thomas's preemptive disclosure of the freedom act had dashed those hopes. Word spread from cotton field to cotton field, and black workers walked off by the hundreds, leaving their hoes where they dropped them.

"Well, Jessica, you must be happy now," Lorimer Davis said.

"You would assume that so shortly after Silas's death?" Jessica said.

"You know perfectly well I'm talking about the abolishment of slavery."

"I am always happy when justice is done," Jessica said.

Lorimer's slaves had left his cotton to dry unpicked in the fields, and no promise of better treatment had lured them back. Without sufficient manpower, the Davis plantation, like many others in the region, stood on the verge of financial ruin.

General Granger's troops were followed by fifty thousand more that surged into Texas to occupy towns in accordance with the martial law policy imposed by the U.S. Congress upon the "conquered provinces" of the Confederacy. Union occupation was the first phase of a period congressional leaders had officially termed "Reconstruction." Federal officers were to replace civil authorities, protect the freed blacks from oppression, and ensure the safety of the agents of the Freedmen's Bureau, a relief organization set up by the U.S. government to help former slaves adjust to freedom. The citizens of Howbutker, furious at the insult when hometown blood had been spilled to defend Texas borders successfully against invasion, held their collective breath over what occupation would mean.

One afternoon in early July as Houston Avenue snoozed in

the heat of high summer, a clatter of horses' hooves striking the brick street broke the somnolent silence. Jessica was upstairs at the heart-rending task of storing away Silas's clothes in a cotton sack when she heard the commotion. Except for the servants, she was alone in the house. Thomas, as usual, was at the plantation, and her daughter-in-law had taken Vernon to see his other grandmother. Jessica paused in the folding of Silas's shirt. She knew at once that the feared occupation force had arrived. Word had gone before their advance that they were on the way. Citizens had hidden their valuables when they heard reports from communities already occupied that private homes were being used to quarter the men, and speculation was rampant that the Yankees would bivouac on Houston Avenue and its officers commandeer the mansions.

Within minutes, there was a scurry of feet up the stairs as the doorbell reverberated throughout the house. The door flew open. Petunia had not bothered to knock. "Miss Jessica," she said, out of breath, "they's some Union soldiers on the porch."

Calmly, Jessica finished folding Silas's shirt. "Very good, Petunia, I'll go see what they're about."

She could not calm the accelerated beat of her heart as she descended the stairs. There had come reports of incidences of vicious abuse by the occupation troops. In Gonzales, a group of Union soldiers had taken offense at a doctor's comment and dragged him from his office by his feet, then shot and killed him in the street. Homes and stores had been ransacked, personal treasures stolen, property damaged, and liberties taken with women. Jessica had months ago stored away a pistol in the bottom drawer of her wardrobe.

She could see the crown of a federal officer's hat through the fanlight and a series of others bobbing behind him. She opened the door. "Good afternoon. May I help you?" she said.

The officer, a tall man who appeared to be in his early thirties, was in the act of brushing dust from the road off his dark blue, gold-piped jacket. But for his uniform, his boyish looks would have been engaging. Jessica was sympathetically drawn to those cursed with her coloring, but in the major's case, his red-brick hair and fair skin with its sprinkling of freckles were more favorable to a man and further compensated by regular features and white, even teeth. When he saw Jessica, he tipped his hat and bowed slightly.

"Major Andrew Duncan, madam. Forgive the intrusion and my dusty appearance, but may I come in?"

"Do I have a choice?"

"I regret not."

Pointedly, Jessica glanced down at his boots, and the officer grinned and scraped his feet on the porch mat. "Will that do?"

Jessica stepped back from the open door, and the major motioned that his men were to stay outside. He entered, bringing in the smell of a man who's spent hard days in the saddle. The officer's eyes swept around the magnificent, mirror-lit foyer reigned over by the portrait of the Duke of Somerset. "Every bit as beautiful as he described," he said.

Jessica's gaze narrowed. "As who described?"

"My cousin," the major said. "Guy Handley. I'm sure you remember him."

Chapter Sixty-Seven

"Guy?" Jessica echoed. "Of course I remember him."

"I came here myself a number of years ago, but only to your backyard. I came to enlist you to spy for the Union army in case of war, but your maid said you were not home. It was wash day, I remember."

Jessica thought back, vaguely remembering a sneering reference Stephanie Davis made about the presence of a strange man skulking out the back gate—"not one of us," she had said, implying that the man was an abolitionist come to engage her in nefarious activities. Jessica had wondered about it for a while afterwards. For once, Stephanie's suspicions had been on the mark.

"I wouldn't have done it," Jessica said, feeling a flush of indignation. "My sympathies with the abolitionist cause did not include committing treason against the country I knew my son would sign up to defend."

"Guy had warned me of such, and that is why I never returned." The major looked around him. "I would ask to sit, but the condition of my trousers might soil your chairs. Perhaps you could conduct me to a place for a chat where I will do the least damage to your fine fabrics."

"There are leather chairs in my husband's study."

"Lead the way, if you please, and how is your husband?"

"He is dead."

The click of the major's boot heels on the polished hall floor came to a halt. "Oh, I am sorry," he said in a timbre of deep regret. "Guy thought the world of him."

"Do you have any idea what happened to Ezekiel and his wife?" Jessica asked.

"They live in Massachusetts on a dairy farm. They are proud parents of twin boys."

"And Guy?"

"A casualty at Bull Run."

Jessica uttered a cry of sorrow. "Oh, no!" Guy had been killed in the first major battle of the Civil War.

The major took her elbow. "Shall we sit?" he suggested gently.

Jessica led him into the study and gestured to a chair in front of Thomas's desk that had replaced Silas's old one and took a seat behind it. The major ran his hand admiringly over the desk's smooth pine surface. "What fine workmanship," he said.

"It was made for my son by Robert Warwick, a friend of the family especially gifted in carpentry."

The major had spotted *James Toliver* etched discreetly in flowing script on a corner of the desk. "I understood your son's name to be Thomas."

"It is," Jessica said, wondering how the major was acquainted with that fact. "James is my son's middle name. Robert had the strange propensity to write backwards. He never finished carving the name by which my son is referred."

"Why not?"

"A Union cavalry officer shot him in the head."

Major Duncan looked slightly discomfited. "It seems an occasion for exchanging mutual condolences for our war dead."

"Please tell me what else is the purpose for this occasion, Major."

Andrew Duncan crossed one leg over the other and set his cavalry hat on his knee. Trail dirt clung to the sole of his boot. "As you undoubtedly know, this is not a social call. My men and I are here to put Howbutker under the guardianship of the United States Army—"

"A euphemism for military rule, I believe," Jessica interrupted.

The major inclined his head. "If you wish, but in any event we are here to maintain order and in doing so will comply with the established rules governing military occupation. Unless challenged, we will respect all persons and private property. Pillage is prohibited. Severe punishment will be inflicted on any man under my command who abuses the restrictions of his power. You have my word on that."

Jessica nodded. "That sounds reasonable, and you seem a man whose word is not given or taken lightly, but why do I hear a *however*?"

"However," he said, "we expect cooperation from the townspeople—no taunting, spitting, or otherwise outward act of provocation toward my soldiers. They fought as hard and bravely in this war as your soldiers, and…if you'll forgive the reminder… they won. In other words, Mrs. Toliver, there is to be no undermining of what we have been sent here to do, which is to keep peace and order and to see that the will of Congress is carried out."

Befuddled, Jessica lifted her shoulders. "I have no intention of taunting, spitting, or otherwise provoking your soldiers, Major Duncan, so why are you telling me this?"

The major uncrossed his legs and leaned forward. "Not knowing of your husband's death, I have come to ask that he join his friends"—he consulted a sheet of paper he removed from inside his jacket and read—"Henri DuMont and Jeremy Warwick. Guy told me they are men of great influence in town. I was hoping

I could enlist their assistance in convincing certain…recalcitrant groups that their opposition to our presence will only end in more bloodshed."

"You are speaking about members of the vigilante groups who call themselves citizen patrols."

"I am."

"Our son Thomas has taken over his father's duties, and the sons of the gentlemen you mention are not without their own level of influence. In addition to Jeremy and Henri, I could have them speak with you. I am sure they will agree with your aims for peaceful coexistence."

"I would be much obliged, Mrs. Toliver," Andrew said, rising. "And now I'm afraid I must impose further on your goodwill."

Here it comes, Jessica thought, wincing inwardly. The major intended to ask—demand—that he and his officers be put up in the mansion.

"I'd like my men to bivouac in the pasture behind this street, and I understand you have a room available over the carriage house. I will require that for my own use. Will you see to its preparation?"

Jessica expelled a secret sigh of relief. "If you insist, Major."

"I'm afraid I do."

From out in the hall came sounds of Priscilla returning with the baby from the visit to her mother's. Vernon was crying. He'd been denied his nap. Jessica heard Priscilla call her name urgently—response to the shock of finding a group of Union soldiers lounging on the front verandah.

"I am in the study, Priscilla," Jessica called.

Priscilla rushed in, and for the blur of a few seconds, Jessica was mesmerized by her beauty. Heat and anxiety had brought a rosy flush to her cheeks and heightened the color of her blue eyes. Blond ringlets of naturally curly hair bounced about her heart-shaped face, setting off skin as flawless as the fresh petal of a Yorkist rose.

"Oh!" Priscilla said, stopping short when she saw the Union officer.

"Priscilla, dear, this is—" Jessica turned to the major and found him staring at her daughter-in-law in hypnotic awe. "Uh, this is Major Duncan," she said. "He is the commander of the U.S. Army battalion that will be occupying Howbutker. Major, this is my daughter-in-law, the second Mrs. Toliver."

Priscilla, dandling Vernon, whiney and fretful in his mother's arms, said, "How do you do?" in a stunned, captivated voice commensurate with the major's wonder-struck gaze.

Major Duncan recaptured his composure. He stepped forward and extended an upturned palm. Tentatively, Priscilla placed her fingers upon it, and he brought the tips briefly to his lips. "I do well, Mrs. Toliver. My apologies for the interruption in your life."

Jessica felt a prickle of alarm. Priscilla retrieved her hand and looked at Jessica as if seeking a lifeline from a sudden spill into deep waters. "I must get Vernon down for his nap," she said in a flustered voice.

"You do that, my girl," Jessica said. "I'm sure the major will excuse you."

"With great reluctance," Major Duncan said with a gallant bow, "but also with understanding. The little boy must have his sleep."

When Priscilla had left the room, Jessica asked, "Are you married, Major?"

"No, madam. I am a career soldier, and my avocation has not allowed it." He replaced his hat and Jessica saw him to the door.

"When do you plan to take occupancy of the carriage house?" she asked.

"Tomorrow morning, if possible."

Jessica almost suggested that other lodging would be more comfortable than the one-room apartment but thought better of it. The major might agree and decide that a bedroom in the mansion would suit him better.

Jessica called Petunia to organize a cleaning crew for the carriage house then went back upstairs to sit among the items of Silas's strewn wardrobe. She felt his presence more when she was surrounded by his possessions. How she could have used his consolation at this moment! The physical current she'd felt between Major Duncan and Priscilla disturbed her. Perhaps, on the major's part, it was nothing more than a virile man's natural appreciation of a beautiful woman, and on Priscilla's, the pleasure of a handsome man's attraction to her, a thrill no doubt missing in her relationship with her husband.

Their marriage had become a painful thing to observe. Thomas had taken his father's words to heart, and no husband ever treated a wife with more respect or courtesy than he showed Priscilla, if woodenly, and she responded as stiffly.

Her son and daughter-in-law waltzed around each other like mannequins, playing at the role of husband and wife without warmth or spontaneity, their baby the only connection between them. During their engagement, they had talked of building a manor home for themselves on the plantation, but there had been no further discussion of it. When Jessica asked Thomas why, he replied that Priscilla preferred to live in town to be near her parents and he did not wish to leave his mother alone in the house on Houston Avenue. But for Vernon crawling and gurgling on the parlor floor after supper, entertaining them, Jessica could not have borne the ponderous evenings in their company.

Chapter Sixty-Eight

From her upstairs window, Jessica could watch the comings and goings of Major Andrew Duncan. He clattered down the steps of his apartment at sunrise to join his men in the pasture, where they had pitched tents and built campfires. There she supposed he took his coffee and ate his breakfast. He merely slept in the carriage house. He had taken over a building in town as his company headquarters near where the Freedmen's Bureau was housed and close to the location he'd selected as the site of a school for the children of freed slaves.

Stories of the major's fairness, derring-do, and short shrift with lawlessness drifted back to Houston Avenue. By month's end, merchants and townspeople had grudgingly come to see the presence of his men as a deterrent to the roaming bands of outlaws, deserters, and ne'er-do-wells tempted to vandalize stores, plantations, and homesteads rendered defenseless because of the drain of manpower by the war. The citizens' patrol remained quiet after a military court found two of their number guilty of dragging a freed slave nearly to death and sentenced them to life in prison in Huntsville, Texas. Horse thieves were chased down and put in stocks under the broiling sun, and convicted poachers of livestock were confined to jail on a diet of bread and water. Meanwhile, the federal soldiers saw to one of their main duties of occupation: the construction of a school for the children of the freed slaves.

Jessica heartily approved of Major Duncan's dogged efforts to see the school erected and planned to volunteer as its first teacher when the building was completed. Voices would rise in objection—the idea of a white woman filling the heads of black children with learning!—but no one expected less of Jessica Wyndham Toliver.

It was not long before Andrew Duncan was a weekly guest at the Tolivers' dining room table. Evenings were the only time Thomas was home from the plantation and the Union major free of his duties to discuss public matters and concerns. Sometimes, Jeremy and Henri and their sons joined them for cigars and port after the meal. Their conversation and laughter often followed Jessica upstairs to bed, and she thought conviviality between men who were once enemies a very good thing. A man of culture himself, it was obvious the major found the Toliver mansion with its many objects of beauty a much appreciated retreat from the grime and tension of his days. Jessica also thought it obvious, though not to her son, that he counted Priscilla as one of the many objects of beauty in the house.

During one of these dining occasions, two months into the occupation, Priscilla dropped the surprise that she wished to volunteer as a teacher at the school when it soon opened.

"Why, Priscilla, how wonderful!" Jessica exclaimed. "We can go together. Major, I had planned to volunteer my services, too."

Priscilla, her flawless brow creasing, turned to Jessica. "If that's so, who will be here to see after Vernon?"

Surprised at the irritation she heard in her daughter-in-law's tone, Jessica said, "Why, Petunia and Amy, of course."

"I do not want my child reared in his early years without a member of his family present. His father is never around during the day. One of us must stay here, and I insist that I need the diversion. You have served your time in community service, Jessica."

Everyone listened to this near tirade with thunderstruck expressions. It was the first time Priscilla had ever put her foot down on anything, and the set of her face and defiant tone brooked no argument. Thomas said, "She's right, Mother. You can serve the cause by helping Priscilla collect books and make lesson plans. Let this be her project. It will give her a chance to show the town what *she's* made of."

He spoke as the head of the house and Priscilla its mistress, a change in status Jessica was only too willing to concede and recognize. She would have been pleased to hear Thomas take his wife's side and delighted in the rare glance of pride he tossed her had it not been for her suspicion that Priscilla's obstinate desire to teach in the school had little to do with instructing the children of the freed slaves how to read and write.

"Could we not leave Vernon with his other grandmother the hours we would be at the school?" Jessica suggested.

"It is my wish he stays here with you. It's clear he prefers your company to my mother's. She is ... well, she doesn't have your way with him."

"Then that settles it," Thomas said. He turned to Jessica sitting at his right. Out of diplomacy she had yielded her spot at the head of the table to Priscilla when Thomas took Silas's place after his death. Her daughter-in-law had never seemed comfortable there until tonight. "Mother, you've earned the right to let others take up the torch for the Negro," Thomas said, his tone softening. "Stay home and enjoy your grandchild."

Across from Jessica, Major Duncan, glowing from a scrub in the bathhouse he'd had his men build behind the stables and never more handsome than in his dark blue dress uniform with its gold epaulettes, remained silent, seemingly choosing to stay out of a matter skirting close to a family dispute. Jessica wondered if the man had any idea what this was all about. Men were so dense when it came to the wiles of women.

"As you wish, Priscilla," Jessica acquiesced, "but keep in mind you will be under the scrutiny of the townspeople."

The veiled admonition sailed over Priscilla's blond head. "No more than you have always been, Jessica. I shall try to handle it with the grace you've shown."

Thomas chortled, "You would warn Priscilla of the disfavor of the townspeople when you've never given a twitch about it, Mother?"

"I was not referring to disapproval, Thomas. I was cautioning your wife not to give cause for an undue wagging of tongues."

Priscilla said, "She means like teaching the black children things they shouldn't learn as she would do, right, Jessica? Not to worry. No one will fault me on that score. I shall teach a simple curriculum of reading, writing, and arithmetic."

Thomas chuckled. "I believe, Priscilla, that Mother is saying to be careful not to give others the impression you're becoming like her."

"I hardly think that's likely," Priscilla responded tartly. Her blue eyes flashed with what Jessica now clearly saw as jealousy of her mother-in-law. Consciously or not, Thomas had given his wife the feeling he compared her to his mother and found her wanting. "It's impossible to copy an original," Priscilla added.

"Well stated, Mrs. Toliver!" the major said, lifting his wineglass to Priscilla. Thomas, with another proud look at his wife, did the same.

"Yes, indeed," he said.

Inwardly, Jessica sighed. Oh, for the love of heaven!

How she would like to throttle Thomas for denying Priscilla

what every wife needs and desires—notice and appreciation from her husband. Did he not see how lovely she was? Priscilla was somewhat empty-headed, sure enough, and too impressed with family name and position, but she had a good heart and caring disposition. Could he not appreciate those qualities beyond her expression of them to his satisfaction in the bedroom? Was he so indifferent to her feelings that he was blind to the human fact that he'd left her vulnerable to the attentions of other men?

Did he not know that, subjected to enough indifference, a woman's heart could turn cold?

These were times like no other; Jessica wished desperately for Silas. Thomas had moved beyond her counsel simply for the reason he didn't feel he needed it. Silas would have talked to him man to man, husband to husband. Thomas would have taken no offense, but for his mother to wade into those risky waters....She could hear her son now: *Mother, what are you talking about?*

Two weeks later, Priscilla approached Jessica about "a delicate matter." When she heard it, Jessica's heart sank. Her gaze raked her daughter-in-law's face to find some clue the girl was aware of the dangerous course she was pursuing. For the past week, Priscilla had been supervising the finishing touches on the school. The Freedmen's Bureau had been registering students, and the first day of classes would begin next week. Priscilla had left to Jessica the tasks of preparing lesson plans, collecting books from neighbors and friends, and securing school supplies, since her daughter-in-law felt her services were needed at the construction site.

"We need more space," Priscilla said in explaining the reason for asking Jessica to give up the bed and sitting room she'd shared with Silas. Jessica would be given the suite she and Thomas had occupied in another wing. "We'd like to turn the sitting room into a nursery for Vernon where he'll have more privacy."

"Privacy? Vernon is only five months old," Jessica said.

"He'll grow."

Jessica was powerless to say no. The house belonged to her, and she was in a position to exercise full authority over it, but for the sake of family harmony, she wouldn't. She was glad Thomas and Priscilla had scrapped the idea of building a manor house on Somerset. Jessica wanted Vernon to grow up in the family home, away from the plantation. Perhaps the child would escape the dominance it had over his father.

Priscilla had strolled to the window overlooking the carriage house when making her request to Jessica, a look of anticipation on her face. Did the girl think her mother-in-law was blind?

"When do you wish to make the move, Priscilla?" she asked.

Priscilla turned to her with obvious relief at Jessica's acquiescence. "As soon as I can get the servants to see to it," she said.

Chapter Sixty-Nine

It was early October 1866 before Jessica could resume the thirtieth year of recording the affairs affecting the Tolivers, Warwicks, and DuMonts. One morning, her heart full, she opened the stiff paper cover of her new notebook in her suite where she had begun tending to her correspondence after she turned the full management of the household over to Priscilla. With the passing of the diadem had come her surrender of the morning room to her daughter-in-law, the only caveat being the removal of her secretary upstairs to her suite. Autumn had arrived with a vengeance, and a cold rain slashed at the windows but a fire blazed in the grate. Petunia had brought her up a pot of steaming tea.

Jessica stared at the blank, white page. Where to begin to record for posterity—and for her own memory when it began to fade—the end of an era she had known for forty-nine years? Today was her birthday. She poured a cup of tea and reflected. Was there any other place to start but the place where she was born?

The "homeland," as many from the Willowshire wagon train continued to refer to South Carolina, had been the most severely punished of all in General Sherman's march through the South. Its infrastructure lay in ruins. Railroads, bridges, roads, wharfs, gins, and warehouses had been demolished. Plantations had been plundered, homes and buildings and fields burned to the ground, livestock stolen or slaughtered, and farming equipment destroyed. None of the three planter families of the Wyndhams, Warwicks, and Tolivers remaining behind had escaped the devastation. Michael now lived with his family in a two-room cabin on what was once Willowshire. One of Jeremy's brothers had been killed futilely defending the family property, and the other had pulled up stakes and taken his family to South America to begin again. Morris died of a heart attack shortly after Sherman's army reached Columbia, the capital of South Carolina, and his two sons did not survive the Battle of Shiloh. Lettie and her daughter had gone to live with her sister in Savannah.

Jessica made a note to herself: *Begin where it all began.*

The fortunes of the Texas Warwicks and DuMonts would make for happier recording. Jeremy and Henri had fared well economically, Henri reasonably; Jeremy especially. Everything Jeremy touched seemed to turn to gold, his insisted form of payment. In April, the U.S. Telegraph Company, in which he held many shares, was absorbed by Western Union, making it the largest telegram company in the country and Jeremy a very wealthy man. He would bat away expressions of admiration for his successful enterprises with the back of his hand. His heart lay in the lumber industry and his optimism had never waned. "The real wealth in Texas, my friends, is in timber," he would say. "You just wait and see."

His surviving sons had married and presented their parents with numerous grandchildren. The oldest, a boy a year older than Vernon, was named Jeremy III. Camellia laughingly referred to the bearers of her husband's name by "Jeremy the father, Jeremy the son, and Jeremy the holy terror."

The blockade had interfered with the importation of Henri's European inventory, but his connections with the French, who were a presence in Mexico and had been sympathetic to the Confederate cause, partially took up the slack. Through diplomatic immunity, French couriers could bring goods across the Texas border, and stock that could not be transported was smuggled. Henri, following Jeremy's advice, had also deposited prewar profits in a northern bank. He shared his friend's enthusiasm for the growth that was bound to come to Texas because of the exodus of people from the South seeking new beginnings in a state not ravaged by war. With that conviction in mind, he had purchased lots in Howbutker to lease as residential and commercial property.

Of the two DuMont sons, Armand alone had married and sired a robust son his parents chose to name Abel. He was the same age as Jeremy III, and expectations were that Vernon and the boys would grow up to enjoy friendships as close as the ones shared by their grandfathers and fathers.

The page still blank, Jessica reflected on what—and how much—she should include of her own family's affairs the past seventeen months. Regardless of jealousies and personal resentments against the Tolivers, community sentiment held they must be given their just due, and the family name had emerged from the war more influential than ever. The outcome of events had exonerated Silas's views. There were many who wished they'd listened to his wise words of counsel and followed his example. Thomas, criticized for not shouldering his gun to fight in the Southland, was recognized as having been among the bravest in defending his native state, and Jessica had been assigned a legendary status in the annals of Howbutker history for... well, being Jessica.

Somerset had been among the few plantations in East Texas to rise from the ashes with a sound foothold on survival. Silas had managed to transport a large shipment of cotton to England before the Union blockade, and thousands of dollars in payment waited to be collected after the war. Combined with the money Thomas had been astonished to learn his mother had stashed away in a Boston bank, her son had the income to replace aged equipment and draft animals, make repairs, and pay his former slaves so well that few had left his workforce. This year the harvest had been good and cotton trade with northern and European markets had commenced with renewed vigor.

Vernon was nearly a year and a half old and the joy of their lives. For all of them, he bridged the abyss of Silas's loss. There were times, watching her grandson, when Jessica thought she would explode from the yearning that Silas could have known him. She had worried that as the child grew he would be affected by the tension between his parents, but by the time he was old enough to become aware of it, their marriage had been coated with a patina of courtesy and mutual acceptance of the other that passed for the appearance of love. For a while, Priscilla had seemed like a new woman, freer, livelier, happier. Jessica had no proof that Major Duncan was the man responsible for the change, but it began the week of the opening of the new school. Priscilla bloomed. Jessica was sure the blooming had nothing to do with teaching numbers, the alphabet, and script to a group of wriggling, tittering, unwashed black children confined in a hot and humid schoolroom. She recognized the nature of Priscilla's giddy laughter, sparkling eyes, and bouncy step from nights she'd enjoyed with Silas.

Jessica kept a tight lid on her speculations. She could only hope for her daughter-in-law's discretion and Thomas's blind unawareness of the reason for the new Priscilla. Gradually the girl shed her timidity, indecisiveness, and apprehension that had increased after she married Thomas—*because* she'd married Thomas, in Jessica's opinion. But her son did notice.

"Teaching becomes you," he said to his wife, and Jessica observed his heightened interest in her. He began coming home earlier, and at first Jessica feared he suspected something, but he had only wanted to be home with his wife and son. Jessica came to excuse herself after supper on some pretext to allow him and Priscilla and the baby time alone in the parlor to enjoy a private evening together.

Their love life appeared to improve. One morning, Jessica came down to find herself the only one at breakfast.

"Where are my son and daughter-in-law?" she asked Petunia.

"They're not out of bed yet," Petunia answered with a sheepish smile. "I've taken care of the baby."

Two months after the school opened, three events occurred almost simultaneously that were to make Jessica forever wonder if they were related. The school burned to the ground, an act of arson surprising to no one since there were factions in the community outraged at its temerity to exist, but it ended Priscilla's teaching career. Shortly after, Major Duncan asked for and received a transfer, and Priscilla announced she was pregnant.

Chapter Seventy

"Mother, she's the spitting image of you," Thomas said, turning the swaddled bundle in his arms to Jessica for her first peek at her granddaughter.

"Oh, dear," Jessica said, peering into the well of pink blanket at the little red face of Regina Elizabeth Toliver.

"Now, now," Thomas chided, his rebuke infused with the proud laughter of a father enchanted by his newborn infant. "I know you've never been happy with your fair skin and freckles and red hair, but Papa loved them, and so do I, and I will love them on this little angel." He touched his lips to the diminutive forehead.

"Maybe she'll be spared my freckles," Jessica said, doubting the hope and herself as the origin of the child's misfortune.

Thomas smiled down at his two-year-old son, who stood gripping his leg, the boy's upturned face filled with curiosity at the object in his father's arms that had so enraptured him. They were alone in the library. The Woodwards were upstairs with their daughter, and soon Priscilla's mother would swoop in to return the child to her daughter's breast.

"All right," Thomas said, "it's your turn, Vernon. Come, let's sit down, and I will introduce you to your little sister."

Jessica watched her tall son take a chair to facilitate her grandson's view of the first female born to a Toliver in twenty years. Thomas's joy in the child's gender was a surprise to her. He had hoped for a boy as a playmate for Vernon. Thomas made no bones about wanting Vernon to have many brothers. He had minded being an only child after Joshua's death and had demanded, "When am I going to have another brother like my friends?" before he was old enough to know not to ask such questions.

"Twenty years!" Priscilla had echoed when Thomas had informed her of the little-known fact of Toliver history after the doctor's announcement she'd given birth to a daughter. "That's an entire generation!"

"You have done what no other woman in the family has been able to accomplish in all that time," Thomas said, fondly blotting his wife's wet hairline with a towel.

"You're not disappointed?" she asked. Priscilla lay exhausted in the birth bed after three hours of intense labor she'd borne with amazing fortitude and patience. Dr. Woodward's competitor had been called in to assist with the delivery and declared to Priscilla's father hovering anxiously in the hall that he had never seen a birthing mother so cooperative with Mother Nature.

"She really wants this baby," he'd said.

Thomas said tenderly, "No, I'm not disappointed. I'm sorry I gave you the need to ask."

"You wanted a son so badly."

"I wanted another child. Given the sons born into the families around here, I didn't dare dream of becoming the father of a daughter."

"You don't mind that she...doesn't look like either of us?" Priscilla asked.

"Not at all. She represents my mother's side of the family."

"I'm so relieved you feel that way," Priscilla said.

Jessica had listened to the conversation from a corner of the room (having yielded the attendant position at the side of her old bed to Priscilla's mother), and asked herself what difference did the child's paternity matter? What did family blood have to do with loving a child?

Everything, if Thomas ever suspects his daughter is not a limb off the Toliver tree, she had thought. So far he had perceived nothing. The attraction between Priscilla and Major Duncan appeared to have escaped his notice entirely. Not even the downturn of his wife's happy mood after the major's departure roused his suspicions. He blamed the destruction of the school. "She was so keen on her work there," he'd said.

"I'm sure that's the explanation," Jessica had remarked but was not surprised when Priscilla, using the excuse of her pregnancy, had rejected a request by the Freedmen's Bureau to resume her teaching duties in an abandoned warehouse until another facility could be built.

Paternity, blood, inherited links would matter to Thomas. Jessica felt the needles of a cold apprehension as she listened to him explain to Vernon his duties as a brother to his little sister. What if Thomas, for no particular reason, should have cause to wonder if the little redheaded girl he called his daughter was really his flesh and blood? What if, on some ordinary day as he observed Regina Elizabeth at play, bearer of his Queenscrown grandmother's name, he should unexpectedly recall Major Andrew Duncan and remember how his wife had come alive during his assignment in Howbutker? What if one thought led to another and on to another, and then suddenly, as surely as he was certain the sun would rise tomorrow, Thomas knew? That sort of instant awareness happened.

It had happened to her. Jessica remembered vividly the moment the realization struck her that Jeremy Warwick loved her beyond the breadth of friendship, though his attention would never stray outside its fraternal bounds. The families were playing croquet on the Warwicks' lawn, Jeremy paired with Jessica, Henri with Camellia, while Bess served the lemonade. Jeremy's ball sailed through the last wicket and hit the stake. He'd smiled at her. "We won," he said, and in that second, like a shaft of sunlight revealing a secret passage in a familiar room, Jessica knew.

And Jeremy knew that Silas had known. That awareness was the reason Jeremy had asked her not to divulge to Silas as he was dying the secret of the money stored in Boston and how it got there. *Just trust me, Jess. In some ways I know your husband better than you. He would mind that you took me into your confidence over him and that I acted upon it without his knowledge.*

But Silas had trusted their fidelity to him not to mind their special friendship, and so it would continue. She'd been shaken by the insight, but Jeremy would never learn of her perception that day. "Yes, we did," she'd said, picking up the ball and waving it triumphantly at the others.

But, oh Lord, what a tragedy if Thomas discovered that Regina Elizabeth had been fathered by another man, and a Union officer to boot. There would be no picking up the pieces and putting them back together again—not for the marriage or for Thomas's relationship with his daughter.

"Poppies," Vernon piped. "Her hair the color of poppies."

"Then we will call her that, son. We'll call her Poppy."

They made a beautiful picture, her glowing son and curious grandson huddled over the infant in Thomas's arms, a perfect subject for a portrait painter. Jessica wondered why she, as a member of the first generation, could not force herself to complete the scene.

"Come join us, Mother, before our little princess is taken from us."

Thomas's invitation was interrupted by the opening of the library doors, and Petunia appeared. "Miss Priscilla sent me to collect the baby, Mister Thomas. It's her feeding time."

Indeed, the child had begun to cry hungrily, tiny limbs flailing in the blanket. Reluctantly, Thomas handed the small bundle over to the maid. "Bring her back to me, Petunia," he said. "I want her to know her father."

Petunia shot a glance at Jessica, and Jessica slid hers away, her stomach curling. "As you say, Mister Thomas," Petunia said.

Civil turmoil marked the rest of the spring and summer as Jessica approached her fiftieth birthday. Major Duncan's successor had been replaced by an iron-fisted general in charge of all the Union forces in Texas. Dissatisfied with the region's attempts to circumvent the directives Congress imposed on its political, social, and economic structure, the general took up residence in Howbutker and immediately inflamed the citizenry by removing its elected county officials and judges and replacing them with his appointees. Only those who took the government-mandated "Oath Test" stating they had never volunteered to bear arms against the United States or "given aid, countenance, counsel, or encouragement to persons engaged in armed hostility" could serve in public office. Thomas was removed immediately as head of the city council and Armand DuMont as mayor.

Those positions, along with others vacated by the commander's sweep, were filled with northern carpetbaggers, termed so because most arrived carrying all they possessed in fabric bags. These persons swooped in to buy destitute farms and plantations and cattle ranches at a fraction of the cost they would have had to pay for the same property and labor in northern states. The county warily and resentfully waited to see what control they would exert over the residents in their new positions of power.

An epidemic of yellow fever added to East Texas's miseries

the year of 1867 and a new foliage-eating pest called the army worm came to harass cotton farmers. Suffocating in the heat with windows closed to keep out mosquitoes, Jessica thought of Secretary of State William Seward's purchase of Alaska from Russia that added 586,412 cold square miles to United States territory and wondered if it were possible to grow cotton there. The children were fretful, Thomas worried and irritable, Jessica weary from her depressing work in a charity hospital set up for Civil War veterans. Priscilla, on the other hand, appeared to have risen above it all, content on the cloud of her improved relations with her husband that gave her sway to exert more authority over the household.

"Whatever are you doing, Jessica?"

Jessica turned at the peremptory voice. Priscilla stood in the doorway of the pantry where Jessica had been counting the dwindling supply of staples still scarce after the war.

"Why…" Jessica said, annoyed that she had to explain herself, "I believe you can see for yourself that I'm checking the larder for the food goods we have left."

"Isn't that my job?"

"It is if you would do it."

"I've been busy with the children."

"Which is why I'm doing it."

Such exchanges were not uncommon between them. Gone was the infatuated, intimidated girl who had come to them wide-eyed at the elegance and refinement of her in-laws—and before the arrival of Major Andrew Duncan and the freeing of certain inhibitions, from which Thomas had benefited.

But October brought cooler weather and the announcement that Priscilla was again pregnant. A surprise visitor awaited Jessica the afternoon of her birthday. She was summoned to the parlor to find a spindle-limbed black woman of her age wearing one of the new princess gowns that eschewed crinolines and cages and gave her bantam, ungainly figure somewhat of a shape. The woman responded to Jessica's open-mouthed astonishment with a wide grin. "You didn't think I'd miss your fiftieth birthday, did you?" Tippy said.

Chapter Seventy-One

The DuMonts had been responsible for arranging the surprise visit and feted the two women in a birthday bash in their château-like mansion that recalled celebrations of the prewar decade. The attire of the guests was noticeably less fashionable and worse for wear, and the hoopless, softly bustled gowns of Camellia Warwick, Bess DuMont, and Tippy stood out like bright carousel ponies on a weathered merry-go-round.

"The war has taken its toll," Tippy commented later of the guests and the reduced number from Houston Avenue in attendance at the party.

"As Silas predicted," Jessica said.

"I noticed the Davises were missing. Did they not come because I was one of the honorees?"

"They did not come because they're ashamed and extremely bitter over their diminished circumstances. I can understand and sympathize with their feelings to a point. They lost their son Jake in the war, such a sweet and good boy. Thomas and the boys miss him still. But Lorimer is responsible for his other losses. He fought Silas's prediction that the Confederacy would lose to the North tooth and toenail and continued to buy land and slaves— on credit—when all reason said to wait for the war's outcome. When he couldn't meet his mortgage payments, all his property passed into control of a commission house in Galveston, including his home on Houston Avenue. The army general in charge of the district has leased it for himself and his officers, a further bitter pill for the Davises to swallow. They are not alone in their grief. Countless other prominent plantation families throughout East Texas have suffered the same fate."

Tippy shook her head sadly. "But Somerset has survived."

Jessica shrugged. "Silas saw to its survival for the sake of Thomas, and Thomas will see to it for the sake of his son. At three, Vernon already appears to be of the same weft and warp as his father. He begs to go with him when he leaves in the morning, but who knows but that the boy prefers his father's company to a house full of women?"

"The boy is like him," Tippy said in her familiar, prophetic voice.

Jessica felt the hairs rise on her forearms. She and Tippy were enjoying the fall sunshine on the front verandah where they had so often chatted, mindless of the neighbors' outrage over one of their own being seen sipping tea with a Negro. Jessica sniffed at their disdain. Those who'd managed to hold on to their homes on Houston Avenue, with the exceptions of the DuMonts and Warwicks, should feel so financially privileged and socially connected as Tippy. Isabel, as she was now called, had become one of the most sought-after fashion designers in America. Her dress and accessory creations, designed for the garment manufacturing firm in New York where she'd first been employed, had been an instant hit and led to other, even more lucrative offers of positions in the world of haute couture. To be called *haute couture* (translated by Tippy to mean "high sewing"), a fashion house had to belong to the Syndical Chamber for Haute Couture in Paris, regulated by the French Department of Industry. Tippy designed for the only establishment in America that could claim membership in that august body. Her clients included the female members of the Astor and Vanderbilt and Morgan families, and she had become friends with Sarah Josepha Hale, editor of the notable Godey's *Lady's Book* and an important and influential arbiter of American taste.

"I don't know that I wanted to hear that," Jessica said, passing over the cream.

"That Vernon is like his father? Why not?"

Jessica stirred her tea. How to answer Tippy? Her quandary was the same as when she returned to her journal after a long absence and did not know where to begin, but, unlike the blank pages, Tippy would listen and respond. Her oldest and only woman confidante would be leaving in the morning, taking the train to New Orleans and on to New York accompanied by Jeremy, who had business in the city. Jessica had only a few remaining hours to take advantage of her counsel.

"Thomas followed in his father's footsteps and married a woman he did not love on behalf of Somerset," Jessica said.

Tippy's eyebrows rose in concert. Like her hair, they were gray, thin, and wispy. "Thomas appears to be as fortunate in that respect as Silas was in marrying you," she said.

"Oh, he's grown to care for Priscilla enough."

Jessica heard a thump from inside the house near the parlor windows where they sat. The servants were moving furniture to clean the rugs. "Have you finished your tea?" she asked.

Tippy peered into the contents of her cup. "Does it matter?"

"No. Let's take a stroll about the garden. The Lancasters and Yorks are showing their best right now."

Away from the house and the ears of the servants, Jessica told of the arrival of handsome and charismatic Major Duncan at a time when her son and daughter-in-law's marriage was at a low ebb. "It was obvious to everyone but Thomas that he was taken with her," she said, "and I'm afraid my daughter-in-law, attention-starved that she was, succumbed to his...interest."

"Did Thomas find out?"

"No, thank God. It was right after the war. He had lost his father and was taken up with many concerns."

Tippy drew Jessica to a stop. "So what is the problem, Jessica? Their marriage seems none the worse, and from what you've said of Priscilla's frigidity, Major Duncan may have done Thomas a favor."

"Oh, I'm not condemning the girl for her affair, if she had one, and it's not my son I'm thinking of."

"Who then?"

"Regina Elizabeth."

Comprehension flashed in the dark depths of Tippy's immense eyes like a trout breaking water. "You mean—"

"I do."

"How can you be sure?"

"I'm not sure." They were at the garden gate. Jessica unlocked it and they entered. "Major Duncan and Priscilla may have simply had an intense flirtation. He may have only made her feel good about herself, freed her fears about sex. I doubt that was all there was to it, but it's possible. Priscilla is an impressionable girl. But what if, by some quixotic quirk of fate, Thomas finds out about them? God have mercy! It would be worse than the house crashing around our ears. Thomas would never feel the same about the child. Tippy"—Jessica turned to her imploringly— "you know about these things. You're from the stars. Will we ever know for sure Regina is a Toliver?"

Tippy frowned as she reflected on the question. "I believe that in time all hidden things are revealed, Jessie, so yes, someday you'll know, but I hope it won't be too late for you to love her."

Startled, Jessica said, "What makes you say that? Of course I love the child."

"Not like you would if you knew for sure she carried your son's blood."

Jessica turned away, shamefaced. "You always could see what others could not. Oh, God, Tippy. I'm so disgusted with myself, but I...When I look at her, I see the freckles and red hair of Major Duncan. I grew to dislike him. He took advantage of the situation and Priscilla let him. Even though I understand how and why it happened and no one seems the worse for it, I can't help but see the child as the fruit of their deceit."

"You're a mother, Jessie. You believe Priscilla, understandably or not, was unfaithful to your son, and that would naturally color your feelings for her and the child, but look at how you love Amy, Petunia's daughter. She's not of your blood or even your race."

"That is true, Tippy, but loving the child of a friend is not the same as loving a child of family. Regina is adorable, and I would never hold her mother's indiscretion against her, but I simply cannot feel for her the bond of blood I feel with Vernon."

"You truly believe Regina is not Thomas's, don't you?"

"I can't shake the certainty of it, and you know I've never been one to give the benefit of the doubt where I believe there is none."

Tippy shook her head sadly. "A pity, my dear, for Regina will love you the most and seek your approval above all others."

Jessica looked over the red and white roses in her garden, their bobbing heads brilliant in the autumn sun. Would there ever come a time she would be forced to lay a red rose at her grand-daughter's feet? Regina, at six months, was already showing signs of Tippy's prediction. Like the housecat that sought Jessica's company when she felt no particular affinity for felines, it was to her grandmother that Regina held out her arms from the crib and parlor floor, in Jessica's lap she stopped crying when no one else could console her.

"Thomas loves his son," Jessica said, "but he worships his daughter, and so does Vernon. I don't want to think about their pain or Regina's if what I believe to be the truth is ever discovered." She closed her eyes. "But for Somerset, Thomas would never have married Priscilla. I've always worried that there will be a reckoning for that decision somewhere along the way. I so hope it will not be Regina who'll bear the brunt of it."

"No reckoning befell Silas for marrying you, Jessica."

Jessica's mirthless laugh cut the crisp air like a knife. "Oh, but it did, Tippy. Oh, but it did."

Chapter Seventy-Two

A soft tap on her door roused Jessica from her journal. Amy, bringing her midmorning tea, she thought. The child was seventeen and had become indispensable to the household. Jessica had offered to send her to Oberlin College in Ohio, the first institution of higher learning to admit women and blacks, but Amy had refused. Her place was here, she said. She enjoyed her life and living "among books and flowers and those I love and need to see after," but Jessica suspected a love interest involved. Amy was "stepping out" with the DuMonts' groundskeeper, and a wedding looked certain in the future. A waste, Jessica had thought, feeling guilty that she had helped create the bond Amy refused to break. She especially felt bad that Amy believed her one of those who needed seeing after.

Amy's and her mother's devotion to Jessica were among the numerous festering points with which her daughter-in-law had had to contend with the passing of the years, and Jessica's position in the household had subtly altered. More and more, she had begun staying in her room until later in the morning.

The date heading the new page in her diary stared back at her. November 7, 1873. Where had all the years gone? Her son was thirty-six, Vernon eight, and David, her newest grandson, five. Regina was…six, Jessica recalled. She set down her pen.

"Come in, Amy."

No response. Puzzled, Jessica got up from her desk. Perhaps Amy needed help with the tea tray. The little pale, freckled face that greeted her when Jessica opened the door was Regina's, a precedent. Her granddaughter had never come to her room before.

"Good morning, Granmama," she said, staring up at Jessica out of eyes large with uncertainty of her welcome.

The look pierced Jessica's heart. What was there about her, what did she do or say for the little girl to doubt her grandmother's pleasure in her company? "Good morning, Regina. What brings you to my door this morning?"

"I...came to bring you a present."

"A present?" Jessica said in a tone to convey happy surprise. "Well, come in and let's see what you have brought." She smiled and offered her hand, and the little girl slipped hers into it. It was a delicate, finely modeled hand. No one in the family quite had the hands of Regina. "You're just in time for tea. Amy will be bringing it shortly. We'll put a lot of milk and sugar in it so your mother won't object to the caffeine."

"That would be very good," Regina said.

Amused—the child had begun parroting her phrases—Jessica suggested, "Shall we sit at the tea table to get the light from the window?"

"That would be very good," Regina said, placing the handkerchief-wrapped gift on the table. She took her seat, carefully arranging the elaborately ruffled skirt of her silken dress, her back held straight. Her mother already had the child in stays and dressed her in the latest selection of children's wear from the recently renamed DuMont Department Store. "Would you like to open your present?" Regina asked.

"I would." Jessica unfolded the lacy square of cloth to find a pack of Adams No. 1 chewing gum. The concoction had just last year come on the market and had, of all people, the notorious General Antonio Lopez de Santa Anna to thank for its discovery. Newspaper articles described the popular new treat as having come about when the former dictator, living in exile in New Jersey, sold a supply of chicle he'd brought from Mexico to Thomas Adams, an inventor, as a substitute for rubber. The inventor noticed that Santa Anna liked to chew chicle, a natural latex gum substance found in evergreen trees in Central America. Having failed in his efforts to harden the material for use in items requiring rubber, Thomas Adams one day chewed a wad of his stock, found he liked it, and boiled a batch to create the marketable phenomenon Jessica held in her hand.

"Oh my, what a treat!" she said, feigning pleasure at sight of the black, flavorless "stretch and snap" preparation that had become all the rage.

"I bought it for you from Monsieur DuMont's store with my pocket money," Regina said proudly.

"How thoughtful of you to think of me," Jessica said, hoping the child did not expect her to chew the beastly stuff in her presence. She heard the rattle of china in the corridor—Amy at last with the tea. Jessica would invite her to stay. Unlike Petunia, Amy doted on the little girl, and the tea would give her and her granddaughter something to talk about, to do.

Regina's eyes strayed curiously toward Jessica's desk. "Are you writing a book?" she asked shyly.

"Sort of. It's a diary."

"What is a diary, may I ask?"

"You may. It's a record of happenings in a person's life."

"Happenings?"

"Events that occur in one's daily existence and in those of family and friends and in the household and town and one's personal feelings about them. It's a written record of memories."

"Do you write about Mama and Daddy?"

"Yes."

"And Vernon and David?"

Jessica hesitated. She knew where this conversation was leading. "Yes," she said.

Tentatively, her look shy, the little girl asked, "Do you ever write about me?"

"Yes," Jessica answered truthfully. "Often."

The child's face lit up. "Really? What do you write?"

"That you are a very sweet and tender child with perfect manners and deportment that you've certainly not inherited from the Tolivers."

Regina laughed gleefully, showing fine small teeth and a little pink tongue. "But Daddy says I am you, straight and true," she said, sobering slightly. "And I want to be like you."

Jessica was stumped for a response. Gratefully, she greeted Amy, bearing the tea tray. "I have a visitor for tea," Jessica said and was about to ask Amy to join them when the look on Regina's face—a plea—stopped her. Don't ask her to stay, it begged, as if the child had read her intent. "Would you please bring us one more cup?" Jessica said. "And add some cookies, too. Regina and I are going to have a tea party."

"I'll be right up," Amy said, with a wink at Regina. "Mind your manners now, little one."

"As if you have to remind her," Jessica chided.

"Who is the boy in the picture, Granmama?" Regina asked, wriggling off the chair under the weight of her skirt and petticoats to inspect a daguerreotype photograph displayed on the shelf above Jessica's desk.

Jessica's breath caught. It had been years since anyone had

noticed the picture, and often lately, she'd found herself remembering Joshua. "That is Joshua. Your father's brother."

Regina cast her a questioning look. "Your other son?"

"Yes, my...other son."

"Where is he?"

"He died, many years ago, when he was only twelve. He was thrown from a horse and broke his neck in the fall."

"Oh!" Regina said, pressing delicate hands to her cheeks in imitation of her mother in moments of dismay. "I'm so sorry, Granmama. You must have been very sad."

"I was. I miss him to this day."

"Was he like Daddy?"

"No. They were very different."

"In what way?"

"Your father has always loved the land. His brother loved the people *on* the land."

"And that made them different?"

"Yes, that made them different."

"Did that make a difference in the way you loved them?"

"I suppose," Jessica said. What kind of question was that for a six-year-old? "But not in the degree," she added.

"Degree?"

"Amount. It did not make a difference in the *amount* I loved them. I loved them equally the same." Jessica felt her face grow warm. The child knew. As much as Jessica tried never to show favoritism, somehow Regina had become aware that her grandmother's feelings for her siblings were not the same as those for her, and that recognition had prompted her questions. Amy arrived with the extra cup and plate of cookies. Regina wriggled onto her seat again. Jessica sat across from her, batting the moisture from her eyes. "Shall I prepare your tea the way I think you would like it?" she asked.

"That would be very good."

Carefully, Jessica went about the ministrations of the tea. The dear child has barricaded herself behind a wall of manners so as not to provoke my disapproval, she thought. How could she ever think I would pierce that tender heart?

"When we have finished our tea, would you like to read one of your storybooks to me?" Jessica invited. "We can sit before the fire and listen to the wind whistle secrets outside the house. We can try to figure out what they're saying."

The little girl's face brightened. "Just me? I don't have to share you with my brothers?"

"Just you and me," Jessica said.

"And we can wrap ourselves in afghans?"

"And we can wrap ourselves in afghans."

"That would be very good indeed," Regina said.

Chapter Seventy-Three

Priscilla paused at the door of Jessica's suite. No matter that every member of the family was gone from the house for the rest of the afternoon and she'd made sure the servants were well engaged downstairs, she glanced up and down the wide gallery before opening the door. She felt the familiar roil in her stomach. Even after five or six of these secret sorties into Jessica's room, she still trembled from the possibility that her mother-in-law may have forgotten something and returned, or—God forbid!—Petunia, Jessica's watchdog. The housekeeper might pop in with fresh linens or roses from the garden or for some other reason and catch her at Jessica's desk.

What plausible excuse could she give to explain stealing into her mother-in-law's room and reading her private journals she'd taken from a locked compartment when she knew Jessica was away? There simply wasn't one, and from the onset Priscilla knew her goose would be cooked with Thomas and Jessica if she were caught, but she'd thought the risk worth the minimal chance of discovery. So far Jessica hadn't had even a whiff that anyone had been at her journals. Priscilla noted their arrangement in the stacks each time she unlocked the top cupboard of the secretary and replaced them in their exact position and the key precisely where she'd found it.

Almost from the moment Regina was born, Jessica had treated her daughter with a wariness not displayed with Vernon. For a while, Priscilla had thought it due to the firstborn grandchild taking center stage in a grandmother's affections.

"Second grandchildren do not cause as much of a stir as the first, do they?" she'd asked her mother.

"Why, of course they do," she'd replied. "Why do you ask?"

"Regina does not seem to hold the same fascination for Jessica that Vernon does."

"That's because she's partial to boys. She's raised only sons, thank goodness. Her nature is not warm enough for daughters, as you can testify."

Priscilla had agreed. She and Jessica had never bonded, much to Priscilla's disappointment, but her mother's explanation did not account for Jessica's fondness for Amy, and her delight in all children, regardless of gender, race, or class.

"You're imagining things," Thomas told her when she'd mentioned the disparity to him. "My mother shows no partiality to Vernon over Regina."

And indeed, when David was born, on the surface of things, Thomas was right. Jessica appeared painstakingly careful in distributing her affection equally among her three grandchildren, but with Regina there was always a little reserve involved. It took a mother to see it.

Jessica's guardedness with Regina had caused a ripple in the calm waters that Priscilla, up until then, had tried to establish in coexisting with her mother-in-law. The small jealousies she'd taken pains to control blossomed into resentments. They were the green-eyed monsters common to any daughter-in-law sharing the domain of her husband's mother. Thomas's implied staunch support of his mother over his wife (though Jessica never provoked a situation that called for it) began to grate. Annoyance at the children's respect for their grandmother when they sassed their mother, and Petunia's and the servants' deference to Jessica when she, Priscilla, was mistress of the house rose to the surface like skin pimples—all caused by her mother-in-law's strange disengagement from Regina.

Why, then, Priscilla asked herself, had she not seen the obvious until last December, in 1874, when her daughter was seven years old? It had struck like a thunderbolt—the key to the mystery that had been staring her in the face since Regina was born. Jessica suspected that her granddaughter was the fruit of adultery, that Major Andrew Duncan, and not Thomas, was the father of her grandchild.

That sudden realization had all but caused her to faint when the families had gathered on Christmas Eve for their annual eggnog party. They were at the DuMonts', and the children were around the tree, opening their presents. Regina was wearing a green velvet dress with a white lace collar and a green ribbon in her hair sprigged with red berries and holly, the only girl among the boys—a princess among her lieges, Vernon and David, Abel, Jeremy III, and their younger brothers.

Bess remarked, "I declare, Jessica, your granddaughter grows to look more like you every year."

Jessica had set her eggnog cup on its saucer with just the slightest deliberation. "I don't see how that could be possible. Regina is so pretty."

It was a perfectly innocuous remark, but Priscilla had fixed her mother-in-law with a stunned gaze she sensed Jessica felt but had purposefully avoided by keeping her attention on the group.

That night Priscilla had lain wide awake frozen with terror beside Thomas. What if Jessica in some unguarded, aggravated moment divulged her suspicions to Thomas? It was then that the idea of reading Jessica's diaries had slowly crept into her numb mind. Jessica wrote in them religiously in preparation of the book she intended to write of the founding families of Howbutker. She must pour out her soul in them. What better place to learn if her fears were founded than in Jessica's written thoughts? The journals were under lock and key, but a year ago, after Regina had been invited to tea in her grandmother's room, she'd watched Jessica store away her current journal, lock the cabinet door, and place the key beneath an ink well. Priscilla had located the key within seconds of entering Jessica's room.

She'd gone directly to the notebook marked 1866, the year the Union occupation of Howbutker began, and found justification for her terror. It was as she'd guessed: Jessica suspected her of having had sexual relations with Major Duncan. The entry that had caused her to stifle a cry was dated August 19, 1866.

I hesitate to commit my dreadful suspicions to paper for fear these pages may be read by eyes other than mine, but my heart is heavy, and I've no where else to unburden it. I believe my lovely daughter-in-law is having an affair with Major Andrew Duncan. I have watched helplessly as this love-starved child has succumbed to the handsome major's attention. She is so blinded by her infatuation with him that she cannot see what is plainly visible to me and possibly Petunia, but thank goodness, not to Thomas. He sees nothing beyond the scope of his duties to Somerset and his delight in Vernon.

And later on, another quickly written paragraph dated April 10, 1867: *Regina Elizabeth Toliver was born today. She is exquisite, perfectly formed. She is fair-skinned and red haired—like me, everyone says. Well...we'll see.*

And further into the year shortly after Jessica's fiftieth birthday, she'd written: *Tippy tells me someday I'll know whether the child is a Toliver. How will the knowledge come to us, I wonder. How will it reveal itself?*

Priscilla had had to dig for these personal comments among recordings of local and national happenings, news of friends, inventions, fashions, books, music—*This year of 1867, Johann Straus, the Younger, has given to our frightening world one of the most beautiful and soothing waltzes ever written, "The Blue Danube,"* Jessica had written on one page. Priscilla had paused, remembering the night she'd waltzed to a Brahms composition in the arms of Major Duncan at the party he'd hosted for the townspeople. Her face grew hot with horror at herself. How could she have been so stupid not to have realized that anyone looking could see the chemistry between them?

Thomas had not looked. Priscilla had peered over Andrew's shoulder at her husband huddled in a corner with other planters and known she was safe. He would not have noticed, in any case. She had grown so tired of handing her cup to her husband to be filled, so weary of loving a man who would never have for her the feelings she wanted and needed. He'd married her to produce an heir. Thomas was the preferred desire of her heart, but— as Jessica had observed and noted—she was starved for the kind of attention Andrew gave her and her husband did not. Was it possible the whole town, looking at Regina, wondered at what Thomas had never seen?

Priscilla had placed the journals back in their chronological order before her luck ran out. Panicked from the information she'd learned, she'd left Jessica's room to consider its implications. Jessica had not acted on her suspicions except to withhold, consciously or not, a definite warmth from Regina that the boys enjoyed, but Priscilla had noticed a thaw toward her daughter in the last year. Perhaps Jessica had become aware of the extent to which Regina adored her, blood of her blood or no, and Jessica would never slam the door of her affections in the face of a child.

Jessica would also never tell Thomas what she suspected. Why would she? Her son and daughter-in-law were contented with each other now. Their family was thriving; their household peaceful. If their marriage was not all they'd like it to be, it was good enough. They'd each gotten what they'd bargained for. Thomas had his two boys as heirs and Priscilla the title of Mrs. Thomas Toliver, recipient of all the name entailed. She had earned and now occupied a special place in her husband's heart. Why and for what purpose would a loving mother and grandmother wish to destroy all that?

Time would erase Major Duncan from the town's memory. He had been gone seven years. The other day someone had trouble recalling his name. Priscilla could imagine no other threat to her peace of mind. Life did have a way of revealing the dust swept under the rug, as Jessica would say, but for the time being, Priscilla saw no reason to expect exposure.

She would never have returned to the notebooks and continued her secret missions into Jessica's room but for a curious reference that had caught her eye and further spiked her interest in Toliver history. Priscilla could not resist investigating, and so she'd gone back to the beginning of the journals to search for its origin and meaning. She'd found numerous mentions, and in the meantime she'd gained amazing insights into the person of her mother-in-law and garnered shocking information that she would file away against the day it might serve as protection for her daughter. She had three more years to go to complete her perusal of the private life of Jessica Wyndham Toliver, and Priscilla would have learned all her mother-in-law had written of the Toliver curse.

Chapter Seventy-Four

In 1876, Rutherford B. Hayes, a Republican, was elected president of the United States in the most disputed presidential election in the nineteenth century. The popular vote favored Hayes' opponent, Samuel Tilden, a Democrat and governor of New York. Three electoral votes were undecided. Political analysts of the day believed a deal was struck under the table that put Hayes in the White House. The Southern Democrats on the commission to decide the fate of the election agreed to give Hayes the electoral vote in exchange for the Republicans removing federal troops out of the South and bringing an end to Reconstruction. The deal led to the Compromise of 1877, an unwritten agreement in which the national government would allow the former Confederate states to govern themselves without northern interference in their political affairs.

The result was that the freed Negro was left unprotected in the South and at the mercy of the Jim Crow laws. These were federal and state statutes designed to segregate the black man from white society, deprive him of his civil liberties, and return him to his prewar social status. The sharecropping system as it was meant to work for the former slave indentured him further to his one-time master. The landowner's manipulation was simple: On credit, he supplied his tenant with the necessary "furnishings" of a mule, plow, seed, house, and supplies to get started, with the contractual agreement that the cost of these expenses would be deducted from his share of the crop at sale time. More often than not, according to the white landowner's figures, the illiterate black tenant's debt exceeded his profit, and he was forced to stay on his land for another repeat of the cycle that would leave him forever in hock to his landlord. Escape from this sort of tyranny was nearly impossible. Workers who ran away from their legal obligations were hunted down by local sheriffs or groups hired for that purpose and returned to the landowner until their debt was paid.

The blacks' rebuttal to this reinstatement of white domination was the mass "Black Exodus of 1879," in which twenty thousand Negroes left the cotton-producing regions of the former Confederacy for the promise of free land in Kansas, Oklahoma, and Colorado. Among them were Jasper's two sons and their families.

"But, why?" Thomas asked in disbelief when Rand, the elder of the two sons, had approached him with news of their imminent departure. "Haven't you been treated fairly?"

"Never better, Mister Thomas, and me and my family and my brother's family, too, is mighty grateful to you. Because of your fair dealin', we got the money to go and get us a good start. We got the education to make sure nobody cheats us, and we owe that to you, too. It ain't nothin' against you that we is goin' but for the hope of havin' our own land which we'd never have as long as we stay on Somerset."

Thomas had heard an unmistakable note in Rand's voice reminding him that if he'd agreed to sell him and his brother, Willie, the land they tilled (the request made numerous times), they would not be leaving. The look in Rand's eye said it was still not too late to make the deal.

"I wish I could see my way clear to sell you those acres you've rented all these years, Rand, but Toliver land has never been for sale and never will be. It was a promise I made my father, and one I hold as well."

"So you've made clear enough through the years," Rand said. "Willie and I will see to the plantin', stay for the christenin' of Amy's daughter, then we be on our way. Might make it to Kansas in time to get in a crop of wheat 'fore winter."

Rand had arrived to say good-bye. They had gathered in front of his family's old home that Thomas had taken over as a plantation office when it had been vacated at Jasper's death. Vernon, fourteen, stood beside his father. In his son's presence, Thomas made a point to set the example he hoped the boy would follow when he was master of the plantation. His son knew he was heartsick at losing two of the hardest-working, most loyal and trustworthy families on the place, but he couldn't allow himself to be surly about it. Rand and his brother and their families were free to go. Rand stuck out his hand, and Thomas shook it.

"I'm sure you've heard stories of the scalawags that ask for money in advance to take you to the promised land, then not show up at the time of departure," Thomas said. "Be aware of them, and you know that if things don't work out in Kansas, you can always come back. Same terms as before."

"I know that, Mister Thomas." Rand returned his old, sweat-stained hat to his head. He looked at Vernon. "My boys said to tell you good-bye, Master Vernon. They'da come, but it was too hard for 'em."

Thomas saw that his son had difficulty swallowing. "I'll...miss them," Vernon said. "I can't imagine going fishing without them."

"Neither can they." Rand turned to Thomas. "Well, so long from all of us, Mister Thomas, and tell Petunia we'll write."

Neither Thomas nor Vernon spoke as they watched Jasper's

firstborn son ride away. He and his brother, Willie, had lived all their lives on the plantation. Thomas had grown up with them as Vernon had with their sons. Jasper had come to Texas with the Tolivers and become an integral part of the history of Somerset. His remains were buried in a place of honor in the cemetery on land he'd helped its patriarch to clear.

"Could you not have sold them the land they worked so they would stay, Daddy?" Vernon, blinking rapidly, asked in a wistful voice.

Thomas raised the boy's chin to look at him. Vernon was nearly shoulder height to him now, but it would not be long before they stood eye to eye. "There are some things too important to put personal feelings above, son. Somerset is one of them. This land belongs to the Tolivers, and not a single acre of it is for sale at any price, for any reason. We are its sole masters. We share its control with no other man. You must remember that."

"I will, Daddy."

Thomas nodded. He had no doubt the boy would remember. His son was so much like him at fourteen. Vernon loved the plantation and had taken an interest in it from the time he toddled down the cotton rows hand in hand with his father. David, his eleven-year-old son—their scamp—had as well. Thomas had been blessed with two sons who had taken to learning the business of running a plantation like hounds to the hunt. David would have been here today, but he'd been permitted to play this Saturday morning in a baseball game, the new sport of the nineteenth century. Both understood what was expected of a Toliver. Thomas would have no son of his living off the bounty of his family's labor without contributing to it. No offspring of his would enjoy the prominence of the name without deserving the right to bear it.

His daughter, too, understood her role as a member of a family that lived by the expectations of its heritage and traditions. Thomas automatically smiled, thinking of Regina. Sons were from the gods, but daughters were from the angels. This morning, she had said to him, "Daddy, Petunia and Amy are very sad."

She had been the first of his children to call him Daddy. It had begun with *da-da*, and the boys had gone with their sister's later form of address. Regina often led the way in how things were said and done in the Toliver household. Of all of the Tolivers he had known, she represented the truest definition of nobility. Kind of heart, strong in spirit, generous and gracious, she held the clearest title to the real meaning of royalty.

"I know, precious," he'd said.

"Petunia's brothers and their families are leaving Somerset. Can't you do something to make them stay?"

"I cannot. Their departure is their decision."

It was one of the rare times he had ever refused his daughter anything, and her disappointment cut him like a knife. For the fraction of a moment, he had actually considered reconsidering— anything to take that pained look from her sweet, freckled face. Instead he had drawn her to his lap. At twelve, she was enough of a little girl still to sit on his knees in the fortress of his arms. Most fathers would have offered a sop, a gift to compensate for the denied request, but that would not work with Regina. No concession could divert her from her original desire. She could not be bought.

"They leave for what they think is a better place," he explained.

Her brow creased. "Than Somerset?"

"Yes."

"There is no better place than Somerset," she said.

He had hugged her. "I hope Petunia's brothers will not find that out in Kansas."

Whenever a blue spell overcame him, like today, Thomas thought of his family, and his mood lifted. He was a very blessed man indeed to have an efficient wife and loving mother at home, the memory of a devoted father, and three delightful children to call him Daddy. Sometimes his heart swelled with such love and pride he thought it would burst.

"Why are you smiling, Daddy?" There was a note of disapproval in Vernon's voice. His tears had barely dried, and his father was smiling.

Thomas placed his arm around his son's shoulders as they turned to go into the cabin. "I was thinking how fortunate I am to be the father of three fine children," he said.

"Heirs to Somerset. Isn't that what we are?"

"You've learned your lessons well, my son. Yes, heirs to Somerset. I wish my father had lived to see there is no curse on the land."

"A curse?"

Thomas wished he had not spoken. Vernon was like a dog with a bone when he wanted to learn more about something. "A jinx," Thomas explained. "Supposedly cast by a supernatural power to inflict harm on someone or something as punishment for their wrongdoing."

"Your father did something wrong?"

"Not at all. He made...certain sacrifices to assure the establishment of Somerset."

"What were they?"

"I don't recall."

"What kind of punishment did he believe the curse inflicted?"

Thomas hesitated. Yellow fever was rampant in Louisiana and sure to hop over the border into East Texas, but all the windows in the family home on Houston Avenue had recently been covered with the new metal mesh coverings called screens to deter the influx of disease-carrying mosquitoes. There was always a danger of cholera returning and other afflictions and accidents that could claim the lives of his children in the blink of an eye, but not by the hand of an imprecation uttered by his father's angry mother almost half a century ago. Yet, superstitiously, Thomas felt a reluctance to voice aloud his father's fear that her malediction related to the procreation and preservation of Toliver heirs. Silas Toliver had worried for nothing. Yes, he had lost his first son, but Joshua, God love his sweet soul, was no real heir to Somerset. Silas Toliver's true heir was alive and well, and his grandsons would carry the name of Toliver and the plantation into the next generation.

"It's a waste of time to talk about nonsense," Thomas said to his son. "There is no such thing as a curse."

PART FOUR

1880–1900

Chapter Seventy-Five

Jeremy glanced around the parlor-cum-ballroom at the group gathered to welcome home Philippe DuMont. The forty-two-year-old bachelor son of Henri and Bess DuMont had returned home for a brief period before reporting to his new job at the Pinkerton Detective Agency in New York after an eleven-year stint with the Texas Rangers, the state's mounted fighting force organized during the Texas Revolution to guard its frontier. There were twenty-two of assorted ages assembled, all from the DuMont, Toliver, and Warwick families. The number and size of the grandchildren had grown too large to be seated at Bess's dining room table, so for the homecoming meal earlier, to many cheeky comments, the youngsters had once again been assigned to the "children's table." The third generation of Toliver offspring consisted of Vernon, aged fifteen; Regina, thirteen; and David, twelve. Those of the DuMont clan were Armand's sons, Abel, sixteen; and Jean, thirteen. The Warwicks' number was composed of Jeremy Jr.'s namesake, Jeremy III, sixteen; and Brandon, thirteen, and Stephen's boys, Richard, sixteen; and Joel, fifteen.

Bess had desired a larger party for her son's homecoming, but Philippe had roundly rejected the idea, disarming his vehement refusal with a chuck of his mother's chin that, as always, so she'd told Camellia with a laugh, had charmed away her disappointment.

They were all very fond of Philippe, but he'd never quite been one of them. Tall, rangy, rugged, totally lacking the elegance of his father's and brother's frames, Philippe had turned out to be if not the black sheep of the families, then the surprise mongrel in a litter of purebreds. From the growth of his first peach fuzz, they'd all observed in Henri's second son a militant nature enigmatically softened by a tenderness toward the fragile and helpless. They'd been amused by his obsessive protection of his little sister, Nanette, and his assignment of himself as discreet guardian of Jeremy's asthmatic son, Robert. Fool with Robert and the hapless malefactor had the fists of tall, strong, fearless Philippe to contend with. Jeremy had loved him for that. The death of Nanette had shadowed the last of Philippe's boyhood years, and the senseless killing of Robert had added to a growing rage against any who would harm the weak. With his brother, Armand, Philippe had returned home after the war to help his father run the DuMont Department Store, the expectation being that the two would assume Henri's position when he retired.

In less than a month, Philippe had left to join the Texas Rangers. He was not cut out to work behind a dry goods counter, he said, or to live in a fine home with servants to polish his boots and turn his bed. He was born to wear buckskin, eat his meals by a campfire, and live under the stars. Besides, Texas needed men like him to defend its frontier against the Comanche and Kiowa and Apache still attacking defenseless wagon trains and homesteads, scalping the men, raping the women, and carrying off children into captivity.

Much to the heartbreak of Bess and the chagrin of Henri, Philippe did not return home in 1870 when the Rangers were replaced by a union peace-keeping force called the Texas State Police. His organization disbanded, Philippe headed north to the Panhandle and sold his services as a gun arm for ranchers trying to defend their land from takeover by the cattle barons.

The election of Governor Richard Coke in 1873 saw the end of the abusive Texas State Police and the reinstatement of the Texas Rangers. Philippe immediately rejoined and added to the myths bred from the capture and killing of notorious criminals and the defeat and removal of the Indians from the plains of Texas.

This last was the cause of the hitch of Jessica's eyebrow as Philippe recounted the Rangers' part in the surrender of Comanche chief Quanah Parker that marked the end of the Texas Indian Wars. Jeremy had observed that Jessica's brows spoke a language of their own. Their twitch, contraction, range of upward movement provided insight into her thoughts. This evening, the infinitesimal arch of one of them indicated disgust at the U.S. Army's destruction of the Comanche villages and the shooting of 3,000 of the Indians' horses, their most prized possessions. No matter the brutality against the settlers and buffalo hunters that Philippe thought justified the slaughter, by the perk of Jessica's eyebrow Jeremy knew her heart was still on the side of the Indians and for all people displaced by the white man's greed and would be to her final day.

To her final day. Jeremy hoped that was a long time in coming. He was losing Camellia. The pulmonary disease that would have eventually claimed the life of his second son was taking his little flower's.

"Quanah Parker..." Bess murmured. "Isn't he the son of Cynthia Ann Parker captured by the Comanche when she was a little girl?"

"Yes," Henri said. "She was kidnapped in 1836 at nine years of age and recaptured in 1860—"

"By the Rangers under Captain Sul Ross," Philippe cut in on a note of pride.

Jeremy, Jessica, and Henri looked at one another, their gazes reflecting the memory of a time only they had shared. "*Mon dieu*," Henri said softly, "has it been forty-four years since the John Parker massacre and that little girl went missing?"

"And we were headed right into the teeth of it," Jeremy said.

"Oh, tell us about it, Grandpa," Brandon, the younger son of Jeremy Jr., begged.

"Some other time," Jeremy said. "You've had enough of a history lesson for one night, and I have to go check on your grandmother." He got up from his chair to the sound of a creak in a leg joint. Jessica had risen also, her quiet demeanor suggesting that her mind was still occupied with Philippe's description of the last battle in the campaign against the Indians six years ago. Jeremy wished Philippe had not been so graphic. The children would relive his account of the massacre in their nightmares.

"Shall I see you home, Jess? It's such a dark night," Jeremy said in the lofty hall of the DuMont château as servants helped them into their warm outerwear. It was February of 1880.

"That would be lovely, Jeremy. I'll let Thomas know. He and Priscilla will want to stay a while longer to visit with Philippe."

They said little on the stroll down the avenue to the Toliver mansion, each weighed by the years of memories Philippe's mention of Quanah Parker had evoked, the sadness of Camellia's illness. Finally, Jeremy said, "I feel every one of my seventy-four years, Jess."

Jessica linked her arm through his. "They don't get any lighter, do they?"

"Or easier, for all our comforts. The only defense against the effects of time is to stay busy."

"And you are certainly that," Jessica said. It had taken forty

years, but with the coming of the railroads, Jeremy was beginning
to see his faith in timber as a major industry in Texas justified
and the Warwick Lumber Company its standard-bearer. By 1878,
when more track had been laid in Texas than in the whole country combined, the company's vast acreage of prime virgin pine
and mighty stands of hardwoods had stood ready for harvesting
and shipment by rail to markets throughout the state. To meet the
demands of the railroads for cross ties, boxcars, and depots and
the surge of orders from commercial builders and real estate de-
velopers in the new towns being founded and counties organized,
the company had begun building additional sawmills and facil-
ities for their workers, all overseen by Jeremy and his two sons,
Jeremy Jr. and Stephen.

"I sometimes think about slowing down, spending more time
with Camellia," Jeremy had said to Jessica a year ago during one
of their gazebo visits. "She wants me to take her to Europe, you
know. I could step aside, leave the lumber business to the boys
to run, and concentrate on my other companies, but we're on the
eve of a great dawn, and I want to feel its sun on my face when it
breaks."

Jessica wondered if Jeremy remembered those words and regretted putting his business interests before the desires of his wife
now that time was running out for her to feel the sun on her face.

Jeremy must have read her thoughts. "She's been a wonderful
wife, Jess."

Jessica heard a sob deep in his throat. "Yes, she has, Jeremy."
Their breaths wreathed out before them, frosty puffs of vapor
swallowed by the dark night. The temperature warranted her
wearing the warm seal cape her family had given her for Christmas and Jeremy his camel hair coat with its rich lapels of sheared
lamb. The crystal air carried the promise of snow by morning.

"Better than I've been a husband."

"Camellia wouldn't agree."

"No, she wouldn't, but I know."

Jessica placed a hand on his lapel. They had reached the front steps of her verandah. "Then let her die without knowing, Jeremy."

A sliver of moonlight caught the flash of surprise in his eyes. "You know?" he said.

"I know."

"But that doesn't mean we can't always be the best of friends."

"We'll always be the best of friends, Jeremy."

He bent his head and kissed the cold contour of her cheek. "Good night, Jess."

"Good night, Jeremy."

Chapter Seventy-Six

It had been a morning of visits with her grandchildren. Vernon first, who tapped on her door as Jessica was dressing. "Granmama, will you help me decide what David and I can get Poppy for her birthday?" and later, at breakfast, when everyone else had eaten and gone, David, her favorite, had stayed behind. Jessica was the only one in the household with whom her younger grandson could discuss his passion of baseball. It seemed that John "Monte" Ward had become the first pitcher to hit two home runs in a game when his New York Gothams defeated the Boston Beaneaters 10 to 9 in May.

"Wouldn't that have been something to see, Granmama?" he'd asked.

"It sure would have," she'd agreed.

"Maybe you and I can go see a game together one of these days."

"I'll count on it," Jessica said.

Now Regina had come to call. From the gazebo, Jessica watched her granddaughter let herself out the screened back door of the house. "I thought I'd find you out here," she called to her grandmother.

Nothing much to think about, Jessica thought, but fondly as she watched Regina pick up her skirts and daintily make her way down the back steps to the brick walk leading to the gazebo. Weather permitting, Jessica always sat in the swing this time of day to have her midmorning tea. Regina had a little of her mother's vacuity in her, but it added an endearing quality to her sweetness of nature denied Priscilla. It was impossible not to adore her.

"I brought an extra cup," Regina said. "You don't mind sharing your pot with me, do you?"

"I'm delighted with the company as always," Jessica said, making room on the swing. "What do you have there? Is that the package of long-awaited patterns from Tippy?"

Regina giggled. "I think it's darling the way you call one of the most famous fashion designers in America Tippy when everybody else calls her Isabel."

"She wasn't always Isabel. Which pattern did you choose?"

"Well, that's what I'd like to talk to you about." Regina removed three envelopes from a glued paper sack, the new type of packaging material for mailing lightweight goods. "I need to enlist your help with Daddy."

Jessica poured Regina a cup of tea. "I can't imagine why you'd need my help with your father. You have only to ask, and he will do your bidding."

Regina smiled. "Not about something like this," she said. "I want Armand's tailor to make the dress for my birthday party from this design"—she handed Jessica one of the three colorfully illustrated envelopes—"but Mother and I agree Daddy will think it's too daring. She'd like me to choose one of the more modest ones, but I want you to convince Daddy that this is the one for me."

Jessica drew her spectacles from her dress pocket to study the illustration on the envelope containing tissue pattern pieces cut approximately to Priscilla's dress measurements. The evening gown was billed as an "Isabel" design, created for the E. Butterick Company in New York. Tippy had been working for the company since 1876 when Ebenezer Butterick offered her the position as head designer of his pattern empire. Since his revolutionary introduction of graded patterns for home use in 1867, it had grown to include one hundred branch offices and one thousand agencies throughout the United States and Canada, Paris, London, Vienna, and Berlin. The gown featured a low neckline and a waist the circumference of a wasp's middle. Jessica could understand why Thomas would object. At almost sixteen, Regina's figure was voluptuous—"another attraction we all agree to blame on you, Mother," her son accused with a father's sigh and roll of his eyes.

"I'm going to be sixteen, Granmama," Regina said. "It's time Daddy realized that I'm not a little girl anymore."

"Fathers never realize their daughters are not little girls anymore," Jessica said. She squinted at the pattern. "What if the seamstress raised the neckline just a little and dropped the shoulders a bit more? That way you still have the right amount of flesh showing for the same effect."

"Oh, Granmama, you're a genius," Regina cried, throwing her arms around Jessica's shoulders. "Thank you for not suggesting *lace*, like Mother did. Can you imagine *lace* on the neckline of a dress like this? It would simply *ruin* the effect I'm trying to achieve."

"And what effect is that? To slay the heart of every boy in the room?"

Regina settled herself comfortably beside Jessica on the swing. "Not every boy," she said. "Only one. Tyler McCord."

"The rancher's son."

"The same. Oh, Granmama, he's...beautiful. So tall and strong—like Daddy."

"Yes, he's quite a handsome fellow," Jessica agreed.

"And even nicer than he is handsome. Granmama, how old were you when you married?"

Uh-oh, Jessica thought. She could guess the reason behind the question. "Eighteen," she answered.

"You're going to tell me that eighteen when you married is different than being eighteen now, aren't you?" Regina tilted her head and gave Jessica an arch look. On days when her mother did not have her "receiving," Regina wore her abundance of brick-red hair loose and flowing, refusing to sit for the hour it took Amy to tether her crowning glory into a french twist on top of her head. An April breeze stirred her tresses, lifting strands away from her pale, freckle-sprinkled face. Jessica never looked into her granddaughter's green-flecked hazel eyes but that she tried to recall Major Duncan's. After a few weeks of his acquaintance, she'd never looked into them again.

"Not at all," she answered Regina's assumption. "Eighteen is eighteen in any generation, though years do not always reflect one's age."

Regina took a sip of tea and gazed at Jessica over its rim. "Were you eighteen when you reached eighteen?"

"In some ways, but not in all."

"Were you ready for marriage?"

Jessica hesitated, then smiled. "I was not ready for Silas Toliver."

"Really?" Regina's eyes grew larger. Jessica knew she loved these moments alone with her when she could pry memories of her youth out of her grandmother. "Was he ready for you?"

"I believe I can truthfully say he wasn't."

Regina's laughter pealed across the yard, the sound young and pure and happy a week from her sixteenth birthday. When it subsided, she said, her tone serious, "Tyler is definitely ready for me."

"That's what's worrying your father. At sixteen he believes you're definitely not ready for him."

"But I will be at eighteen. Granmama, I want to marry Tyler. Daddy, of course, is having a fit. He doesn't think Tyler is good enough for me."

"Well, now," Jessica said, "that brings up another father principle when it comes to daughters. Fathers think no man is good enough for their little girls."

"Did your father think Grandfather Silas wasn't good enough for you?"

Jessica took a moment to sip her tea. Regina waited, her gaze anticipatory of her answer. "I'm sure he didn't," Jessica said, patting her lips with her napkin, "but your grandfather surprised him by making me happy. What color and fabric do you think you'll choose for the dress?"

"Oh, I'll have to consult with Armand on that," Regina said, her attention instantly diverted to the pattern. "I think a dramatic color in satin, don't you, with elbow-length gloves in the same fabric…"

Jessica heard without listening. Her thoughts were on Jeremy Sr. He had hoped that one of his grandsons, Jeremy III or Brandon, would win the heart of Regina—"a mingling of our families' blood, Jess. What could be a sweeter twist of fate?" The twinkle in his eye had made clear his wish that in a great-grandchild he would have a part of Jessica Toliver to have and to hold.

Camellia had died in the spring of 1880, three years ago. Jeremy's sons had homes of their own, and their father rambled around in his baronial mansion by himself with only a cook and housekeeper to see to his domestic needs. When he wasn't working twelve-hour days, and his children and friends weren't allaying as many of his empty hours as he'd permit, he filled his time at home reading voraciously. Of all the families, he was the best informed. It was from Jeremy that Jessica learned of the experiments of a Gregor Mendel, an Austrian monk, whose research in cross-breeding garden peas had led to the discovery that the basic principles of heredity governing color, shape, and height in plants can apply to traits in people and animals. Jeremy showed her a chapter in a book that explained how certain traits in human beings, termed dominant and recessive and relating to everything from hair color to temperament, could disappear in the second generation but reappear in the next.

"So now we have an explanation for Regina's red hair and freckles and winsome figure," Jeremy said.

Jessica was usually uncomfortable with any reference comparing her granddaughter's physical features to hers. It was only a skip and hop to Major Andrew Duncan in the memory of anyone who remembered him. But Jeremy had given her even more of a red herring to throw the dogs off the scent. She'd borrowed the book and showed it to Thomas. "I think you'll find this interesting," she said. "The marked chapter explains how I'm to blame."

In a rare display of affection, though Jessica loved the girl dearly, she placed her arm around her granddaughter's shoulders and hugged her to her. In a week, Regina would be sixteen. In another two years she would be married. She would leave her family to go live with her husband on his ranch. She would have her own family. As she grew older, enmeshed in the duties of wife and mother, time would assert its will on her face and figure. The simple passing of the years would eliminate any sudden connection to the Union major who came to Howbutker long ago. What could possibly spark it? Regina had only to get through the next two years, and Jessica could foresee no situation or occasion that would bring up the question of her paternity.

"I'll put in a good word for the dress with your father," she said.

Chapter Seventy-Seven

Thomas regarded his wife in frustration. "You are asking *me* to pick up a hat for you at the milliner's? That ladies' shop? What if I don't know what it looks like?"

"The hat or the shop?"

"The hat. The shop is at the end of the first spoke street off Circle, isn't it?"

"That's the one. And it's not a hat, dear. It's a *headband,* and you don't have to know what it looks like. Mrs. Chastain, the milliner, will know.

"Can't you send a servant?"

"They are all busy helping me with the party. Thomas, please—I *need* that headpiece today so Regina can try it on before tomorrow and adjustments made if it doesn't fit. It's a surprise. I ordered it last month to complement her dress. It will be the perfect touch."

"It's for Regina? Why didn't you say so?"

Priscilla sighed in frustration. "All I have to do is say it's for Regina, and my will is done. I didn't tell you because you can never keep secrets from the girl."

"She worms them out of me."

"Only because you hint that you know something she'd like to know."

"Mrs. Chastain, you say? She's the woman I'm to speak with?"

"She's the owner of the shop. She's expecting someone to pick up the band. She'll have it ready, and you won't have to linger."

"What color is it? The band."

"A light summer green over a rather goldish haze."

"Sounds pretty. It will bring out Regina's hazel eyes."

Priscilla rose hastily from her desk in the morning room, a large, ornate replacement for Jessica's slim Queen Anne secretary. "Darling, if you don't mind, I need that headpiece as soon as possible. I've got a dozen things to do today to finish preparations for the party, and I'd like to check that item off when Regina returns from her piano lesson. *Everybody* on the guest list is coming. *Nobody* would miss it."

"As long as everybody is coming to celebrate our daughter's birthday and not out of curiosity about the house," Thomas said.

Priscilla pressed a hand to her heart to express horror at the idea. "Of *course* everyone is coming to celebrate Regina's birthday. I've done no more to redecorate the house than anyone else has on Houston Avenue," she said. "No one is coming to be impressed."

"Uh-huh," Thomas said, uncrossing his legs and rising. "And all I have to do is simply walk in and pick up the piece?"

"It will be wrapped and ready to go."

"I hope the woman doesn't have undergarments on display."

"It's a *hat* shop, Thomas."

It was a nice day for a canter into town, and Thomas was glad to get out of the house that no longer seemed like his boyhood home. With the exception of his mother's suite, his wife had completely redecorated the place, upstairs, downstairs, even his study when he'd been on a business trip to Galveston. Nearly every feature of the sunny house of his childhood with its deep white moldings, Wedgwood blue walls, cream-colored sofas and chairs, and silk draperies in garden pastels had been replaced with the heavy colors of the Victorian period. Their very names—"blood burgundy," "moss green," "ash rose," "shadow gray," "autumn brown"—depressed Thomas. Massive, ornate furniture, dark woods, heavily stained glass, damask-covered walls, weighty fabrics embellished with tassels, cording, fringe, beads, and spangles had supplanted his mother's slimmer, lighter, more graceful décor. "The place has been turned into a damned museum," Thomas had complained to Armand when his decorator's work was finished.

"It was what your wife wanted, my friend," Armand said.

Still, it had been almost twenty-seven years since the house had been refurbished, and Thomas had not wanted to stir up a hornet's nest by refusing Priscilla's request to "redo a few things." When he'd gone to ask his mother's permission, she had said, "Let her have her way, Thomas, and do not think of me. You'll be living here long after I'm gone."

Her observation had induced a sadness he'd not been able to put aside. His mother was sixty-seven. Every day of his life, he missed his father. Jeremy and Henri, his father surrogates, were aging. How destitute he would feel when they were gone. He had his friends—Jeremy Jr. and Stephen and Armand, the best— and his children, of course, but his darling daughter would marry soon, and Vernon and David in time. They would leave his home, and then he would be left with Priscilla.

These thoughts were on his mind when he entered the small establishment to which he'd been dispatched, simply named the Millinery Shop. The place had not been in business long. What he knew of it came from Armand, who was now running the department store. The Millinery Shop was a competitor to his friend's line of women's hats, but Armand waved away the challenge as one would shoo a fly. "There's enough business for all, and Mrs. Chastain features certain styles I don't carry. The proprietor is a war widow. Her husband was killed at Manassas. No children. Quite a lovely woman, actually. I wish her well."

A silver doorbell announced his presence. Thomas had only a few seconds to register the pleasant fragrance and utter femininity of the place before a woman emerged from a lace curtain drawn across an opening to the rear of the shop.

"Good afternoon, sir. May I help you?"

She spoke in a deep contralto, her voice the most beautiful he'd ever heard. To his complete astonishment, Thomas felt his skin tingle. "Uh, Mrs. Chastain?"

"Yes."

"I'm…Thomas Toliver, and…I've been sent to pick up a package for my wife."

The woman smiled. Thomas felt pressure mount beneath his rib cage.

"I know who you are, Mr. Toliver." She reached under the counter and withdrew a small package. "I believe this is for you. It's already paid for. I hope your daughter will be pleased."

"Oh, I'm—I'm quite sure she'll be very pleased." He could not believe himself. He had conversed easily with the richest and most powerful, the venerable and erudite, the famous and notorious, and yet here he stood tongue-tied in the presence of a millinery shop owner of no more consequence to the world than a feather in the plumage of one of her hats.

"Would you like to see the item your wife purchased for your daughter? I understand it's to be a surprise."

"That's what her mother says, and yes, I'd like very much to see it."

"Let's unwrap it, then."

She set the package on the counter and with light, deft strokes, untied the ribbon. "What do you think?" she said, holding up the wired confection of satin rosettes in the green and gold color his wife had described.

Thomas took the exquisite design in his hands. "It's the color of my daughter's eyes."

"Hazel, so I'm told."

"Yes, hazel."

"Not as pure green as yours, then."

"No, no...They are her own."

"I understand she has red hair."

"Yes, like my mother."

"This color should complement her red hair beautifully."

He should give the piece back, allow her to rewrap it again, Thomas thought. "How does it...work?" he asked.

The woman took back the arched creation. "Like this," she said, and gave a mock demonstration. "The piece is designed to hold the hair back and serve as a frame for the face. It should be lovely on your daughter. Shall I rewrap it?"

"Yes, please."

Thomas watched her hands at work, the bone structure delicate as bone china. She still wore a gold band on her wedding ring finger. She handed the package to him. "There," she said with a smile that turned his heart over. "I look forward to seeing a picture of your daughter wearing her surprise in the social section of the Sunday paper."

"I have a better idea," Thomas said. "Why don't you come to my daughter's party and see your handiwork for yourself? It's tomorrow evening at seven. I'm sure my daughter would love to have you there to thank you in person."

"That is very kind of you, but...what would Mrs. Toliver say?"

"My mother?"

"No. Your wife."

"Oh. Why, she would be delighted as well."

"May I...consider the invitation, Mr. Toliver?"

"Yes, of course." Thomas picked up the rewrapped package. "And it's, uh, Thomas, by the way."

She held out her hand. "Jacqueline," she said.

He pressed it gently. "Jacqueline. Perhaps you will give serious thought to the invitation?"

"Perhaps. Good-bye...Thomas."

Thomas tipped his hat. "Until tomorrow evening, I hope."

Chapter Seventy-Eight

"You did *what*?" Priscilla demanded.

Before the mirror, Thomas calmly continued knotting his black dinner tie. "I invited Mrs. Chastain, the milliner, to our daughter's birthday party. I thought she'd like to see her artistry worn in person."

"Thomas..." Priscilla positioned herself between her husband and the mirror. "Jacqueline Chastain is a nice enough person, but she is a *milliner*, a...a woman of *trade*."

Thomas placed the back of his hand on his wife's arm and gently but firmly moved her out of his line of vision. "So?"

"*So?* So people like her are not to be invited to Regina's party! *That's* what's so!"

His task completed, Thomas leveled his gaze at his wife. "Now, how would you have felt if someone had said that about you as a doctor's daughter—a saw-bones, some would say."

Priscilla flushed. "Don't you speak that way about my father, God rest his soul."

"I'm not speaking of your father, but of you, Priscilla. Try to walk in the shoes you may have filled if you'd not married into the Toliver family."

Priscilla's eyes blazed. "And think of the children *you* wouldn't have had if you hadn't married me," she said.

"Believe me, Priscilla, I do every day. Rest easy, my sweet. From the look of Mrs. Chastain, she doesn't eat much."

While Thomas mingled among the guests, he looked for her entrance. A place had been set for Jacqueline Chastain at dinner as far away as was possible from his chair at the head of the table. Thomas was tempted to move her place card closer to him but realized that would invite speculation from his wife. What had gotten into him? He was entertaining dangerous ideas—or was he? Was it so wrong—immoral—to admire a beautiful woman not your wife? To enjoy the simple pleasure of her company? In the nineteen years of his marriage, he had never looked at another woman in—the way a man shouldn't once he had taken a wife and had children by her. He couldn't have explained the impulse that had caused him to invite Mrs. Chastain to his daughter's party or his excitement at the prospect of seeing her again. He had spoken only a few words to her, spent only minutes in her company, but he couldn't get her voice out of his head, her lovely face and pleasing manner out of his thoughts. He almost hoped she wouldn't appear, and if she didn't, there was no reason to think they would meet again.

Thomas concentrated on his daughter, laughing, glowing in a circle of her friends, Tyler McCord planted by her side. He sighed. The boy was a good catch. He was from a stable, loving family, and he was obviously head over heels in love with Regina, and she with him. Everyone in the Toliver household liked him, the boys especially. Tyler and Vernon could talk land, and he and David baseball, and the McCords already treated Regina like one of their own. As a father, Thomas could ask for no more than that. The burnished green satin headpiece set off his daughter's waterfall of red ringlets dazzlingly. In the center of the band was a small diamond pin he and Priscilla had presented her in honor of her sixteenth birthday.

"Thank you, Mother and Daddy," Regina had said in her effusively appreciative way when they'd opened presents earlier. (Vernon and David had remembered her with silk stockings and her grandmother with enameled hair clips.) "When I wear this pin I will always remember the wonderful party you gave me on my sixteenth birthday."

Priscilla had taken the ornament to attach to Regina's dress, but Thomas had stopped her by suggesting she pin it in the center of the headband. "Daddy! What a darling idea!" Regina had cried, and Thomas had ignored the speculative look Priscilla shot him while his idea was put in place.

How he wished Mrs. Chastain were here to see the display of her creation. Priscilla had told Regina that it had been designed just for her and bragged that no one else in town had anything like it. The newspaper pictures the photographer had taken of his daughter would not do it justice.

"Excuse me, Mr. Thomas," Barnabas, Petunia's husband and the Tolivers' houseman, whispered into his ear. "The Mrs. Jacqueline Chastain you were expecting is at the door." He handed Thomas her calling card.

Thomas's heart jumped. "Well, then, by all means, let's go collect her, Barnabas."

She stood in the chandelier-lit, overfurnished foyer with a dignity meant to hide the uncertainty of her reception, Thomas perceived at once. He felt his ire rise. He would make sure no one gave her reason to feel unwelcome in *his* house. He walked toward her smiling and held out his hand. She wore a white dress that forswore the lavishly trimmed, bustled, tightly corseted gowns every woman in the party was wearing in favor of a loosely fitted creation that flowed from her shoulders—her own design, Thomas guessed, and admired her courage in swimming against the stream. Her dark hair was arranged in a coronet atop her head and entwined with yellow satin ribbons.

"Mrs. Chastain," he said, taking her hand. "How good of you to come."

"It is my pleasure, if slightly dampened by nervousness, Mr. Toliver," Jacqueline said.

Thomas presented his arm. "I've just the thing to correct that, Mrs. Chastain. Let's head for the punch table."

Priscilla greeted their guest with her practiced hostess charm that did not bother to hide her pointed surprise the milliner had had the audacity to show up. "I so hope we haven't put you out to come on such short notice, Mrs. Chastain. My husband can be...overly enthusiastic sometimes."

"Not at all, Mrs. Toliver, and I admire enthusiasm. It is such a generous trait."

When Thomas escorted the new arrival to meet his daughter, Regina threw her arms around her. "I love, love, *love* my hair-piece, Mrs. Chastain. Thank you *so* much for all the creativity and time and *effort* you put into it."

"Seeing it worn in your hair makes the time and effort insignificant, Miss Toliver."

"Oh, do please call me Regina, and may I call you Jacqueline? It's such a beautiful name. French, isn't it?"

Thomas could have hugged his daughter. When Jacqueline turned to meet Vernon and David, who'd been waved over for introductions, he drew Regina to his side and kissed her temple. "I love you, Poppy."

"I love you, too, Daddy."

When he introduced Jacqueline to his mother, Thomas caught the imperceptible quirk of a maternal eyebrow directed at him, in his youth a definite precursor of a talk to come. She put Jacqueline at ease immediately by complimenting her dress.

"I see you agree, as I do, with Oscar Wilde's view that these 'dress improvers'"—Jessica swiped at her bustle—"are a modern-day monstrosity. My friend Tippy—Isabel—is now designing dresses free of these abominations. Do you know of Isabel?"

"Indeed I do, Mrs. Toliver," Jacqueline said, looking amazed. "You *know* Isabel? Personally?"

"I most certainly do."

Elated, Thomas watched the two women put their heads together in an animated discussion of his mother's history with Tippy. Before long, other guests gathered around, the wives admiring Jacqueline's dress, the men admiring Jacqueline.

At the end of the evening, Thomas said, "How did you arrive, Mrs. Chastain?"

"By livery. I told the driver to return by ten."

"Jackson is probably drunk in the local tavern by now. I will summon my driver and carriage to take you home."

He would have preferred to go himself, but that would have tempted fate. He saw her out to the carriage and gave his driver explicit instructions not to leave until Mrs. Chastain was safely ensconced in her quarters above her shop. They shook hands. "Good-bye...Jacqueline. Thank you so much for coming."

"You were kind to invite me...Thomas."

She smiled at him, the moonlight glowing in the darkness of her hair, on the yellow satin ribbons. "Perhaps we will have the opportunity to meet again," he said.

"I hardly think that's likely, but the thought is nice. Good-bye...Mr. Toliver."

Thomas watched the carriage pull away and swallowed the ache in his throat.

Chapter Seventy-Nine

David Toliver, aged fifteen, dressed quietly in the darkness of the bedroom he shared with his older brother, Vernon, but apparently, not quietly enough.

"David, what are you doing?"

His brother's voice, strong, authoritative, startled him. There was nothing that got past Vernon, David thought irritably. "Dressing," he said shortly.

"Why?"

"I'm going to the old mill lot to practice."

"No, you're not. Daddy will have your hide. You know he expects us out at Somerset to help with the ginning this morning."

"I'll be back before he knows I'm gone."

Vernon sat up in bed, running a hand through his black, sleep-tousled hair. "It's too dark to play baseball, and I don't want you going by yourself."

David finished buttoning his shirt. "Who're you? My father? Just because you're eighteen doesn't give you the right to tell me what to do. Sam and Nick are going to meet me there, okay? We'll practice a few hours, then I'll be back in time for breakfast. Don't tell on me. Promise, brother?"

"I don't like it, David. Not one bit. That old mill pond attracts all kinds of critters at night, and it's dark as pitch outside. Also, I heard rumors the Ku Klux Klan could be out tonight."

"We won't be playing in the pond, David, and it's five o'clock, almost dawn. Don't you hear the chimes? And the KKK isn't going to bother one of the Toliver sons."

"What with the bales we'll be lifting, why do you feel you have to practice at all? Won't you need to rest your arm before the game Sunday?"

David pushed his arms into his jacket and grinned at his brother. Of the two, Vernon had the edge on looks. David's short, stocky build and heavy facial features were in notable contrast to his brother's tall, sleek figure and chiseled physiognomy, not to mention the attraction of Vernon's unruly raven-black hair, which David teasingly called "the Toliver crown." By comparison, his younger brother's baby-fine cap was a nondescript brown.

But David's personality made up for the unfair disparity. His ready grin lit up eyes the purplish blue of bluebonnets and suggested the quick wit and impish humor just below a reserved manner that made him more the favorite among their friends than his serious-minded brother. He was the pet of the girls if not their sweetheart; the indispensable spark of the party if not the beau of the ball. He was the occasional despair of his mother and the daily cheer of his father. His grandmother and siblings adored him.

"If you played baseball, Vernon, you'd understand. A baseman's arm needs daily training and conditioning, especially if you play third. It takes a strong arm to get a ball from third to first."

His brother drew the covers back over his head. "Just be careful," he said under the muffle of the blankets.

David soundlessly let himself out through the side entrance of the house rather than risk leaving by the back kitchen door. Amy and her husband and their daughter Sassie's quarters were right off the pantry, and since her mother had died last year, Amy could wake up at the pad of a mouse's feet in the parlor. She'd try to talk him out of going, and that would create a ruckus that his parents might hear in their room upstairs right over the kitchen. The threat of the "white knights," as the sheeted members of the Ku Klux Klan called themselves, kept everybody off the streets until daylight, and Amy had an unholy fear of them.

"You may be a Toliver, but what if you come across them and witness something you shouldn't, and they see you," she'd said to him on another morning when she'd caught him sneaking out of the house to meet the boys at their playing site. "Once they get the liquor in them, that ignorant bunch of riff-raff hidin' under them white sheets wouldn't care if you were Jesus's son, they'd make sure you never told nothin' to nobody."

David hadn't let on that he already knew most of the identities of the riff-raff under the hoods because his baseball buddy, Sam Darrow, had told him, swearing him to secrecy. Mr. Darrow rode with them. David figured he had nothing to worry about because of Sam's dad.

David set his cap more firmly, stuffed his fingerless fielder's glove into his jacket pocket, and, with his baseball bat anchored over his shoulder, set off into the chilly darkness. He breathed in deeply of the bracing morning air. Jiminy jumping frogs, it was good to be alive, especially at this time of year. He loved fall when the leaves began to blaze and the days turned crisp— perfect baseball weather—and he had years and years to enjoy playing the sport. He didn't have to give it up when he became a man. That amazing recognition had come to him at his sister's sixteenth birthday party in the spring. He'd happened to look across the room at his father standing with his best friends, Armand DuMont and Jeremy Jr. and Stephen Warwick, all in their middle forties and still hale and hearty, and did a little calculating. He had over thirty years to swing a bat and pitch a ball to first base before he reached their age. The boys' group he played with now, made up of the sons of his fathers' friends, would just grow into men's teams like the one Marshall had formed last year. Until then, Howbutker would probably never have an adult team. Men like his father couldn't see the point of grown men trying to hit a ball with a stick of wood and then run to touch a sack of sawdust without getting tagged. They couldn't see the skill and strategy involved, how the pitcher can baffle and fool a batter, or know the great feeling of striking a home run or hitting one deep. They just didn't get it, though all the fathers were fine with their sons' interest in the sport as long as nobody got hurt.

He was one lucky fellow, David had decided at the party. He got to do the two things he loved best in all the world: grow cotton and play baseball. He had the best parents and brother and sister and grandmother in all the world, too, though he'd get an argument over that claim from his friends in the Warwick and DuMont clans, who thought their families pretty rare.

Sam Darrow and Nick Logan were waiting for him at the playing site, impatient to lose the shivers in their jackets from the heat of play. Behind them, the derelict mill loomed in the darkness, its outline blurred by steam rising from pond water still warm from Indian summer when struck by the cold front that had come through in the night. The abandoned lot next to the mill and pond had been commandeered years ago by the local boys as their playing and gathering field. Sunday's game against Marshall would be officially played in the city park that offered a bandstand and room for spectators.

Sam and Nick were the only ones on the team willing and brave enough to skip out without their parents' knowledge to meet this early in the morning. David knew his mother did not approve of his association with "their kind." She was haughty like that. The boys were not from Houston Avenue, where the other players lived. Their homes were in the country, and their fathers did not wear frock coats and vests to work. One was a brakeman for the Southern Pacific railroad, and the other worked in a tannery. As with David, their fathers had chores waiting for them after breakfast on Saturday when everybody worked until dusk, and their mothers absolutely refused to let them out of the house once supper was over and night fell. No sneaking out then. In the Darrow and Logan households, Saturday nights were for bathing and polishing shoes for Sunday school and church. So it was either at the crack of dawn today or never that they'd all get one last chance to practice before the game tomorrow afternoon.

"Hey, boys!" David called, feeling his grin crack his cold face. The others responded likewise, ready for the workout to begin. The drill this morning was for Sam to practice his pitching, Nick his hitting, and David his fielding. These were their special abilities, skills at which they were the best on the team. Dawn was breaking when the boys shed their jackets and David slipped on his fingerless, thin leather glove recently manufactured for the protection of a fielder's hand. Nick got in position to bat, Sam to pitch, and David to catch or chase after the ball.

At the first crack of Nick's bat, the ball sailed over the pitcher's and David's heads and landed in the darkness of the pond's bank. "Great hit!" David called, running after the ball before it could disappear from sight. "Do that a few times tomorrow and the game is ours!"

Dang, where did it go? David wondered, straining in the darkness and shade of cypresses to find the brown leather ball buried in the damp high grass and swamp flora. He didn't dare lose it. It was an A. G. Spalding ball his father had given him for Christmas, the one they meant to use in tomorrow's game. He heard one of the boys cry out, "David, look out for snakes!"—Nick, he thought it was—when he saw the ball and reached for it with his left hand to spare his fielder's glove from getting wet.

Too late he saw the black menace the ball had disturbed and froze in horror as a water moccasin lunged straight at him, its open mouth brilliant white in the dimness, and sank its fangs deep into the back of his hand. The snake held on until David tore it from his flesh and flung it toward the pond. He heard it plop into the water as he staggered backwards out of the danger zone staring at the puncture wounds beginning to ooze blood. Within seconds, his hand felt as if it had been jammed into a bed of hot coals.

The boys ran screaming toward him. "I've been bit," David said, already tasting metal in his mouth. He felt his heart rhythm change, his lungs begin to strain. His vision blurred and his bowels loosened. He heard Sam wail as nausea rose, "Oh, my God! Oh, my God!" and thought of the game he would not live to play.

Chapter Eighty

After the funeral, early one morning, Thomas rode out to Somerset and dismounted on the rise of land where his father was buried. The red oak leaves were turning, as were those of the sumac, black gum, and hickory buried among the pines lining the road to the plantation. He knew that he would not live enough years for orange-and-gold October mornings not to bring the memory of the day before the sun fully rose when his youngest child met the instrument of his death. Thomas removed his hat and squatted before the headstone. He stared at it, remembering in particular a part of the conversation he'd overheard between his mother and father twenty-two years ago. He recalled fragments of his father's words.

My mother prophesied a curse would fall upon Somerset for the sacrifice I made to fulfill my ambition of having a plantation of my own. . . . I paid no attention to it. . . . But then, our first child miscarried, and there was another miscarriage after the birth of Thomas . . . and after that . . . you . . . seemed unable to conceive. And then when we lost Joshua . . .

Thomas had never forgotten the sound of his father's anguish in his confession to his mother. *The possibility possessed me like a demon that perhaps we were cursed . . . and being punished for . . . the selfish and willful trades I made for the sake of the land. . . .*

Thomas shook his head to dislodge any thought of believing his son's death was the fault of a curse, but his mind would not let go. He had come here today where he'd often brought concerns, anxieties, hopes, triumphs, most often seeking guidance and answers, as if his father could counsel him from the grave. He rarely left without an easier heart, a firmer resolve, a clearer sense of direction. Today he came to seek release from the ridiculous notion that had bedeviled him unmercifully since his little boy was brought home already in the throes of death from a morning of baseball practice, but as he stared at the headstone, Thomas had the awful feeling he'd come to the wrong place.

In his mind's eye, he could see his father as he best remembered him: tall, straight, in command, the wisdom of the ages etched in his handsome, strong face, the eyes direct and steady. Today, though, the memory of that clear green gaze held no affirmation of Thomas's opinion that the Toliver curse was an absurdity. On the contrary, he believed his father may have argued the point with him.

It was a fact that he, too, like his father, had sacrificed another person's happiness for his own self-interest, and he had lived to regret it, which had been curse enough. Thomas often wondered, especially now when sometimes he thought Priscilla hated him, how much happier she would have been if she'd married a man who loved her. He had robbed her of that happiness, and for that theft he had paid with his own personal happiness, which had been a sacrifice of his own. But had the "selfish and willful trades" he'd made for the sake of the land resulted in David's death? Of course not. Men married women for less reason than love all the time, and their children died. No hex was involved. Henri and Bess had lost a daughter; Jeremy and Camellia Warwick a son. Were they under a curse, too?

Thomas stood, replaced his hat, and looked out over the infinite rows of cotton where his real solace lay. The workers were making the second pass at the still-abundant fields. It was a beautiful sight. The width, expanse—the *power*—of all that whiteness stretching farther than it was possible for the eye to see filled his soul, he could not deny it. He remembered his father explaining to Priscilla when they were first engaged: "Tolivers are not seamen. We were not born to ply oceans and sail ships. For better or worse, we are men controlled by some inherited need to master the land—great parcels of it—and make it our own as our ancestors did in England and South Carolina."

How could a man deny who and what he was, what he'd been born to do, what he needed to survive, what he believed with all his heart he must pass on to his progeny? If his grief swelled at the sight of the legacy his younger son had not lived to share with his brother, it was due to an irony of fate, not a curse. He'd been robbed of an heir he'd married a woman he did not love to produce, but his loss had nothing to do with the sacrifices he or his father had made on behalf of Somerset. Thomas vowed to continue to remember that.

Chapter Eighty-One

The last day of 1883, Jessica removed a notepad from the stack of journals in the upper cabinet of her secretary, adjusted the wick of her kerosene lamp against the gathering twilight, and headed her final entry of the year.

DECEMBER 31, 1883

A light has been extinguished in the Toliver household that all our Christmas candles have not relieved. What a sad holiday season this year—worse, even, than when Silas died. Silas had lived; David had not. The shock of my grandson's death still stuns, and our grief will linger a long, long time—forever for his parents. Parents do not get over the death of a child. How I yearn to comfort my son and his wife, but there is no solace I can give. I excused myself when the minister came with his Bible. I did not wish to hear his hollow words. Thomas's face was as gray, Priscilla's as blank-eyed, Vernon's as tear-stained when the preacher left as when he came. Regina had escaped to Tyler's arms where she's spent most of her time since her brother's funeral. Henri and Bess and Jeremy's wordless presence has been consoling. They know. They have been where Thomas and Priscilla are now. Thomas mourns for Vernon also. He remembers the loss of his brother, Joshua.

Adding to the household sadness is the distance I see quivering between Thomas and Priscilla like heat on pavement in the hottest days of summer. My son is puzzled by her angry withdrawal. Their grief should be uniting them. I, too, am perplexed. It is as if Priscilla blames Thomas for the death of their son, that somehow she has found out about the Toliver curse and believes it responsible for what has happened. But how could she know unless...

Jessica laid down her pen and stared unseeing out the dusk-filled window. Like the sudden lunge of the snake that had killed her grandson, an unthinkable possibility leaped into her mind. Dear God! Had Priscilla read her diaries? From what other source could she have learned about the curse? The knowledge could not have come through Thomas. He had been kept ignorant of the foolishness that had haunted his father. But would the girl be that unprincipled, that ignoble? Was Jessica imagining things? Was she misjudging her daughter-in-law?

Another cause could account for Priscilla's animosity toward her husband. The night of Regina's birthday party his wife had seen the attraction between Thomas and Jacqueline Chastain. To Jessica's knowledge—and it would not have escaped her— Thomas had not acted upon his fascination, but ever since, Jessica was convinced that Priscilla had become the milliner's enemy. The situation had not appeared so at first. Priscilla began buying all her hats from the Millinery Shop, so many that Thomas had remarked on her extravagance at supper one night.

"I'm delighted you are giving Mrs. Chastain the business, Priscilla, but must you support it as if you're the only customer in Howbutker?" he'd said.

"I'm trying to be a pied piper by leading all my friends to her door," Priscilla had replied.

But Jessica noticed that Priscilla never wore the hats, and word had come to her by way of Bess that someone had written letters circulating around the county that defamed the morals of the widow who owned the millinery shop. They claimed Jacqueline had seduced her husband and warned women that as long as "the wanton" was in town, their husbands were in jeopardy of her wiles.

"Who would do such a thing?" Bess said. "One wonders, of course, if there is truth to the letters even though Mrs. Chastain does not seem the sort, but who knows? She is very beautiful and unattached."

Jessica had had an idea who. A letter had not come to her, a further implication that Priscilla's hand had held the pen. Her daughter-in-law had bought the hats to throw suspicion off herself. Bess had destroyed her copy of the malicious swill, so Jessica could not compare the writer's signature to Priscilla's. Jessica had been in a quandary of indecision. If her daughter-in-law was innocent of such evil, confronting her could drive a wedge between them that would never be removed. And if the girl was guilty, Thomas would be unable to live under the same roof with her, and what would that alienation do to the children? Jessica believed she had no choice but to remain silent and hope the perpetrator's scheme would have no effect on the prosperity of Mrs. Chastain's shop.

But if Priscilla *were* guilty of that sort of skullduggery, how far a leap was it to steal into her mother-in-law's room, unlock the cabinet in her secretary, and read her private journals? The idea of it was so chilling that Jessica rose abruptly and began to pace. Good Lord, the buried secrets the girl would have unearthed! And why had she read them in the first place? Surely her interest in her husband's lineage was not *that* strong!

In her mind, Jessica sorted through the information her

daughter-in-law was now privy to if she'd read the diaries. The sum and private nature of the content appalled her to the bone, not the least of which was Jessica's suspicion that the girl had had relations with Andrew Duncan and believed him to be the father of Regina.

Jessica forced herself to remain calm. She could still be imagining demons that didn't exist. Priscilla had never hinted of the information she'd learned by so much as a sidelong glance. She'd never used it to her advantage against Jessica, whom she'd come to dislike, but then, why would she and risk discovery? What had led her to embark on such a perilous mission as reading her mother-in-law's diaries? She would have known that discovery would lead to her disgrace—and Thomas's complete rejection—if caught. What *had* caused her to put her marriage, and her zealously enjoyed position, in jeopardy?

Jessica strolled to the window overlooking the drive leading to the carriage house. Sometimes in the early hours, she thought she could still hear the clip-clop of Major Duncan's horse carrying him to his quarters late at night. Suddenly the answer to the puzzle popped into her head. Of course. The major! Red-haired, freckle-faced Andrew Duncan was the reason Priscilla had read her diaries.

Jessica wondered why it had taken so long for the light to dawn. Somehow, she had given Priscilla cause to wonder if her mother-in-law suspected her affair with the major, so she had gone to the only logical source for confirmation and found it.

Jessica plopped down in a chair, her mind spinning. Now what? Exposing the woman to Thomas was out of the question. Merciful heavens, the devastation that would unleash! There would be the scandal of Priscilla's adultery, the question of Regina's paternity, marital estrangement—all on top of David's death. Besides, Jessica had no proof her son's wife had read her diaries. Priscilla could—and would—deny everything, and Jessica must consider the children. Once again, she would have to let these particular sleeping dogs lie. There were other dogs Jessica feared her grandson's death may have roused since Priscilla had now learned of the Toliver curse.

One by one Jessica began removing the journals from her secretary and placing them in chronological order in pillowcases. When they were filled, she locked the bundles in her wardrobe and concealed the key in the finial of her bed post. If Priscilla came visiting and found them gone, she would know soon enough that her unforgivable deed had been discovered.

Chapter Eighty-Two

It was spring again. The white dogwood and spirea, redbud and purple wisteria were blooming. As Thomas rode into town from Houston Avenue, he wondered if he would ever feel the way he had last year at this time when his daughter turned sixteen. Then, he had felt in the bloom of a full life with perhaps the exception of his marriage, but a man couldn't have it all. But that had been a year ago, and then the darkness came with David's death that had left the surviving members of his family feeling as though they'd been buried in the black core of the earth. They had emerged after a time, but none of them was the same as before.

It will just take more distance from that dark place, Thomas thought to himself. Then perhaps life would return as it had been, or at least a semblance of it. For now, he had little enthusiasm for things the way they were then: his marriage, civic obligations—even, sometimes, Somerset. He went through the motions, but his heart wasn't in those occupations that had given him purpose and enjoyment. A carpetbagger was running for his spot on the city council and Thomas was of a mind to let him have it without a fight. Vernon had practically taken over the running of the plantation, and as for his marriage, he simply hadn't the energy to stoke a flame from the dying embers any more than

Priscilla seemed to want its warmth. It was still a surprise to him that she'd rebuffed his attempts to console her after David died. She'd turn away from him, and sometimes he'd catch her staring at him accusingly—as if she blamed him for their son's death. After a while, Thomas attributed her coldness as coming from the sobering realization he'd endured for some time. They were losing their firstborn to manhood, and their daughter's vital presence would be gone from the house when she married next year. Priscilla would be stuck with her dull husband and his aging mother.

This morning he was on his way to have luncheon with Armand. Another black cloud was descending. Henri DuMont was terminally ill, and Armand was going through the throes Thomas had suffered when his own father was facing death. Like then, when Armand had offered the solace of his friendship, Thomas was going to tender his.

First, he had business with the man running his cottonseed mill located the other side of Howbutker. Thomas had established the mill in 1879 when cottonseed was in high demand for every use from food fodder for animals to stuffing for mattresses. Cottonseed oil had overtaken flaxseed as the chief source of vegetable oil in the United States, and a market had opened up with the new invention of oleomargarine that called for the oil as a substitute for animal fat in its production. Today he was to confer with his foreman about expanding the mill's capacity to meet its increasing avalanche of orders. Thomas felt he should be happy to discuss plans to enlarge this lucrative source of income, but the mood was not there.

Automatically when Thomas entered the town circle, he glanced down the spoke street leading to Jacqueline Chastain's shop. He had never dared turn his horse in its direction for fear that a mere glimpse of her through the mullioned panes might give him cause to stop. It had been a year since he'd last seen the back of her dark head outlined in the eisenglassed window of his carriage. She had sent a note of condolence after David's death, and he'd resisted the insane impulse to go to her and cry out his grief on her lovely bosom.

This morning he gave in to the urge to ride by her place of business. What the blazes did it matter, anyway? Perhaps he would not feel the same when he saw her a year later. He was not the same man. She might not be the same woman. Besides, he would not stop and go in. He would simply allow himself a brief look and keep riding.

Moments later, Thomas reined his horse before the shop. He stared in disbelief at the sign in the window: CLOSED. The display windows gaped vacant of the luring frippery of women's hats, umbrellas, gloves, and purses exhibited there last spring. An air of desertion hung about the place as if it had been closed for some time. Thomas dismounted and tried the door. Locked. He peered inside at the empty shelves and bare counter. What in hell? He backed away from the entrance and cast his eyes upward to the second floor, relieved to see an array of perky geraniums in the window box. Someone was living there.

Thomas secured his horse at the hitching post and walked around to the side of the building, where a flight of stairs gave access to the apartment above. He listened and looked for signs of life, a movement behind a curtain, a domestic sound, but heard and saw nothing to indicate anyone was home. Something brushed his leg. A cat. It leaped to the bottom step and flew up the stairs to the landing, where it began to mew demandingly at the closed door. Thomas held his breath as it opened, and Jacqueline Chastain stood framed in the doorway.

Thomas called softly, "Jacqueline?"

She stepped out onto the landing and peered down. "Thomas? What are you doing here?"

"I...I saw the sign in the window. I had no idea that...your shop had closed."

"Yes, for four months now. My business...fell off."

Dismayed, he placed a foot on the bottom rung. She wore a look of defeat, despite her straight posture and beauty that was unadorned this morning. She wore a dressing gown and her dark hair loose about her shoulders.

"But it looked as if you were doing so well," he said.

"I was...for a while."

They stared at each other. Thomas said, "Will you be staying in Howbutker?"

"Only a little longer until I can make other arrangements. Armand DuMont has been so kind to allow me to stay in the apartment, but I can't impose on him much longer. I'm sure I'm preventing him from renting the space."

"Armand DuMont?"

"He owns the property. I'm so sorry to hear his father is ill."

Only Armand, God bless his generous heart, would rent property to a competitor, Thomas thought. He'd had no idea. He said on impulse, "May I come up for a cup of coffee?"

After a small hesitation, she said, "You may."

She served him steaming coffee in delicate china cups. They sat in the small room facing the street that served as a parlor. Thomas noticed packed crates tucked here and there, crowding the limited space. "Where will you go?" he asked.

"Back home, to Richmond, Virginia. I've a sister there. She and her husband have agreed to take me in. I'm hoping to find work in a millinery shop in town."

"When...will that be?"

"In a few weeks when I can dispose of the rest of my inventory." She gestured toward the wooden boxes. "A general store in Marshall has agreed to take them, and then I'll have the money for my fare."

His heart felt squeezed. "I'm so sorry things didn't work out. You are so talented. I would have thought you'd have plenty of business."

She smiled at him sadly. "I did, too, but…" She shrugged her shoulders. "It was not meant to be. How have you been getting along since…the tragedy?"

"I'm…managing," he said with a faint smile.

She nodded, the simple response and a brief close of her eyes carrying a world of understanding. Thomas took her for the kind of woman who would not try to comfort him with platitudes. The cat, a gray tom, leaped to her lap and curled there with a proprietary air. She sipped her coffee. Thomas set down his cup. He should go. There was nothing more to be said, though volumes strained to be spoken. He knew nothing about this woman. People could fool you. They could surprise and disappoint you. Tried-and-true instincts could betray you. But of this he was sure about Jacqueline Chastain: She was too special to live in a loft or back room of her sister's house and too talented to work for pennies selling another's wares in a millinery shop.

He leaned forward. "Mrs. Chastain—Jacqueline—if you could find a suitable position here in Howbutker, would you stay?"

"Yes, of course," she said, and he'd hoped to hear a leap of hope in her voice, but she sounded resigned to her fate. "However, I do not expect such a position to be available."

"Why not?"

"There are…certain influences afoot in this town that would prevent my being offered one."

He frowned. "Like what? Whose?"

She rose, holding the cat. Their visit was over. "I'm not at liberty to say, Mr. Toliver, but I do appreciate your concern. Thank you for inquiring after my welfare." She led the way to the door and smiled a final good-bye as she held out her hand. "Time will not close the hole in your heart," she said, "but I hope the years will fill the space with happy memories of your son."

"You have not heard the last from me, Mrs. Chastain," Thomas said, refusing to accept the finality in her tone. "You must keep the faith."

"I'm afraid I've lost that, Mr. Toliver," she said.

Chapter Eighty-Three

His meeting with the foreman of his cottonseed mill forgotten, Thomas headed for the DuMont Department Store. He always lost his breath when he walked into its rarified air, an occurrence that happened seldom more than twice a year when he shopped for Regina's and his mother's Christmas presents. After his first failed attempts at pleasing his wife on other celebrations that called for gifts, she preferred putting a bug in Henri's or Armand's ear about something she liked. They in turn would pass on word to him, and he would say to put it on his bill, wrap it up, and send it to the house. Thomas could not recall any item that he had personally selected to give to Priscilla to commemorate special occasions.

The DuMont Department Store was a gilt, marble, and mirrored palace whose fine wares and opulent appointments were set aglow by dozens of gas-lit crystal chandeliers. It boasted separate departments for men's, women's, and children's clothing, along with sections for jewelry, gifts, home furnishings, and furs. Under its roof were housed a tearoom, hair salon, bookstore, design and tailoring rooms, and administrative offices, all spread on three floors reached by a sweeping, elegant staircase.

Thomas regarded the store as a Texas phenomenon. What businessman would ever dream of building a retail establishment like the DuMont Department Store in a small town in East Texas and expect to turn a profit to justify its expensive scale and inventory? But Henri DuMont had done just that. From the beginning his instinct for pinpointing his customer base, knowing what his patrons wanted and would pay for, had been the guiding light behind the store's success. Henri knew the value of advertising and publicity and had always been in step with the modern demands of the times in which he lived. He and Armand had been among the few retailers to realize that mass production, ushered in by the Civil War, would change the way Americans dressed, shopped, and ate. They understood that men and women had moved on from the lengthy fittings and costly trimmings of custom-designed, couture clothing and had therefore primed the store for the advent of ready-to-wear garments that could be purchased immediately, right off the rack.

Customers came from all over, giving Henri's competitors in Texas cities and those in Louisiana and Mexico a run for their money. Around Easter and Christmas, it was not uncommon for flocks of families to come to Howbutker for a weekend's roost in the Fairfax Hotel to do their shopping in the DuMont Department Store, or for gaggles of ladies to arrive by train on buying sprees that made short work of the inventory in the store's gleaming cases. The DuMonts' home décor department was in constant demand, and no well-to-do Texas rancher or farmer ever dared send his daughter off to finishing school without first outfitting her from the store's selection of up-to-the-minute feminine attire. Nowadays, customers did not have to visit the store to buy what they needed. They could order right out of the DuMont Department Store's mail-order catalog, an innovation begun by Aaron Montgomery Ward in 1872.

Thomas took the flight of stairs to the second story, where the store's glassed offices overlooked the main floor. He found Armand in his own office, passing by Henri's, where the founder's chair behind his desk yawned sadly empty. Armand, his lean, aristocratic face showing the strain Thomas had known in watching his father die, glanced at the mantel clock when his secretary ushered him in. "You're early," he said. "You must be hungry."

Thomas got right to the point. "Armand, I need a favor."

Armand leaned back in his chair and hooked his thumbs into the pockets of his silk waistcoat. "Ask, and it is yours."

"Not so hasty, my friend. What I have to ask may not set well with you, but I hope it will."

"Ask, my friend."

"It is about Jacqueline Chastain. As you know, her shop failed. I believe she's nearly destitute. It's been very generous of you to allow her to live in the apartment until she can make other arrangements."

Armand dismissed the tribute with a wave of his hand. "She is a deserving woman."

"I'm glad you think so," Thomas said. "I spoke with her this morning. Her future plans sound pretty bleak. She intends to go live with her sister and brother-in-law in Richmond, Virginia, and hopes to find employment in a millinery shop there."

Armand was listening patiently, and Thomas suspected his friend, who knew him so well, had already anticipated the favor. "I wonder if you have a position in the store that calls for her expertise and could offer her a job," Thomas said. "I know nothing about women's hats, but from what I saw of those in her shop when I picked up that head thing Regina wore on her birthday..."

Armand leaned forward and placed his elbows on his desk. "I wish I could have stopped what was happening, but I couldn't."

"Well, no, you couldn't throw business her way."

"I'm not talking about that. I'm talking about the deliberate plot to boycott Mrs. Chastain's shop. Somebody mailed letters that started a whisper campaign against her. Very unsavory stuff. The blasphemy obviously fell on the right ears, and"—Armand lifted his well-tailored shoulders—"you saw the result when you went by her shop."

Thomas felt heat rush to his head. "Letters?"

"Very damaging not only to her place of business but to her personally. The poor woman is persona non grata now and has become a practical recluse."

"How did I not know about this?"

"Why would you?"

"Do you know who was responsible for the letters?"

Armand held his eye. "I've an idea."

"Who?"

"I've never lied to you, Thomas, so don't ask me."

"But you know?"

"I've definite suspicions. Now, as to your request, I'll be happy to hire Mrs. Chastain. We can use a designer of her talents. I thought of offering her a job, but under the circumstances, with her reputation in tatters, I...didn't think she'd wish to stay in Howbutker. Shall I sound her out?"

"I'd be most grateful, Armand," Thomas said, trying to think of who in town would go to such lengths to destroy a woman like Jacqueline Chastain. He would go to the house and ask Priscilla. She belonged to every women's organization in the county, fertile grounds for gossip. If anyone would know, she would, and when he learned the name of the perpetrator...

They shook hands, but Armand tightened his grip as Thomas made to pull away. "Thomas, my friend, I advise you not to investigate this matter further."

Thomas studied him, puzzled. "Why? Whoever it is deserves to be run out of town!"

Armand released his hand. "Are we still to meet for luncheon? I'll drop by Mrs. Chastain's on the way to the Fairfax and have her answer for you."

"And I may know the name of the culprit by then. I'm on my way home now. I'm sure Priscilla will have a good idea who's behind this. My wife did all she could to keep Mrs. Chastain in the black. She must have bought over a dozen hats."

"Really?" Armand raised a sleek eyebrow. "How...generous of her. One o'clock at the Fairfax, then?"

Thomas urged his horse to a full gallop toward Houston Avenue and was halfway there when he drew on the reins so sharply his mount almost lost its footing. A shocking coldness, like a dunk into icy water, shuddered through him. Good God! Priscilla! Priscilla wrote the letters! He had only to ask himself who would want to see Jacqueline Chastain run out of town for the answer to shout at him. He had only to recall Armand's odd demeanor and warning couched as advice, Jacqueline's remark—*There are certain influences afoot in this town that would prevent my being offered one*—to know that his vindictive, spiteful, jealous wife was responsible.

Priscilla! That brainless wife of his who thought herself superior to a shopkeeper who possessed the grace and kindness to keep silent about her maliciousness to her husband. Thomas was certain Jacqueline suspected Priscilla. Thomas recalled the bills of sale his wife had signed for the hats, the purchase a ruse to deceive him and others from guessing her to be the culprit behind the poisoned pen. Obviously, Jacqueline had come in possession of a letter, and she would have compared its writing to his wife's signature on her copy of the bill. No doubt Armand had done the same. Priscilla would have tried to disguise her penmanship, but its many flowery, telltale curlicues would have given her away as the writer.

Thomas kneed the horse on and steadied his breathing to regain control of his rage. He had to be careful how he confronted Priscilla. He must remember that she was the mother of his children and still grieving the loss of a child. For the same reason, he must think of Vernon and Regina and avoid causing them further pain from seeing their parents at each other's throats. They were already sadly aware their mother and father were not as happy together as their best friends' parents. The wives and husbands in the Warwick and DuMont households were heart mates. His children could not say that of him and Priscilla.

But Priscilla must not be allowed to get by with this heartless act of malice against an innocent human being. He would find a way to make sure she did not.

Chapter Eighty-Four

Late that afternoon Henri DuMont, aged eighty-three, closed his eyes for the last time as he spoke to Jeremy, who stood by his bedside. The first to know he was gone, Jeremy gently placed a hand on his brow and said, "Good-bye, old friend." Cries immediately went up. Armand sobbed uncontrollably before his tearful sons, Abel and Jean, and Philippe, veteran of many wars, bowed his head in an attitude of inconsolable grief. Armand's wife stood beyond the bed waiting to offer her arms to her husband and sons while Bess, stiff-shouldered, lips pressed together, stoically drew the sheet over the face of her husband of forty-eight years.

In the hall outside Henri's bedroom, Thomas and Jessica waited for the inevitable news with Jeremy Jr. and his wife. Upon hearing the sounds of mourning, Thomas placed his arm around Jessica's shoulders. "He is with Papa, Mother."

"Yes," Jessica said, her voice forced through the pain of her grief. "Such a good friend he was, so noble and generous."

Thomas wiped his eyes and left his mother to be with Bess while he went downstairs to the drawing room to impart the news to Vernon and Regina and their Warwick contemporaries, Brandon, Richard, and Joel. Regina discerned his message before he spoke and rose to embrace him. "You want me to walk home with you, Daddy?" she asked when he said he must go down to tell her mother.

"No, Poppy. Stay with Abel and Jean. They will need your comfort."

Thomas walked the short distance to his house, his footsteps dragging. God, he wished he could be with Jacqueline Chastain. One of the dearest men on earth had died, and the earth was poorer for it, and he wanted to be in the presence of a woman who appreciated that loss and understood his pain.

When he'd met Armand at the Fairfax, his friend told him Jacqueline had accepted his offer to design hats for the store and manage the counter of women's accessories. As part of her salary, she would retain the apartment over the shop with the understanding her earnings would increase to cover the cost of lodging should the property be rented.

Grateful, deeply moved by his longtime friend's generosity, Thomas had asked, "Armand, what with Jacqueline Chastain's reputation compromised, aren't you taking a chance she will be bad for business?"

"I have faith that my customers will know a lady when they see one," Armand had answered.

It was not a title he could apply to his wife, Thomas thought in repugnance as he let himself into the house. Sassie, Amy's daughter, eight years old, ran forth to welcome him. "Miss Priscilla is upstairs, Mister Thomas."

He touched her cheek. It was wet with tears. The DuMont servants had passed along word on the avenue that Mister Henri had died. Henri had always seen that Petunia and Amy and now Sassie had special treats from the store, especially at Christmastime. "I liked him so much," Sassie said, her mouth quivering. "He was such a nice man."

"Indeed he was, little one," Thomas said. "I'll go up. No need to tell the mistress I am home."

He found Priscilla trying on hats. A black assortment of them was on the bed. Christ! A clothes fiend, his wife was already deciding what to wear for the funeral. She turned to him from her mirror, assuming a face appropriate for the sadness of the occasion. "Amy brought up the news, Thomas," she said. "I'm so sorry. I know how fond you were of Henri. How is Bess?"

"How do you think she is?"

She shrugged, dropping her mask. "I was just asking."

Thomas gestured toward the hat collection. "What are those?"

"What do they look like?"

He was so tired of this sort of verbal volley in their limited conversations. "Which ones are from Mrs. Chastain's shop?"

Priscilla turned back to the mirror. "None. They're from the DuMont Department Store."

"Where are the ones you purchased from the Millinery Shop?"

She glanced at him over her shoulder. "You say the name as if you're familiar with it."

"Where are they, Priscilla?"

"In the wardrobe over there. Why do you care?"

He opened the wardrobe doors to find a melee of women's hats stacked unmindful of the crush to feathers, ribbons, and flowers. Their price tags were still pinned to them. Priscilla had never meant to wear them. She never intended to serve as a pied piper to lead other women to Jacqueline Chastain's door, as she'd claimed. Thomas carefully pulled a black hat from the pile. "Here," he said, "this is the one I want you to wear to the funeral."

Her face paled slightly. "Why?"

"As advertisement of Mrs. Chastain's talents. Isn't that why you bought them? I met with Armand today, and he tells me

that someone has been sending around poisonous letters maligning Mrs. Chastain's character, the idea being to drive her out of
town. Apparently, it worked. Her shop is closed. I can't imagine
who would do such a reprehensible thing, can you, Priscilla?"

Thomas saw the movement of a quick swallow make its way
down his wife's creamy throat. "No, I can't, but why wear the hat
if…if she's out of business?"

"Oh, she's not entirely. Armand has hired her as a hat designer
and overseer of one of his women's departments. That means she
gets to stay in town, and I think it would be very gracious of you
to wear her hats as a statement of your support. Let Howbutker
see that you don't believe a word of the drivel those letters contained. Did you receive one, by the way?"

Priscilla swallowed again. "No, I did not."

Thomas began removing the hats from the wardrobe, setting
them on tables and chairs. "The perpetrator knew better than
to send one to you, I'm sure." He studied each of the feminine
creations, memorizing their details, conscious of his wife's appre-
hensive attention. "I don't recall you wearing any of these," he
said.

Priscilla emitted a nervous laugh. "Why would you? You
never notice such things."

"I'll remember these. Where are your others—the ones you do
wear?"

Silently, her expression tense, Priscilla pointed to another
wardrobe. Thomas tugged at the bellpull, then opened the
wardrobe doors. Without a word, he began pulling hats from
shelves and tossing them onto the bed with the others. Amy appeared. "Someone rang?"

"I did, Amy," Thomas said. "Please collect the hats on the bed
and distribute them to your friends or take the whole bunch to
your church for its rummage sale, whatever pleases you. Miss

Priscilla will not be needing them. When you have finished, place the hats on the table and chairs in the vacated space in the wardrobe."

Amy's enlarged eyes said *Uh-oh*, but she replied, "Yes, Mister Thomas. I'll go get some cotton sacks to put them in."

When the door closed, Thomas narrowed a needle-sharp eye at his wife. "I don't believe anything else needs to be said or done concerning this matter, do you, Priscilla?"

Taut-faced, Priscilla said, "I suppose not."

"Very good. Now if you'll excuse me, I'm going to ride out to Somerset to visit my father's place of rest."

Chapter Eighty-Five

In the years immediately following Henri's death, the circle of Howbutker's founders' sons grew even more tightly knit. Thomas, Jeremy Jr., and Armand had turned fifty, Stephen not far behind. Their sons, in their early twenties, were deeply involved in their families' businesses, allowing time for the fathers to spend more time with one another. Members of the clans broke into social groups based on ages. Jessica, Bess, and Jeremy occupied one. Thomas, Armand, Jeremy Jr., and Stephen formed another, and their sons—Vernon and Jeremy III, Brandon, Richard, and Joel Warwick, and Abel and Jean DuMont—comprised the youngest.

Thomas relished his association with his three friends. Without them, he would have been a lonely man. His daughter had married—happily, he was elated to observe—and was expecting her first child next year, in 1887. Accompanied by Jeremy and Bess, his mother was on a round-the-world cruise that would take the better part of a year, and afterwards, the three were to visit Tippy in New York and Sarah Conklin in Boston. She would not be home until the week of Thanksgiving.

Vernon had taken up residence during the week in Jasper's old house, outfitting it with louvered windows and other amenities suitable for the heir apparent to Somerset. He had never been quite the same after David's death and seemed to prefer solitude, throwing all his energies into the cultivation of cotton. It was an exciting and lucrative time to be growing the largest revenue crop in Texas. Even with improvements in the ginning process and the invention of a compress that could reduce 500-pound bales into units half their size for easier shipping by the ever-increasing rail system, planters could hardly satisfy world demand for the fluffy white bolls. Thomas was still engaged in the day-to-day management of his life's work, but not engrossed as he once had been. Thomas envied his friends their continued interest in their vocations even though they had slacked off to enjoy the benefits of their success.

Thomas recognized that a happy home life had a lot to do with a man's enthusiasm for other pursuits, a blessing his friends enjoyed that he did not. As when they were first married, he and Priscilla were strained in the other's presence. They treated each other with painful respect that Thomas believed barely hid the malice his wife felt for him. He'd found her out and now she hated him for discovering her capable of vile acts. She would never regain a high opinion of herself in his eyes, and so she consoled herself by thinking the worst of him. Once his children were no longer at home and his mother had left on her trip, Amy had asked if Thomas wished to take his meals with Priscilla at the small table in the breakfast room, but he declined. The intimacy would have been unbearable. They continued to eat in the dining room, one at each end of the long table. At night they slept as far away from the other as possible in the bed they shared. Thomas longed to sleep apart, but he could not bring himself to suggest an arrangement that would be the final repudiation of his wife.

The four friends formed the habit of lunching together every Wednesday at the Fairfax. Thomas would ride in from the plantation and hitch his horse before the DuMont Department Store.

He could have ridden farther on to the hotel's dining room, but he enjoyed collecting Armand and walking with him the one block to its entrance. At least that was the excuse he gave himself when he knew full well the occasion provided him the only opportunity to see Jacqueline Chastain.

In the two years of her employment in the store, she'd become a mainstay. "I don't know what we'd do without her," Armand said. "Her creativity reminds me of Tippy's." It had not taken long for Jacqueline's dignity, sincerity, and decorum to cause customers to doubt the inflammatory content of the poisonous letters. At a party in the DuMont home, Thomas heard a matron extolling the expertise of "that fine clerk you hired, Armand," and finished by declaring that "whoever the villain was that sent those nasty letters maligning Mrs. Chastain ought to be horse whipped." Thomas had carefully avoided looking in Priscilla's direction.

It was Wednesday again. Thomas stepped inside the chandelier-lit retail edifice with eyes trained to look first at the women's accessory counter. Jacqueline Chastain saw him and smiled. She had been expecting him. Usually he said something like "Good afternoon, Mrs. Chastain," and lifted his hat slightly. "How goes your day?"

"Perfectly, Mr. Toliver, and yours?"

"Enhanced now, Mrs. Chastain. So nice to see you again."

"And you as well."

That was all. Observers looking on would see Thomas barely break stride as he passed the counter over which Jacqueline Chastain presided. They had never exchanged more than a few words. Sometimes she would be assisting customers, and he would merely lift his hat on the way to the staircase.

But always the sight of her and the sound of her voice lifted his heart for those brief seconds before it fell. After a few months working in the store, Jacqueline had moved from the apartment above her former shop to the one Tippy had occupied that was located nearby. It boasted a white fence and small cottage garden beside the front walk. Thomas knew Jacqueline did not possess a conveyance and was glad she had not far to walk after store hours. Today, there were not as many in the store as usual and no customer in the women's accessory department, and Jacqueline stood behind the gleaming glass counter looking like a queen devoid of subjects.

"Mrs. Chastain—" Thomas began, but his voice caught. He was feeling especially melancholic today. Earlier at the plantation he'd had a talk with his son. Lately, Vernon had been squiring a pretty girl about, the daughter of a dairy farmer the Toliver family had known for years.

"Do you love her?" Thomas had asked.

"I…don't know, Daddy. What does love for a woman feel like?"

Thomas could not answer him. He had not had the experience. Thomas said instead, "I can tell you what love doesn't feel like."

And so, man to man, Thomas had shared his story of how he'd married his mother to produce an heir to Somerset. "I believed we'd grow to love each other, but I was wrong," he'd concluded.

"Do you regret it?" Vernon asked. He had expressed no surprise at his father's confession. As hard as his parents had tried to hide it, their children had been aware of the disaffection between them. "I mean, was your sacrifice for Somerset worth it?"

"Yes, the plantation was worth it, son. The times dictated what I had to do. Certainly I wonder how my marriage—and your mother's—would have turned out if I hadn't jumped the gun when I did and married for the reason I did. But my solace is that if I hadn't married Priscilla, I would never have fathered my three wonderful children. You will never know how much I love you until you have children of your own, Vernon. And…another comfort, son. I can die knowing my sacrifice for the land of my fathers and my struggle and labor were not in vain."

Thomas had looked out across the picked fields, the wind stirring the white residue between the stripped plants that resembled drifts of snow, and felt a resurgence of the old pride. "I have but one regret," he admitted.

"What is that, Daddy?"

"That I will die without ever having been with a woman I love."

That was Jacqueline Chastain, Thomas thought, taking the rare opportunity to gaze fully into her face. She must be over forty by now, he guessed. Time had not dulled her beauty. Her loveliness had been strengthened by a womanly wisdom detectable in her poise and manner, her smile and eyes and incomparably warm voice.

"Mr. Toliver," Jacqueline returned, the slight contraction of her eyebrows telling him she wondered what had affected him.

"It will be Thanksgiving soon," he said, appalled at the inane observation.

"Yes, I hear it's around the corner."

"My mother will be home from her world cruise."

"I'm sure you're anticipating her return with great excitement. She'll have worlds"—she smiled at the pun—"to tell you."

"And I'm to be a grandfather. My daughter is expecting her first child in April next year."

"How wonderful for you."

Armand would be waiting for him. He must go, but still he lingered. How was her cat? Thomas asked. Lazy and fat, she said. Her garden? She was seeing a bounty of stocks and sweet Williams this year. Their fragrance was delightful. Had she been keeping up with the scandal brewing in Paris over John Singer

Sargent's painting of Madame X? Fascinating what riled people up so, didn't she think? Yes, she agreed. She thought the painting lovely, and the black dress the critics were making such a fuss over very appropriate to the woman's beauty. The French were usually so...embracing of the unorthodox.

Thomas wondered what her life was like when she went home after the store closed. How did she keep busy in her little house? Was she lonely? Had she made many friends? Was she being courted? Armand described her as "fiercely independent," preferring to do the "man jobs" around the house herself rather than accept the assistance of his maintenance crew.

Thomas perused the display case. "I'd like to buy something to welcome my mother home. What would you suggest?"

"We just got in a collection of beautiful fans, lightweight but quite effective for our summers. Would you like to see them?"

"Most certainly."

Thomas bought a fan, and then he saw Armand come down the stairs, his gaze lighting instantly on the aisle where he suspected his friend would be. "It's been a pleasure, Mrs. Chastain— Jacqueline," he said.

"Mine as well, Mr. Toliver—Thomas," she said.

When he arrived home late in the afternoon, Priscilla was waiting for him.

Chapter Eighty-Six

Thomas, after stabling his horse, always entered his mansion through the kitchen door. In the spotless, savory environs of hanging pots and pans, scrubbed chopping block, cavernous sink, and work surfaces, he could count on being greeted by Petunia when she'd been alive and whom he still missed, and now by Amy and her daughter, Sassie. Amy would inquire about his day and was genuinely interested in his report. Sometimes he'd sit down with a cup of coffee to listen to her share gossip telegraphed through the grapevine always humming from house to house on Houston Avenue. Occasionally, especially since his mother had been gone on her trip, Thomas would unburden himself of worries regarding Somerset and concerns of the city council. He knew his confidences would never go past the screened back door. There was always something delicious to snatch on his way through the kitchen, and today he noticed a heaping plate of his son's favorite pecan cookies. Vernon was coming to supper and would stay through the weekend.

"Mister Thomas, your wife would like to see you in the morning room," Amy said by way of greeting. Her anxious tone and pointed gaze warned him to be on guard. If Priscilla had her way, she would send Amy with her husband and daughter to the plantation to pick cotton alongside her uncle Jasper's families. Jasper's two sons, Rand and Willie, had returned to Somerset after finding Kansas overcrowded and inhospitable and the farming opportunities not as advertised. Priscilla may be mistress of the house, but the staff answered to Amy, whose first loyalty was to Jessica. Thomas was aware that the domestic situation nettled the hell out of his wife.

"Amy said you wished to see me," Thomas said, entering the morning room.

He hated what Priscilla had done to a room that had served as a sanctuary to him when he was growing up. Light had spilled everywhere through the window sheers, now darkened by heavy draperies, and there had been comfortable chairs on which to sit. He remained standing. Priscilla got up abruptly from her oversized desk, her clenched jaw giving notice of her anger.

"I have taken much abuse from you, Thomas, but I will not take this," she said.

Abuse? He had never so much as touched a fingernail of his wife's hand in anger, and she spent money as freely as rice thrown at a wedding. Thomas said, "And what is it that you will not take from me, Priscilla? Enlighten me, please."

She approached him. Her slightly thicker waist and larger hips betrayed her entry into middle age, but her face still held evidence of her former beauty. It had been a long time since her startlingly pretty looks had quickened his pulse.

"Jacqueline Chastain," she said through tightly gripped teeth. Involuntarily, he jerked his head back. "What about her?"

"You're having an affair with her—or at least would like to." Thomas let out a little guffaw. "Who told you that?"

"I have my sources, but I don't need them. Any blind idiot can figure out why you stop by the DuMont Department Store every Wednesday to meet Armand."

Thomas's brow rose. "Because it's his place of business, perhaps?"

"Don't play the innocent with me. You could meet him at the Fairfax for your weekly luncheon session."

"Diners are requested not to hitch their horses by the restaurant if possible, for obvious reasons. As you know, the windows face the street. Besides, Armand and I enjoy the walk."

Priscilla's lip twisted. "You can give any excuse you want, but it holds no water with me, Thomas. I know that you stop by Mrs. Chastain's counter every time you enter the store. Your face goes through a metamorphosis. You've been described as looking like a schoolboy bringing his favorite teacher an apple."

"By whom? And how in the world do you know a word like *metamorphosis*?"

She looked ready to slap him. Her teeth clenched tighter. "Never mind how I know and don't think the rest of Howbutker doesn't know either, but I'll tell you this, Thomas…" Priscilla stepped closer, so near that Thomas could see the fine hair on her lip, the tiny pores on her nose through a thin film of perspiration. "If you make a fool of *me* by consorting with Mrs. Chastain, I will make *you* sorry for the rest of your life. I'll hurt you beyond belief, beyond your endurance. Trust me on that, you hear me?"

Thomas stepped back from her fury. He had not been the husband she'd banked on when she agreed to marry him, he granted her that. He'd tried to make up for it by indulging her spending, tolerating the exalted position she gave herself as the wife of Thomas Toliver, the snob she'd become. He despised snobs, people who thought themselves better than others by luck of birth or marriage, positions they had not earned for themselves. Translated, *snob* meant literally "without nobility" and that applied to Priscilla. He could not tolerate such arrogance even from her and met it with a tongue given to wry taunts.

"You continue to amaze me, Priscilla. First *metamorphosis* and now this. What makes you think *you* have the wherewithal to make good such threats to me?"

She closed the space between them and now he could smell the alcohol on her breath. She had been at the sherry. "I know things about your family that would singe the hair on every single head in this county if they were known."

Thomas's gaze widened inquiringly. "Really? You've made discoveries in my family's history to provide you that kind of fodder for salacious tittle-tattle? I'd love to hear them. In regard to meaty tales of that sort, I've always thought the Tolivers rather dull fare."

She moved away from him, fear from the realization that she'd said too much flitting across her face. For the thousandth time, Thomas wondered how he could have been so self-duped to believe this woman the perfect wife for him. He supposed the surprise of her interest in his family's history, especially his ties to English royalty, had convinced him he had proposed to the right woman. No detail of family legend or fact had escaped her curiosity. He'd been delighted when Priscilla jumped on the slightest tidbit of Toliver and Wyndham background dropped innocently at the table, usually resulting in his father diverting the conversation to a history lesson.

Thomas had gone away to war happy that Priscilla was willing to instill in their children knowledge and appreciation of the roots from which he came. Such understanding bound descendants to family and to the land, committed them to continue what their father and his father before him had begun. Whatever was to be his fate, Thomas remembered thinking, Priscilla, under the tutelage of Silas Toliver, would not allow his children to forget who they were and the duty they owed their family name.

What a fool he had been!

"You were saying, my dear?" he inquired politely.

His wife's bluster was like a sea swell whose force has suddenly collapsed. Her Dutch courage had deserted her. She stepped farther away from him, her posture crumpling, and sputtered, "You—you just be careful of your step…that's all I'm saying, Thomas. I will not have you embarrass our children."

"I would never embarrass my children, Priscilla, and please hear what I'm saying to you. If I ever hear a word of your suspicions of a liaison between Mrs. Chastain and me uttered to anyone else, I will make you wish you hadn't. I am not thinking of myself or you or even our children. I am thinking of Mrs. Chastain, who is totally innocent of your unfounded accusations. Whatever makes you think she would indulge in an affair with a married man? I am, therefore, not likely to be guilty of the charge you've leveled against me."

Thomas let the icy implication hang in a silence in which Priscilla appeared too stung to speak. "And tell your little spy in the DuMont Department Store that I'll have her fanny fired if I ever get wind of a whisper of slander against Mrs. Chastain," he went on. "I'll hold her personally responsible."

A throat cleared behind them. Thomas and Priscilla whirled to the sound. Vernon stood in the doorway. "I've come for supper, Mother and Daddy," he said.

Chapter Eighty-Seven

Thomas liked his son-in-law, and he was grateful his daughter's marriage gave him the opportunity to know the boy's parents. Until that occasion, Curt and Anne McCord had been mere acquaintances. They lived on a large cattle ranch in a sprawling house with unmarried twin boys a few years younger than their older son, Tyler. Even Priscilla was delighted with the family into which her daughter had married. Besides being wealthy and highly respected, the McCords loved and treated Regina like the daughter and sister they'd always wanted but never had. Tyler and Regina's living quarters had been reconstituted from a barn on the grounds into an enchanting cottage under the artistic direction of Armand DuMont's home designer. Thomas loved the open, airy feel of both his daughter's and her in-laws' houses with their spacious screened-in back porches that allowed a view of the green expanse of the ranch without the annoyance of flies and mosquitoes.

At the McCords', Thomas felt at home. Today, his family had been invited to a Sunday afternoon barbecue at the ranch. It was April 1887, and his first grandchild was expected within the month. The afternoon's gathering would probably be the last without the addition of a baby in their midst. Jeremy Warwick Sr. and Bess DuMont had been invited as well. The McCords'

courtesy in including them—the Tolivers' extended family—in
the party was another of the many reasons Thomas appreciated
and liked them. Every day he offered a prayer of thanksgiving for
his daughter's fortunate marriage and happiness. For Regina he
had no worries. The same was not true for Vernon.

After dressing, Thomas walked down the hall to his son's
room. Vernon, too, enjoyed the outings at the McCord ranch. It
was never a struggle for his parents to get him away from Somerset as it was for other events.

"Thomas, the boy is growing cotton out of his ears," Priscilla told him. "We've got to do something—*entice* him with
something—to get him interested in a diversion outside that
damned plantation!"

Thomas agreed but did not remind his wife that "that damned
plantation" paid for her extravagances she felt it his duty to indulge as fair compensation for other lacks in her life. Vernon
opened the door at his knock. What a fine-looking lad he was!
Vernon resembled his grandfather more than he did. Thomas
could see legacies of the Toliver line in himself—the Duke of
Somerset's green eyes, black hair, the shadow of a dimple in the
center of his chin—but he was shorter and of less elegant build
than the svelte figure in the hall painting to whom Silas Toliver
had been and now his grandson was almost a spitting image.

"About ready?" Thomas said but saw that he needn't have
asked. Vernon was dressed for riding with the McCord twins,
who were close to his age of twenty-two. They'd take a canter
about the ranch before the meal was served, a good social distraction for Vernon. The boy was lonely. He'd been especially close to
his siblings and now his brother was dead and his sister married.
He had little time to be with his Warwick and DuMont cohorts,
and he'd dropped the dairy farmer's daughter after he and his father had talked at the plantation last November.

"Yes sir," Vernon said. "I'm ready. Everybody downstairs?"

"All but us. Jeremy and Bess have arrived, and the carriage is out front. I thought you and I could ride behind. I've had your horse saddled."

"That must mean you want to talk to me."

"It's been a while."

His son had not mentioned the confrontation between his parents he'd happened upon that afternoon last November. It was like him not to. Vernon never minded anybody's business but his own. Thomas and Priscilla had both stood frozen, wondering how much their son had overheard. Priscilla had tried to smile. "We...weren't expecting you this early," she'd stammered.

"Apparently not," Vernon had said and simply turned and gone up to his room. They'd had supper together, a strained affair, and the next morning Vernon was gone before Thomas came down for coffee. But today he meant to broach the subject of Jacqueline Chastain and clear the air of any thought his son might have of his father having an affair with her.

After that terrible afternoon, Thomas had reconsidered the circumspection of even the brief trade of words he enjoyed with Mrs. Chastain. Others, besides Priscilla's spy, might notice and speculations would fly. He must think of her reputation, but he simply could not discontinue their Wednesday exchanges without a word of explanation. He considered one last stop by her counter or a note sent to her house, but what if he said or wrote something that made more of their conversation than she'd intended? He had presumed she felt as he did, but what if he was wrong? He had no talent to finesse the truth of her feelings, and what could they do about them if hers were the same as his? He was a married man and Jacqueline Chastain a vulnerable woman alone in a town all too willing to pounce on her for the slightest suspected impropriety.

So he'd done nothing. He'd started meeting Armand at the Fairfax, and he had not seen Mrs. Chastain since.

With Jessica, Jeremy, Bess, and Priscilla ensconced in the carriage, Barnabas driving, Thomas and Vernon on horseback in the rear, they set off. It was an impressive little cavalcade. At Priscilla's insistence, Barnabas wore livery, a red uniform piped in black and set off with a cravat of fluffy white lace. Two high-tailed, head-tossing black stallions pulled the shiny black coach trimmed in gold. Again, due to another of Priscilla's unyielding proposals, its doors bore the Toliver coat of arms, a red rose intertwined with instruments of war imposed on a dark green background.

It was a fine Sunday afternoon. They'd attended church services together that morning and Thomas was remembering the minister's reading from Proverbs: Train up a child in the way he should go, and when he is old, he will not depart from it.

Vernon was proof of the Scriptures. All the ills of farming—the back-breaking work, crop failures, worry over weather and money—were not enough to make his son consider another occupation like so many other sons of the area's farmers. Many had been unwilling to work the land of their fathers and had given in to the lure of jobs in the cities or gone off to college to pursue professional careers. But in some ways, Thomas did not wish his example to instruct his son. He must caution Vernon to be careful of the sacrifices he made for the plantation. Vernon must do nothing to tempt the shadow his grandfather—and even Thomas, in weak moments as he'd gotten older—believed hovered over Somerset.

But that was a subject for another time. This afternoon, Thomas wanted to sound Vernon out on the topic of how much of his mother's tirade he'd overheard and if he were curious about her threats. Priscilla had been drunk, but not so much that her harangue had not carried the weight of belief in what she was saying. Her warnings had left Thomas puzzled. He would not dignify them by demanding Priscilla explain herself, but what things did she know about his family that would singe the hair on every single head in the county? In what way could she hurt him beyond belief, beyond his endurance?

Vernon smiled over at him. "So, shall we talk?" he invited.

Thomas drew his horse out of hearing range of those in the coach. "Son, about that argument you overheard between your mother and me…"

"None of my business, Daddy."

"It's your business to know that your father—"

The rapid approach of hooves behind them interrupted his speech. Their horses registered the disturbance and attempted to rear, and Barnabas directed his team a little over to the side of the road.

"What in thunder is their hurry on a Sunday afternoon?" Thomas exclaimed. Nearing them at top speed on their horses were a man and a woman riding abreast. Thomas recognized them as the late Dr. Woodward's replacement and a local midwife.

The doctor identified the coach and reined to a sharp stop while the midwife thundered on by. "Mr. Toliver, you might want to come with me," he said, "but hurry."

"Why?" Thomas asked, suddenly gripped by a terrifying premonition.

"It's your daughter. The McCords sent word she's having her baby and a hard time of it. I'm on my way to their ranch now." Without waiting for a response, the doctor flicked his reins over his horse's shoulders and sped off in a cloud of dust.

Priscilla had poked her head out of the coach, blue eyes dilated in alarm. "Thomas, did I hear right? It's Regina?"

"You heard right," Thomas said, his tone clipped. "Vernon, stay with your mother. Barnabas, be careful of the road in your haste." He gave the sides of his horse a swift kick and raced off after the doctor, a rush of foreboding like a great wind filling his ears.

Chapter Eighty-Eight

He arrived minutes behind the doctor. The McCord men—Tyler, his twin brothers, and their father—were standing in a group on the wraparound porch of the main house, heads down and shoulders slumped. As Thomas leaped to the ground, his frantic stare lit upon Curtis McCord first. The rancher's hand was clamped around his lower jaw, the pose of a man in great despair, and a jab of terror struck Thomas in his gut. Seeing him, Curtis cut through his brood and hurried down the steps.

"Thank God you're here, man. You're in time—"

"For what?"

"You better hurry," Curtis said. "I'm sorry to have to say it, but you better hurry."

Thomas pushed by him. He had a glimpse of Tyler's tear-washed face as he ran up the steps and into the house, the guilt heavy in his son-in-law's red-rimmed gaze that dropped the instant he made eye contact with his wife's father.

A servant, recognizing him, merely pointed up the stairs to a room at the far end of the hall. Even before Thomas reached it, his stomach heaved at the warm, astringent stench of blood and body fluids, an odor he had not smelled since his days in the midst of the wounded and dying on the battlefields of Texas in the Civil War. He charged toward the open door and was met by the tall, taciturn Mexican woman that ran the house with an implacable hand. She moved to stand in front of him. "You cannot go in, *Señor*. Doctor here now. No men allowed."

"The hell you say. I'm her father." Thomas shoved the house-keeper out of the way and tore into the room. A cry ripped from his throat. On the bed, his daughter lay under a sheet whose bottom half was soaked in blood. Her eerily pale face, framed by a mass of sweat-darkened hair and her freckles standing out like a sprinkling of cinnamon on a white empty plate, appeared to float from the pillow. She moved her head at hearing him, but her eyes stayed closed.

"Daddy…" Regina acknowledged his presence with a weak lift of her hand, and Thomas rushed to clasp it, the figures of Anne McCord and the doctor and midwife blurs on the other side of the bed.

"I'm here, Poppy. I'm here," Thomas said. He knelt by the bed, his throat clutching. "What can Daddy do for his little girl?"

"Keep…holding…my hand," Regina murmured, her eyes still closed, her slight breathing labored. The doctor moved to lift and peer beneath the sheet.

"Forever if you wish, sweetheart," Thomas said, stroking her cold, clammy forehead. "I'm not going anywhere."

"The baby…was…born dead," Regina whispered. "A boy…"

"Sssh, rest now, sweetheart. It will be all right."

"Mother?"

"On the way. Granmama and Vernon, too."

He heard Priscilla's hysterical voice from the floor below, followed by a rush of anxious footsteps up the stairs. When Thomas glanced toward the door, he saw the doctor shake his head at the midwife and felt the earth drop from beneath his knees. Seconds later, Priscilla burst into the room, his mother behind her, but they had come too late. Thomas turned back to his daughter and observed her chest fall in its final breath.

Beginning to keen, Priscilla shoved Thomas out of the way, toppling him, and gathered her daughter to her bosom to rock her as she had when Regina was a child. Thomas hauled himself to his feet and fell into a nearby chair, covering his face with his hands as tears began to stream. He heard Anne and the doctor say something to his mother before they and the midwife slipped from the room, and then Jessica came to stand beside him and place a hand on his shoulder. He felt its gentle weight like a crushing stone. Its significance reached beyond commiseration, beyond mere understanding of his grief. He lifted his tear-streaked face. "Are we Tolivers cursed, Mother?"

She closed her eyes against his interrogation. Her face sagged, and Thomas was suddenly reminded of how old she was—seventy in October, the month another of his children had died.

"I don't know," she said.

"I do!" Priscilla suddenly shrieked. She whirled to them, still clutching her daughter, loathing in her streaming eyes, the contortion of her mouth. "You Tolivers are cursed, cursed, *cursed*!" she screamed. "And my baby boy and now my daughter are dead because of it. God, I wish I'd never married into this family! I wish I'd never laid eyes on *any* of you, God damn you!"

Vernon would be arriving soon. He must not hear his mother carry on so. Thomas forced sound from his throat. "Priscilla... please. You're distraught. You don't know what you're saying."

"The hell I don't!" Carefully, Priscilla laid her daughter down and levered herself up to face them. Her hat was askew, the front of her beribboned bodice soiled with the sweat of her daughter's ordeal. Her eyes gleamed maniacally. Her lips twisted obscenely as she continued in a screech mindless of the rain of consequences to fall.

"Jessica's father paid Silas Toliver to jilt the woman he loved to marry your mother, Thomas. Did you know that? The price was the money to buy Somerset—that holy altar before which you Tolivers worship."

Priscilla had flounced to Thomas's chair to speak directly into his face. "Your grandmother predicted a curse would fall on the land because of what he did, and your father came to believe her when he lost his son and the other children he would have had if he'd not betrayed the woman he was supposed to marry. Until the day he died, your father believed his children—the heirs to Somerset—were born to die because of the jinx he'd incurred when he made his deal with the devil."

Riveted to his chair, Thomas asked aghast, "How do you know all this?"

"She read my diaries," Jessica answered calmly.

Priscilla blinked and regarded Jessica as if only then realizing she was in the room. Thomas saw rage give way to befuddlement in his wife's sudden notice of his mother.

"You read my mother's diaries?" he croaked.

Priscilla backed away unsteadily, squeezing her eyes shut and pressing her fingers to her temples as if unsure of where she was. "No! I've heard rumors, that's all."

"I'm afraid not," Jessica said. She stepped to the bed and trailed the back of her hand down her granddaughter's cheek. Bending, she kissed the ash-pale brow. "Sleep well, dearly beloved child." Straightening, she regarded Thomas and Priscilla with a face as stolid as a marble bust. "Be careful of what you say. Vernon is in the hall."

"Keep him out there for a little while, Mother, and shut the door," Thomas said as she turned to leave.

Priscilla had cowered away from him. When the door closed, he asked, "Is it true, Priscilla? Did you read my mother's diaries?"

"No! And why should that be important anyway? Our daughter is dead." Priscilla clamped her hands to her face and began to wail again. Heavily, Thomas pushed up from the chair. He wished he had the stomach to fold the mother of his daughter in his arms, but he did not. His feelings for his wife were as dead as the body under the blood-soaked sheet.

"We must speak with Tyler to ask permission to take our daughter home," he said.

Four days later, on the afternoon of the burial when the mourners of Regina Elizabeth Toliver McCord had seen her interred in the family cemetery with her stillborn son, the members of the Toliver family gathered listlessly in the parlor of the mansion. They sat sprawled in the stiff, horsehair chairs and couches, too emotionally drained to move or speak. Priscilla and Jessica had not removed their hats or Thomas and Vernon their stiff cravats. Amy entered silently bearing a tray of tea and specially baked scones and left the room.

Thomas and Priscilla had not spoken a word beyond necessity since the evening the little procession returned to Houston Avenue pulling the wagon that carried their daughter's body home to be bathed and dressed for viewing. Stiff-lipped and dry-eyed, they had met the flood of visitors to the mansion from opposite sides of the room. The evening of their return, Thomas had slept in one of the guest rooms. The next day, he instructed members of the household staff to remove his things from the room he shared with Priscilla to his new quarters.

"Somebody needs to say something," Vernon said.

Jessica poured the tea. "One lump or two?" she said, sugar tongs raised.

"Neither," Vernon said, standing. "I need to get out to the plantation."

"I am going to have a rest," Jessica said. "Perhaps you should, too, Priscilla."

"Yes," she agreed listlessly.

"Thomas?" His mother cast an eye in his direction.

Thomas drew up his legs to stand. "I will not be home for supper," he said.

Priscilla threw him a wild-eyed look. "Where will you be?"

"Out," he answered.

Chapter Eighty-Nine

"You've been seeing *her*, haven't you?" said a voice from the shadows of an alcove opposite Thomas's room.

Thomas spun around. The alcove was a deep utility space with shelves for setting tea and coffee trays. As children, David and Regina had played hide-and-seek there, the first place they'd look for the other. "You've taken to spying on me, Priscilla?" Thomas asked, inserting his key into the lock.

Priscilla emerged from the shadows into the hall lit by a wall sconce. It was nearly midnight. Thomas found something sinister about the rustle and glow of her shiny dressing gown in the light cast by the single candle. She'd lost weight in the two months after their daughter's death, and her face had a haunted quality about it. Thomas sympathized with her pain, but only as a parent sharing the grief for the death of a mutual child. He could not bring himself to comfort her as a husband. Priscilla's mourning was compounded by her regret that she'd let the cat out of the bag about reading his mother's diaries. Thomas no longer wondered where she'd learned the hair-singeing things about his family he had never known. He no longer cared that she could hurt him beyond belief and his endurance. He was already there.

"I'm not spying," Priscilla said. "I feel I must hang around my husband's door on the off chance of speaking with him. I would have waited inside your room, but you feel the necessity to lock it."

"I've sufficient reason, wouldn't you say?" Thomas said. "We'll talk in the morning. It's late and I'm tired. Go to bed."

A flush darkened Priscilla's cheeks, but she set her jaw. "We'll talk now. I want to know if it's the truth."

"If what's the truth?"

"That you've been seeing Jacqueline Chastain."

"If by *seeing*, you mean if I happen to catch a glimpse of her in town?"

"I heard you gave her a ride in the carriage last Sunday."

"I offered her a ride as she was on her way to her church and I mine. It was too hot to walk."

"How very convenient that you happened along on the very Sunday I was too depressed to go to church."

"Think what you will, Priscilla." Thomas opened his door. He'd had enough of this conversation.

"Don't you care what people are saying?" she demanded.

Thomas stepped into his room and pulled her in after him. He did not wish his wife's strident voice carrying to his mother's suite at the other end of the hall. He shut the door. "What are *they* saying, Priscilla, or is this simply another one of your unfounded speculations?"

"Where have you been tonight?"

"Playing cards with Jeremy Jr. and Armand and Philippe. Philippe is home on furlough."

"You weren't with her?"

"I've never been with her."

"I don't believe you."

"Well, that's your prerogative."

"Where do you go when you're not home or at the plantation or about your council duties?"

"Well, let's see what's left. I suppose I would be at one of my lifelong friends' homes."

"You seem to be spending a lot of time with them."

"So it would seem."

"Why do you spend so much time at the plantation? I thought Vernon was running things now."

"He is, but he needs me."

"You've turned him against me."

"*You* have turned him against you, Priscilla. He was outside the door at the McCords and heard every word of your tirade."

As usual, Priscilla's belligerent stance crumbled. She wrapped her arms around her thinner girth as if to hold herself together. "Thomas—I...I...was, as you said, distraught. Why wouldn't I be? My daughter had just died. I couldn't have known what I was saying. I shouldn't be held responsible."

"Did you read my mother's diaries?"

"*No!*" Priscilla said, her vehement denial flushing her face. "Everything I said was based on rumors. The families are fodder for gossip. You ought to know that."

"I do," Thomas conceded, "and if it's any comfort, I...have also wondered if some...hand of vengeance is not responsible for the tragedies that have occurred in the Toliver family because of the sacrifices my father and I made for the plantation, but only in moments of despair. I put no stock in such superstition, not for a minute. My brother's fatal fall from a horse, the deaths of our son and daughter, my mother's incapability to preserve and bear more children—no more a mystery than the DuMonts losing their daughter in a hurricane or the Warwicks a son at the hand of a Union officer in wartime. Young women die in childbirth every year. What happened to David could have happened to any boy playing by that pond."

A strange stillness had come over Priscilla. An odd light appeared in her eye. She drew to a straighter posture. "You mentioned that you, too, had made sacrifices for Somerset. What were they, Thomas? Was I one of them?"

Thomas heard a faint echo of hope that he would deny her suspicion. He turned away and began to unbutton his vest. How he had hoped she would never put that question to him. Priscilla had borne his children. Whatever else she wasn't, she'd been a loving mother.

"Tell me, Thomas. I want to know."

He unbuttoned his cuffs. "Yes, Priscilla, you were the sacrifice I made for Somerset."

There was silence, like the kind following a loud thunderclap. Thomas kept his back to her, unwilling to see what injury he had wrought.

Priscilla said in a surprisingly steady voice, "You wanted an heir in case you were killed in war, and no one else but I was available or suitable at the time. Was that it?"

"That's right. I thought we could make a go of it."

"And because of the sacrifice you made marrying me, two of our children are dead."

"I don't believe that."

"Well, I do. And so does your mother. I lied, Thomas. I read her diaries."

Thomas jerked around in time to see tears of deep hurt welled in her eyes and struggled to temper his reaction. He'd destroyed any doubt she may have had of his reason for marrying her. Suspecting was one thing. Knowing for certain was another. He was surprised that after all these years, she still fostered hope he'd married her for love.

"I'm sorry, Priscilla," he said. "I deceived you, but I hoped our children and the life I've provided you—the life you seem to enjoy—was compensation. I know I've denied you certain plea-

sures and joys you would have known if I'd...felt differently or
if you'd married someone else, but why in God's name did you
read my mother's private journals? Was it to gather information
for that history of the Tolivers you're writing?"

She drew a handkerchief from the sleeve of her dressing gown,
on hand for emotional moments that struck without warning.
Thomas, too, made sure to have one available in his coat pocket
for sudden attacks of memory and loss.

Priscilla dabbed at her eyes, then deliberately thrust the handkerchief back up her sleeve. She was through crying for him, the
gesture said to Thomas. "I suppose I could give that excuse, but
I'm tired of lying," she said. "You don't seem to have that tendency, so I'll try the truth for a change, see how *you* like it. I read
Jessica's diaries to learn if she suspected me of having sexual relations with Major Andrew Duncan."

Thomas stared at her, shocked speechless.

Priscilla eyed him innocently. "Jessica did, actually. Suspect the
truth, I mean. I found her reflections on the matter in black-and-
white in her journal of 1866."

"Priscilla...did...you have relations?"

"I most certainly did, so don't think I've reached my age without entirely having experienced those pleasures and joys you denied me."

A memory of the dashing, red-haired army major who had
bunked in the carriage house during the Union occupation over
twenty-one years ago wafted through Thomas's shock. Twenty-
one years ago...

"You never once noticed, did you?" Priscilla said, smug satisfaction glowing in her eyes. "You were so involved with your
holy plantation and so indifferent to me, you never once flicked a
glance in the direction of Andrew and me, but your mother did.
Why do you think she held Regina at arm's length all her life?"

Priscilla's face swam into focus. "You're not telling me that Regina was—"

"Major Andrew Duncan's? Yes, I am."

Thomas staggered back as though acid had been flung into his face.

"There now," Priscilla said. "That knowledge should relieve you of a little grief for Regina's passing and certainly any guilt you may feel because of your lack of attention to me."

"You—you're lying, Priscilla. You're just saying all this to get even with me, to hurt me...."

"Well, I warned you I possessed knowledge to do that, didn't I?"

"Regina was my daughter! *Mine!*"

"From whom do you think she got her red hair and freckles and skin tone?"

"My mother!"

"Or from Major Duncan. We'll never know for sure, now will we?" Priscilla moved closer to glare into Thomas's face, small teeth gritted. "I loved you, Thomas. I wanted *you*. Not your money or family name or the *compensations* you threw me as a sop. Sure, I had my...repressions when we married, but with the warmth and assurance of your love I could have overcome them as I did with Andrew. He gave me back to you a changed woman that you enjoyed for a few years." She patted his shirt front. "It will take a while to adjust to *the truth*, Thomas, but we'll go on as we always have, and I better not ever hear of you dallying with Jacqueline Chastain. You owe me your fidelity."

Thomas brushed away her hand. "I will start proceedings tomorrow morning," he said.

Priscilla tilted her head inquiringly. "What proceedings?"

"Divorce proceedings. I'm charging you with adultery."

Chapter Ninety

Priscilla pleaded. "Think of Vernon," she said. "Think of Regina, what this will do to her memory."

"I'm expecting *you* to think of them, Priscilla."

There was talk, of course, when word got around the county that Thomas and Priscilla Toliver were ending their twenty-six-year marriage, but an out-and-out scandal was diverted when Priscilla agreed to allow Thomas to divorce her quietly. Thomas laid out the terms. He would not state his grounds for seeking the divorce before the county judge if she would simply, without contesting his petition, leave his house and his life with no legal recourse to return. In the space of the public record requiring the reason for the dissolution of their union, he would agree to having the standard, commonplace explanation written. It would state the marriage had become "insupportable because of discord or conflict between the personalities that destroys the legitimate ends of the marital relationship and prevents any reasonable expectation of reconciliation."

"No reasonable expectation of reconciliation, Thomas?" Priscilla queried in a broken voice.

"None."

And so it was done. Priscilla chose the city of Houston as her new place of residence for its accessibility by train that made it convenient for Vernon, her brothers, and few remaining friends to visit her. Thomas set her up in a small but elegant house in the most prestigious neighborhood in the city, opened an account in her name, and arranged to pay for a three-servant staff and horse and carriage.

The divorce became final ninety days after the county judge signed the document releasing Thomas from the marriage, and on the ninety-first day, he called upon Jacqueline Chastain. They were married three months later. Once again, the DuMont Department Store had lost its top designer.

Four years later, in 1892, Vernon handed the conductor his ticket and settled down in his first-class compartment. The train had begun its chug through the outskirts of Howbutker, its rails following the course of a lake. Vernon noticed through his seat window that the water-loving cypresses were dropping their leaves, the first trees in Texas to do so in the fall. On just such a morning nine Octobers ago, his little brother had died. David would have been twenty-three years old had he lived. The little shooting heart pain that always came with the recollection of his brother added to Vernon's low spirits. He was on his way to Houston for a weekend visit with his mother. He loved her and felt sorry for her, but he dreaded the hours cooped up in her little house seeing what she'd allowed herself to become.

His mother had lost everything that had fostered her vanity. She had dressed and adorned herself as befitted the wife of Thomas Toliver and their social position in the top rung of Howbutker society—the state, in fact. Beyond her children, she had breathed to impress, be seen, and included. She now lacked those inducements to preen and look her best, and her weight gain and indifferent appearance showed it.

There was nothing Vernon could say or do to encourage an interest in charity work, intellectual pursuits, or the making of new friends in her changed environment. His mother preferred to live hidden away from the stigmas of her divorce and the humiliating remarriage of his father to his "paramour" and to nurse in private her grief for the loss of two of her children and the station to which she'd once belonged.

Vernon blew out a sigh. Now was not the time to be away from the plantation. It was harvest time, and a bold new pest had entered the state from Mexico through the Texas valley town of Brownsville. It was called the boll weevil, a nasty little beetle about one-fourth inch long with wings and a prominent snout. Cotton and corn farmers had encountered insect threats to production before, but against this one there appeared to be no defense. Vernon would miss the meeting of planters and farmers held tonight to discuss a plan of attack with a representative of the United States Department of Agriculture, but he could not leave his mother alone on the eve of his brother's death. His father had the comfort of his stepmother, Jacqueline Chastain.

Vernon had been despondent at the breakup of his parents' marriage, even though he accepted it as inevitable after going to his grandmother and begging her to clarify what he'd overheard from the room where his sister lay dead. He had been shocked that his mother had read his grandmother's diaries (like his father, he did not believe her denial), but now that certain secrets had been exposed, Vernon insisted Jessica tell him what the Toliver curse was all about. His father had been too devastated to approach.

And his grandmother had obliged him, chronicling the casualties leading to the day of that terrible argument that had held him transfixed in the hall of the McCords' ranch house. The notion of Somerset being under some jinx originating from his great-grandmother in South Carolina before Texas was even a republic was balderdash, of course. He chalked it up as just one more grievance his mother could hurl against his father. Vernon had already been made aware of the reason he'd married her and been pretty certain his mother knew as well. He understood his father's motive and his mother's resentment. What he hadn't known and had been captivated by was the turbulent start of his grandparents' apparently happy history together.

Vernon had been relieved that David and Regina were not around to suffer the pain of the divorce and would be spared seeing their mother the way she was now. The whole sad business had left him determined never to marry unless it was to a woman he loved and who loved him, but that provoked another worry: What if he should never find that woman? What then? He was twenty-seven and no one was in sight who even came close to meeting his requirements. He was the sole surviving heir to Somerset. What would happen to the plantation if no Toliver came after him to inherit?

It was not a worry he wished to add to his despondency at the moment, and he removed a report from his briefcase to study the skimpy information cotton scientists had gathered on the boll weevil. The weevil, Thomas learned, could fly only short distances, but weather disturbances like hurricanes, prevalent in the Gulf of Mexico in September, could carry it far beyond its existing range. He was deep into reading when a discreet rap on his compartment door interrupted his concentration. "Come in," he called, still engrossed.

Bertram, the Negro porter with whom Vernon had become friendly on his trips to Houston, stuck his head in. "Excuse me, Mr. Toliver, but I wonder if you'd mind sharing your first-class compartment with a woman who'll be getting off in Houston. She's back in third with a rowdy bunch of hooligans bent on impressing her, despite her disinclination for it. She's quiet, sir. I'm sure she won't disturb you from your work."

"Oh, sure," Thomas said, waving a hand without looking up from his papers. "Send her in."

Escorted by the porter, she arrived minutes later. Vernon glanced up, meaning to nod politely in welcome then return to his report. Instead, his eyes widened and his jaw slowly dropped.

"Thank you so much, sir," his visitor said, seeming not to notice his rapt gaze. Her hat was askew, and she appeared slightly out of breath. She set down her portmanteau and umbrella and took a seat opposite and down from him, by the door, as if she did not wish to intrude upon his space. Without another glance at him, she adjusted her hat, a straw affair too prim for the alluring abundance of glossy auburn hair massed in a bun that looked as if it might shake loose at the next jolt of the train. Fashion had veered from the overabundant extravagances of frills and flounces his mother still favored, and the woman's simpler traveling suit with its form-fitting bodice, hour-glass waist, and slim-lined skirt was most becoming to her well-endowed figure. Vernon thought he had never seen a more desirable woman.

The hat in place, his compartment companion folded her hands in her lap and took a deep breath of apparent relief that emphasized the fullness of her bosom. She caught him staring, and her full lips arched into a small smile. "I promise not to be a distraction," she said in a warm, throaty voice that conjured dazzling possibilities beneath the bed sheets.

Vernon untangled his legs, sat up straighter, and cleared his throat. "I invite you to be as much of a distraction as you like."

An auburn brow registered her surprise. He guessed her to be in her early twenties. "Then…do you suppose you might summon the porter for a glass of water?" she asked, pressing a hand to her ivory throat. "I feel so very parched."

"Water for a parched throat? May I suggest something perhaps more quenching?"

"Like what?" she said, amber eyes curious.

"Champagne," Vernon said, reaching for the porter's cord.

"At eleven o'clock in the morning?"

"The hour is pressing toward noon."

"Oh, well, I—" Her hand fluttered to the high collar of her blouse. "If you insist..."

"I most assuredly do insist," Vernon said with a smile.

Her name was Darla Henley. She was returning to Houston from a visit with her aunt, a widow, who still managed to operate a farm that had been in her family for two generations. Her father was a postmaster in Houston. Her mother was deceased. She worked in a publishing firm after having earned a secretarial diploma.

"And what do you do in the publishing firm?"

"I read and correct copy—material submitted by writers."

On their second glass of champagne, he asked, "Why aren't you married—a woman like you?"

She sipped her champagne. She had moved at his invitation to the window seat opposite him. "I was promised, but I broke it off."

"Why?" Vernon asked, soberer than he'd ever been in his life.

Darla Henley clearly was not. Tipsily, she explained, "I discovered in time that we were not suited."

"Really? How did you know?"

"I was quite sure he was not the sort of man to order champagne to quench a lady's dry throat at eleven o'clock in the morning."

Vernon laughed, suddenly feeling he hadn't a care in the world, a state of being he'd not experienced in a long time. Did her comment mean she was looking to snare a man of wealth or a man of panache? He hoped to find out. Reaching inside his coat, he withdrew a slender leather case from which he extracted a card. He handed it to her. "I wonder if you'd permit me to call upon you while I'm in Houston, Miss Henley?"

"Why, Mr. Toliver, I'd be delighted," she said.

Chapter Ninety-One

He had meant to stay in Houston only for the weekend and depart Sunday to be home in time to ride out to Somerset for a look at how the first picking had gone, but Vernon remained in the city four days. When he returned to his home on Houston Avenue, Jacqueline met him with a small cry of relief. "Vernon, we've been so worried. We thought something had befallen you."

"I should have sent a telegram. I'm sorry. Jacqueline...may I speak with you?"

Vernon drew her aside into the library for a private word. He had been met with a ring of black, anxious faces—Amy's, Barnabas's, Sassie's, and those of several other servants. His grandmother was upstairs and his father at the plantation. When he and his stepmother were alone, Vernon said, "Jacqueline, I... believe I've fallen in love."

"Ah," she said. "So that was the cause for the delay. Who is she? How did you meet?"

Jacqueline was one of the easiest people in the world to talk to. At first Vernon had bowed his neck not exactly against her, but certainly not for her. But within weeks of her coming to live in his childhood home, he understood what had drawn his father to her. Vernon had expected her to take over the house with wide-sweeping, arbitrary changes, impose her will, tastes, and authority, but she had not. She had simply blended in, won the hearts of the servants immediately, the approval of his grandmother, and, gradually, her stepson's admiration. She brought a calm and soothing presence into the home, and, despite the grief lines permanently engraved in his father's fifty-five-year-old face, Vernon had never seen him so happy—if he'd ever seen him happy at all.

"On the train to Houston," he answered his stepmother's question. "Jacqueline, do you believe in love at first sight?"

Jacqueline pursed her lips. "At your age, I believe in physical attraction at first sight."

"Why at my age? Why not yours when you and my father met?" Vernon had learned from his mother that she'd made "the mistake of her life" when she sent his father to Jacqueline Chastain's shop to pick up a headband for his sister's sixteenth birthday party. "Something flared between him and that woman that she made sure stayed lit," his mother had accused.

Jacqueline answered, "Because at your father's and my age, we recognized something beyond the physical that we both longed for and could give to the other."

"How do you know when it's more than the physical?"

"That knowledge comes only with knowledge of the other person."

Vernon threaded his hands agitatedly through his hair. "I don't know that I can wait to get to know Darla Henley. I'm so…so besotted by her now. Jacqueline, I could hardly leave her to get on the train. I wanted to put her in my satchel and bring her home with me. I never thought I could feel this way about any woman, but I cannot think, I cannot breathe when I think of her."

His mother had warned that Darla could be a gold digger, but she wasn't, Vernon was certain. He decided to play down the impression of wealth he'd given her by the first-class compartment on the train, the French champagne, his fine clothes, and see what she made of it. He called upon her the second night he was in Houston and rather than taking her to the elegant restaurant atop the Townsmen, the elite gentleman's club to which he and his father belonged, he squired her to a more modest eating establishment. He wore an informal set of clothes he kept at his mother's for lounging about the house and transported her to and from her father's narrow, three-story "railroad house" in a hired cab. If Darla was surprised or disappointed in her expectations of the man who appeared at her door from the more affluent one with whom she'd shared a compartment on the train, she did not give a hint. She seemed only delighted that he'd honored his request to see her again. He'd skillfully avoided talking about himself on the train, and she'd been too polite to ask what he did for a living. Later in conversation he'd volunteered that he worked a cotton farm with his father in East Texas.

"Very difficult work," Darla had said. "My aunt would attest to it."

After relating these details to his stepmother, Vernon said, "Do you think she'll be offended when she finds out I'm a man of wealth?"

"You mean do you think she'll believe you dressed down and conveyed her about to places you thought suitable for a woman of her station?"

"You're so quick, Jacqueline," Vernon said. "Yes, that's exactly what I mean."

"Be honest with Darla, Vernon. Explain that it wasn't *her* station you were thinking of, but your own and the reason for your concern. Give her the choice to be displeased with you or understanding of your need to know the basis of her interest."

"Still," Vernon said, feeling contrite, "it was a rotten thing to do."

"Yes, it was," Jacqueline agreed. "There are other ways besides watering down one's credentials to determine a person's genuine feelings."

"I will keep that in mind, Jacqueline. Thank you," he said and hugged her.

Vernon was back on Darla's doorstep the next Saturday, having dispatched a letter notifying her of his return. He'd decided to wait a little longer before making a clean breast of his status for fear of how the chips would fall. *Status.* How he loathed the word. It reminded him of his mother. To avoid having to share his limited time with his mother, guiltily, he booked a room in a hotel within short walking distance to the Henley residence. In the early afternoon, he tugged the rope of its front doorbell.

"Am I too early?" he asked, when she opened the door and immediately set his pulse to racing.

"Not quite early enough," she said, smiling. "I've been looking for you since morning."

She had packed a picnic lunch and knew of a delightful little park not far away. The fall weather was perfect for walking. They didn't need to spend money on a cab, she said. They found a grassy spot in the shade of a tree and spread a blanket. After the sandwiches and cake, Vernon lay with his head in her lap while she read to him. "I'm a poetry reader myself. Do you mind?" she said, waving a slim collection of Henry Wadsworth Longfellow's poems before him.

"I'm a poetry listener myself," Vernon lied. "Read to me."

She stroked his hair, massaged his temples, smoothed his brow while she read the passages aloud, the sound of her sultry voice floating over him like music from some heavenly body beyond time and space. He melted into the bliss of her thighs beneath his head, only the fabric of her skirt and petticoat separating him from her warm flesh. He had never known a more perfect afternoon.

"Do you attend church on Sunday?" he asked, hoping she did not and he could spend the brief hours of the next morning with her before he had to catch his train to Howbutker.

"Sometimes," she answered. "My father is not a churchgoer."

They stood before her front door. The porch lantern was burning. They had been to supper at a café in the neighborhood. "Will you...attend tomorrow?" he asked.

"No, I was hoping you'd agree to have breakfast with Papa and me."

"I'd like that very much," Vernon said, relieved, and reached above her head to turn the lantern down low, casting them into semidarkness undiluted by light from the harvest moon. "I would also like to kiss you," he said.

She answered with a demure bat of her tawny lashes. "Well... if you insist."

"I most assuredly do insist."

He lowered his head, drowning in the amber eyes before they closed and she submitted to his lips with a passion that would have made him think her easy if he didn't believe she felt as he did—that they were made for each other. Vernon remembered his father saying, "My son, there is no desert drier than a loveless marriage. Marry for love, or not at all."

"Even for Somerset?" he'd asked.

"Even for Somerset."

Vernon also recalled gazing over Somerset's fields after a particularly parched season. The rain had come in the night, succoring the dry earth, filling the troughs between the cotton rows with life-sustaining water that would reach their roots, and he'd tasted the sweet quench of their thirst. Vernon felt that sensation now.

But he would follow Jacqueline's advice. Knowledge of a woman came only with knowing her. He would not make the mistake of his father. Their lips separating, her body still molded to his, Vernon looked into the amber eyes and said the words he hoped to say to her every night the rest of his life, "I'll see you in the morning."

"I'll be waiting."

The next morning as Darla waved Vernon off in a hired cab, her father stole up behind her. "When are you going to let him know you know who he is?" he asked.

"When he tells me," Darla said. "That will be soon enough."

She thought he had looked familiar on the train. That thatch of coal-black hair, startling green eyes, the cleft chin, his sheer handsomeness were too memorable not to rouse the feeling she'd seen his picture in an article that had come across her copy-editor's desk. Her publishing firm also lent its services to newspaper offices. She had deliberately excluded that information when explaining her duties to Vernon. After their meeting, she'd asked about Vernon Toliver from her boss, who knew the family name well. The Tolivers were "old Texas," he told her—moneyed and prominent in their corner of the state—and directed Darla to back issues of newspapers containing coverage of the family from the days of the Republic to the present time. By the end of the week and her second outing with Vernon Toliver, she was well versed in the history of the cotton-growing Tolivers from How-butker, Texas.

Darla was not at all hurt that Vernon had kept his prominence and wealth a secret from her. She considered the omission smart. He didn't know her from Adam's ox, but he needn't worry. She was not after his money. She merely wished to become his wife and care for him the rest of his life. He needed her, and she would fill him to the brim. She would have many children—boys, she hoped. She didn't believe she was cut out to be the mother of girls. They were too devious, and she knew she would not be happy sharing her husband's love with another woman, even a daughter. When Vernon became assured of her love, he would reveal himself to her. Until then, Darla would allow time and nature and her own instincts to guide their course.

Chapter Ninety-Two

'Tis been a year of the ringing of the bells—the set of three in the belfry of the First Methodist Church of Howbutker. The church claims them, but they really belong to the community as a means of alerting the citizenry to the hour of the day, outbreak of fire, flood, and criminal mischief. Bank thieves were caught this year when a teller slipped out during the robbery and rang the bells, drawing people out onto the street, including the sheriff, and the felons ran right into the arms of his deputies.

In the spring the bells announced the tying of the marital knots of three couples before the altar of the church. Three of the sons of the third generation of the founders of Howbutker exchanged wedding vows with their brides: Jeremy III in April, Abel in May, and Vernon in June. I would have worn the same dress to all three occasions if Tippy hadn't sent frocks for each.

"Now, Jessica," she'd remonstrated in a letter included in the parcel mailed from her spacious offices on Broadway in New York City, "I want to see pictures of you wearing one of these dresses for each wedding. Knowing you, you'll drag some old thing out of the closet and make it do for all three nuptials. You must do the boys proud."

As if anyone would notice what an old broken-down grandmother on the grooms' side of the aisle was wearing. But I was most honored when Abel and Jeremy III asked me to sit with their families for the ceremonies since I am the last of the clans' matriarchs. Bess DuMont is gone. It was I who found her body in her garden when I had gone to meet her and Jeremy for coffee. The three of us had taken to meeting on Tuesday mornings in one of our backyards, a habit we'd fallen into after we returned from our world cruise. I arrived a bit early and was told that Bess was still gathering flowers for the coffee tray, the little touch she loved adding to the French pastries that Jeremy devoured. I found my beloved friend lying beside her dropped basket of peonies and snapdragons. She lay with her face turned and her eyes open as though suddenly struck by a desire to press her ear to the ground. A butterfly flapped its wings frantically on her shoulder, a bereaved beneficiary of the philanthropist who had provided the beautiful garden.

And so the bells tolled for Bess, too.

Not long after, Armand went to collect the body of his brother, Philippe, who was killed in a shoot-out with members of a notorious group calling themselves The Wild Bunch, a gang of violent outlaws led by a fellow named Bill Doolin. Philippe was still with the Pinkerton Detective Agency and had been called to Oklahoma to help law enforcement agencies deal with the group terrorizing the state. I quote what Armand said at Philippe's funeral: "I'm glad the angels came for Mama before she had to bury the son she always believed would die by the gun with which he lived."

And this year claimed the life of my old nemesis, Stephanie Davis. Lorimer succumbed years ago—"of a broken heart once he was forced to share-crop his own land sold to a carpetbagger"— so Stephanie said, and we all agreed, those of us remaining from the Willowgrove Wagon Train. Stephanie died in the Old Folks Home, established for the growing number of aging widows left impoverished by the war, of whom Stephanie most certainly was one. The Sisters of Charity run it, and I volunteer there once a week to offer what little comfort I can to the residents. For a long while, I was a reminder to Stephanie of all she had lost, and she would turn away when she saw me, but gradually, her bitterness faded before the realization that I was among the few who remembered her son Jake and "the way it was." So we spent long hours remembering Jake and Joshua and our time together in New Orleans and the years of struggle in Texas afterwards.

Stephanie left me with a gift—a box of memories I may never have opened but for her. It inspired me to begin putting into order the material for the history of the founding families of Howbutker. At seventy-six, I cannot afford to delay. I'd anticipated Priscilla's compilation of family history to sort through as well, but to Thomas's and my surprise, she took the collection with her after the divorce. Thomas believes his former wife will make a ceremony of burning them.

So the bells rang for marriages and funerals, births and deaths this year of 1893. It closes on good notes and bad, like years do. On the good notes, my son and grandson are happily married. Their wives appear a perfect fit for them. Jacqueline Chastain is a walking blessing to us all; Darla, only to Vernon. If Darla had her way, she would isolate her husband from his family, keep him all to herself as possessive women in need of the undivided attention of their spouses tend to do. She knows Vernon would never allow it and so is careful of her attentions to his father and Jacqueline and me, as well as to the Warwick and DuMont clans my grandson regards as family.

She's a crafty woman, is Darla Henley. Vernon was beside himself when she agreed to live apart from us on Houston Avenue. He was sure that Darla, coming from modest surroundings, would want to reside in the mansion, but she assured him that as long as they were together, it didn't matter where they lived. Jacqueline kept her counsel, but I am convinced she saw, as I did, that Darla's amenable acquiescence was a means to avoid sharing Vernon with the other members of the household, especially the women.

Well, who can blame her? Three women in a house, one deviously controlling, would make for an uncomfortable home life for the men folk. Frankly, Jacqueline and I were both relieved at the newly-marrieds' decision to rent a townhouse in Howbutker, one owned by Armand DuMont, until they decided when and where to build a home of their own.

On a bad note, the year ends with the country in a financial panic. The lessons of history are wasted on the white man. His greed will not allow him to learn from history's mistakes so as not to repeat them. The causes of the Panic of 1893 are the same ones responsible for the economic crisis in 1873. Over-building of the railroads, over expansion of buildings, factories, and docks, over-mining and over-planting of crops—bought on credit backed only by the promise of staggering revenues—have led to the collapse of the financial markets here and abroad. Naturally, Somerset is affected.

Thank God for the financial savvy of Jeremy Warwick, who at eighty-seven, still has the sharpest mind in the business world and an understanding of the greed of man. He warned Thomas of the abnormal growth and over speculation going on in every industry and advised him to sell his stocks and bonds before the inevitable crash. Thanks to Jeremy, Thomas did, and there is money to continue operating Somerset and paying expenses.

But that is not to say there is much wiggle room for unwarranted spending. Somerset faces many challenges. The national and international cotton markets are now flooded because of the too rapid expansion of production owing to the convenience of railroad shipping, mechanization of equipment, improvement of crops and farming techniques. Egypt and India have emerged as competitive sources for cotton, and the boll weevil will be a demoralizing worry for years to come.

I have joined those in taking up the new craze of the bicycle as a mode of transportation. I had only to mention my interest to Tippy before she immediately mailed me two costumes designed for cycling. The skirt is cut to resemble a pair of bloomers, and I feel as if my legs have been thrust through pumpkins, but the design is practical for managing the pedals.

At any rate, on my bicycle, I pedaled out to Somerset one day last fall, and the sight of the snow-white fields flowing to eternity nearly stopped my heart. The wind rustled through the tree tops of the bordering pines, and I could almost feel Silas's hand caressing my face. I felt a surge of pride as I looked upon the fruits of my husband's and son's and grandson's labor, and I, who never pray, asked God to sustain this land of the Tolivers for generations to come. Regardless of the curse that haunts it, the sacrifices made to preserve it, Somerset deserves to be.

And so, with that, I conclude this, my last journal. In the interest of time, my pen in the future will be devoted to the writing of *Roses*.

Chapter Ninety-Three

Thomas gave a start when he read the name of the sender on the envelope. *Priscilla Woodward Toliver*. It was addressed to him, not Vernon. Thomas had arrived home after a frustrating day and did not need another aggravation added to the strain on his temper. What did Priscilla want? More money?

He took the envelope into his study to pour a Scotch and water before opening it. Damn, if people you thought you knew couldn't still fool and disappoint you. He'd gone to his neighboring planters today to present a USDA recommended plan for reducing next year's weevil damage. To control the pest's population, the strategy called for burning and plowing under cotton stalks immediately after harvest to avoid the beetles having a chance to hibernate, but success depended on a community effort. Weevils could migrate to the next planter's fields, so for the plan to be effective and the crop protected, each farmer had to agree to burn their residue at the same time.

Thomas had been shocked at his neighbors' lack of cooperation. Jacob Ledbetter, who owned Fair Acres, a plantation between Somerset and the strip of Toliver land along the Sabine, balked, saying, "All those fires going at the same time would be a hazard to our homes and buildings and livestock if the wind blew the wrong way."

Jacob had a point, but what other choice did they have if they were going to reap a harvest above the cost of production next year?

His other neighbor, Carl Long, a carpetbagger from Minnesota who had practically stolen his plantation from the Tolivers' long-time friend Paul Wilson after the war, had actually attempted to blackmail him. Thomas took a stinging sip of the Scotch and water to alleviate the sour taste of Carl's offer. "Tell you what, Thomas. You buy my plantation, and you can burn the place down for all I care. Otherwise, no deal. I don't have the man-power to do what you're suggesting."

Thomas would have liked nothing better than to have bought the Longs' land and Fair Acres, too, if it were for sale, which it wasn't, but he had no money to buy extra acreage. He had stalked away from both men in a foul temper. To hell with Carl Long, but he might strain relations with Jacob Ledbetter if he went ahead and burned Somerset's fields. Since the settlement days, the Ledbetters had allowed the Tolivers egress through their land to their property on the Sabine with its gin and cottonseed mill and dock. Jacob could close that route if his neighbor chose to pre-serve his plantation at the destruction of his.

Were there any heads harder to drill through than farmers' noggins? Thomas remembered the prewar days of his father's appeals, arguments, threats against secession, but did any landowner listen? To their miserable regrets, they did not, and they weren't listening now. Planters' heads were as deeply buried in the sand as they were then not to recognize their livelihoods were more threatened by the assault of the boll weevil than any force of the Union army. Once again, and probably as futilely, the only recourse open to a Toliver was to beseech the Texas legisla-ture to establish mandatory stalk-destruction dates for cotton and corn producers.

Thomas ripped open the envelope and withdrew a single page. The house was quiet. This was the afternoon Jacqueline and his mother attended their reading club and stayed for tea. *Thomas, Priscilla wrote, I need to see you as soon as possible. It's very important. May I expect you Sunday? Please respond by telegram. You must come, Thomas. Time is of the essence. PWT*

Thomas folded the letter thoughtfully. Sunday. That was in three days' time. He had not seen Priscilla since he'd installed her in Houston eight years ago. Though invited, she had not come to her son's wedding. Thomas never asked about her, and Vernon did not volunteer information. Vernon and Darla made regular trips to visit his mother and her father. Oddly, but apparently happily, Priscilla and Barney Henley had become friends and spent evenings together playing cards. Vernon and his wife seemed to enjoy their time in Houston with the pair and made no complaint about having to make their dutiful visits.

Jacqueline would encourage him to go. She would never say it, but she'd see it as his duty to honor Priscilla's request. He shared part of the fault in the breakup of their marriage, and Priscilla had asked for nothing extra in the eight years afterwards. She had abided by the terms of the divorce and quietly and completely disappeared from his life.

Thomas felt a sense of foreboding. What could Priscilla possibly want with him? And why the sense of urgency? Thomas dreaded seeing her. He was sure time had not been gentle, and he felt responsible for its heavy hand. Still, he wouldn't have traded these past eight years he'd been free to love and be with Jacqueline for all the guiltless consciences in the world. He loved his wife more every anniversary and, at fifty-nine, regretted only the quickly diminishing number of years left to spend with her.

He rang the servants' bell. Sassie appeared, a reminder of how fast the years had flown and would continue to fly. Sassie was nineteen and engaged to be married next year. Only yesterday she'd been toddling behind her mother, Amy, who herself had been in her early twenties.

"Sassie, when my wife returns, tell her I've gone to the telegraph office," Thomas said.

Priscilla had dressed in her finest but terribly outdated dress. Thomas paid no attention to female fashions, but even he knew that the hard bustle of women's skirts had been replaced with pleats, thanks to the sensible likes of Tippy. Priscilla greeted him with a cool smile and cooler hand. She did not look well and had lost the weight Vernon had mentioned to Amy she'd gained.

"A cup, Thomas?" Priscilla invited, sitting down in her dim parlor at a table laid for afternoon tea and motioned that he do the same.

"No, thank you."

"Then Scotch and water, perhaps?" Priscilla pointed casually to a sideboard as in the old days when he would come in for the day and help himself to the decanter before supper.

The familiarity of her manner touched a chord. "I believe I will," he said.

Settled in the small room, he with his crystal glass and she with her china cup, Thomas asked, "Why did you wish to see me, Priscilla? I'm taking the late train back to Howbutker."

Her lip quirked. "I didn't expect you to stay, Thomas, only to come."

"Well, I'm here. What do you want?"

She reached behind her to a bookcase and removed a leather volume almost too heavy for her hand. "Here," she said, handing it to him. "A present for Vernon—my going-away present."

Thomas took it and stared at the gold-embossed lettering. *To-*

livers: A Family History from 1836. He shot her a startled gaze. "You actually completed it?"

"It helped to pass the time. I hope Vernon will keep it for posterity. I want him to know about his family roots. The title is not exactly accurate. The historical facts go back to the beginning of the Tolivers and Wyndhams in England."

"How—how did you compile the material? Where did you find it?"

"You mean other than from your mother's diaries?"

Thomas could feel heat shoot to his face. She had been nothing but gracious. "That's not what I was asking, Priscilla," he said.

"I know," she conceded, her tone less arch. "Mainly I used the *New England Historical and Genealogical Register*. It's an organization that employs genealogists who contact sources here and abroad for records and documents from such places as parish registers, archives, headstones. The photographs were collected from newspapers and from the DuMonts' and Warwicks' albums they were kind enough to part with and, of course, from your mother."

"She'll be very impressed," Thomas said, hearing a huskiness in his voice. The book was a masterful compilation of family genealogy, maps, pictures, anecdotes, history, and data beautifully bound. It must have taken several years to compile and assemble. He smoothed a hand admiringly over the cover. "The cost of this must have taken a pretty penny out of your pocket."

She flicked a hand to indicate the room, grown shabby through the years. "The money was no matter. As you can see, I don't spend much, either for living or personal expenses. You'll observe that there is space in the genealogical chart for additions. It won't be long before you'll be adding another name to the Toliver tree."

"Yes," Thomas said, clearing his throat. "Darla should be delivering next month."

"And Jeremy III and Abel are to be proud papas as well, are they not?"

"They, too. If the children are sons, the dads are hoping the boys will forge the special bond they knew growing up."

A wistful shadow crossed Priscilla's face. Thomas could tell she was remembering the days when she'd been a witness to the special friendship their son had shared with his two best friends. "They enjoy an enviable companionship, Vernon and Jeremy III, and Abel," she agreed. "I hope along with you that the next generation of boys will be so blessed."

"Is the book why you asked me to come, Priscilla? If so, I thank you. It will be a treasured volume, but I really must be going."

He pushed back his chair, but she raised a restraining hand. "There is something else, Thomas. My main purpose in asking you here is to tell you something you need to know."

He had suspected there would be another shoe to fall. "And what is that?"

"It's about Regina, your daughter."

Chapter Ninety-Four

The muscle of his heart contracted. "Regina?"

"Your daughter, Thomas," Priscilla repeated.

Thomas stood up, so abruptly he struck the handle of the tea strainer, splattering brown stains and tea leaves on the white damask cloth. "I do not wish to discuss Regina with you, Priscilla. I have to go. I'll see myself out."

"Before you hear me confess that I lied to you about her paternity?"

Thomas had picked up the book and almost reached the door. He froze in step, then slowly turned around. "You lied?"

"I wouldn't have, if I'd known you'd divorce me. That you would do such a thing—even consider such a maneuver—never occurred to me. People in your circle do not divorce."

Thomas stood motionless. "It was not a maneuver, Priscilla. It was a straightforward rule of action to your admission of adultery."

Priscilla got up from the table, a little shakily, Thomas noted. The flesh had darkened beneath her still bright blue eyes. Was she ill, he wondered, or simply showing the physical effects of her reclusive life, evident in the drawn shades, the musty odor, and the forlorn impression that sunlight and people rarely entered her house?

"I wanted to hurt you—and deeply," Priscilla said, using the table for support as she stepped around it. "I knew the only way I could strike at that cold heart of yours was through Regina."

Thomas's jaw tightened. "I don't know what your game is, Priscilla, but I'm not playing. Frankly, I don't give an ant's piss whether you slept with Duncan. Regina's paternity doesn't matter. She was my daughter in every sense of the word, if not my flesh and blood."

"Now who's lying?" Priscilla said. A mixture of triumph and appeal shone in her eyes. "You know damn well you wrestle in your sleep at night—cry—from the devastating possibility that the daughter you loved, worshiped, adored had been fathered by another man. By day your memory of her is tainted with the thought that the blood of a Union soldier, the enemy you fought against, a Yankee, ran in her veins—that the daughter to whom you attributed the finest of your families' traits was no more a Toliver...a Wyndham...than I am."

Thomas swallowed hard, unable to veil the pain she must surely read gripping his throat. Yes, for years after Regina's death, even now, the image of his daughter could not come to him in memory without the grief of her death compounded by the wretchedness of wondering if the child of his heart belonged to another father.

"If it pleases you, Priscilla, then of course it matters," Thomas said, "and you may take satisfaction in the assurance that yes, indeed, you hurt me where I could feel no greater pain." He opened the door.

"That's why I asked you here, Thomas—to tell you the truth. You've got to believe it," Priscilla called in a strained voice as he stepped into the foyer.

Thomas took his hat from the hall tree. "Why should I?" he said.

"Because I'm dying and I want to make things right."

He paused and turned to study her. "Are you lying to me, Priscilla?"

"Well, I suppose you'll know shortly, won't you?" she said with a derisory toss of her head. "Thomas, I'm too weak to argue with you. You can believe me or not. I slept with Andrew Duncan three times, and they were not when I could have gotten pregnant, so Regina could be no one's daughter but yours."

Thomas stepped back into the parlor for a closer look at his former wife to determine if she was lying or telling the truth. With Priscilla, it was hard to know, but he did not doubt she was sick. He noticed the more pronounced pallor of her skin, the deeper sockets of her eyes and hollow cheeks. He felt a wave of pity for her, but he could not let sympathy override his knowledge of the deceit of which she was capable.

"How do I know you're not merely telling me what I want to hear? That this...*confession* isn't a way to make amends for a despicable claim you now wish you hadn't uttered?"

Priscilla closed her eyes tiredly. "Think what you like. I've said my piece. You can believe it or not. What the hell do I care if you live out your life always wondering. You have *Jacqueline*"— Priscilla spit out the name—"to comfort you." Carefully, slowly, Priscilla walked over to draw the bellpull, then fell into a chair, swallowed by a puff of silk and crinolines. "Now you must leave so I can take my pain medicine. My girl is good to see I take just the right amount."

The book under his arm, his hat in hand, Thomas felt himself at a loss what to think. Did he believe her or not? He wished she'd made a stronger case to relieve his doubt. Was she really dying...his son's mother? He said, "Priscilla, I...are you telling me the truth...about everything?"

"I have said what I had you come to hear, Thomas. I don't owe you anything more than that. What you do with it is your look-out. Now get out."

"I am sorry your life is ending this way...."

Priscilla waved aside his expression of sympathy. "My only regret is that I didn't marry someone who would have appreciated me like Major Andrew Duncan did."

Thomas said, "I regret that for you, too, Priscilla."

"But I was a good mother, and I delivered three beautiful children."

"Yes, you were, and yes, you did, Priscilla. No one can fault you for that."

"Send Vernon to me. Tell him to come as soon as possible and without his wife. She'll make him the happiest husband alive, but everybody else in his life better watch his back."

"That's what my mother says."

Priscilla grinned sickly. "Good ol' Jessica. She's not one to miss a trick."

The maid entered, carrying a tray of medicines, and went straight to her mistress sitting listlessly in a chair by the window. She set the tray on a table and drew the draperies even closer against the afternoon sunlight, adding to the parlor's gloom. Priscilla had closed her eyes and seemed to have forgotten Thomas's presence. While the maid unscrewed the cap to a bottle, he went to her chair and pressed her hand. She did not respond. He turned to leave and she said without opening her eyes, "There is one way you can be sure Regina was yours, Thomas."

He halted in his tracks. "How?" he said.

"Read the history," Priscilla said and opened her mouth wider to receive the spoonful of liquid sleep.

Chapter Ninety-Five

It was early evening when Thomas arrived home. Supper had been kept warm for him, but he declined it, and after giving Jacqueline a long, thankful embrace, he went up to his mother's suite carrying Priscilla's memorial to the Tolivers. Closeted in his first-class compartment on the way home, visions had hurled out of the past against the twinkle of lights in distant houses seen from his train window. A scene shot before his eyes of Priscilla complaining to him of his mother caring more for their sons than for their daughter. He had dismissed her observation as foolish. His mother loved all her grandchildren equally. She'd simply had more experience raising boys and was more comfortable around them. Occupied fool that he was, Thomas had never given a thought to his mother's slight detachment from Regina. He'd noticed only how his daughter's little freckled face lit up and her arms reached out for her grandmother when she came into sight. Vignette after vignette of family times flashed to him that justified Priscilla's concern, and he'd been a blind idiot not to have seen it until now. The light should have dawned when Priscilla admitted reading his mother's diaries to learn if she'd discovered her affair with the major.

A chill gripped his spine as Thomas realized his mother had suspected from Regina's birth that her granddaughter could be

Andrew Duncan's child. *Could be*, for how could she know for sure? Thomas had lived these many years with the doubt of his daughter's paternity buried in him like a festering bullet impossible to extract. He had resigned himself to it, but he could no longer live with the gnawing, burning pain. He had to know what his mother knew. He wanted to believe Priscilla—he was desperate to believe her—but that leap was too high for his credulity unless his mother could offer some proof of her own that his daughter was or was not born of his flesh. As Priscilla had said, his mother never missed a trick.

Jessica answered his knock in her bedclothes, but she was still up, having her evening pot of hot chocolate. She looked surprised to see him.

"Yes, son? What is it?"

"Mother, I must talk to you."

"I'll be delighted to listen."

Thomas had never told anyone of Priscilla's admission of adultery or her denial of him as Regina's father that night in his bedroom. For eight years he'd shouldered the burden of her disclosures in secret, but he could no longer bear his pain alone.

"You knew all along of her relationship with Duncan, didn't you, Mother?" Thomas said when he bared the reason for the divorce and Priscilla's retraction of her lie.

"And you're wondering why I didn't tell you," Jessica said. "What good would have come of it, son? Besides, I only suspected their attraction. I did not know for sure."

"But you treated Regina as if you did."

A hint of color on his mother's lined cheeks betrayed her shame. "Yes, I did, and I hope you will forgive what I can never pardon in myself. I was as sure then that Andrew Duncan was Regina's father as I am now sure he wasn't."

"Why? What evidence of her paternity changed your mind?"

Jessica laid the Toliver history tome she'd earlier thumbed through on a side table. Thomas thought it a deliberate diversion to gather her words. His mother was not one to speak of serious subjects without first considering them.

"It doesn't matter now how I know," she said, flickering a sad smile. "A grandmother's intuition, perhaps, but Priscilla has given you all the evidence you need. Your heart can rest easy."

"You're saying I should believe her?"

"Oh, yes, son. Priscilla told you the truth."

"How do you know?"

"In these cases, my dear, you have to determine the truth by what you know about the person. You know Priscilla hates you as only a scorned woman can. If Andrew Duncan had been Regina's father, why would she feel the need to pull out the thorn of your doubt? It was through no regard for your pain she attempted to release you from it, but concern for her immortal soul. Can you imagine dying with something like the lie she told you on her conscience? Do you credit Priscilla with that much courage? I'm sure she hopes you'll reject her confession and live in misery the rest of your life, but she's cleared her skirts with her Maker and that's all that matters to her. Believe her, son, and treasure a father's memories of his daughter."

Thomas contemplated his mother. He would never have positive proof that the daughter interred next to his son had been blood of his blood, flesh of his flesh, but he was sure enough of Priscilla to believe the logic of the living legend sitting across from him. His mother had never steered him wrong. What was more, she was convinced that Regina was his child, a vote of confidence good enough for him. A feeling of deliverance swept through him like a man drawing fresh air into his nostrils after being buried alive. He stood up on the brink of tears and bent to kiss the cheek of the woman who had given him life. Of course he forgave her. She had suffered the doubt of Regina's paternity longer than he and now must live out her life regretting the affection she'd denied the best of the Tolivers.

He wiped away a drop of moisture that had fallen on her cheek. "Thank you, Mother. Sleep well. I certainly will."

"Must you be in such a hurry, son? Where are you off to this time of night?"

Thomas retrieved the volume. "To see Vernon. I must tell my son his mother is dying."

Jessica listened to Thomas's footsteps fade away and fancied they sounded lighter despite the sadness of his mission. How thankful she was to have lived long enough to relieve her son from the pain she'd been ignorant of all these years. She was grateful, too, for the inspiration that had enabled her to shift the proof of her granddaughter's paternity onto Priscilla. Thomas believed her, and now his mother no longer had to dread the conversation she may have had with him if he'd pressed her for the truth as she believed it.

I knew long ago that Regina was your daughter, Thomas. Tippy told me that one day I'd know for sure whether she was of your flesh and blood.

How? How did you know?

Because Regina died, my son. If she'd been another man's daughter, she would have lived.

But, of course, she'd never have that conversation with Thomas. As a mother, she would never relieve her son's doubt by burdening him with guilt. Thanks to Priscilla, she'd convinced him through reason, the only language Thomas understood.

Priscilla had pointed him in the right direction when she told him to read the history of the Tolivers. The proof he sought was right before him in the genealogical charts, but Thomas would never see it. Her son did not believe in the curse, but Priscilla did.

Eight years ago, the night they brought Regina's body home for burial, Vernon had come to her room bleary-eyed with grief at his sister's death and the certainty his parents' marriage was irrevocably over. What curse was his mother screaming about, he'd wanted to know. He'd been twenty-two at the time, stunningly handsome, but grief had reduced him to the little boy who used to crawl into his grandmother's lap when in need of "sugar time," as Amy called it.

Jessica had related the basis for the superstition and watched the skepticism grow in her grandson's expression.

When she'd finished, Vernon had summarized. "Let me be sure I understand, Granmama. This…hex on Somerset started when my grandfather married you rather than the woman he'd promised to marry and as a result, his son died and you were unable to bear any more children after my father?"

Jessica had conceded that the notion did sound far-fetched when considering that other families suffered similar tragedies, but there was the matter of Thomas's children dying in his generation.

"Caused by my father marrying my mother for the reason he did?" Vernon had stated incredulously.

"That's what your mother believes."

Vernon had blown out his cheeks in apparent relief. It was so easy for the young to mistake a simple explanation as the full answer to a troubling question. "Thanks for telling me, Granmama. I was afraid there was more to it. My poor mother is deranged, as she has every right to be." He'd stood up, clearly satisfied, and given her a grin marked with sadness. "As you used to read to us from Aristotle, Granmama: 'One swallow does not a summer make.' So, I'm thinking the deaths in two generations, though they could be construed as consequences for wrongful marriages, do not constitute a pattern—or a curse. But just to be sure," he said, "in the third generation, I won't repeat the sins of the fathers. I'll marry a woman I love."

As Vernon left, he looked back with a smile, reminding Jessica of Silas. As Thomas aged, he had fleshed out, and she could see the influence of the Wyndham males in his heavier shoulders and thicker girth, but Vernon's figure, like his grandfather's, would remain true to the slim, graceful stature of his aristocratic forebear.

"And I will add this, Granmama," Vernon said. "However wonderful the woman was back in South Carolina that my grandfather didn't marry, he made no mistake in marrying you."

Jessica still felt a pleasurable warmth in remembering her grandson's compliment and recalled her relief when he'd closed the door. She'd been afraid that Vernon would ask her if *she* believed in the curse. Two weeks afterwards, a headstone was erected to mark the grave of Regina Elizabeth Toliver McCord, and Jessica had cut a basket of red roses to lay at its feet.

Chapter Ninety-Six

The wives of Vernon, Jeremy III, and Abel delivered healthy nine-pound boys within weeks of one another in the fall of 1895. Darla requested their son be named Miles after her grandfather, and Vernon consented with no argument. The boy looked nothing like any member of his family but had inherited the high forehead and rather pointed nose of his wife's father and other Henleys Vernon had seen in photographs. Jeremy III's son was called Percy after an English ancestor, and the Abel DuMonts christened their male heir Ollie.

The three infants took to one another right away, as had their mothers. Vernon was much relieved that Darla liked his best friends' wives and enjoyed their company. He'd been worried that she would feel inferior to the finishing-school graduates who came from families of great wealth. Jeremy III's wife was a high-spirited girl from Atlanta named Beatrice whose father owned a fleet of commercial ships. Abel had married a saucy debutante and manufacturing heiress nicknamed Pixie who hailed from Williamsburg, Virginia.

There was much for a woman to envy about Pixie and Beatrice. Their husbands could afford them the best of everything, and if not their husbands, their own purses were available and bulging. Beatrice's father presented the Warwicks III with a new house as a wedding present. He had met the Warwick clan in the prenuptial celebrations and decided that Warwick Hall, while large and magnificent, was too crowded for his daughter to begin her marriage. The baronial edifice housed the surviving members of three generations: Jeremy Sr., his two sons, Jeremy Jr. and Stephen and their wives, and the patriarch's four bachelor grandsons, of whom Jeremy III was one. His daughter would get lost among so many Warwicks and have little voice in the running of the household.

An antebellum home was razed on Houston Avenue and a magnificent new structure erected in its place. Every modern convenience was installed, wired, or introduced. The two-storied, columned showplace boasted flushing toilets, running tap water, and electric lights. No expense was spared on its décor, furnishings, or landscape.

Abel and Pixie chose to remain in the family's château-styled mansion with Armand, who had lost his wife to cancer the year before, and Jean, his other son who had never married. Pixie, an only child whose parents were deceased, said she loved the idea of "queening it over a house full of men."

Her subjects worshiped her and allowed her full sway to command as she saw fit. One of her first duties, tactfully assumed, was to bring new life into the house. The deaths of Armand's mother, Bess, in 1893 and his wife in 1894 had shadowed the household. Before their demise, hardly an antimacassar had been changed for years out of respect to Henri. Pixie sensitively set about removing reminders of illness and loss. That meant replacing dark with light, the old with the new, the outdated with the modern— all without offending the tastes of the former mistresses. The result was an expensive marvel of grace and beauty that brought tears to Armand's eyes. "Finally, we can breathe again in my old home," he said.

The Warwicks and DuMonts were able to live lavishly. Their families were among the wealthiest in the state, though both clans eschewed conspicuous consumption. Timber had become Texas's largest and most important revenue-producing enterprise, and the DuMont Department Store the leading shopping mecca in the state. It was the close of the Gilded Age in America, an era of unprecedented consumerism fostered by the growth of the railroads, finance, manufacturing, trade, new inventions, communications, and the discovery of oil. While Texas, along with the South, did not participate fully in the flourishing economy of the rest of the country, the state's potential for financial growth was boundless. The only business sector struggling to pay its bills throughout the land was the agricultural industry. Drought, the boll weevil, low cotton prices, and exorbitant rail costs had begun to eat into the profits of Somerset.

When they married, Vernon had hoped to give his wife everything her heart desired since she asked for and expected nothing but his love and attention, which he willingly and happily gave. To his surprise, since he'd not known how she'd react when he was eventually forced to explain the state of their finances, Darla accepted with grace the fact that she'd not married a rich man after all. "At least not one as prosperous as we Tolivers used to be," Vernon told her, "but the tide will change, and the Tolivers will be in high cotton again—literally."

It would take a few more growing seasons for Somerset to reap the huge profits of former years that had made them wealthy, but Vernon and his father were confident the harvests would come. Good rains were expected. They read of new uses for cotton and cottonseed every time they opened the pages of *The Farmer's Manual and Complete Cotton Book*, and competition in the U.S. for their product was dwindling as more farmers turned to other crops. Vernon and his father were getting a handle on the boll weevil through more efficient cultivation, the use of fertilizers to hasten ripening of shorter fiber varieties, and earlier planting in fields located away from swampy areas and woods where the beetle thrived. On the political front, Congress had begun enacting antitrust laws to break up the railroad monopolies that charged prohibitive freight rates, a great boon for farmers. If Darla would just be patient, Vernon told her, he could promise she'd be dressed in the finest the DuMont Department Store had to offer, and of course, eventually, as nature had its way, they'd move into the mansion on Houston Avenue.

What did she need patience for, Darla said, batting her tawny lashes and drawing Vernon's tall head down to her lips. She had everything she wanted right here in their dear little house with her husband and son.

Vernon could hardly believe the marvel of his wife or the happiness she brought him. It took him several years to recognize the design behind her determination not to be bested by the best. Her beauty aside, for which she had no challenge, she did not attempt to compete. The Tolivers' reduced circumstances were no secret among their intimate friends, so Darla simply made more impressive what she could do with little than Pixie and Beatrice could do with much.

With amazing thrift—"from growing up poor," she maintained—Darla could make a loaf from a crumb. With culinary wizardry, she orchestrated meals of inexpensive ingredients that brought *oh*s and *ah*s from those who could set more bountiful tables. She purchased house and dress fabrics from a warehouse in Marshall where merchants like Armand sent last year's bolts to be sold at discount prices. When complimented on her window draperies and gowns that rivaled the finest worn by the more affluent, she was not above admitting that "with the help of Isaac

Singer" her creations were made with her own little hands at her sewing machine.

Their household staff consisted of only two servants, one of whom was Amy's daughter, Sassie, who helped Darla look after Miles. Two maids were not sufficient to keep the house in the impeccable shape Darla demanded, so without a thought to her pride, so Sassie reported to Amy, "The mistress, she pitch in like a seaman bailin' water outta a leakin' boat." No one visited the single-storied white clapboard rent house of the Vernon Tolivers' residence without going away exclaiming over the shine and order of the place with its ambience of peace and harmony.

Vernon idly wondered at his wife's seemingly obsessive need to lord her skills at making much out of their limited resources over their best friends' plentiful abundance. Among the three families of the Tolivers, DuMonts, and Warwicks, there had never been the faintest whiff of any member's attempt to "outdo" the other. One's economic circumstances and what one did with them were no consideration to the friendships. Vernon was grateful that Jeremy III and Abel had married wives who appreciated and supported their tight bond and were of the same unpretentious ilk as they.

Vernon ascribed Darla's excessive drive to her desire to make him proud of her. She never wanted him to regret not marrying someone prettier and richer. He assured her daily and nightly that she was all he could ask for in a wife. No woman walked the earth who could make him feel more like a king in his home, among his friends, and in society.

He saw two clouds gathering that threatened to throw a cast over his domestic happiness. Despite their earnest efforts, Darla had not become pregnant again, but neither had Pixie and Beatrice, setting Vernon's mind to rest over the vague, ridiculous possibility there could be something to the Toliver curse. The other was his disappointment in his son. Miles was now a full four years old. By his age, Vernon had often spent gleeful whole days with his father at Somerset. He loved being petted by the workers, eating watermelons right off the vine, seeing the animals, playing with the black children, but, most of all, he'd enjoyed riding in the saddle with his father into the fields. The same had been true of his father with his father. But Miles' visits to the plantation ended in tears and tantrums within minutes after Vernon set him down from the wagon. A waterfall of whined complaints met every effort to coax his son into enjoying himself. He didn't like being in the saddle. The horse scared him. The leather chapped his legs. The workers' children played too rough. The pigs and goats smelled. The sun was too hot. The flies and mosquitoes bothered him. He was hungry. He was thirsty. He was bored. He wanted to go home.

"He's too young to feel what you do for the plantation, Vernon," Darla said. "Give him time."

But Vernon had a sickening sense—perhaps unfounded, he would convince himself—that time would not change the boy's dislike of being with his father on the land he loved. Darla was apathetic about the day-to-day toil and routine of the plantation that Silas Toliver had carved from the wilderness and his son Thomas had preserved at such great sacrifice. She exhibited polite but little interest when Vernon attempted to share events of his day that affected their livelihood. In those ways, he suspected Miles was like Darla. What would become of Somerset if his son and only descendant had no desire to follow in the footsteps of his forebears?

But eventually, one of the clouds lifted. Darla announced she was pregnant.

Chapter Ninety-Seven

"Darla is hoping for another boy," Jessica said to Jeremy.

"A girl in the families would be nice," Jeremy said. "They bring fresh air into the place. What is Vernon wishing for?"

"A daughter would not be amiss with him, but our little girls have a way of dying."

"Ah," Jeremy said, his customary response to statements requiring no further discussion. Jessica had learned to read its range of emotions as he had the expression of her eyebrows.

"Vernon has confided to me that if the baby is a girl, he'll insist she call him Daddy," Jessica said. "He does not like it that Miles calls him Papa. Says it makes him sound and feel old, but *Papa* was Darla's preference."

"Ah," said Jeremy again.

"Indeed," agreed Jessica.

It was autumn again, three months from the close of the nineteenth century, a much anticipated event nationwide that had sparked the friends' earlier conversation in the gazebo. Jessica had informed Jeremy, who enjoyed her sharing the contents of her readings with him, that the purists would have the new millennium begin January 1, 1901, because the Gregorian calendar numbered century years from 1 to 100. She was glad the pragmatists were not following the convention and were going with the ancient astronomers' idea of numbering years from 0 to 99. She might not be alive to usher in the new century in 1901.

"Now, Jess," Jeremy cautioned.

"Just stating the practical, Jeremy. The old body is wearing out, so it reminds me every morning I get out of bed."

"Yes, well…" Jeremy recrossed his legs on the swing of the gazebo, uncomfortable with the mention of the inevitable, Jessica recognized. She was eighty-two, and he ninety-three. She changed the subject. She'd received letters from Sarah Conklin and Tippy. The chamber of commerce had selected Sarah among Boston's Women of the Century, and Tippy was launching a new line of feminine wear to support the vanguard of women emerging in society determined to be socially useful and personally autonomous.

"Comfortable, practical, and aesthetically pleasing," Jessica quoted Tippy's description of her designs to which Jeremy returned his usual "Ah" in approval. Eventually, Jessica got around to the reason she'd sent word she'd like to see him. She reached for a small jewelry box she'd brought to the gazebo.

"Jeremy, dear, I wonder if you'd do me a favor?"

"Anything, Jess. You know that."

"Would you sell this for me?"

Jessica opened the lid of the box containing the emerald brooch her father had presented her on her eighteenth birthday. Recognition and surprise flared in her old friend's gaze.

"Jess! That's the brooch you wore when I first met you!" he exclaimed.

"You have a good memory, Jeremy."

"How could I forget?"

For a few seconds, Jessica thought his eyes misted over. She averted her glance to the brooch the morning sunlight had set on green fire in her hand. "I never wore it after that night," she mused. "I've been keeping it as a little nest egg. It should bring quite a sum if the sale is transacted by a man adept at negotiating deals."

"Why in the world would you wish to sell it, Jess?"

"For money to publish my book, *Roses*. I don't have enough of my own, and no publisher is willing to pay *me* for the privilege of printing a history of our families. Who would buy it? And for obvious reasons, now is not the time to ask Thomas for the money."

"Ah, Jess…" Jeremy took the brooch from the box and inspected it admiringly. "It's so beautiful, so rare. It looked lovely on you the night of your eighteenth birthday party. Why don't you keep it and let me give you the money to publish your book?"

"No, Jeremy, dear. That would be going against Silas's wishes and the agreement he and you and Henri made when we first settled here—the pact never a lender or borrower be to the other. It has stood the families in good stead. Besides, upon my death, I don't want the brooch to be an issue between Jacqueline and Darla. Knowing Jacqueline, she'd let Darla have it, and I'd rather bury it first. Will you sell it for me?"

"Of course I will. I know just the man who will buy it for the price of its value."

"And Jeremy?"

"Yes, Jess?"

"No adding extra bucks of your own to the sum. Promise?"

"I promise, Jess."

He went by train to Houston the next morning. Jeremy made a point to patronize the hometown merchants whenever he could, but the nature of his business today required discretion and anonymity. He was on his way to an establishment from which he had purchased gems of rare quality to give as presents to his late wife. He did not suffer Jessica's quandary when it came to the dispensation of Camellia's jewelry to his two daughters-in-law and now Jeremy III's wife, Beatrice. Camellia would have been proud to see her collection worn by the women her menfolk had married. In all ways, Jeremy considered himself a very lucky man.

Thane and Thaddeus Oppenheimer were twin owners of a jewelry shop only the wealthy entered. Thane sold and Thaddeus bought. It was Thaddeus Jeremy told the elegantly dressed salesgirl he wished to see, and after flicking a glance at his business card and over his expensive attire, she led him directly into the man's gemology laboratory at the rear of the shop.

"My God, this is exquisite!" Thaddeus declared, studying the brooch through his loupe, a small, handheld magnifying device used by jewelers to assess a gemstone's quality. "I shouldn't tell you that. You'll ask the earth."

"Which Thane will sell for that and a couple of planets more," Jeremy rejoined.

"He will indeed," Thaddeus murmured. He stated a price.

"Done," said Jeremy.

"This will go into the case immediately," the jeweler said. "It could be gone by the end of the day."

"Most likely," Jeremy concurred.

Jeremy lunched at the Townsmen, his club in Houston, the money for the brooch thick in his wallet. He took his time and enjoyed a brandy and coffee afterwards in the lounge, where he chatted with other captains of industry and met a representative of the state's new rich. He was a man from Corsicana in East Texas who, in the process of tapping a shallow artesian well on his property in 1897, hit a pocket of oil and gas. After a pleasant exchange with the newcomer, Jeremy checked his gold fob watch and decided he'd allowed enough time for the brooch to be inventoried, cleaned, polished, priced, and displayed under the bright lights in one of the gleaming cases of the Oppenheimers' shop. He'd best hurry.

Thane was behind the counter. Jeremy saw the brooch displayed in an individual glass case set on a pillar at the front of the store to entice customers as they walked in.

"I'd like to purchase that emerald pin if I may, Thane," he said.

Thane looked puzzled. "But...you just sold it to us, Mr. Warwick."

"And now I want to buy it back—for the asking price, of course."

"Uh...yes. As you wish, Mr. Warwick."

Jeremy wrote the jeweler a check for the amount of the brooch and said, "No need to have it wrapped up, Thane. It's going right into the safe when I get home."

In a voice of barely restrained astonishment since his customer had walked in, the jeweler said, "Not to be worn at the neckline of a lovely woman, Mr. Warwick?"

"Only in memory, Thane," Jeremy said.

Jessica counted the bills in surprise. "You were paid this much, Jeremy? You promise you didn't throw in your own money?"

Jeremy held up his hands. "I promise," he said. "You have there the exact amount the jeweler paid for the brooch. Believe me, he'll sell it for a lot more."

Jessica said in a faintly musing voice, "I wonder who will buy it."

"Perhaps a man who loves a woman very much," Jeremy said.

Chapter Ninety-Eight

On New Year's Day, 1900, Jessica began in earnest to put together the history of the founding families of Howbutker. The organization of the book would require the first quarter of the year and the actual writing of the text the second two. Her hope was to have the manuscript to the publisher at the beginning of the final three months to allow plenty of time for *Roses* to be assembled and printed and ready to present to the three families at their annual gathering on Christmas Eve.

Her budget allowed for the purchase of a Remington typewriter and the services of a typist and proofreader. After conducting not very extensive interviews with the town's limited pool of qualified applicants, Jessica chose a young woman in need of supplementing her secretary's salary to type her weekly output. To correct her grammatical mistakes, she hired a reporter of equal age eking out a living at the Howbutker *Gazette*.

Thomas had said, "Darla made a living reading copy for a publisher before she and Vernon were married, Mother. Why don't you use her services?"

Jessica had given him a look that he'd misread. "Oh, right," he said. "With the baby coming and all she has to do, Darla doesn't have time."

"How perceptive you are," Jessica said.

Jessica, the secretary, and the reporter made a convivial group that Amy was happy to ply with pots of tea and bakery goods twice a day for a week. The rest of the time, Jessica was closeted with her notebooks and writing tablets and pencils, emerging from her room only at meal times.

"Time seems to be of the essence to your mother," Jacqueline observed to Thomas. "You would think she 'hears time's winged chariot hurrying near,'" she quoted from a poem by Andrew Marvell that she and Jessica had enjoyed reading together.

"She is nearly eighty-three," Thomas said. "Perhaps she does."

"Perish the day," murmured Jacqueline.

Jacqueline missed her mother-in-law's company. They were great reading and gardening and cycling companions, and Jacqueline had begun to feel lonesome. Thomas spent every day at the plantation now that cotton was once more a necessary commodity in the world of commerce. The new century saw cottonseed production superseded only by lumber in fiscal importance in Texas, and the Toliver cottonseed mill hummed night and day to meet the demand for its output. Textile mills to rival the North's had been constructed in the state and the Southland, and Somerset led the way in supplying the millions of bales of cotton required annually to satisfy foreign and domestic requests. The fortunes of the Tolivers were turning around.

At the beginning of April, when Jessica had been at her writing task for three months, Jacqueline presented Thomas with a proposal that would indirectly affect the outcome of her life. Darla was one month from her expected delivery date and had endured a hard pregnancy. She'd been confined to bed for the last thirty days, and Sassie, with the assistance of only one maid and her own four-year-old daughter, Pansy, to see after, was running her legs off to appease the demands of her fractious mistress. The rent house was too small to provide living space for more help, so Jacqueline suggested the entire family move in with them on Houston Avenue—"just until the baby is born and Darla can get back on her feet," Jacqueline said. Thomas would see more of his grandson, and Amy would love having her daughter and grand-daughter under the Toliver roof.

Thomas was reluctant. God knew he was obtuse when it came to women, but from the start he'd pegged the reason for his daughter-in-law's willingness to live elsewhere but in the mansion of her husband's family. She was not a woman to share her possessions, and those she considered her husband, son, and house.

However, Thomas was concerned for the baby's well-being in its mother's womb. All that bad temper and fretfulness he heard about from Amy, passed on by Sassie, couldn't be good for the child's health and development. Vernon must have another heir. Thomas loved his grandson, Miles, but the boy was so obviously a Henley, of the same weave as his mother. Young as the child was, neither father nor grandfather could see Miles growing into the kind of man essential to the helm of Somerset.

So Thomas agreed, and within weeks the Vernon Toliver family was ensconced in a wing of the mansion on Houston Avenue. Though she remained uncomfortable, Darla's temper settled. She even relaxed enough from the pressure of her domestic responsibilities to look forward to the arrival of her newborn. Up until then, there had been some concern over the lack of maternal enthusiasm for the human being growing in Darla's womb causing her to suffer every undesirable symptom of pregnancy and the disruption of her well-run household. Miles had been such an easy child to carry.

In early May, after eight hours of unrelenting labor, Darla was relieved of her burden. Too drained and exhausted to assume an appropriate expression of joy, her disappointment in the gender of the child was visible to all members and servants of the To-liver family when Mary Regina Toliver was put into her arms. The baby's father and grandfather and great-grandmother stood by the bedside, marveling at the infant. A cap of black hair, the trace of a chin dimple, the elegant shape of the head, hands, and feet marked her for a bona fide Toliver.

Jacqueline stood at the foot of the bed and saw the same rapture upon her husband's face that was present when he'd looked at his daughter Regina at her sixteenth birthday party so many years ago. Thomas would not be able to part with this child of his lineage, even for the distance of her parents' home across town. The Vernon Tolivers were under their roof for good. As they were moving in, Jacqueline had seen Darla assessing her temporary surroundings in the light of the new developments in their lives. The Vernon Tolivers' improved economic situation and their growing family dictated they move to a house in keeping with their status and needs. What more appropriate place than the mansion of her husband's birth to which he had claim? Jacqueline read the handwriting on the wall. The new grandchild would be the deal maker. Jacqueline would no longer be in charge of her home.

Her apprehensions came to be. Darla, quietly and subtly, without drawing attention from her husband and father-in-law, set about making it clear to Jacqueline that as a stepmother, she was a usurper whose place had been won through the failure of another woman—the true wife and mother of the home, now dead. It was only proper that she, the wife of the heir to Somerset and bearer of his descendants, should take her rightful position as mistress of the house.

Jacqueline was sixty years old. She had neither the desire nor the stamina to pit herself against a woman of Darla's indefatigable determination to dominate home and family. She could have gone to Jessica, who would have explained "rightful position" to Darla, but she would cause no domestic rift. The children were under their mother's strict control, and access to them was limited, so Jacqueline formed other interests, one of which was travel. Freed of domestic responsibilities and with her husband busy all day at the plantation or with civic duties, Jacqueline was at liberty to take overnight trips by train to museums and art galleries and sites of interest in San Antonio and Houston and Austin. Members of her reading group often went along and sometimes Beatrice and Pixie, whose young company she relished.

In early September of 1900, Jacqueline asked Thomas to take a train trip with her to Galveston to see the city's acre-sized flower garden that had won national acclaim. The excursion was really an excuse to get a few days' separation from the woman she'd been foolish enough to invite into her home. Darla had become dreadfully bossy of late to the servants, especially Sassie, and it was difficult to watch Darla's overt favoritism of Miles when she allowed Mary to cry her heart out in her crib and forbade anyone to pick her up. They could stay at the lavish hotel on the Galveston shoreline built for the visitors flocking from all over the country to see the spectacular flower display, Jacqueline told Thomas.

Sadly, Thomas said he must decline. It was harvest time at Somerset, and he couldn't go off and leave Vernon to handle things alone. Perhaps his mother would go with her.

Jessica was finishing *Roses*, Jacqueline reminded him.

Perhaps Darla could break away for a few days, Thomas suggested.

Absolutely not, his wife said quickly. She wouldn't dream of taking Darla away from the children. She would go by herself unless she could interest members of her reading group to share the experience.

In the end, Jacqueline traveled to Galveston alone. It was not the first time she'd traveled without benefit of a companion, much to Thomas's concern. Before leaving, she visited Jessica in her room, and her heart softened at the lined face that looked up from the final pages of a draft covering sixty-five years of the sojourn of the Tolivers, DuMonts, and Warwicks in East Texas.

"You suppose anybody will want to read it?" Jessica asked.

"Those that matter," Jacqueline replied.

"How long will you be gone?"

"I'm not sure."

Jessica peered at her over the thin gold rims of her spectacles, dark eyes knowing and wise. "Long enough to cure what ails you?"

Jacqueline smiled crookedly. Nothing got by Jessica. "I can't be gone that long. I'll telegraph when I'm coming home."

"We'll miss you," Jessica said.

Thomas drove her to the train station and saw her seated in her first-class compartment. His concern for her safety was relieved by the conductor's promise to keep an eye on her and the promise of a friend in Galveston to meet the train and escort her to the hotel.

The telegram was never sent. On September 8, as the unwarned 37,000 residents of Galveston went about their business under blue skies despite high tides flooding some of the inland streets that morning, a hurricane was gathering force in the Gulf of Mexico. The assault that would become the most devastating natural disaster ever to strike the United States made landfall midafternoon while Jacqueline was enjoying tea served in the Palm Room of the Galveston coast hotel where she was registered. The hotel was the first obstacle in the path of the storm.

Chapter Ninety-Nine

It had taken Jessica two weeks after the disaster at Galveston to pull herself together to confront Darla. Finished with dressing, she sent Amy to summon her grandson's wife to meet her in the morning room.

"The morning room, Miss Jessica? Not up here in your study?"

"The morning room, Amy."

Darla swept into the room she'd wasted no time seizing as her command station and looked stunned to see her husband's grandmother sitting in the desk chair she'd assumed as exclusively hers.

"You wish to see me, Jessica?"

"I do. Have a seat, Darla."

"I'm afraid I can't. I have so much to do—"

"*Sit down, Darla!*"

Darla sat. Jessica swiveled her chair to address her. "Just so you know, I blame you for my daughter-in-law's death. But for you, she would not have felt compelled to remove herself from your domineering, insufferable presence."

Darla's mouth dropped open in protest. "I beg your pardon?"

"You don't have my pardon. *Ever!* I am taking back my house. Get your things out of this room this morning. Otherwise, I will have them removed and not in the orderly fashion you would prefer. And in the future, the servants will report to me. Is that clear?"

Darla rose dismissively and drew to an indignant height. "Vernon will have a say about this."

"Vernon has no say about *anything* concerning this house. This house belongs to me, and I will make the decisions concerning it. If you don't like that arrangement, you and your family are at liberty to move."

Aghast, Darla said, "You wouldn't dare do that to your grandson and his children."

Jessica quite deliberately got to her feet and went to stand before Darla. She gazed into the amber eyes, feeling hers like agates in cold water. "You wouldn't dare force me to do it, but be assured that if you are of the courage to do so, Darla, I will carry out my promise. And do not for a moment think you can hold the threat of withdrawing Vernon and the grandchildren from Thomas or me over my head. Vernon would never allow it. You would see a side of your husband you do not wish to know, and he would see a side of you that you've taken great pains to conceal. Have I expressed myself clearly?"

Darla drew back from the piercing gaze, hand clutching her throat. "I believe so."

"Very good," Jessica said.

"Here you go, Mrs. Toliver," a representative of the Hawks Publishing Company of Houston said to Jessica as he handed her a volume bound in wine-colored leather with a title embossed in gold leaf. "First copy of *Roses* hot off the press. Mighty handsome, if I may say so."

"You may," Jessica said, thumbing through the pages whose contents had been distilled from the hundreds of journals and diaries she'd edited for the book. "A very handsome volume indeed and just in time for Christmas. Will you see to the delivery of the rest of my order to my home in Howbutker?"

"With pleasure, Mrs. Toliver. This book was a commission of great pride and enjoyment for us here at Hawks. As a Texan, I'm grateful you took the time and effort and trouble to leave us such a legacy."

"I hope the founders' families will share your appreciation," Jessica said. "*Roses* is my Christmas present to them."

Clutching her copy of the book, she wished the man happy holidays and walked out onto the sidewalk suddenly feeling a little crestfallen. Her project had turned out exactly as she'd hoped— better, even. The quality of the publication and the attention to detail showed that it had been in the hands of those who cared. A good firm, Hawks Publishing. But now that she'd completed her year's mission, she felt like a balloon with its air expelled. What did one do with a deflated balloon?

Jessica wished for Jeremy's company. He'd lighten her mood. He would take her to the Townsmen to celebrate, and she might even get a little tipsy on champagne, but he wouldn't mind. She would have asked him to come with her on the train to Houston, but she hadn't wanted to spoil the surprise of her present to him.

It was just as well, Jessica thought, searching the street for a hansom cab to take her to the railway station. She needed to get back to Howbutker anyway. Thomas worried so about her when she was off alone, and she wished to cause him no further distress. He had pleaded with her to wait until a time he could escort her, but that would have been too late for her purpose. It was the middle of November 1900. She would comfort herself with the thrill of accomplishment on the train journey home. It had been no small feat she'd achieved, Jacqueline would have said in praise.

Jacqueline.

Besides Jeremy and Tippy, her last best friend was gone. The pain of Jacqueline's loss pierced through her every morning upon awakening, and Jessica knew from her grief at Silas's death what Thomas must feel upon opening his eyes. Thank God for Mary. That beautiful baby had saved her son from drowning in sorrow.

Darla had arranged for his granddaughter to be made more available to him since Jessica's little talk with her in the morning room. She set aside a period in the evening called "Granddaddy Thomas time" when Mary was placed in his arms to be rocked to sleep, and Miles sat at his knee to tell him about his day. Thomas's recitation of "Mary Had a Little Lamb" led to the whole household, including Darla, referring to the baby as Mary Lamb.

Vernon credited the loosening of the maternal reins to his wife's sensitivity to his father's loss. Jessica couldn't tell whether Darla's charity was due to her husband's appreciation for her thoughtfulness or was simply another strategy to dupe him, but her motives didn't matter. She was nicer to live with. Darla relaxed other rules regarding the children, especially Mary, who had been permitted little contact with people outside of her parents. She turned the child's daily care over to Sassie, who adored her, and did not shoo Miles' friends, Percy Warwick and Ollie DuMont, away from the crib when they came to visit. Percy especially seemed enchanted by the black-haired little sister of his friend. He brought her toys and made funny faces to make her laugh and oftentimes Miles had to call him away to join him and his friends at play. Vernon had lost his bid to have Mary call him "Daddy," but through no design of Darla's. Mary had emulated her brother's reference to him and gurgled "pa-pa," which Vernon interpreted as baby language for "Papa."

The temperature had dropped into the thirties while Jessica had been conducting her business, and she pulled the collar of her coat closer. Rain was threatening. She'd gone off without her umbrella, and naturally, no cab was in sight. She walked to the intersection, where a taxi was more likely to be had, but the rain caught her en route. She was drenched by the time she waved down a cabbie and got another dousing when she was let off at the train station. The conductor, a man of long acquaintance with her family, brought her a towel and a blanket and a cup of hot cocoa to stave off the shivers, but the morning after her arrival on Houston Avenue, Jessica awoke to a chest filled with congestion.

"It's nothing," she told a worried Thomas and Amy. "I've got lungs tough as a war horse's."

They believed her. To their recollection, Jessica had never had a cold. The box of her self-published books arrived by train the next evening. The station master was kind enough to have his son deliver them, and during the early hours of the next morning, to the accompaniment of a deep cough, Jessica set to work.

The DuMont Department Store was to introduce in December the lovely innovation of wrapping Christmas gifts in red and green tissue paper rather than in the brown parcel packaging ordinarily used. Jessica had purchased her order for the tissue early, and paper and ribbon were on hand to wrap and label copies of *Roses* for the head of each household of the founding families of Howbutker. There was one for Thomas, Jeremy Sr., and his sons, Jeremy Jr. and Stephen; and Armand and Abel and his bachelor brother, Jean. Two copies were reserved for the city library and state archives housed in Austin, and Jessica would mail one to Tippy.

"Amy," Jessica said, back in bed and burning with fever, "I want you to see to it that that stack of gifts over there"—she indicated the chair piled with her red-and-green handiwork—"gets under the tree when the families gather for Christmas Eve."

"Why, Miss Jessica," Amy said, "you goin' be doin' that your-self jus' the way you like."

"No, Amy, I won't." Jessica thought of Tippy, born with only one "air bag" so she called it, still going strong at eighty-three. But then, Tippy had been born in the heart of a star and lived under celestial protection all of her life.

In her last days, delirious, her lungs full of infection beyond the scope of the times to cure, Jessica's mind floated back to the past. She saw Silas again standing beneath the dark green leaves and waxy white blossoms of the magnolia tree in the courtyard of the Winthorp Hotel on the eve of saying good-bye. Joshua stood be-side her wearing an oversized buckskin jacket. Those gathered round her bed wondered at her small, distant smile. Jeremy took her hand and held it to his heart. "She sees someone," he said.

ACKNOWLEDGMENTS

The suggestion that I write a prequel to *Roses* came from my husband. I had been beset by readers of my first novel asking if I planned to write a sequel to the story, but I had no inclination to continue the war of the roses. That narrative was done. However, when I heard my husband say that he'd like to know how the Warwicks, Tolivers, and DuMonts came to Texas, that idea intrigued me. How *did* those families get to Texas?

And so, to find an answer to the question, I began my research that took me along the road the family patriarchs must have traveled before Texas was even born. It has been an interesting and exciting journey. To those who went along with me, my thanks. You know who you are, but I will name some of you anyway. There is no particular order in which you offered the comfort of your support, interest, and encouragement, so I will begin with my husband, Arthur Richard Meacham III, who provided all three in abundance. Joining him were my dearest companions, Ann Ferguson Zeigler and Janice J. Thomson, without whom I'd write in a vacuum and my writing days would be lonely. Always, of course, I am thankful for my agent David McCormick, of McCormick and Williams Literary Agency, and Deb Futter, editor-in-chief of Grand Central Publishing, and her assistant, Dianne Choie, who are simply among the kindest and most helpful and knowledgeable in the business. Thanks, too, to my publisher, Jamie Raab, who I understand read the manuscript by flashlight in the midst of Hurricane Sandy and gave the go-ahead to publish. Also, I'd like to acknowledge Leslie Falk of McCormick and Williams whom I've never met but who has always been a gentle and constant wind at my back. My gratitude, Leslie.

And to the fans and readers of my literary efforts everywhere, thank you one and all. I am in your debt.

READING GROUP
GUIDE

Questions for Discussion

1. What were the consequences of Benjamin Toliver leaving the entire family estate to Morris? Who suffered the most as a result of his action?

2. Was Silas justified in forgoing his marriage to Lettie? In the long run, was it fair to her? In the reader's view, which was Silas's greater objective: self-preservation or his yearning for a plantation of his own?

3. What traits of character did Jessica possess that made inevitable the abiding friendship between her and Tippy?

4. Willie May speaks of "knowing her place" and respecting "boundaries." How is her philosophy put to the test? What was at risk?

5. Discuss the aspects of the Underground Railroad. Can you make any modern-day comparisons?

6. We see Lettie only briefly, but the reader learns a lot about her. What do you make of the philosophy she lived by: "Dread and do, or don't and regret."

7. Carson Wyndham arranges for the burning of the Conestogas when it becomes apparent that Silas will not break his engagement to Lettie. What motivation was behind his action?

8. At the end of chapter 22, Silas asks himself if he was wrong to ensure for his son the birthright and future his own father had denied him, no matter what the cost might be. What answer do you think he would give at the end of his life?

9. Jessica and Silas's relationship changed over the course of their trip to Texas. In what ways? What was the key element in their association that caused each to view the other differently?

10. Discuss how Jessica's abolitionist views shaped the story from her life in South Carolina to her new home in Texas.

11. At what specific points in the story does Silas come to have a different view of Somerset and why? If you have read *Roses*, were there similar points in Mary's life?

12. The author weaves period elements such as political issues, national events, natural disasters, mores, manners, and apparel into her novel. How effective were they? Did they add or detract from the story?

13. In answering the question of what *Somerset* and its sequel, *Roses*, are about, how would you respond?

14. Eventually Jeremy learns that Jessica knew of his love for her. In your opinion, why did they not act upon that love? What

prevented them from becoming lovers or marrying? In *Roses*, can you point to a similar situation between Percy and Mary?

15. When Silas asks Jessica whether she believes in curses, Jessica answers, *"I believe what we call a curse is really a withholding of natural blessings ... like rain that should fall at the proper season, but it does not."* Discuss her definition from your own viewpoint.

16. At the end of chapter 51, Silas tells Jessica he's going to buy back Ezekiel's wife, Della. Jessica embraces Silas, and *"The moment gave Silas the feeling of a ship coming home to harbor at last."* Explain what he meant by that feeling.

17. For those who have read *Roses*, how well did it mesh with *Somerset*? Were there any loose ends or were they tied neatly together?

18. At any time, did you feel empathy for Priscilla? Why or why not?

19. Some of *Somerset*'s story unfolds in Jessica's diary entries. What advantage, if any, does that give the reader?

20. For you, the reader, what were the most satisfying moments in the story? The most moving? The most informative? Did the novel's ending provide closure? Why or why not?

A Conversation with Leila Meacham

Q: You spoke in the acknowledgments about how this prequel to *Roses* came from a suggestion by your husband, Dick. Can you go into further detail about how you came up with this story? Did you work backward from the beginning of *Roses*?

A: As with my other novels, I sat down one day and simply began to write the prequel to *Roses* with little, if any, forethought of what to type on the computer screen. I could compare my husband's remark, "I'd really like to know how those families came to Texas" to a clothesline on which I could hang whatever I chose. It seemed to me the logical place to start was where the journey began—in South Carolina with Silas and Jeremy scheming their escape from the state of their birth—but I'm not even sure I put that much thought into it before I began. Certainly I knew that I would have to weave threads of *Roses* into the novel, but those ties would not be forthcoming immediately, so I had the task of setting the scene to come. But that is what I find magical about the creation process: making something out of the void. So it was with Part One of *Somerset* that set the story on the road to Texas.

Q: On a similar note, can you describe how you did the research for this story? So much of what happened the book was affected by the political and social changes of the times. Which came first, the research or the story line?

A: My research went along with the time frame of the story. For instance, I read reams of what was happening in the United States during 1835. Those events led to other historical discoveries that provided background for the story and often influenced the direction of the plot. I found myself so absorbed in the realities of what was happening in our nation that it was relatively easy to transpose the atmosphere and aura of the events and period to the computer page.

Q: The Toliver marriages in the story make for such contrasts. Do you believe it's possible for an "arranged" marriage like Silas and Jessica's to thrive the way it did? Do you think that a couple's relationship can so strongly affect their children's (and grandchildren's) relationships, as in the story?

A: I cannot speak to the success of arranged marriages. I believe Silas and Jessica's marriage succeeded, despite the mighty divide between their convictions, because of mutual respect and physical chemistry that blossomed into everlasting love. Along with those attributes came mutual recognition of and appreciation for the other's personality and strengths that somehow managed to fit hand in glove. Those elements were lacking in Thomas and Priscilla's union. Other than their children, they had little upon which to build their relationship. Yes, I believe that to some extent the way children will grow up to view and commit to marriage is affected by the state of their parents' well-being with each other.

Q: A passion for the family business seems to run in all of Howbutker's founding families. Do you think this was more common during the story's time period, when options were fewer and travel, like Silas and Jeremy's cross-country journey, was uncommon? Do you think that there is a similar passing down of work from one generation to the next to-day?

A: It stands to reason that children of parents who own successful business enterprises—not only in the time of the Tolivers, Warwicks, and DuMonts, but certainly today—grow up with the expectation they'll inherit the family business. The passing of the ancestral torch has been going on since the dawn of time. There may be a maverick in the group, such as Philippe DuMont who preferred riding with the Texas Rangers to clerking in his father's department store, but history is full of generations of offspring still filling patriarchal shoes.

Q: Jeremy's decorum and respect for Silas are so admirable in light of his love for Jessica. Did you ever consider letting the two get together after Silas's death? Do you think Jeremy was happy in the end, despite never being able to act on his love for Jessica?

A: I believe friendship—the strength, endurance, and sacredness of it—is one of the strongest elements in both *Somerset* and *Roses*. Jeremy's friendship to Silas would never have allowed him, even after his wife's and Silas's deaths, to act upon his love for Jessica. He respected that Jessica, who loved only Silas, would stay faithful to her husband's memory, and he would not tread upon it. He offered his abiding friendship that he knew was more valuable to her than an offer of marriage.

Q: Do you think there was anything Priscilla could have done to win Thomas's love and respect? Could Jessica have done anything to convince him to reconsider his treatment of his wife?

A: No, to both questions. Priscilla and Thomas were like two plants who should never have been stuck in the ground together. One required sun; the other needed shade. Neither could nurture the other. As for Jessica, a mother or mother-in-law has only so much influence over married children.

Q: Over the course of two books, is there a particular element of the Toliver/Howbutker world that you'll miss the most? Did anything or anyone surprise you in the course of writing two books about this family and its surroundings?

A: As an author, I enjoyed exploring the worlds and periods in which these families lived. If I came away with a lasting impression from the writing of these novels, it was an awareness of the trade-offs of progress. It giveth, and it taketh away. But there was also the reconfirmation that improvements and advances in the quality of living have little effect on the human condition, no matter the times. Telegraph lines may give way to telephones, the horse and buggy to automobiles, the farm to the city. Morals and mores may change, roles reverse, and revered institutions fade away, but human problems and needs, conflicts, and dreams stay the same. The three families lived in a quieter and simpler society, one perhaps to be envied in the frenetically busy time in which we live, but at the end of the day, their deeds were the deciding factor in their happiness, as ours are today.